The Persistent Past:
Discovering The Steele Diaries

Also From John D. Beatty

Fiction

The Stella's Game Trilogy

Stella's Game: A Story of Friendship
Tideline: Friendship Abides
The Safe Tree: Friendship Triumphs

The Liberty Bell Files: J Edgar's Demons

Crop Duster: A Novel of World War II
Sergeant's Business and Other Stories

The Past Not Taken: Three Novellas
This Redhead: The Dialogues

The Steele Diaries

Steele's Battalion: The Great War Diaries

Non-Fiction

The Devil's Own Day: Shiloh and the American Civil War

Why the Samurai Lost Japan:
A Study In Miscalculation And Folly

The Fire Blitz: Burning Down Japan

The Persistent Past:
Discovering The Steele Diaries

John D. Beatty

•JDB• Communications,•LLC•
WEST ALLIS, WISCONSIN

For Frank,
With Love

A WEDDING

Historians study past events so intensely that when new ones happen to us we spend too much time analyzing and not enough just being there.

That morning, I recalled that in June of '82, Melanie and I were married at St. Barbara's Chapel on the Crest University campus. Connie's wedding in May of '96 was at St. Barb's, too. And both brides were pregnant: Meli, twelve weeks; Connie, six months, with twins. I was 27 when I got hitched; Meli was nearly 27. Connie was nearly 26, and her groom, Mike Klein, was barely 26.

That's where the similarities ended.

Between my proposal and our ceremony was two weeks. The planning took an evening. Our bridal party comprised the two of us, my father as Best Man and Meli's oldest sister as Matron of Honor.*

Mike had proposed to Connie a year before and planned for that long. My daughter Maria was Connie's Maid of Honor. The ring-bearer was Connie's son Johnnie; my son Charlie was Mike's Deputy Best Man. The flower girl was the daughter of Meli's brother, Al; my son Jason was one of Mike's ushers.

All this was running through my head when I heard, "who gives this woman to this man?"

"*I* do," I croaked, giving Connie's hand to Mike, joining Meli in the pew. I tried to pay attention to the service, but I kept going back over our lives.

---

* For our whole backstory, see *The Past Not Taken: Three Novellas.*

"I now pronounce you husband and wife under God's holy ordinance. Seal your promise with your kiss." That woke me up again, and so did the organ.

"Ladies and gentlemen," the good Reverend pronounced, "*Mr. and Mrs. Michael Klein.*"

What a road we've traveled, I thought, as we all applauded.

"At least she got free of that curse," Will Gerard said to me at the reception. We watched the dancers, including my Air Force officer sister Darla, who just blew in from Ohio.[*]

"Which curse was that?" I'd met Texas Ranger Captain Will just three days before. At about five-nine and about a measly 150 pounds, he didn't fit my image of a Ranger. But his eyes had an intensity and that gray tint that Connie shared with her mother—Will's niece, Joan, my neighbor as a teen and my first love.

"The curse of Judson Emmerich," Will said. I had just completed all the obligatory wedding reception dances with the bride, Meli, and her mother, the grandmother of the groom, my mother, both of my sisters and both of my sisters-in-law.

"He was that bad?" Meli, tripping the light fantastic (so to speak) with her brother, distracted me.

"He was a right bastard, all right," Will sighed. "You never knew my sister?"

"No." Joan didn't talk about her birth family. Meli glanced at me, then at thirteen-year-old Maria. Our daughter was taking a turn with a neighbor/classmate, Ted Bergmann, on what I thought was their first date. They seemed closer together than I thought a first-date dance should be . . . cheek-to-cheek, chest-to-chest closer. Then I heard Will . . .

"Bev was a sweet kid; and I was wild. Our paw sent me to his brother in Texas to straighten me out; he was a Ranger, too. I was eighteen when I last saw Bev; she was sixteen."

"Know anything about Jud and Bev?" I asked, looking over at eight-year-old Johnnie, wandering between knots of adults. Jason and Charlie, five-going-on-six and eight, were doing similar tours

---

[*] I had never seen Darla in uniform before that day, except in pictures.

around the party. Charged with watching the boys, Maria glanced at them when she could.

"They got married in '53, and as soon as Bev got pregnant with Joan in '54, Jud took off. Joan was eight when Jud held up that bank in Batavia in '63, shot those two guards and got sent to the slammer for life."

"He died in a Tennessee federal nursing home in '90," I sighed.

Will smirked. "Couldn't have happened to a nicer bastard. Then Bev got sick and Joan had to go into foster care. All Joan had of her family after that was Bev's name in the middle, and mine in a little notebook with my address in Texas. I never knew how she got that or kept it. But Bev's handwriting and the pictures in that bag was how I knew who Joan was when she showed up on my doorstep in a snowstorm the Monday after Thanksgiving."

"Joanie showed me that notebook," I smiled, recalling a balmy, sweet afternoon in her room, sharing secrets and learning how to make out. "She called it her escape plan. I wondered how you reacted when Joanie just. . . ." *Maria's resting her head on his shoulder . . .? First date, my . . . .*

"My fiancé wondered about a pregnant fourteen-year-old with a shopping bag full of all her possessions who knocked on my door calling herself my niece. But I'd just started with the Rangers and couldn't take her in then, the best I could do for her was find a good foster family."

"Well, I . . ." I started, glancing at Maria and Ted again. *They're OK as long as I can see them . . .*

Will gestured to his wife, a vivacious redhead, laughing with my parents. "That gal never got over Joanie's just showing up, so I married this one two years later." He sipped his drink. "Anyway, you know the rest." He shrugged. "Now, I've got a question for you: Connie's birth father. You know anything about him?"

"He got locked up a few years ago."

"Not that it matters anymore," Will sighed, grinning at Connie as she greeted guest after guest with patient conviviality. "She's become *quite* the young woman."

"Indeed, she has," I agreed, watching her and Mike on their

rounds around the party, "considering . . . "

"Yeah," Will mumbled. "Considering . . . hi, Connie; Mike." The band announced the last dance and the garter-and-bouquet tosses just a few minutes before.

"Uncle Will," she smiled, pecking a cheek as she and Mike made their final rounds of the party. She had done her hostess duty to everyone all day, pleasant to everyone despite her growing weariness that anyone with eyes and a soul could see. "Thanks again for coming up. *Hey*, Dad," she turned to me. "Mike got something in the shop you should see."

"Like what?" I asked.

"A bloody-great steamer trunk I bought a week ago" Mike added. "Meant to tell you earlier, but . . . "

"You've been busy . . . "

"Yeah. You'll have a look when we get back next month?"

"Sure." *Who could refuse a groom on his wedding day?*

"Who's that?" Will nodded to the small crowd gathering at the big room's main entrance. "Royalty of some kind?"

"As always," Mike grumbled, "*Mother-Dear* has got to be the center of attention at least once during every event." Christina "Tina" Klein, Mike's mother, whom I'd met at fundraising events over the years, was an intense, ostentatiously wealthy woman estranged from her own family, including her only child, who divided her time between condos in New York and Mayfair and her *chateau* in France. "They made a big noise out of my high school graduation, like it was some group effort. I hadn't seen *Mother-Dear* for three years before I graduated."

"Huh," I said. Mike's paternal grandmother, Devota Crest Klein, the only member of his family who responded to the wedding invitations, approached the gathering gaggle with the stately dignity of the matriarch she was. "Let's let 'em . . . "

"I thought this party was breaking up," Will said.

"I did, too," I sighed.

As *their* champagne arrived (everyone else's had been poured half an hour before) and more Kleins spilled through the doors, I wondered if they *meant* to upstage the couple's departure.

"We should go over there, Mike," Connie sighed. For my part, the Kleins were merely Connie's in-laws. Though Tina chaired Crest Corporation, destined to regulate part of our existence, I understood she would not interact with me often.

"Yeah. Folks; excuse us." Mike could share little bits of his vast treasury of stories about his profession at the drop of a hat, which I had a hard time nailing down.

"Sure," Will said as we watched them go. Mike called himself—and Connie insisted he was—a dealer in antiques, art, and novelties. "Just be careful you don't get gored."

"Good advice," Mike called over his shoulder. I thought of him as an ally-picker/rummage and estate sale maven—which he was, too—who sold enough stuff often enough to do it for a decent living. The wealthy worthies waited for the bride and groom to come to them, since, well, collectively, they owned perhaps ten percent of the school and the granite quarries that supported it. They naturally expected to be waited upon by the adopted child of a mere head of a large university department.[*]

As we watched the Kleins toast the happy couple, I thought that overall, Mike was a good guy who taught Johnnie how to throw a Frisbee and helped my kids with their baseball, and that's what mattered.

Sometimes he got lucky. Once in a great while, he got very lucky.

When we got back to the house that night and after I fed the cats, I switched on the living room TV and saw a news story about dedicating the Keck II telescope in Hawaii. The boys watched in fascination while Maria stared, distracted.[†]

"It is the largest optical array in the world, Dad," Charlie said with authority.

"Maybe it can see back in time," Jason said.

"How would it do that?" Johnnie scolded. The boys were having a sleepover.

---

[*] They had a reputation as a pompous limb of the Crest/Jenson clan's family tree that included the founders of the school, the quarries and the community.
[†] Pre-teen boys are often interested in space things; teenage girls are interested in what makes *them* spacey.

"Didn't Ein-guy say you could do that?" Jason asked. Johnnie and my sons were familiar with each other, but boys don't need to know each other well.

"Einstein used that analogy to show his theory of curved space," I said. "It's late; you boys better . . . "

"It's nine o'clock on Saturday night," Johnnie complained. "Still too early to . . . "

"*I* say it's *bedtime*," Meli declared from the doorway, having shed her turquoise gown and donned capris and a t-shirt. "Now, go brush your teeth and get *ready for bed*."

As the boys scampered past Meli for their bathroom, Maria just stood in the screen's glow, her metallic blue-green dress shimmering, her hazel eyes unfocused. "You OK, honey?" I asked.

"I'm *fine*, Dad." She answered. "Weddings are special times." Meli's eyes, as she leaned against the doorway, grew wider. "Nice to have someone to share it with."

"You two were mighty, ah, *familiar* for a first date, sweetie," I said. "Did Ted try . . .?" Meli looked curious.

"*No*, Dad," Maria grinned. "We see each other almost every day, in Algebra and French and on the bus, and we eat lunch together most days. What was *your* first date like?"

"Your Aunt Karen and her boyfriend took Joanie and I . . ." Meli crossed her arms and put on her enigmatic grin.

"Connie's mom?" Maria ignored her mother.

"Yeah. We went to an amusement park a couple of weeks before the first men landed on the Moon. I've got pictures if you . . ."

She smiled a little, with a gleam in her eye. "You tie everything in your life to something in the past, don't you?"

"The past is what I do, honey. It's very persistent."

"Yeah," she said, watching the screen again, distracted. "Did you guys make out and stuff?" Meli cocked an eyebrow . . . slightly.

"That came later . . . "

"Did you . . . *after* that?" Meli made an *I have to laugh but I shouldn't* face.

"Not . . . we, ah, fooled around some, but no . . . ah . . . "*

---

* There comes a time in every parent's life when this kind of question

"Home runs?" she asked. Meli snorted.

"No."

Maria glanced at Meli, then back at me. "I like Ted a lot. I just . . . do you like teaching history?"

"Well, I do it a great deal," I said, relieved we were out of the teen dating minefield. Meli shook her head as if tasting something bitter. "And I write about it."

"I know; I've read your books. I like American history this year."

Meli nodded; I frowned at her. *Why didn't I know this?*

"Well, there's a lot to like about the American story . . ." Meli gave her little shrug.

"I think that Herbert Linn guy's full of it." Maria glanced at me. "What do you think?"

She was talking about the highly controversial book she'd brought home as an optional text, *A New History of America,* that was very uncomplimentary to America's past. "I think his viewpoint is not just baseless, but purposefully distorted." Meli blinked.

"Me, too. G'night, Daddy; Mommy; love you." She kissed my cheek, then Meli's, and turned towards the stairs to her suite* as the boys came out in pajamas. Little silver-gray Midge followed Maria, his tail up in the air.

We listened to Maria go down to her room and watched the boys jockey for position in the living room while big black Smudge watched and waited patiently, tail wrapped around her feet, for them to settle down so she could nestle next to one or the other of them.†

We repaired to the kitchen for a last toast, waiting for the boys to nod off so we could turn the TV off and go to bed ourselves.

"Hey," I mumbled when Meli crawled into bed.

"Hi," she whispered, reaching for me . . . *sans* nightie . . . .

"The boys . . . "

"Half a house away and dead to the world. Now. *c'mon* . . . "

Afterwards, with the windows open for the fresh breeze off the

---

comes from their child. But I told the truth without details.

* A basement apartment with a separate entrance from the back yard.

† The spayed hussy didn't have a preference.

mountains* and listening for the night sounds with my lover's arm across my chest, I tried not to think of the past, but . . . "Did Maria talk to you about her date?"

"You ask me about another woman's date . . . *now?*"

"Well . . . "

"They've been *an item* in school since September."

"Why didn't *I* know this?"

"You didn't ask. They had fun. Ted's a good guy."

"I saw them dancing . . . do you know his family?"

"No, and I saw them, too, but *you*," she grunted, straddling me, "need to ravish me again."

I wondered after that just how Meli kept herself as fit as she did at going on 41. We were both getting a little pudgy around the middle, though I walked, she ran, and we swam as much as we could. And the kids kept us going. But that night was like she'd been before . . . "Honey, are you *late* again?"

"Late as in pregnant? Not to worry, babe,† she pecked my cheek. "I'm just happy." She reached for me under the sheets. "How about you? Are you happy, despite thinking about other women after making love to your one-and-only and forever wife?"

"Our daughter's not any other woman."

"She *is* another woman."

"I've seen that this evening."

"So? You happy, babe?"

"As happy as I can be at eleven-thirty on a Saturday night, with a houseful of contented kids and a naked and satiated wife purring beside me."

"Purr-purr-purr . . . "

"Eggs, Johnnie?" Meli asked. Despite our late-night activities, she and I were up before the boys. But the cats don't scratch their door,

---

* The Gray Range to the north and east; the Jenson Range to the south and west, were parts of northern Appalachians.
† I'd had a vasectomy after Jason was born, so no spontaneous reversals or young bucks hanging around.

wanting to be fed at the crack of dawn; just *ours* if we don't get up early enough.*

"Scrambled, please, Gramma," he answered.

"Mom," Charlie asked, "what am I supposed to call Mike now? Is he my . . . uh . . .?"

"He's our brother-in-law," Maria answered, working the toaster for breakfast. "Just call him 'Mike.' It's what you've always called him."

"Is *his* mom our Gramma, too?" Jason asked.

"Um . . ." I said. "She's Johnnies's step-grandmother, but she's not a relation to us."

"Mom," Charlie asked, poking at his potatoes, "How come you're Johnnie's Gramma but my Mom?"

"Johnnie is the son of our sister, which makes him our nephew," Maria grinned, putting a stack of buttered toast on the table. "I'm his aunt and you're his uncle."

"Technically, yes," I said. "He's Jason's nephew, too."

"How does *that* work?" Johnnie wondered, munching toast.

"It just does," Maria sighed.

"And Mike is your *step*-father, Johnnie," I added. "The twins will be your *step*-siblings."

"Yeah. Mama Connie said that." Johnnie shoveled in some eggs.

I'd heard *Mama Connie* before, but I never quite . . . he called his adoptive mother *Mama* or *Mom*, depending on his mood.

"*Grampa*," Johnnie asked, "what's Darla to me?"

"Your aunt," I said.

"*Great*-aunt," Maria corrected, starting another batch of toast.

"Yeah: your grandfather's sister," I said. "Did you talk to her?"

"Yeah. I never heard of a girl in the Air Force. She says there's lots 'em."

"*That's* so," I answered.

"Connie's adopted, too," Charlie announced. Meli and I looked at Charlie . . . not angry; surprised.

Johnnie paused for a moment, his eight-year-old gears clashing and clanking. "Yeah?" he said curiously, glancing at Meli, then me.

---

* If dogs have families, cats have staffs.

"She was the daughter of my oldest friend," I said. "Joan—her mom—passed away and your mom came to live with us."

"She had you in her tummy when she came," Maria said, glancing at Meli, who made a stern face. We'd figured that was Connie's story to tell, if she ever did, but Maria nodded at Meli and me.

Johnnie looked at Melanie, expressionless. "I wasn't born?" he asked.

"You were born a little later," Meli said.

This was a lot for an eight-year-old to take in at breakfast. "Then who's my . . . my . . .?" he stumbled for the right words to *that* dreaded question.

"He was in Texas," I answered. "We don't know who he was."*

I watched Charlie, glancing back and forth between me and Johnnie. Jason was crumbling his bacon into bits; I admired his restraint. I saw Meli, wishing I could come up with a magical phrase to explain rape to an eight-year-old. The cats, watching from their climbing tree in the living room, seemed to watch Maria.

"He was a *dumb bully*," Maria declared, putting her hands gently on Johnnie's shoulders. "Your Uncle Will punished him for being such a bully."

Dumb bully. A handle any eight-year-old could understand. *Punished for being such a bully*. An elegant explanation for what happened to teenage Connie's rapist.†

"Will's your mother's uncle; your great-uncle," I added.

"Mama Connie was pregnant . . . with *me?*" Johnnie asked.

"Yes," Maria said gently, calmly, firmly.

"A dumb bully put me in Mama Connie's stomach," Johnnie said.

And the world stopped. Even Jason sat motionless. The cats stared out the window.

"Yep," Maria sighed, looking at Meli, then me, before she leaned down to Johnnie's ear. "Your mom brought you here to get you away from that dumb bully."

---

* Untrue, but . . . .
† His family dynasty gave up all claims to Johnnie, a devastating blow, aside from his being shot in the *tuchus*.

The Persistent Past

"Huh." Johnnie glanced at me, then at Meli. "Why?"

"He was a real bad dude," Maria said softly, staring at me.

Johnnie leaned his head back to grin up at Maria, holding her hands. "I'm lucky to have such a *brave* mom and *gorgeous* aunt."

"Thanks, but call me 'auntie' just once and I'll bite your ears off," Maria said, kissing one.

"Can we play baseball?" Johnnie asked, pushing his empty plate away. "I wanna see *Auntie Maria* hit . . . ."

"Sure," I said, as the load I'd carried for that few instants just . . . fell off . . . sort of, amid many "I'll hit it out of the park," and "bet you can't," taunts.

But what did Maria just do?

"She *told* you . . .?" I asked when Meli and I cornered Maria in her suite.

"I guessed, and she confirmed, last year." Maria shrugged, going into her bedroom to change out of her pajamas. When Johnnie was in town last Christmastime, Connie was engaged and pregnant, and those had to be explained. I knew Connie's pregnancy was both confusing and exciting for him, but there were still questions in his mind he had yet to ask.

"It wasn't your place to . . . ." Meli said through the door.

"Connie and I worked that out," Maria answered. "It was the simplest way to explain it. She said I could tell him if he . . . "

I blinked, breathless for a moment, glancing at Meli. "So . . . "

"I think I've known since I knew what rape *was.*" Maria came out in shorts and a tank, breathing deeply before gazing out her big sliding egress window, her hands on her hips: a pose she often assumed when she was going to say something Very Grown Up. "In Life Skills in 5th Grade, when they started talking about the difference between *good* and *bad* touches; when you *want* to be touched and when you *don't*. I remember Connie just wasn't that excited about even having Johnnie, but she was going through with it, regardless."[*] She turned to face us. "Connie had all the signs of a settled rape survivor. She accepted what happened and knew it

---

[*] Maria was barely five when Johnnie was born.

wasn't her fault." She wiped a tear away. "My sister—adopted or not—is the *bravest* woman I know."

"It may have been what happened, Maria," Meli said, "but there's a lot more to rape than just that."

"Your explanation for Johnnie was elegant," I said, "but sexual assault is about control; more about *violence* than just . . . "

"You can't reduce it to 'mean bully' and walk away, honey," Meli continued. "For most women, it's very traumatizing. Some never get over it."

"Yeah, but *Connie* . . ." Maria protested.

"Connie is an exceptional woman." I said. "The guy was shot right after he . . . "

Maria looked astonished. "I didn't know that."

"Connie's friend didn't *kill* him," I said, "but he never sat down the same way again. You may have figured out the mechanics of what happened, but there's a lot more to that kind of attack. You remember her being all bright in the mornings, right?" Maria nodded. "Yeah, she worked hard at that, especially for you, because you were so little."

"I remember after she . . ." Maria started. "Connie was so sad when they took Johnnie away that I gave her my favorite stuffed horse."

"She still has that horse," Meli said. "She calls it her lifesaver, because you gave it to her when she was miserable. Listen," Meli braced herself, hands on her hips. "You need to be more careful with such things around the boys. They learn a lot more than we think. They aren't equipped to assimilate it all."

"Ass . . . *what?*" Maria asked.

"Integrate into their thinking, sweetheart," I said, reaching for her; Meli did the same. "I'm just glad you . . ." I stopped, her tearful embrace becoming suffocating.*

She wept for a while before Jason dashed down the stairs, yelling, "*C'mon* you . . ." and he stopped.

"Just a minute, Jason," I called over my shoulder. "Maria's upset . . . "

---

* Nor did I appreciate how strong she was until then.

The Persistent Past

"We'll *be* there, Nasty," Maria choked, seeming to constrict around us both. "Just give us a minute."

"Gotta change myself," Meli whispered.

"Blue bikini?" I asked . . . rhetorically.[*]

"In your *dreams*, big guy," Meli grinned, pecking Maria's temple, then mine. "And you, too, babe; no pajamas in baseball."

"*Often* in my dreams . . ." I mumbled; both women grinned.

Jason dashed up the stairs with Meli behind him as Maria uncoiled from around me. "Come up when you're ready," Meli called.

"Too cold for a bikini of any color today," she smiled, sitting down to pull her socks on. "Come July, when it's warm, I'll talk her into her *black* one[†] with me, OK?"

"OK, sweetie. When Jason learns what nasty means . . . "

"I'll find another name for him," Maria said, reaching for her shoes. "I still wipe his butt at least once a week. Leave sibling management to me, Dad."

As we climbed the stairs, I wondered . . . *Connie didn't tell me about any other of Mike's finds . . . ever.*

Why now?

---

[*] She wore a skimpy blue bikini the winter we got closer, and not since.

[†] Meli's black two-piece was hardly a bikini.

THE TRUNK

Che day I finished my last TA* evaluation I ventured down to Mike's shop, a fixture in Granite Ledge's Old Town. "Mike, *when* are you going to call me Curtis for Crissakes? You've been dating to my daughter for five years. *When?*"

"When I feel comfortable with the concept of calling a former professor by his Christian name, sir—Curtis," he answered. Mike displayed posters, old and new musical instruments, paintings by local artists (living and dead), antique knick-knacks, and bric-à-brac[+] in his storefront shop. There was an 18th Century spinning wheel in remarkable shape in one display window, and a nearly-mint 19th Century quarter-sawn oak sewing machine cabinet in the other.[‡]

"Try it *today*, will ya?" Mike was an expert on New England furniture, a skillful restorer, and a good businessman in a marginal business.

"OK; sure. Well, whad'ya think?" He pointed to an enormous, battered, bound by cracked leather straps *monster* of a steamer trunk. It was missing one of its four big strap handles and one of its brass feet, the size of a small spittoon. A dolly with casters—obviously made for it—kept it off the floor. "Good workmanship," I said, trying to twist the box; it wouldn't bend. Years of travel (I guessed) had gouged and scratched the red oak box in several places, but it

---

* Teacher's Assistant. Graduate students learning to be professors.
+ The difference between knick-knacks and bric-à-brac is a matter of taste, but the latter are said to be less useful than artistic.
‡ I'm a weekend woodworker, so I knew a little of what I was looking at.

21

seemed sturdy. "You know, Maria told Johnnie about . . . "

"She called and told Connie, yeah. We figured he'd ask, eventually, and we talked about it before they left. The Templetons had their own views, *suspected* what happened, but wished we'd given them a heads-up before Johnnie found out."

"Blame *Charlie*; *he* started *that* ball rolling."

"That *blabbermouth*. No actual damage done, though, we don't think."

"How did you get into this racket?" I'd never thought to ask.

"My father's business, sir. I started working here in high school; took it over when he passed."

"Curtis, Mike. Plan on finishing your degree?"

"I think about it once in a while."

"Your tuition's covered now." Connie wrote a newsletter on our archival holdings and was the school's cheerleading coach.

"But not credits or books . . . "*

"True." I glanced at him. "You majored in . . .?"

"English, sir—Curtis." I had him in an American history class in 1989–'90, where he held his own in the discussion group.

"Is your family investing in Connie's salvage venture?" Submerged Stone, which pulled sunken granite blocks out of the twenty miles of the Sonoco River to the Atlantic,† was one of several of her businesses. Kleins owned real estate and financial firms besides their interest in the quarries.

"Gramma Devota's got a little piece." Since Connie's salvage venture was not her only successful business, Devota knew a sound investment when she saw one.

"Huh." I turned to the contents of the trunk that Mike had spread out on a folding table. Steamer trunks were at least a half-century after my period (though I was doing some work on the Industrial Revolution in America). As a professor of American history, a document archivist, and a historical graphologist (though not the personality part of that description), the paper items Mike

---

* Which could equal tuition for a full-time student . . .
† At $300 a ton and more, a 100-ton Grade F/Level 3 Jenson granite block was well worth the cost of salvage.

found in it were in my field . . . kinda.

"Old books and papers," Mike explained as I scanned the contents that reeked of bibliosmia,* "but once I dug around . . . "

"Yeah." I spotted a citation for an Army Distinguished Service Cross, dated 1919, making the material WWI and a century out of my period. I opened one book to a random page.

> 22nd November, Colline Mortelle, Flanders.
> Met Lieut. Col. McFadden commanding the
> 2nd Battalion of the 3rd Canadian Regiment
> (2nd/3rd Canadian), Newfoundland Black
> Watch, the battalion we're supporting. A no-
> nonsense officer; knows Talbott from earlier.

Flanders? Newfoundland Black Watch? November . . . when?
"Where'd you find it?"

"Estate sale on the Steele Farm up by Camp Penobscot."

"Never been." I had passed the sign off the freeway often enough; thought nothing of it. "Tell ya what, Mike," I said, spotting several silk streamers and an unusual flag. "I'll give you $100 for the contents, and you *keep* the trunk." The head of a large university department could hardly not spare a C-note. And *this* alone . . . "You should have the medals and the flags looked at."

"Yeah; I know some guys," Mike said. "Well, sir—Curtis—this damn thing's the size of a piano.† Give me $150 and take the whole thing off my hands."

"Mike, your mother-in-law—my *dear* Melanie—will murder me if I bring that beast home. You hang onto it; see if you can clean it up. Might fetch a good price." Besides furniture and local art, Mike often bought old and interesting items like this one for $10, cleaned them up, then sold them for $50, sometimes more.

"Yeah, maybe. He glanced at the bottom of the trunk, the massive lid propped on a chair (there was an empty bracket for a prop inside). Unlike most steamer trunks, whose arched lids just cover

---

* The odor caused by the chemical breakdown of compounds in paper as it ages.
† It was only the size of maybe a truck engine, not a piano.

their contents,* this one's lid was nearly the height of the body. He thumped the bottom softly with a fist: it resonated hollow. "Huh." He grabbed a rag and dust brush and gently worked on the flat surface, brushing aside a loose piece of lining paper over an old-fashioned keyhole. "Ah."

"Secret compartment?"

"Yeah." Mike dissapeared into to the back of his shop and came out rummaging through a small box. "There's only so many bit keys this small." After he found two of the right size, he inserted one, then the other; the second did the trick. The same bitter smell came wafting out. "More of the same," he declared, seeing another stack of notebooks inside.

"Mike," I said, as I read another page in the first notebook.

> 10th April, Pioneer Park, St. Louis, Misso.
> Met a Corporal acting as MP this morning at breakfast. Satisfied by my pass, I asked him where I could find a shower-bath. He pointed me to the YMCA that offered them for five cents. Riverboats pass the park about three a minute. I wonder where they are going. I wonder where I will go after Officer's school.
> I got Dad's wire and his very generous $100. Now I can buy what uniforms I can get before I have to ship out. Took a chance and bought another three diary books; I might not have a chance later.

"I can't guarantee anything, but I might seek a grant for these. There's enough for a collection. With a grant, I can probably come up with another $1,000 for all of this stuff."

"Fair enough."

I gathered all the bound books and other paper into a dozen paper grocery bags.

And I knew why Connie had told me about it.

*   *   *

---

* The rounded lids placed them on top of other luggage in a ship's hold.

"*You're* home early, honey," I said to Meli, carrying a bag in the house.

"Dentist this afternoon," she answered, looking up from her magazine. "Didn't feel like going back to work."

"Give us a hand?"

She followed me into the garage, grabbed two bags. "What's all this stuff?"

"Mike found it in an old trunk," I said. "Not sure, but it looks like it might be important."

"Sure *smells* old," she said, wrinkling her nose.

"That it is." We brought it all into my den, placing the bags on chairs, the sofa, the side tables, and the floor. "Older than we are."

"And bending down to . . . *oof* . . . put this stuff *down* . . . tells *me* my age. Kids will be home soon." She surveyed the sight. "What do you think it is?"

"Material from WWI."

"Huh." She gazed around my shelves. "Not much here on WWI." She peered into one bag. "What are you going to do with them?"

"Well, there are some medal citations in here, so there's that. I paid Mike a hundred for this lot. If I can work up a grant, there's more in it for him."

She made a face. "Is there a hundred worth in it for *us?*"

"I don't know, honey. I have to investigate it."

"Your *money*, your *time*, babe." Melanie took little interest in my work; she didn't understand most of it. As a planner for the City of Granite Ledge, she had little use for my kind of history. "Hope it's worth what you paid for it, and your time."

"It'll take some work to figure it out, honey."

"Should keep you busy this summer."

"It might be more than *that*, honey."

She crossed her arms. "How *much* more, babe?"

"*That* much more."

She sighed, then grinned. "*Hope* so, babe. I have to start dinner."

Now, to back up a bit . . .

I was the head of the largest non-geology department* at Crest University. When I became the Jenson Foundation Professor *and* Chairman of the American History Department and Chief Archivist of the Crest/Jenson Archives, I had only been an Assistant Professor for nine years, and had only held my Ph.D. for that long. Most academics graduating in 1982 would wait that long just to get into a tenure-track position.† Yes, I was the son-in-law of the Professor and Chairman before me. And yes, I was decades younger than all my contemporaries at other schools.

But I had very few major publications to my name (though many articles, a regular graphology column and a few minor-if-well-received books; not enough to justify the position I held). Meli and my fellow professors all knew all this. I needed a Major Find or Something Truly Original to keep the wonderers from getting too vocal, as they would with new hires, in the sweet bye-and-bye.

But this was undoubtedly 20ᵗʰ Century material, and my dissertation was on financing the Barbary Wars over a century before . . . this wasn't my field.

After dedicating many years to archives, I figured I could investigate this material.

I was shuffling through the material when Maria came home from baseball practice, still in her uniform. "What's all this?" she asked.

"Mike found it."

She wiped her hands on the towel around her neck. "Anything *int*eresting?"

"This," I said, and held up a slip of paper that read *Le Baggage avec Benoit, 6 Avril 1919, une coffre à vapeur, 200 F.*

"*Avril* is French for April," she said. "Let me use my French for something more useful than ordering awful food." She came back a few minutes later. "*Baggage avec Benoit*, is probably Benoit's Luggage. *Coffre à vapeur* is steamer trunk; *F was* an abbreviation for *Franc.*" She paused, looking curious. "Someone paid two

---

* Crest was built on quarry training and teacher education. The Crest/Jenson Archives that I was in charge of were built on that foundation.
† By that time, the glut on the history Ph.D. market was such that there were at least two grads for every available position.

hundred Francs for a steamer trunk from Benoit's Luggage on April 6ᵗʰ, 1919."

"Think that was a lot?"

She shrugged. "I dunno; might be *cool* to find out, though."

"I wonder if it was *the* steamer trunk Mike found where all this stuff came from."*

"Can't say," she mused, scanning a bound book. "This looks like a diary."

> 6ᵗʰ April 1905. Dearborn, Mich.
> I got this book today for my ninth birthday.
> Mama says I should write and practice every
> day to improve my penmanship.†
> We saw a flying machine at the fair park
> today. Papa's truck can carry 7 of us in the
> back if we don't sit. Helen and Irving sat in
> front when we went to the park.

At the bottom of the page was a series of looping circles that the Palmer Method emphasized for his cursive style.‡ "This may be this diarist's first volume," she said. "He was Charlie's age."

"You have brilliant instincts, honey," I said, holding the book up to see the spine. A faded Roman numeral "I" was barely visible in fading, rusty ink.

We peered at the diary in her hands for several moments before I said, "If these are from eighty years ago . . . we need to be wearing gloves, sweetie."

"Why?"

"Because the oil in our skin might harm the old paper."§ I had a box of cotton gloves in a desk drawer. "Here." We put gloves on, and she shuffled through the same bag carefully, coming up with another diary that started:

---

* I'd been a working scholar long enough to know that not everything is what it seems.

† His wasn't a childish scrawl, but it wasn't picture-perfect, either.

‡ Like most children of the '60s, I got Palmer in school.

§ As I mentally kicked myself for not thinking of it before . . .

6th April 1908. Dearborn, Mich.
Today I am 12 years old. I start this third
volume of my diaries by apologizing for not
numbering them before. Organizing my
thoughts by writing them down gives me time
to think. Diane says, since I am as old as
Romeo was, I should marry soon. That scares
me.
Charlie says he'll join the Army as soon as
Papa lets him or can't stop him next year.
Charlie has always had a no-good
relationship with Dad. He says he needs to see
the world and get away.

"He was your age . . . huh."

"My age," she whispered. "Same age as Romeo."

"I believe he was fifteen . . . "

"There was a real Romeo?"

"Oh, yeah."

"You mean Shakespeare wrote about real stuff?"

"He did. Many of the plays were based on history."

She looked over the bag. "There's lots of these in here."

"Yeah . . . OK," I mused. "Who was he apologizing *to*, do you think?"

"Anne Frank wrote some of her diaries to Kitty."* She blinked, sitting on the arm of the sofa; the only free sitting space in my den just then. "Who keeps diaries? Why? I know why *I* do, but . . . "

"Is that rhetorical, or . . . "

"Two of these start on the sixth of April. We can surmise from that, three years apart, that kept doing it for a while." She gazed at the bags, then at her gloves. "Should this stuff be here in your home office if it's so old, Dad?"

Like I said, brilliant instincts. "Wanna help me haul this stuff to the Archive building, honey?"

"Sure." We hauled the bags out to my car again and drove the

---

* Frank began late diary entries with "Dear Kitty," probably referring to a popular fictional character of her time.

The Persistent Past

mile and a half to campus and the quarter-mile to the Crest/Jenson Archive Building. We then hauled it all to the big, open Holding Room, where we stored new material for decontamination.* After putting the bags into plastic baskets, she asked, "what are you gonna do with this stuff, Dad?"

"I dunno, but I might owe Mike a grand for it." The continual rush and hum of the dehumidifiers, the quiet *whoosh* of the cleaning racks, and the buzz of the rows of bug zappers in valences were the only other sounds one could hear in Holding.†

"Think it's worth that?" She adjusted a hair braid . . . somehow,‡ then hugged herself in the room's chill.

"I sure hope so." I paused, looking at the dozen bags. "Should I go for a grant?" I asked myself.

"Why not?" Reading another diary, she said, "Huh? He joined the Army at eighteen."

"Yeah?" I said, watching her and avoiding the temptation . . . "We're gonna be late for dinner." *Don't be like Eve and hand me an apple, sweetheart.*

"Um . . ." she read aloud:

16ᵗʰ *April, Ft. Wayne, Mich.*
Tomorrow I will draw my uniforms. It's cold
and drafty here in the barracks. The windows
leak and the stoves aren't lit between March
and November to save fuel. The dust would
appall Mom and Vanelle, but the barracks
are barren. Still, we must clean them.
Other fellows talk about women a lot. I smile
and nod, pretending I know what they mean.
Few of these fellows know how to read. Perhaps
I will teach them to read. Perhaps they will
teach me about women.

---

* Poorly-stored writing stock is often infested with insects and contaminated with mold.
† The cleaning racks pulled a steady draft of air through the material under constant UV lights, killing most insects and mould spores.
‡ Some of the things women do about their hair always baffled me, since mine was always so thin. By then it was nearly gone.

I am astounded by the sheer volume of profanity and vulgarity these fellows use so readily and easily. Not a paragraph is uttered that does not have some profane expletive related either to sex or women's anatomy, and many of those words I do not know.

"What do guys talk about when they talk about women?"

"We *like* them. In that world with no women in it . . . "

"No women at all? Why not?"

"There weren't any women in the Army until WWII."

"*That's* weird. Do they talk about specific women or my sex collectively? I mean, what's to talk about? Women are just women, aren't we? We've got breasts; guys have . . . "

"Not all women are the same, sweetie. In his case, I think what he's talking about is . . . he just left home, and the illiterate guys he's with may have been around, made some conquests . . . "

"Conquests of what?"

"Conquest, in this case, means they have enticed* women into having sex with them."

"Seductions?"

"*Yes.*"

She looked surprised. "Guys talk about that?"

"In my experience, they *talk* more about it than they actually *do* it."

She twisted her mouth into a scowl. "Yeah, so do girls. Why are they *swearing* so much?"

"Men without women tend to do that."

She paged through the diary in her hand some more, reading in random places, then said, "I'd really like to . . . we'd better go or Mom'll be *pissed*." I loaded that diary into a vacuum rack, closed the door, and left. On the way back, she gazed out the window, but, like her mother, I could hear the gears of her mind grinding. "Is that kind of thing fun?"

---

* Or paid, but I didn't mention that.

The Persistent Past

"*I'd* call it rewarding. Uncovering the past one story at a time, making connections with the present where it happens."

"Happen a lot?"

"Often enough to keep interested in looking for it."

"How did you learn to *do* all that stuff?"

"Five years of preparing for nine years of college; thirteen years of doing, of teaching . . . "

"Huh. Think *I* could learn it?"

"*I* think she meant it," I said that night in bed. We'd played baseball in the backyard that evening. Meli pitched to everyone; she had a good arm for softball.[*]

"Why would she *want* to?"

"I don't know yet. I started on *my* path at thirteen . . . "

" *You* were a nerd."

"After Joanie left, true." I had only two girlfriends as a teenager: Joanie and Marcia, who were both as into history as I was.

"I'm not sure I'm ready for *two* historians in *my* family," she sighed.

"What's *wrong* with . . .?"

"Babe, I love you, but we go to parties that aren't for school and you get shuffled off to a corner with the vegetarians, model railroaders, and other pariahs because all you can talk about is . . . "

"And what's wrong with model railroaders? I am one."[†] Silence. "I'll start her off with the drab stuff about paper and bindings and ink. Maybe that'll scare her off for ya."

"OK."

"Tony, what do you know about WWI?" I stopped in Tony Zane's office for a chat the next day.

"I wasn't *there*, despite student claims to the contrary." Tony had a bright sense of humor and a quick wit, an analytic mind, and was planning to retire at the end of the next fall semester. He was

---

[*] Wearing a crop top, like Maria's . . . .

[†] We had a 4 × 8, two-track N-gauge layout in the basement that the boys and I built and ran in the winter and in bad weather.

also a brilliant teacher of what we called Modern American History—since 1865.* "It was between 1914 and 1918 and killed many, many people. Anything more, you'll have to be more specific."

"I seem to have happened on a stash of WWI material."

"Ah!" Tony had over twenty years on me, but his sparkling eyes always seemed child-like. "How big a stash of what kind?"

"I've got a dozen grocery bags of it over in Holding."

"Let's have a look."

The walk in the warm New England spring air wasn't long, but it seemed we traversed the Quad faster than usual. I pulled one bag out of its basket, donned gloves and spread the contents on the paper that Tony pulled off a roll. We perused many bound books, faded and brittle with age. Two medal citations caught my eye—a British Military Medal and a French *Croix de Guerre*—now spread on brown paper. I found the DSC citation again, placing it next to the other two.

"There's *something* here, Curtis," Tony mumbled, holding a medal citation up to the light. Tony wasn't often serious about anything, but this time . . . "something big."

"How big?" I asked. *Big enough?*

Tony fingered through a bound book. "Well, this seems to be a diary of a young man in the US Army before WWI. Know how many of those there are?"

"No . . .?"

"This is the only one I've ever *heard* of, pal," Tony breathed. "Here's one from 1915; here's . . . ho-boy: from 1917 . . . and he's in combat in France! Look:"

> 22ⁿᵈ November '17, Iroquois Line, Flanders.
> Noise here is continuous even a mile or more
> behind the "front line," a racket like a factory
> that smells like [expletive]† gunpowder and
> phosgene gas.
> Met Brigadier Butcher commanding the
> brigade. Fine fellow if abrupt.

---

* The debate about what's "modern" rages among historians.
† This story removes the vulgarisms that pepper the diaries.

The Persistent Past

I am told that, because the British losses have been so bad here, ours may be a very long shift: as much as twelve days, rather than the usual four for any outfit. Talbott says he didn't know, doubts if Dona did, either. I believe him. [expletive] *me!*

He backed away from the table, shaken. "This is like finding the *Titanic*, Curtis, a momentous find."

"Needs to be authenticated," I said softly. "My son-in-law found this stuff in an old steamer trunk." I showed him the receipt that Maria had translated. "Maybe this one."

Tony peered at the paper. "Could be."

"Think it's worth a grant?"

"I'd back a grant to do the preliminary work. We'd need another opinion."

"How about Norm?" Norman Altenburg was the Holman Foundation Professor of Military History at Crest, and chairman of our small Military History department.

"We can ask him, but he's not really interested in anything on the ground." A Holman Foundation/US Air Force Foundation endowment funded his chair, named for Granite Ledge's sole Medal of Honor winner.* "But his department might help. This isn't your patch . . . "

"True, but I've always thought 'my patch' balkanizes our business too much."

"I agree."

"This kind of grant comes with deadlines." A Jenson Foundation basic research grant† often had very short deadlines, like months. "Need the do the work pretty quick . . . "

"Yeah. Who's gonna do your job in the meantime?"

"Good question." Someone would have to take over some of my department head tasks, like hiring new TAs and adjuncts,‡ lining up

---

* And who was also a shirtsleeve relative of the Jenson clan.
† As opposed to a sustaining grant.
‡ Crest hired adjuncts to teach *sub*-courses and sections under professors and assistant professors.

new curricula, vetting new syllabi, *and* my job with the Archive. That's not to mention the three graduate classes I was supposed to teach, *and* the Jenson Scholar I'd been mentoring since '93 and the new one I'd get in two years, *and* there were the TA contracts from the new Corporation all the department heads were supposed to be meeting about soon, they said . . . trivial stuff like that. "You volunteering?"

"Not me, pal; I'm trying to do less work, not more. Polly? Sam?"

"I could ask them. We need something to call this . . . stuff."

So we kept looking . . . all morning . . . looking.

The name that kept showing up was Edmund A. Steele, called *Ned* in some places. "For working purposes," I said, "I vote we call it the Steele Collection."

Tony nodded. "Good enough."

While it made sense to just say, "this is Ned Steele's stuff," *sense* wasn't what the careful researcher used—yet. I had to authenticate the material, and that meant we had to tie this material to actual archives with verifiable authenticity, or find another way to make sure they were what they appeared to be. Even then, authenticating could mean many things. Testing the physical age of the material would be expensive, if it were possible at all.[*]

That afternoon we made copies of the medal citations and sent them off with form-e-mail queries to the American, British, and French defense departments. We drafted a grant on my computer, hit "send" with a copy to Norm Altenberg, and called it a day's work.

We could wait for years before we got either more information or money. Often, the business of history is simply waiting and begging.

"How was practice today, Maria?" I asked that evening. I found my children—and Ted—kicking the ball around in our backyard before supper.

"Our last baseball game is Friday." She kicked the ball to Charlie, who side-passed it to Jason.

"We'll be there," I said. Jason kicked the ball back to Maria.

"Me too," Ted declared, "on the other field playing with the boy's team."

---

[*] Dating paper only 80-odd years old was nearly impossible then.

The Persistent Past

"Soccer starts again in August," Maria said, booting the ball over Charlie's head.

"*I've* got a baseball game Saturday, Pops," Charlie yelled, chasing the ball. "You gonna . . .?"

"Sure," I shouted. "Haven't missed too many games yet. What are you guys gonna do this summer?"

"*Baseball*," he yelled, kicking the soccer ball to Jason, who stopped it with surprising skill for a six-year-old.

"*Baseball*," Jason said, back-footing the ball to Maria.

"*Swimming*," Maria said, stopping the ball under her foot. "Time to get ready for dinner, guys."

"I'll head for home," Ted declared, waving.

"Stay for dinner, Ted," I said.

He and Maria looked at each other; the boys just watched. "I can call?"

"Sure." We started dinner; Maria had a limited culinary repertoire, but she could follow a recipe; Ted helped more than I ever did with a girl's cooking at thirteen, which I thought was a development.

"What's your dad do, Ted?" I asked at dinner. The lasagne and broccoli were not bad.

"He owns a car dealership in town, sir," he answered. "Bergmann Motors?" The boys tried to look busy. It was the first time Maria had had a male guest at a home dinner.

"Got my minivan there," Meli said. "Do you have brothers and sisters?"

"Two of each, Mom," Maria said. "Ted's in the middle. His mom teaches math at the Academy."*

"She's just asking because we've never met them, Maria," I said.

"No, we haven't," Meli declared, glancing at me. "We would *like* to meet them."

"I'll have Mom . . ." Ted started.

"Or *I* can call *her*," Meli interrupted.

"Yes, ma'am," Ted said, bracing himself. "Dr. Durand; Mrs.

---

* Granite Ledge Academy, a private prep school.

Durand; I like your daughter and your sons. I'd like your permission to . . . "

"*Teddie,*" Maria said under her breath, "we talked about . . . "

Teddie? "Our permission for *what,* Ted?" I asked. Meli suppressed a grin while trying to look both interested and puzzled. The boys just looked back and forth. Maria seemed frozen in time and space.

"Your permission, ma'am; sir, to see Maria this summer."

I glanced at a bemused Meli, then at the puzzled boys. "*Well,* guys, should we grant this young man permission to see our Maria?"

Melanie acted the part of a matriarch. "Young man," she asked, "what are your grades like?"

"I had a 3.65 average this year, ma'am," Ted answered. "Not the best, but . . . "

"He's very studious, Mom," Maria said. "*I* think he studies too much sometimes."

"Well, 3.65 will get you into most schools if you can keep it up," I said, trying the role of guidance counselor. "How about extracurriculars? You play baseball, but what else do you do?"

"He builds trains," Jason said. "Like *ours, only bigger.*"

"I see," I said, gazing at Meli, then the boys.

"Where do you live, Ted?" Meli asked.

"*Mom,*" Maria moaned, "they're three blocks west and a block north."

I nodded judiciously. "What do we think, then?"

"I don't see any objections to him seeing her," Meli nodded, "if we meet your family *soon.*"

"*I* think he's *cool,*" Charlie said.

"He's OK," Jason added.

"Well, then," I said, nodding to Ted, "you have the family's permission to *see* our Maria providing we meet your family in the next, say, two weeks."

Maria looked a little mortified, but far more relieved.

After dinner, the kids dashed back outside for baseball. Meli and I watched from the porch, swilling cold drinks in the shade and swatting away early mosquitos. "That went well," I said as the kids pointed out their diamond for Ted. It wasn't a diamond, but four base-sized squares of MDF laid out in a pattern that looked like one.

"Better than well," Meli agreed. "I'll call his mom tomorrow."

"Tony thinks that stuff's a find," I said, watching Jason at the plate. "We put in for a grant."

"Good." We applauded Jason's hit just over Charlie's head and just beyond Maria's glove. "Now what?"

"We sent copies of medal citations to Washington, England and France." Maria snatched up and threw the ball back to Charlie, who threw it to Ted, who pitched it at Jason, who swung and missed.

"How long will that take?" Charlie takes over at bat; Maria pitching; Jason and Ted fielding.

"Can't say. Now I need to find help should I get a grant." First pitch, low and outside; Charlie tips it in a bunt, dashing for first base.

"School help?" Maria dashes for the ball, tossing it to Ted, who throws it at Charlie, barely missing his feet and . . . safe!

"Yep." Charlie takes the field with Ted; Maria is at the plate; Jason's on the mound . . .

"You gonna ask Polly?" The windup; the pitch . . .

"Yeah." Maria connects on a dropping ball, popping it up . . . Charlie and Ted are back, back, back . . . Maria tags first . . .

"We had lunch last week. Her boy's sweet on Maria." Back, back . . . Ted's under it . . . Maria heads for second . . .

"Isn't he Charlie's age?" Back . . . back as she rounds second . . .

"Crushes don't care about age. Don't you remember crushes?" Maria's dashing for third . . . "Like Joan?"

"Joanie wasn't a crush."* Maria's rounding third and heading for home . . . !

"No, but Polly was." Polly was five years older than I and my student mentor† who helped me catch up after my bout with mono in '77–'78. We got naked once in the spring of '80. Maria's halfway home . . . !

"Not a crush at 25." Ted calls for the catch; he's under it . . . !

---

* Crushers and crushees don't get naked together.
† Meli's father was my faculty mentor.

"You had the hots for her as soon as you got to Crest at eighteen."

"That was *then*, honey." And . . . it bounces out of his glove!

"Meet with her, babe." And Maria's safe at home!

"Hi, Sam," I said, knocking on his door the next day. "Got a minute?" Sam Becket was the Florian Mills Professor of American History, who got the job after Amy Gilchrest passed away in '93.

"Sure, Boss," he grinned, hip-deep in boxes of books. "C'mon in to my disaster." He fit the look of a history professor—right down to the horn-rim glasses and willowy hands. "Find a seat somewhere."

I located an armchair with only one box on it and moved the offending object. Sam moved two more out of his desk chair. "Sam, how's the wife?" A year before, doctors had diagnosed her with MS.

"Her mobility isn't too bad yet, but her stamina ain't there anymore."

"You never had kids?"

"Not for a lack of trying. But we found out she couldn't, so . . ." He shrugged.

"If there's anything we can do?"

"We're good. We have help when we need it, but she can fend for herself most of the time." The school's health insurance was exceptional.

"Sam, I need a favor." I explained what I might have been up against if I had won a grant. "So, my duties would need another set of hands. It's a big ask . . . "

"Um," Sam said, surveying his boxes. "This *isn't* the disaster it looks like 'cause these are everybody's books." Sam was the department's book screener.

"I'll allow all full profs to hire your own TAs and field adjuncts as needed . . . "

"OK . . . I also want in on the Truxton project." The Truxton Archive was several thousand documents of unknown provenance and authenticity. Certain documents there might have altered our understanding of the past, but the majority proved ordinary. Our few researchers studied and classified the items at a rate of about ten a year on average. My little team of researchers started plowing through them in 1982. "I can take a section from you, I suppose."*

"*Done.*" Sam was a political historian, specializing in the early Constitutional era and leading up to the Jackson period. We were finding very interesting Madison-era documents in the Truxton. His input would be priceless.

"Hey, OK." He stood and offered his hand. "I meant to congratulate you personally on your daughter's marriage. We sent a card and a little gift."

"Thanks, and I'm sure she and Mike appreciate it."

"If there's anything else you need, just let me know and I'll try to wedge something in."

If you want something *done*, ask a busy guy.

"Hi, Polly," I grinned at her reflection in the window. We met in the faculty lounge around lunchtime the next day, having arranged it by e-mail.

"Hey, Curtis," she said, bussing my cheek from behind me. Polly Winfield had been the 1968 Jenson Scholar and was now the Sturmer Grace Professor of American History. She sat in an armchair opposite me, tugging at the legs of her shorts.† "Rumor has it you've struck gold," she smiled, pulling her hair back over her shoulders. "I hear it's WWI stuff, never seen before."

"Word gets around, dosen't it?" I described what I found, what Tony and I had done so far. "If I'm gonna . . ." I started.

"*Do it,* sugar,"‡ she leaned forward and whispered with a wink. Her scoop-neck tank top drooped briefly, effectively.§ "You need it. Publishing something like that . . ." she added, leaning back, "puts you on the map. Remember what that diary I found in Utah did for my career?"

---

* A section of grad students would mean up to three class days a week and up to fifteen papers every other month. It was a lot.

† Two decades before, a Crest professor could never wear shorts in school buildings, regardless of gender. But times change.

‡ It was that name that started us going that day.

§ *Sans* brassiere, in the faculty lounge . . . times do change.

"It got you your chair," I nodded. She found an immigrant railroad worker's Cantonese/pidgin English diary in a forgotten corner of the archive at the Golden Spike park in Utah. Her translation and later research led her to other material in California and China that earned her enough credibility to get the Sturmer Grace Institute to endow her chair at Crest in perpetuity.

"Right. These diaries could save yours."

"Have you heard . . .?"

"In this job market, anything could happen."

"True." I tried to look away, but she was just . . . so . . . "How's your kids these days? How's that hubby of yours?"

"They're just fine; thanks for asking. Now," she leaned forward again, even further. "*Sugar*, you've *got* to do it. Meli says so; I say so."

"You talked to *Meli* about . . .?"

"An hour ago, *sugar*."

"Only if you'll take some of my *load, lover*." *

"For you and Meli, *sugar*," she touched my knee, "anything. I'll take a section and sit in on the Dean's weekly marathons for you."

"How about the TA contracts? Can you go over them with the Corporation?"

"Sure." She winked . . . slowly.

Then I had my help.

"Talk to Polly?" Melanie asked. With the boys in bed and Maria in her suite, we were not that interested in the reruns on TV.

"I did," I said, "so did you."

"You expected me to do anything else?" She stretched out her legs, flapping her skirt in the fan's breeze.

"Maybe not. You jealous?"

"I was when you told me about your tryst." She took her bra off with that maneuver where they don't take their tops off.

"It was more than . . . "

"It was a day of sweaty sex in The Cubes† with my buddy Polly, the first to get me drunk. What else would you call it?"

---

* That's what I called her for an afternoon, a night, and a morning.

† Nickname for the Steuben Graduate Housing Complex.

The Persistent Past

"And a night and a morning," I corrected. "We were scratching an itch."

"Twenty-four hour affair?"

"Um . . . about twenty-*two* hours."

" *We* never fooled around for twenty-two hours straight . . . "

"And we didn't either. We slept least four hours."

She sighed. "I imagined doing that when I was that age." She reached under her skirt, pulled her underwear off. "Just once, I wanted to spend a day and a night making love with someone I truly cared about . . . loved."

"Then . . . now?"

"The kids would interrupt us." She threw her underwear at me and turned the TV off. "C'mon; let's sprint."

"How about we take a weekend, go somewhere without kids?" she whispered, passing the boy's rooms. "Weekend after this . . . "

"Our anniversary?"

"When better?"

"The kids?"

"Maria's old enough to watch the boys for a weekend; Connie will look in . . . ."

"You already asked?"

"Yep."

"Can I go with you, Dad?" Maria, her swim bag over her shoulder, would normally either walk or bike or shuttle bus* to the pool. But that day it was raining, threatening lightning.

"Sure."

It was drizzling when I stopped at the Hermann Field House . . . and Maria didn't open the door. "Dad, can I go *with* you?"

"I'm working . . . ."

"On those diaries." She looked determined, so much like her mother. "I want to read more of them."

"The Holding Room's gonna be a *cold* in those shorts."

"I brought sweats."

---

* Shuttles went all over Crest, Granite Ledge and its environs round the clock. Kids eight and over could get passes.

We entered the Archive Building through the side entrance, which required ID and a passcode.* Maria pulled her sweats on as soon as we got to Holding. I gave her gloves and a pad of paper and sat her down in a cubicle, gave her a diary. "Now, note any names you find and how often you find them. It's important to align real people to the names in the text, as the more we do *that*, the more authentic the documents become."

"Uh-huh; OK," she said distractedly, paging through the diary.

The early stage of any document collection exploration project was both exciting and boring, since much of any set of documents was mundane. I grabbed a few loose sheets that started in January, like any diary, and showed signs of being torn out of a binding. They also emitted a peculiar smell that wasn't just of aging paper.

"Smell this," I asked Maria, holding an errant sheet in front of her. She sniffed, wrinkling her nose. "Spit-up?"

"Do these look like teeth marks?"

"Little teeth; yeah, somebody's been chewing on 'em."

"Explains the smell, too. Welcome to historical research in the raw, Ms. Durand."

She grinned, and we both went back to reading; interesting . . . fascinating . . . captivating . . . absorbing . . . .

"Flu survivors?" I wondered aloud. Maria shifted in her chair, leaned back, frowning. I saw a tear roll down her face. "Honey? You OK?"

"I'm fine," she sighed at length. "Just reading about this hill he's on." She looked at me. "This is the most . . . *interesting* and *horrible* thing I've ever read."

"A *lot* of this work is like that, but a lot it is . . . puzzling. Like this, with no date, but probably 1919."

> *I find it hard to believe it was just two months ago we were preparing to attack the last bastions of the Kriemhilde Stellung. I have not heard shooting for nearly two months*

---

* The main entrance, where the great unwashed came, was staffed seven days a week.

The Persistent Past

and yet sometimes at night, I can hear the
machine guns rattling in the dark.

"Shell-shock, I guess."

"They call it something else now, Dad: PTSD. Listen to this, from 1918 . . . "

29ᵗʰ May, Bois de St. Bourges.
I walk among the casualties in the aid
stations, making sure no one is suffering
more than they have to. Thorsten's hurt;
Grimes is in a bad way; Willis is out for a few
weeks, or months. Dugan's lost his right arm;
out of the Army for good.
Again, many dead among the officers, like
Lieut. McCarthy and Capt. Duran from the
staff, and I struggle to feel both more and
less. I know feeling is dangerous for me here
and now but [expletive] *I want to weep and*
cannot find the strength!!!

She read the entry aloud, blinking, and wiped another tear. "Guys he knew . . . killed . . . "

"Maria, are you *sure* you . . .?"

"I love this stuff, Dad," she sniffed, then grinned. "As smelly and as raw and a scary as this is, this is *orgiastic.*"

"You know what *orgiastic* means, honey?"

"Thrilling; super-exciting."

"Well, yeah, but the root of the term is orgy." I paused. "Know what that means?"

"People having sex in a . . . *oh!*" She blushed with sudden recognition, shifting in her chair. "Kids say that all the time in school."

"Shows you what middle schooler's vocabulary is like, dosen't it? Here: this is probably from 1919."

18ᵗʰ January
Death, death, nothing but death. I am
surrounded by death. This has been one of the

*longest, most grueling nights of my life bar
none.
Dad sent the wire to the Senator, and he had
Angie show it to me.
Mama was 38; Di was 23; Helen was 14; Irving
was but 12. They died of the flu in October.
I had heard it was bad back home, but not
this bad. Flu killed more Americans in three
months than the Germans did in a year.
I didn't know how life-affirming being with a
woman can be, especially after such news.
Angie is my rock, my buddy like Di was, but of
course not like Di was.
But now, I can weep in Angie's arms.*

I stopped, watching for her reaction. She wiped her face with her sleeve again, swallowed hard, and said, "Helen was just a year older than me." She blinked again. "*Flu* killed all those people?"

"It did. They called it the *Spanish* Flu. Killed more people than the *war* did, I understand." I paused. "Irving was a year younger than you."

"Yeah," she said softly. "His mother; Di *is* Diane, his sister; Helen and Irving were his sister and brother."

"Yeah? How do you know?"

"I read it in here; July 1917 . . . "

"I wonder who the Senator would have been?"

"Here," she read from her notes. "He met Miss AG on the train on July 28th." She paged back. "*Here.*"

*28th July, Eastbound train.
I am sensible of what I am about to say
because of my understanding with G, but I
have met quite the most remarkable young
woman, Miss AG, the daughter of Senator G,
who put George's name forward for the naval
academy. I expressed the family's
appreciation for his sponsorship; she will pass
it on. Miss AG has Red Cross training and says
she wants to volunteer for overseas. I am*

completely enchanted by her smile and her
violet eyes. If I never see her again, I shall
never forget those eyes.

"Huh," I said as she finished reading. "Looks like they got married in France in January, probably in 1919, by this diary entry."

She smiled, but wiped away another tear. "Good that she was around for him when . . . . that telegram . . . "

"Yeah. Not especially orgiastic, though, is it?"

"Dad, I'll never use *that* word again."

"Not at least until you take part in one, eh?"

She threw her head back and erupted into laughter. "Don't worry, Papa,"* she said at last. "I'm not gonna do *that* until I *do it* with one guy I like a lot."

Good to know, honey. "So, what do you think of this work after," I glanced at my watch, "three hours of it?"

"I want *more.*" She turned back to the diary.

"Um," I asked, "that diary entry's November, yeah? How did you get that far in three hours while taking notes?"

"Well, I didn't start at the beginning and I didn't read everything in between," she said, looking at her notes. "I started in . . . July. He'd *just* got promoted and was furloughed to a place near Detroit,"

"Ah." She rubbed her sandaled feet together. "Cold?"

"Chilly in here," she agreed.

"A constant 65 degrees in the archives. Want to take a break? Warm up some?"

We walked to the lobby, which was air-conditioned to a temperature of a slightly wetter 70. The receptionist wasn't there; the sign said *Press button for service.*

We watched the rain pelting down as lightning flashed over the mountains, and we heard the crack of thunder rolling across the campus. Then we heard the Noon Shot as it *cracked* and *rolled* across Granite Valley. Having lived there for so long, it had become like church bells ringing every fifteen minutes, so familiar we barely

---

* Not a term she used often.

paid attention. But we knew it was Jenson Stone's North Quarry firing a midday blast—as they did about every other weekday from May to October—freeing another few hundred tons of granite from its mountain. No one minded, because nearly everyone knew that twenty-five percent and more of the school's budget came from quarry endowments, and a third of Granite Valley worked either at the school or in the quarries.

I wondered what was going through Maria's thirteen-year-old head after reading *that* when she said, "Ned and Angela were *twenty-one* when they met. *Twenty-two* when they got married. Ned asked G's father if he could write to her."

"Yeah, it was a different . . . who's G?"

"A girl he met in Michigan. Did you ask Grampa Bert's permission to marry Mom?"

"Um . . . no," I said, clearing my throat. "No; we just said we wanted to raise you together, and he poured us a drink."

"Does Gramma Helen know I'm not yours?"

"They figured it out at different times."

Silence. "Thanks for adopting me, Dad."[†]

"You're welcome."

"This *kind* of work, this research," she whispered. "So many questions. So many pathways."

"It's not for the faint of heart or the lazy," I agreed, glad she'd got off that tangent.

"Does it always seem . . . personal?"

"We often try to put the lives of those in the past into a current context to understand why they did what they did, but that's a mistake," I answered. "There's a concept called *zeitgeist,* which is a German word for 'time' and 'ghost' or 'spirit.' It defines the prevailing . . ."

"*Spirit* of the *time,*" she finished. "Like that guy said: the past is a foreign country, they do things differently there."

"LP Hartley said that; and it's true," I sighed. "Historians and their students have to struggle against interpreting the actions of the

---

[*] The South Quarry, across the river, fired at 9 AM and 3 PM; the Morning and Afternoon Shots.

[†] She asked me to after briefly meeting her birth-father when she was eight.

past using current sensibilities."

She gazed at the rain; looked up at the lightning. "If every boy I talk to had to ask your permission, like Ned did for G . . . "

"How many are there?"

"I don't hang out with all the boys at my school, but I know their names, talk to a lot of 'em. I've known most of 'em since kindergarten." She paused. "But then, on the train, after Ned met Angela, he said 'my understanding with G.' What did he mean?"

"An agreement between a man and a woman then meant, um, like going steady."

"What?"

"*You* call it exclusive."

"Oh. So why didn't he ask Angie's father's permission?"

"*That* was the contrast between what people do in peace and in war. Ned was going off to war; so was Angela; G in Michigan wasn't. Attitudes change then. Life, when faced with death, becomes more immediate." I remembered that from a unique military history class I had to take.[*]

"Like with Connie and Jenny and Jerry. Jenny was sent to the Gulf; Connie and Jerry got together . . . "

"You knew about that?"[†]

"Yeah. I want friends I could share a friend with; be *that* trusting."

"That would be extraordinary, Maria," I said, stroking her back. "I was glad when it played out for them."

"It's good to have friends, be friends before going all the way, isn't it, Dad?"

"Yes, it is, honey. It's very important to be friends first."

"I like Ted, Dad; a lot." She turned to me. "I want a relationship like Ned and Angela had *before* I . . . "

"Well, we'll have to find out how long that lasted. A lot of wartime marriages don't endure."

---

[*] War and Society was part history and part sociology, covering the effects of war on societies.

[†] The three had been buddies since high school. Jenny joined the Army Reserve to help pay for college and was called up; Connie and Jerry fell into each other's arms while she was gone. Maria was eight.

"OK," she said, rubbing her hands together, "let's get back to work."

"Batter *up!*" the umpire called at the bottom of the 7th. The score was 3-2 with a runner on second; Maria was up to bat for the Falcons.

"So, tell me about Maria's excursion yesterday," Melanie said, watching her stride to the plate. "How fast did she get bored?"

"She didn't," I said. Maria tapped her cleats with her bat, rolled her shoulders as she took her place in the box. The Vixen's star pitcher snagged the throw from short, turned to face her opponent; she's struck out five that day.

"Really?" Meli said, glancing around for the boys. Jason, in his mascot suit, aped his sister with his oversized plastic bat.

"She was genuinely interested," I said. "She has good instincts." Maria took her stance; the pitcher started her windup . . . .

"Huh." Jason, watching, waved his bat . . . .

"I think she might be good at it." Here's the pitch . . . .

"Huh." Maria checks her swing; ball one . . . .

"She said she wants to be friends with the guy before she has sex." The Vixen catcher throws it back . . . .

"She *said that?*" The pitcher winds up . . . .

"Yep. There's a couple in there. She . . ." And the pitch . . . .

"A couple of what?" Maria draws back . . . Jason draws back. . . .

"People . . . ." Swings and connects . . . the crowd goes wild as the ball arcs over the infield and drops over the head of the Vixen's center fielder!

"*Go, go, go, baby, GO!*" Maria rounds first . . . the runner crosses home . . . center field dashes for the ball . . . .

"*Dig in,* Durand!" the Falcon coach yelled. Maria tags second; the batting coach waves her in . . . center field scoops it up . . . !

"*Run, Stinky, run!*" batboy Charlie yells from the Falcon's bench as Maria rounds third; center field arcs the ball to the pitcher . . . .

"*GOOO . . . .!*" Everyone's on their feet . . . she's dashing for the plate; the pitcher catches, twirls around, her braids slashing her face . . . cuts loose . . . .

"*Slide!*" the Falcon coach yells; it's gonna be close . . . she dives and . . . here's the ball . . . the catcher's in front of it . . . she's got it and . . . !

"*Safe!*" the umpire calls! And the Falcons win!*

"Inside-the-park homer," I sighed. "I know a little about baseball, but . . . "

"Yeah," Melanie said, still applauding as Maria took the backslaps and high-fives from her teammates. "And here I thought that stuff was about WWI."

"It's a bunch of diaries written by a young man *in* the war," I said. "He meets a woman . . . "

"Oh," Meli said. "Not some camp-follower, I hope . . ." Maria hugged her brother in his Falcon suit . . . .

"Daughter of a senator, we think," I answered as Maria waved at us and kissed Charlie, much to his embarrassment . . . .

"Oh. So she likes the . . . wait; you said something about friends and sex . . .?"

"She said she wants to . . ." I started.

"Later," Meli answered, getting up to leave.

A lot of our important conversations were like that—interrupted by kids.

"So, *what* was it Maria said?" Meli asked. We were watching TV reruns again in the living room. Maria, Jason and Charlie were having pizza with the team after the upset win over the favored Vixens. I summarized our dialog. "Huh. She's thought about it." At the commercial break, she got up. "Want anything from the kitchen?"

"Pass."

She came back with a soda pop. "How well does she handle it? She dosen't get bored?"

"Anything but. She got a little weepy sometimes. It's the first time she's seen a first-hand account of the past that hasn't been filtered by the entertainment industry or some other writer."

"Huh." Silence. "So the *boring* stuff lessons didn't work. Is there anything big in there?"

---

* Games were seven innings.

"Can't say. The nature of original sources is you can't really tell what's in it until you read it and get some validation."

"And she still swam after?"

"For an hour. I talked with Adelle while I waited."

"Is she on the mend?"*

"It would seem so. She looks the same; just a little older."

"I wish Maria would just choose one sport."

"She has different friends in different sports."

"That's true." She changed the channel. We didn't talk about much after that, but I could hear Melanie's gears grinding all night, and smelled them when we kissed goodnight.

"Philip Bergmann," Ted's father extended his hand across my threshold that rainy Saturday. "Pleased to meet you."

"Curtis Durand," I answered, taking his hand. "So glad to . . . "

"Sarah Bergmann," Ted's mother smiled, boldly crossing my threshold, a little girl in tow. "Your kitchen is . . . *there*, I see it." She was shaking hands with Meli, setting down her loaf of bread and donning an apron before I could . . .

"Please excuse my wife, Curtis," Philip said, leading a girl and a boy into the house. "This is Nona, my eldest daughter, and David, my youngest son."

"Nona; David," I nodded; the girl, arms crossed, smiled indulgently; the boy offered his hand. "The kids and your brother are downstairs if you want to join them. I think Ted and the boys are working the trains; can't say what Maria's up to."

"Thanks," Nona sighed, and David grinned, clomping down the steps.

"Philip, can I offer you a libation?" The cats, as they often did when guests arrived, watched from their tree.

"White wine, if you have it, please."

After going into the kitchen for the one thing I did not have in the living room, I offered a toast. "To our children who brought us together."

---

* Adelle Freeman, the school's Athletic Director and swim coach, had breast cancer treatment the previous winter.

The Persistent Past

"To our children, indeed, Curtis," he smiled, a rather pleasing look on his drawn face. "You'll have to excuse Winona; she wasn't that eager to attend." We both listened to the girls giggling from the basement. "She's a year ahead of Ted and Maria, though I think they know each other from last year."

"Philip, would you care to retreat to my den?" I asked, listening to the goings-on in the kitchen just before Sarah came out with the little girl.

"Can I take Alicia downstairs?" Sarah asked. "She's getting underfoot."

"Right over there." I pointed to the stairs across from the front door. Turning to Philip, I nodded. "Now, the den."

Philip gazed around my bookshelves, my photos on my walls. He was tall and seemed emaciated. "You teach at the University, I understand," he said.

"I do, yes. American history. You have a car dealership in Granite Ledge."

"With my brother. Curtis, I *have* to say this," he intoned, looking out my window, inhaling deeply. "I believe your daughter and my son are an attractive couple. She seems to be a *very* bright girl."

"Yes, I, ah, think the same. Ted's a smart kid."

"He is, yes." He glanced at me. "And they both say the work you do is very stimulating."

"Well . . . um," I stumbled; history work is called a lot of things, but *stimulating* isn't one of them. "The job of history can be . . ."

"Yes; I majored in history after my stint in the Army. Satisfying, but not very lucrative . . . then the family business got in trouble." Philip scanned the bookshelf behind me, as if thinking of something . . . else. "Not all professions are as they seem."

"Indeed, not," I agreed.

"We are not observant Jews, Curtis; I believe Sarah told Melanie this when they spoke." Their telephone conversation the Monday before took nearly an hour, chattering like old friends who had never met.

"I gathered that." Her pseudo-explanation of her call told me more about moms talking about their kids than it did about the Bergmanns as a family. "You have an older son?"

"Yes; Redmond is twenty, works for the streets department. *And* he attends Granite Ledge Community College, studying law enforcement. He wants to go to the state police academy. He also works at our dealership on weekend evenings." Then he smiled. "My children, Curtis, are not only blessings, they have been my salvation." He sipped his wine, glanced once again at the shelves behind me. "A Jew talking about salvation," he mused. "But there it is." He leaned back. "Tell me about these diaries that Maria tells us about."

I gave him a capsule rendition of what we had found so far. "It's an ambitious project, I admit, but I believe it will add to the corpus of what we know about the Americans in WWI. He drops a lot of names, such as Pershing and Patton and Marshall, that I can't verify he ever met." I sipped my wine. "Working on it." Midge at that moment strolled into the den.

"My *grandfather* was in that conflict," Philip said, watching Midge as he jumped up next to him.* "My *father* was in Korea." He breathed deep. "*I* was in Vietnam."

"My Dad was a Seabee in the Pacific; *Meli's* father flew in B-29s; I had an uncle who was killed in WWI. I never served." Undisturbed by this intruder, Midge crouched on the sofa arm.

He shrugged. "Not everyone had to." Once again, he scanned the bookshelf behind me before he finished his wine. "May I ask for more wine?"

I fetched the bottle and came back to find Philip studying Meli's father's memoirs that I had edited; it was on the shelf behind my chair. "I have *more* of those," I said.

"Ah, I have one, thank you," he answered, letting me fill his glass. "Melanie's father autographed my copy at the American Legion post when it came out." He sipped his wine. "I only mention it because, well, I saw that book on your shelf and I . . . I do that from time to time; become distracted." He smiled, stroking a purring Midge as Smudge walked into the den. "I was determined to speak of our children we met." Midge stared wide-eyed at Smudge as she jumped up on the *other* sofa arm.

---

* It was one of his daytime spots.

The Persistent Past

"Well," I started, interrupted by a peal of laughter from the basement, "I don't think we have anything to worry about."

"That was fun," Meli said, slipping into bed that night.

"It was . . . and the kids didn't kill each other."

"Three girls and four boys aged fourteen to four hung out with no blood spilled or tears shed, and dinner went well. Kids even helped clean up."

"Maria knows Nona from where?"

"They took that goal-tender clinic with the county soccer league last year."

"And Frisbees in the rain," I added. After dinner, *everyone* was in the backyard in the warm drizzle and tossed plastic discs around for an hour. Melanie and Sarah conspired to hoard all three discs when darkness fell.

"Maria did good." We listened until the boys settled. "Did you know Sarah before?"

"Slightly; PTO. She's younger than we are. Philip's older. They'd known each other; old family friends."

"And Red's twenty? She started young."

"He'll be twenty next month, but yeah; she was nineteen, a freshman in college, when she had him." It amazed me how much information could pass between two women in a phone conversation and one meeting. She grabbed my hand. "Philip's a nice guy."

"Yeah. He thinks Maria and Ted are an attractive couple."

"I do, too; Sarah called them *handsome.*" She squeezed my hand. "Sarah mentioned that Ted's getting an interest in WWI."

"Huh."

"They are each other's first close-to-serious relationships. We don't believe they're *biblical*, Maria probably stops Ted at second degree,* or he stops on his own."

"Over or under?"

"Maybe lights-off under by now."

Silence. "Do you even know where your blue bikini is?"

---

* First degree—swim attire/no contact with skin beyond lips. Third degree, no attire/full contact with everything.

"Tossed it after Maria was born; it would never fit again." Silence. "Charlie's last game of the season tomorrow."

"Uh-huh."

Silence, but for the night sounds outside. "I was *twelve*, I think, when I first got felt up over my swimsuit."

"You had enough at twelve to . . .?"*

"Didn't matter how much I had. I was more curious than scared, wondered what it felt like for a boy to . . . "

"I'll guarantee he was terrified."

"When did you try, either over or under?"

"Joanie and I were fourteen, making out in the hammock in my backyard one night in our swimsuits it was so hot. Next thing I knew, we were stark naked and . . . ."

"Nothing in between? Not even a little oral . . . .?"

"Nope."

"Under didn't happen for me until Junior Prom. Strapless gown; kinda inevitable in '73."

"You were still curious?"

"Eager; I put his hand . . . here . . . "

"Do you still feel the same about me now as you did then?" We'd driven to the Chateau Montague resort up the Sonoco River that weekend.

"Then . . . when?" It was a ski lodge/recreation area on Mount Killeen[†] that attracted tourists year round.

"When we first . . .?" We were on one of several hiking trails late Saturday morning, after snooping through their little faux mountain village/tourist trap.

"Met in the Exec?" As the 1973 Jenson Scholar, I had my first meal at Crest with Polly, Meli, and her father in the Jenson Endowment Executive Building's Executive Dining Room.[‡]

---

[*] I'd seen pictures of Meli at twelve. I believe the term is late bloomer.
[†] In the Grey Mountain range.
[‡] Meeting their faculty mentors at the Exec was a tradition for Jenson Scholars; I'd only been in that lofty palace four times in my 23 years at Crest.

"No, not then; I was terrified then." After we arrived at the chateau the night before, we enjoyed a delicious four-course dinner with wine (which we never did at home), followed by an evening in our in-room jacuzzi, then by a relaxing sleep.

"Of me?"

"Of having to see a boy my age in my living room as often as I saw Polly for the next decade.˙ But I thought you were *cute* in those *tight cords* when you came down to the house after . . . "

"I thought you were cute in that short-short skirt."

"Culottes . . . "

"Whatever they were. But . . . no, when we first . . .?"

"When you went *noble* and proposed, bended knee and the whole spiel nine years later?"

"Now as then? Sure; more." We reached two posts marked *Diversion C* on each side of the narrower, steeper trail uphill of the main trail. A drop-bar secured by a padlock stretched between the posts.✝ The trail led us to a bowl twenty yards uphill, just about three feet lower than the trail to it. A screen tent, gently swaying in the fresh breeze of pine scents, covered the bowl. Varnished stumps passed for chairs and tables. We gazed around us at the spectacle of a tree-covered New England mountain on a balmy late spring morning. "I always liked you."

"It took *me* a while." She pulled the blanket out of her bag; I pulled the bottle of wine from mine. We spread the blanket out on the needle-covered ground and opened the wine. She took off her shirt, leaving a blue bikini top. "New, *just* for *you*, babe," she winked, pouring the wine into paper cups, sitting on stumps.

"Well, *thanks*," I said, pulling my shirt off. "Bring your boyfriend up here, do you?"

"Mike proposed to Connie in one of these." She slipped off her skirt—she had blue bottoms, too. "Now, I'm bringing you." I doffed my pants; thought I'd try a smaller Speedo-like, ventilated thong-thing. She stared, grinning. "*Those* are smaller than *mine*."

˙ Jenson Scholars are encouraged to hang with their mentor's families.
✝ We had the key, having reserved the diversion for the day.

"Supposed to be cooler."* We sipped, watching the scenery as the sun twinkled through the dense canopy overhead and the translucent tent, breathing in the deep richness of the pines on the soft breeze. "But yours looks *bigger* than your old one . . . "

"Three kids and fifteen years later it has to be a little bigger . . . I sometimes feel like I *trapped* you with Maria."

"What a *wonderful* trap."

"I'm *serious.*"

"So am I." I reached for her hand. "When I married you, your father enabled me to do what I'd planned to do since I was a teenager, and I've loved every day of my life since."

"I don't know *when* I loved you, babe," she sighed, "but I *think* it was before you asked." We sipped.

"I *think* I loved *you* that Christmas break." We sipped.

"Maybe it was then for *me*, too. It was my *tiny* bikini and your little Speedo that did it for us."

"Don't matter how big it is or was, I love what's *in* it." We finished our cups of wine.

She stood and untied her top and bottoms, one string at a time, and stretched her arms high; I stripped. "This place is amazing," she said, walking to the edge of the enclosure.

"I just hope nobody's gonna come down behind us," I walked up behind to embrace her.

"If they do, they'll get one helluva show." We stood inches from the screen wall, not moving, before she moved back to the blanket and lay on her side, holding out her hand. "*Come* to me, babe."

Making love on a mountainside to the one person in the world I wanted to spend my life with, snoozing, drinking more wine, snacking on cheese and bread, chatting about us and the kids, doing it again before the sun set behind the mountain and the bugs came out.

Then I knew that was what it was all for.

"Sex is not the same at forty as it is at nineteen," Meli sighed early Sunday morning, with the sun pouring into our bedroom skylight. We hadn't gotten a *great* deal of sleep.

---

* They did sweat less, but they crept up my . . .

"You're forty-one in three months." I gazed at her, half covered by the sheet. "It felt the same." We'd done more talking than we'd done for a while, and more of that than we usually did in a day and a half.

"That's because you're a *guy*," she sighed, turning her head. "Gals . . . "

"Ah."

"But my passion has become more intense." We watched fluffy clouds passing overhead. "Never done it outside before, not in broad daylight."

"Can't recall doing it outside in daylight, either. *Moonlight,* though, almost."

"I'm *glad* we did." She sat up and stretched, her brown locks cascading down her back.

"Me, too. So why now?"

"Because, after you get that grant, you're going to get involved with those diaries. They will take most of your attention and your energy." She turned to me. "Oh, you'll still be around, be with the kids and me, going through the motions with us; make love to me pretty regular. But your *mind* will be over there." She stroked my forehead. "We need to get in as much loving before that grant comes as we can." She ran her finger down my face. "Understand?"

"I'm glad you believe I'll get the grant, but why would I change . . .?"

"You need this Big Thing, babe," she smiled, reaching for the sheet. "We need this; all of us. But *now* . . ." she threw the sheet off and straddled me. "*I want* . . . "

Afterwards, we dozed off in each other's arms; the sun glazing the sweat on us. The next thing I heard was her voice in my ear. "Babe, I love you. Our first time, remember? Up in the Cubes the morning *after* we told my parents I was expecting, and you pro-posed?" She slid on top of me. "I gave you every chance to back out." She sat up to straddle my hips. "That first time . . ." she deftly maneuvered . . . "and you had a little grin, *that* one . . . I knew . . . what love . . . beyond mere lust . . . felt like . . . *oh!*"

So did I.

"Meli, Maria seriously wants to help me with those diaries." We were heading back home after our erotic weekend, and yes, we slept at least seven hours out of thirty-six.

"She *said* that?"

"Yeah." I never remember feeling so relaxed and drained and in love as I was that afternoon.

"What would she be doing beyond reading?"

"Transcribing; indexing; inventorying. She can read the cursive pretty well."*

"How much help would she give? How much time?"

"We haven't worked that out yet. I can pay her out of the grant if I get it. It might already owe Mike a grand."

"How much would you pay her?"

"$5 an hour . . .?"

"She gets that babysitting or cutting grass, when she can get the work." There was a glut in those local markets, too.

"Maybe $7?"

"Maybe. Wonder what she'd give up?"

"*Not* her studies." She was an excellent student, doing well in every subject but math, where she was average, at best. "Some athletics?"

"Don't think so; she loves the camaraderie. I'd want to know *why*, though, besides the money."

"So *ask* her."

After the welcome home excitement, gift-giving,† and getting the luggage in, we sat on Maria's sofa—with her between us. "You said you wanted to help with those diaries," I started.

"Yeah," she answered, looking back and forth. "Did you guys have *fun?*"

"We *said* we did, honey," Meli said, looking at her sideways.

---

* Crest insisted that Granite Ledge schools teach cursive writing that many of our college students regarded as code; we had freshman and graduate remedial classes in it.
† Most of the excitement was for the little trinkets expected after any trip. That's the sole reason those tourist trap gift shops exist.

"It's good for couples to do that, isn't it? Get away from it all for a little, I mean . . . so you *can* . . . without kids around?"

"When you have kids, you'll get it, honey," Meli patted her arm. "Any trouble with the boys?"

"No, but before those *tattletales* tell you, Ted was here for about half an hour while Connie was here on Saturday night."

"Here, where?" Meli asked.

"Living room: lights on, Mom."

Meli looked at me. "And . . .?"

"*No* exposure, Mom. He helps me with math."

"That all?" I asked, winking at Meli.

Maria glanced at Meli, then side-glanced at me. "We made out for a few minutes. *OK?*"

"As long as you're straight with us, baby," Meli said. "Now your father . . . "

"Maria," I said, "the Steele Collection would like to contract you to transcribe diaries and index the material *if* we get a grant."

She blinked, surprised. "*Contract* me? For *money?*"

"We're prepared to offer you $7 an hour for five hours a week."

She blinked, stared at Meli. "How much for *twenty* hours a week this summer, Dad?"

"Maria, twenty hours would cut into a lot of stuff you like, wouldn't it?" Meli asked. "You have swimming, and . . . "

"Swim practice for the teen league[+] is two hours three evenings a week, Mom," she answered. "I *like* swimming for the exercise and the friends, and Coach Freeman's gonna put the team at The Rock[‡] through *hell* next year."[§] She shook her head and spoke into the air. "I just like to be with friends."

---

[*] When we *first* talked about boys, we said "be straight with us *when* . . . ."

[+] Maria swam in the Crest-organized *teen* league, playing soccer at school and baseball in a multi-county league; Charlie played ball in the Crest *youth* league; Jason played in the *pee-wee* league; I swam in the *faculty* league; Meli in the *family* league.

[‡] Granite Ledge High School.

[§] Adelle was an Olympic swimming medalist who *finally* got an AAU-approved swim squad together at Granite Ledge High, but *not yet* at Crest.

"Maria," I said, "we will only pay you to work *fifteen hours* a week during the summer. When school starts, you'll go down to *five*."

Maria glanced at Meli, then at me, then looked down. "And there's *Ted*," she sighed, leaning forward, "and the rest of my friends. Not all of them play baseball, *or* soccer, *or* volleyball, *or* swim."

"*Friend*-maintenance is important, honey," Meli said. "Why do you want to work on these diaries? They're by a man who . . . "

"He wrote what he saw," Maria said. "What he saw was pretty terrible. But it's . . ." she cast about for the words, looking at the ceiling, "it's terrible and it's wonderful and it's fascinating, all at the same time."

I could see a bit of Meli's heart fall. "But once the bloom is off that rose, honey," I started.

"Then I'll tell you and quit, Dad," she interrupted. "But I want to see where Angie and Ned end up. Some of that stuff . . . it's kinda . . . "

"Those people *then* . . ." Meli said, with a little edge.

"He wrote about being fully exposed, Mom," Maria said with a smile. "I *know* how *it* works."

Meli smiled a little. "You want to know how . . .?"

"Things were different then, Mom," Maria grinned, taking both our hands. "They didn't have TV or movies or magazines or the internet like we do now."

"That's true, Meli," I nodded. "French postcards were as close as you could get to *Playboy* in 1918."

"Let alone *Hustler* or *Nugget*," Maria added. We both looked at her, open-mouthed. "Allison's brother gets 'em." She rolled her eyes. "She filched some from his closet . . . ."*

"You know that's just . . ." I interrupted.

"Yeah, Dad." Maria grinned and shook her head. "Those women are airbrushed silicone-sisters,† and the guys . . . besides," her voice dropped an octave, "there's Jason and Charlie, and I've

---

* Allison was a neighbor/classmate/bestie with a 21-year-old brother at home.
† I hadn't looked at those magazines in years (honest!), but I knew that most models had augmentations by the '90s, and they were showing much more than when *I* looked at them *for the articles* . . . .

The Persistent Past

seen boys' suits too far down." She looked at me again. "Dad, I want to help you with those diaries." Maria's eyes were so expressive, so warm, so . . . *demanding* when she talked like that.

"You'd sacrifice a lot of time this summer, Maria," Meli said. "You're sure you want to . . .?"

"I also want to find out why a fellow diarist kept writing," she answered with her most even voice.

"This is original source material, Maria," I said. "Some of it might be . . . *savage*, if you get what I mean. If we can authenticate what he wrote . . . "

"Yeah, Dad," Maria answered. "He was writing about some awful stuff; death all around him. I just want to know if . . . it just made him feel better or what?" She crossed her arms again. "When I'm writing in my journals, I wonder about Anne Frank's Kitty. Was Kitty real or just someone Anne made up? The nature of who diarists are writing to is what I need to know."

Meli and I looked at each other. "Reason enough, honey?" I asked.

"I suppose, babe," Meli answered—with gritted teeth.

"So," I said, looking back at Maria. "What do you say to $7 an hour?"

Maria offered her hand. "*Deal.* When do I start?"

"We'll go down to the Archives Monday, get you some credentials so you can go in there on your *own*, grant or not."

"Both surprising and . . ." I started after Meli slid into bed.

"Not so surprising, yeah," she finished. "Our journaling daughter wants to get into history in a big way."

"I could use the help," I said. "An inventory and mechanical validations will take two months, minimum, if it was just me."

Silence. "Do you see signs of . . .?"

"Maybe." We were very wary of any changes in her behavior outside the norms of growing teen girls.*

"Let's watch for it." Silence. "What are you thinking?"

---

* Both Maria's biological father and grandfather suffered from mental health issues.

"Smell the gears grind?"

"*Hear*'em."

She nestled next to me. "*I* think she wants to work with *Daddy*, using that bit about motivations as an excuse to get close to you."

"Huh." Silence, listening to the night sounds of the house, waiting. "Wanna . . .?"

"*Just* cuddle . . . if you can *do* that."

"Since we haven't slept through the night in the past two, I can."

"I should wake you up for some fun at midnight, just for that."

"Now, let's set a few ground rules, guys," I said, packed in Melanie's minivan that Saturday morning. "Stay together; always keep an adult or Maria in sight, and only Mom and me are getting buyer tags. Got it?"

"Yeah;" "OK, Dad;" "Sure, Pop."

We got to Steele Farm by 10 that morning. Mike gave me the receipt for what he paid for the trunk,* I'd gone to estate sales as part of my training at Crest: Practical History Research, a 500-level course I taught now. I'd gone to a few more in my role as the curator of the Crest/Jenson Archives. But I hadn't gone to one as just me for ages. But this trip was to validate the provenance of that old trunk and the contents, camouflaged as a family outing.

Steele Farm looked both prosperous and ramshackle at once. I'd seen farms in New England, the Midwest and the South, but this one wasn't the usual farm I'd seen anywhere. Other farms we'd passed getting to Steele's had structures huddled together. Steele Farm was more sprawling on a three-acre cleared lot. The slab-sided, two-story main farmhouse had a wing added to one side, making it look lopsided. A falling-down wooden barn sat forlornly next to a newer and larger steel pole barn. Add to that several wooden and metal sheds and lean-tos, a couple more brick buildings, a brick-and-frame cottage in a corner, a mixture of rail, concrete block, stone, and chain-link fences and retaining walls, a broad concrete apron and a gravel driveway. On one side of the lot were fields planted in shin-high corn; on the other two sides were woods with dense underbrush in some places and cleared in others. A

---

* It read *Locked Oversized Steamer Trunk, $20.*

The Persistent Past

hundred yards of grass, dotted with cars and trucks, separated the nearest structure from the road.

We parked the minivan near the road, and Melanie, Maria, and I paced slowly up the drive as the boys dashed to the tractors, trailers, and other machinery under awnings, which seemed odd since most developers wanted to unload the stuff as fast as possible. Most of the modest crowd were looking at the machinery and equipment in the awnings and outbuildings.

Maria went after the boys when they passed out of sight; Meli and I walked up to the main house. Most of the furnishings inside were older, but not yet antique, though there were a few antiques in not-bad, cleaned-up shape. There was a nice end table, a well-worn dining room set, and a newer sofa in the front room. Over the fireplace was a painting of a man, a woman, a girl, and two boys in an oval frame. Unlike most of the other items in the house, it had neither a sale sticker nor a tag.

While Meli wandered into the kitchen, I entered a small room off the living room and stopped, staring at an untagged, framed document on the wall.

Now, in my career as an archivist and a history educator, I'd been lucky several times with interesting and even important finds in dusty archives. As a person, I'd been lucky a few times: finding the love of my life, having healthy children, and having a career that I'd dreamed of since I was thirteen.

But never had I ever been this lucky.

The framed document was the quit deed for Steele Farm. The owners were Edmund A. and Angela G. Steele, dated November 10th, 1952. That told me that the steamer trunk and the diaries must have come from *this* Steele family . . . and Ned.[*]

"*That* item's not for sale," a woman's voice behind me declared. "Untagged . . . "

"I *know*," I said. "What would it take to talk to someone in the family?"

"I dunno . . ." I must have looked ill because she asked, "are you all right, sir?" as she sat me in a wooden swivel chair in front of

---

[*] The Steele name was on several businesses in the area.

an enormous roll-top desk. "You look like you've seen a ghost."

"I have," I declared, pointing at the portrait over the mantle. "There: Ned and Angie Steele."

The woman turned and looked. "Um . . . I don't . . . "

"I bought the contents of a steamer trunk you sold to Mike Klein," I said, producing the receipt. "It's full of his diaries and other things."

The woman was probably my age or a little older, with wisps of gray in her brown hair. She brushed it back out of her face reflexively. "Mike Klein? I know Mike; been dealing with him for . . . "

"He's my son-in-law."

"Oh," she said, looking back and forth at me, then at the portrait. "So . . . "

"So that document on the wall," I hitched my thumb over my shoulder, "means that trunk and its contents are from a real person—*him*."*

"It's like a voice from the past, then," she nodded. "I'm Sue Benotti, managing this sale." She offered her hand. "Their youngest son was the last owner."

"Ma'am," I said, shaking her hand. "Most businesses would just clear it out as fast as possible. Why would . . .?"

"Talk to the owner, Ridgeway Renovations, out back."

Out back of the house where Sue led me were a desk, a chair, and several boxes of objects under an awning. "Colin, this is . . . I'm sorry; I didn't get your name," Sue said.

"Curtis Durand," the guy declared, offering his hand. "I heard you got a job at Crest."

"Um, *yes*, I . . . "I agreed, shaking his hand while searching my memory for Ridgeway. "I'm afraid you have the advantage of me."

"I was a year behind you at Crest," Colin declared. "Finished my Ph.D. at State, but could never land a job in academia, so I started this renovation racket. What brings you out here?"

I gave another capsulized version as my (dim) memory of him came back; Colin grew more interested in my story by the moment. "Well," he said at last, "I should have tried harder to get inside that

---

* *From Steele*, yes, but not yet verified as to historical accuracy.

The Persistent Past

trunk, then." He searched his table for a moment, muttered, "I keep finding stuff like . . . *this*," and handed me a manila envelope. "Tell me what you think . . . "

I pulled out the faded yellow sheets with *The Brownshoe Army By Edmund A. Steele* typed on the first page. "That's his name," I muttered, fanning through the hundred-odd typed pages with notes, strike-outs, cross-outs and proof marks. "Where'd you find . . .?"

"The desk in there," Colin said.

"What do you want for it?"

"Finder's credit. Is that . . . Melanie Hubbard?"

I turned to see Meli behind me. "She's Melanie Durand now."

"Colin, I brushed you off so much you went to State and I had to brush you off more until I said *yes* to those dates we had," Meli declared.

"Yeah," Colin nodded as Meli bussed his cheek. "Wished we'd had more . . . "

"We didn't have any *chemistry*, Colin," Meli smiled.

"More's the pity, Meli. Curtis, this place has history; more than any other I *have*. We need to get the Granite Ledge Historical Society to take it over; why I've been slow-walking the sales. This Steele guy was a *pillar* of the community. I've had people come up here and talk about all the meals they had here; all the picnics and all the cars and trucks he fixed *gratis* . . . "

The more I learned about this guy, the more I wanted to learn.

"Colin said he'll contact the family," Meli said on the way back home. We departed with a stoneware washbasin and pitcher that Maria liked, some old toys that Jason thought were cool, and a baseball autographed by a player I'd never heard of, but Charlie wanted it. Meli found a framed mirror for our hallway; a space we'd needed to fill for a while. We'd spent $85 on our treasures.

I'd also signed for the typescript and arranged for large format photos of the portrait and the quit deed, and a note of intent to buy them at some future time.*

---

* Where the Collection might keep the objects if we aquired them, though, was unknown, as the Archives had no provisions for 3D objects.

"Yep. He'll contact the historical society, tell them about our finds, about his role in the community."

Meli studied the Polaroids of the portrait I took. "I think the girl looks a little like Maria," she said. "And the older boy, something like Charlie. The younger boy . . . just a boy. But the woman looks like Connie."

"Huh. Did you know Colin well?" I asked.

"Not *that* well."

"Not *how well*, Mom?" Charlie asked.

"Just well enough to rate his *kissing* on the lower end of my scale," Meli said with remarkable aplomb.

"Kissing's got a scale?" Jason asked. "Like a weight?"

"*Kinda*, yeah," Maria said, watching Meli in the rearview. "It's more like . . . like . . . "

"A curve," Meli declared. "A grading curve."

"Yeah. Every girl's got her *own*," Maria added.

"Mom's not a girl," Jason protested. "She's a mom."

I barely held back a laugh; Meli just looked . . . yeah, like that; Maria faked a cough. "Moms are still girls, Nasty," she grinned, thumping her brother's noggin softly. "They were girls before they were moms, but they're still . . . "

"Mom's a girl like you and Megan?" Jason asked.

"She's a woman like Connie, and like I will be," Maria sighed, "and Megan will be . . . ."

"Where's Dad on your curve, Mom?" Charlie asked.

"Well," Meli smiled, glancing at me. "Right on top most of the time, but sometimes . . . "

"*Some*times he's not; right, Mom?" Maria grinned widely. "All boys are like that."

"Yeah?" Charlie asked. "Where's Ted on your scale?"

"I, ah," Maria made a face, "I haven't decided yet. Not enough . . . "

"You guys did it enough when Mom and Dad were gone," Charlie declared.

"He just stopped over for . . ." Maria sighed, nudging her brother.

"*The night*," Charlie declared.

The Persistent Past

"Ten minutes to talk about math," Maria said, exasperated, elbowing Charlie once more.

"He did?" Jason asked. "I didn't see him . . . "

"You gotta pay attention, dummy," Charlie teased.

"Lights off or on?" Meli asked, grinning.

"On," Maria loudly answered, holding her hand over Charlie's mouth.

With three kids from six to thirteen, that was what most of our weekend excursions were like.

"What's this about?" I asked no one in my office, opening *The Brownshoe Army* to the first page, labeled "Introduction."

```
    Until the 1958 Pentomic and then the
1961 ROAD reorganizations, no one would
recognize the way the Army ran. Men got
promoted in most line infantry companies
because they were friends with the
commander or platoon leader, or they were
good at something either officer liked,
like boxing or baseball or football.
Ability to soldier or lead wasn't
important; friendship was. The situation
was just as bad, if not worse, at higher
levels.
    It was an Old Boy's Club with guns.
```

That felt like a revelation. At least that told me he lived into the 1960s, kept his nose (if not his hand) in Army affairs. Reading further . . .

```
    When I enlisted in 1914, my first job
as a Private waiting for assignment was to
ensure the Fort Wayne officers' latrines
had papers, if the enlisted men did or
not. Now, these outhouses barely had roofs
or walls, but they had to have papers for
the officers.
```

The manuscript was part diatribe and part memoir, and jumping ahead, ended cryptically . . .

In Japan in 1947, Angie and I were in regular contact with Corky and occasionally my brother George, but hardly ever heard from son George, who was just transitioning to jets in the Air Corps, but seemed to want out. Some fools divided Korea in 1945, so there was that mess in front of us. But Japan was a lovely, if shabby, place to live. Carl turned 17 that year and wanted, of all things, to join the Navy. I couldn't keep him from doing it.

Dugout Doug barely knew I was there, but said I should have stayed on the retired list when he threw me out of Korea. According to Charlie Willoughby, he still hadn't forgotten that "boy General" business in '18. I don't believe he forgot it to the day he died.

Ned wrote a lot of *The Brownshoe Army* text as disorganized stream-of-conciousness like this, which I found odd for someone who wrote diaries for at least twenty years. Without a date on it, I couldn't tell when he wrote it other than some time after 1962.

I looked into several references on both world wars and could find no mention of a *Steele*. It was as if he didn't exist, or perhaps someone had erased him.

THE GRANT

I smiled at my mother-in-law as she entered my office. "Thanks for coming, Helen," This was the day I would present the hard work I'd done making sure all this paper could be what it seemed to be to a leading expert on diaries and memoirs.

"Welcome, Curtis," she nodded. "Just glad someone can use my esoteric knowledge of diaries and diarists."

"You wrote the *only* scholarly work on the subject, dear," I gestured to a chair. She wrote the only forensic analytic study of the contents and structures of diaries, also analyzing diarists by how they wrote. Archivists around the world had been using her guidance for years. German authorities referenced her work in 1983 while the "Hitler diaries" were being analyzed.

"While true, Curtis, can the charm," she grinned. "I'm ready to get to work.* Show me what you've got."

"OK," I said, pushing a spreadsheet in her direction. "Mechanically, over the twenty journals and fragments of journals I have, he used dip pens, fountain pens and pencils. His *very* early diary entries are in either pencil or dip pen, but transitioned to fountain pen after he received one when he graduated from 8ᵗʰ Grade in 1912 . . . "

"Grammar school," Helen mused quietly. "Where most stopped; where my brothers stopped."

"Well, Ned didn't, and he didn't stop his journals, either."

---

* Helen retired soon after Bert's death in January, only teaching tutorials. She never taught forensic journal/diary analysis anywhere formally, though she consulted in it.

"Did he go to college or Normal School?"*

I paused briefly, remembering that Helen was 77; she knew all this stuff; she'd lived it. "*Normal* School," I answered.

"Eh," she mused. "Born in 1896, you said?"

"Yes."

"So . . . two years or more at the Normal School . . . huh." She appeared lost in thought for a moment. "What else have you got so far?"

"Ned's hand got steadier in each pre-1914 journal, his numbers more certain. He learned to make cursive italics[†] at eleven . . . "

"About the time I did," Helen sighed.

"OK. This was also when he stopped making Palmer loops with either pencil or dip. He learned German and umlauts when he started Normal School . . . "

"*Where* was this?" Helen asked, not raising her eyes from my spreadsheet.

"Detroit area."

"His school must have been near Saint Mary's Church, where the German nuns taught." I stared as she looked up. "Bert and I grew up in the Detroit area, Curtis. You didn't know that?"

"No; you never mentioned it."

"We lived in Bloomfield, just outside Detroit. I *knew* Bert from the neighborhood and the Franklin Normal School we attended." She gazed out the window at the sunshine on the quad. "We wrote when he was at Crest—just friends then—and while he was in Air Corps training. He proposed by mail and we got married while he was on furlough in '44."

"That I knew of. Just didn't know *where*."

She nodded. "I moved here when he left because we knew he'd come back. I finished my degrees here . . ." She trailed off, staring out the window, and sighed. "Got that goddamn *wrong* telegram here . . . had so many friends here."[‡] She smiled. "Was *so* happy when

---

* A kind of teacher's college.
[†] Ironically, these are *non*-slanted letter patterns, rarely seen and absent in most method books.
[‡] Bert was reported missing presumed dead in 1945.

I got the *right* one a year later. But I'd already spent his insurance."

"Isn't *that* something?"

"The Steele's would have lived miles away. Didn't know them." She glanced at me. "There's a farm. . . ."

"Where Mike got the trunk. We went up there last week."

"*Nurse* Steele was on the maternity floor at the old Jenson Memorial Hospital when Rose was born in '50. Lovely woman. Got me a shot or two of whiskey during my twenty hours of labor with Rose. I remember her *eyes . . .*"

"Ned remembered *them*," I said. I described the diary entry where Ned wrote about meeting an enchanting redhead with violet eyes he'd always remember.

"Bert and I met them both at a VJ Day event at Camp Penobscott in '55 eight weeks before Melanie was due. I wasn't surprised to learn she'd served as a nurse during the war. And their youngest son; he'd had three years' service by the time he was old enough to enlist. He'd just got out of the Navy when we met him." She looked back at the spreadsheet. "OK, let's keep going."

That persistent past. "Ned's writing pressure changed considerably over the years, and depending on where he was writing. He made some entries on a solid, stable surface; others probably on a knee, and others almost certainly in moving vehicles. Some, no doubt, on the ground and a few, I think, on walls and floors."

"Any other written materials for comparison?"

"Yes, and they are consistent with his journal writing at its best."

"Good, good . . ." Helen smiled. "Good work so far, Curtis. What else have your surveys told you?"

"There are large damaged areas in some journals, stained by ink or food—coffee, often—blood or other things I can't describe, and baby spit-up. . . ."

"Really?" she grinned. "Go on."

"Several journals have pages missing, often at the *end,* but just as often torn out in other places. Several are only half-full; others crammed the last entries together. There are no patterns to the distortions, as one might expect in forgeries."

"So far, so good, Curtis," Helen sighed, tracing a finger across my spreadsheet. "These Roman numerals; where did they come from?"

"He numbered each journal volume consistently, starting his whole-number journals on 6 April, his birthday."

"Whole number journals," Helen looked puzzled.

"He started at least three in January: XA, 1915 that I don't have, XIIIA, 1918, and XIVA, 1919 that I think I have in fragments."

Helen nodded sagely. "Tells us something about the mind of this journal-keeper, dosen't it?"

"Um, yes, it does. Most diarists write in quiet repose; Ned appears to have been writing even when he was under fire or ill. He got the habit early in life and, as far as I can tell, kept it up for at least twenty years."

"Right. Think he just stopped?"

"Unlikely. There are probably more journals . . . somewhere."

"All *you* have to do, dear boy, is *find* them."

"Uh-huh."[*] I sighed. "I made transparencies of random pages from the journals I have chronologically." I got up to my overhead projector. "Then I made optical comparator measurements of every different letter, number, and punctuation mark." I turned on the projector, putting a transparency on the plate. "They are consistent at least 90% of the time, and they evolved over time. After making 20× and 40× transparencies, I studied the letters, numbers, and punctuation marks."

She grinned. "This makes it a lot easier than what *I* had to work with in the '40 and '50s."

"Yep," I agreed. "Using all that . . . his letters comparatively developed over time, like you say they *had* to, and their consistency from page to page and volume to volume, I conclude that this collection is far too mechanically complex to be a stack of forgeries. I will put my reputation on it."[†]

"Brilliant, Curtis; I'll put mine on it too. You have learned well. Now," she declared, "the hard part."

"Yes," I said, sitting down. "Now I have to authenticate—somehow—just what Ned was writing about."

---

[*] There's always something else . . . somewhere.

[†] This forensic graphology work was not an attempt at researching Ned's character, but the evolution and comparison of his handwriting.

"Right." Helen declared. "Linguistic analysis here *might* be helpful, but . . . 1906 until . . . when?"

"1927 is what I have."

"We *might* see his language skills evolve, like most others who started as children. But after age 30, it stops for most people."

"Well," I said, "Ned stayed in the Army from 1914 onward. I think he'd be continually exposed to pop culture, wouldn't he?"

"There's that. We'll just have to see." Helen stood up. "Now, it's the historian's turn until I see transcriptions or they come out of Holding. But you've got a lot of teaching tools here, Curtis," she pointed at my stack of transparencies. "You can show the hard *work* of the history profession that Bert beat into all your heads."

And I would use those tools shamelessly . . .

"Dr. Durand," Morse Hardin[*] said, reading a paper in front of him. "According to Doctors Zane, Altenberg, and Friedenthal,[†] *and* Helen Hubbard, you may have made the discovery of a lifetime."

"I don't know about *that*," I answered modestly. "It's a great deal of original material, yes, but . . ." We were in the Long Room in Jenson Hall, where graduate degree candidates defend their last essays. More accommodating drawing-room-style sofas, tables and chairs replaced the dark furnishings and small lamps used in those more adversarial proceedings.

"To quote Dr. Friedenthal," James Jenson[‡] interrupted, "'this treasure trove of Great War material, if authenticated, will be a boon to anyone researching the United States Army in the early 20th Century. It may contain priceless insights into significant figures who shaped our century.' Any thoughts on *that?*"

"Only that Harry Friedenthal is prone to gilding lilies." Most members chuckled.

---

[*] Moe was a great-grandson of Tiberias Jenson, the Chairman and public face of the Committee of Regents, all of whom owned shares of the school.
[†] Harrison Friedenthal was the military historian in Oklahoma selected to review the material.
[‡] James, another great-grandson of Tiberias, was a minority owner of Jenson Stone that owned and operated the quarries.

"How did you come upon this material, Dr. Durand?" Alan X. Jenson[*] asked, grinning. "Just so I'm clear on the provenance." I repeated the story of Mike's purchase. "OK," Alan said, looking at another paper. "We got a request—an offer to buy—these papers."

"Ah, sir," I cleared my throat, "Buy?"

"Yes; the Marshall Foundation in Virginia heard about this find. Offering a tidy sum for the material, too. There's another from the Liberty Memorial in Kansas City . . . "[†]

"Dr. Durand," Moe asked, "how do you see the Crest/Jenson Archive growing?"[‡]

That was an excellent question that I had asked myself and dreaded having to answer because I really didn't know. A bulk of the Crest/Jenson Archives had to do with 18th and 19th Century America and a little before and after, though we felt the Truxton Archive might go deeper in either direction. And I was the chief keeper . . .

"I think, sir," I answered, "that we may view this boon as an opportunity to expand our reach into the 20th Century with the centennial of WWI coming up in just twenty years,[§] and personal accounts of soldiers have interest in any period."

"Ah," Alan said. "An excellent point." Private schools—and Crest took no federal money—are always grubbing for money, either from alumni or from other institutions. Archives like the Crest/Jenson drew attention, and attention drew donations and endowments from alumni, foundations and philanthropists. But they also brought in more documents related to the documents already in hand. That was how collections and archives typically grew, but sometimes documents just fell into our laps . . . like these. The Crest/Jenson grew by an average of fifty documents a year. A topical

---

collection pegged to a major event could bring in more money from grateful users,* especially during an anniversary year. Our revenues about doubled during the independence Bicentennial, nearly that during the bicentennial of the Constitution, and were on track to grow by at least 20% during the Barbary Wars bicentennial coming up; even my dissertation had sudden interest.

"Shifts away from our chief strengths, though," Christian Fisk[+] said. "Would we find enough scholars to *work* that collection . . .?"

"Norman Altenburg has expressed interest," I answered. "It will give his little department some . . ."

"Ownership is a problem there," Moe intoned. "*You* are pursuing the grant. *Your* son-in-law found the documents. It looks more like *your* personal . . ."

"If the Foundation makes this grant," I interrupted, "the Steele Collection will *owe* Mike Klein a thousand dollars, and *me* a hundred."

Alan sighed. "Give us a minute, Jane." He nodded to the stenographer, who kept a record of all such meetings. Jane, nonplussed, put her hands in her lap. "Curtis, you need this."

"I do, Alan." Though we were not friends, we were friendly. "I need a major project like I should have had before I took over the Department. My name on . . ."

"What would you *do* with this collection, Curtis?" Moe asked.

"Moe, I've thought long and hard about this and . . ." I inhaled deeply and plunged ahead. "I think this is an important diarist who, in the depths of the First World War, found enough time and sense to record what he was seeing, what he was feeling. The Department of Defense will be interested in this guy, in this collection, so we may get ready access to a means of validation much faster than the National Archives. I . . ."

"DOD's interested?" James asked. "That wasn't *in* the grant request . . ."

"An error of omission, sir," I lied. I was not on a first-name basis with James, and I had yet to hear from DOD. "I wrote the

---

* Not required.
[+] Christian was a great-great-great nephew-in-law of Tiberias Jenson.

grant request *before* I verified the name . . . "

"Ah," James said. "Go on."

"Well," I stumbled, regretting the interruption of my great flow of ideas. "Diaries are often like letters to a future self, reassuring their reader that what they remembered really happened . . . "

"Do you think so?" Christian asked. "I've wondered about that."

"I believe there are many purposes, but I think *this* one started out as one thing and ended up as something else," I said with growing certainty, based on my conversations with Helen. "We see an evolution from a boy practicing penmanship at his mother's behest, to a young man who first used a telephone as a teen, to a raw soldier bemoaning the *Lusitania's* sinking before he . . . "

"Are we sure these are genuine?" Alan asked. "When I was in Vietnam, we weren't supposed to keep diaries for security reasons, though some did."

"Reasonably certain, Alan," I said. "There's an awful lot of material; more than any forger would or could credibly create. Helen and I are sure they are not forgeries, but as yet, I can't tell if they're *accurate.* I sent copies of his medal citations off, but I have heard nothing from the DOD or Ministry of Defense or the *Ministère des Armées* yet on the DSC or Military Medal or the *Croix de Guerre . . . "*

"Wait . . . what?" Alan asked. "A British Military Medal *and* a *Croix de Guerre?* This guy won both?"

"That what it looks like," I said. "I have both the medals *and* the citations. I contacted all three armies at the same time . . . ."

"Forging one would be easy but *three* would be risky, especially if they were just . . ." Alan declared.

"Abandoned in an estate sale," I finished.

"You're right, Curtis," Alan said. "So, you're going to use the diaries and the other material for something academic or popular?"*

"*Good* question," I said honestly. "I'll have to see. First, though, I need to transcribe some, authenticate *that* material with other sources, transcribe some *more*, and so on."

---

* *Popular* can make money; *academic* can treat insomnia.

The Persistent Past

"Sounds tedious," Moe said heavily. "And slow. How long before you'd have something to show?"

"I *can't* know," I answered. "It depends on how easily I can validate the entries." I cleared my throat. "My daughter, Maria, has an interest in helping . . . "

"Pretty girl, Maria," Alan grinned. "Good center fielder, too; plays baseball with my Doreen."

"Jane: start up again," James said. "Dr. Durand, how do you intend to spend a grant from this foundation?"

"Funding queries, information wanted ads, travel to the different archives, and transcribing." This was one of the many things they already knew, but they had to ask for the record. "I don't think physical testing of the material would be very fruitful, as they are not old enough . . . "

"How much have you budgeted on preservation?" Alan asked. It was already in my grant request, too.

"About 15% for packaging and rent in the Archives."

"Dr. Durand, who would take over your other duties while you work on this project?" James asked.

"Dr. Becket and Dr. Winfield have said they can help me out," I answered.

"Very well," James said finally. He looked around at the other members, then said, "Dr. Durand, we grant the Steele Collection $25,000 as a part of the Crest/Jenson Archive. You may draw $2,500 immediately, and you have two months to produce an inventory[†] for a second draw, and six to show a plan for a product[‡] before your last draw, whereupon the Jenson Foundation may provide a continuing grant. Is this agreeable?"

"Yessir," I answered. "Thank you, sir."

---

[*] *Rent* was a dollar a month a linear foot for collections not directly acquired by the Archive. *Packaging* included the $5 acid-free paper envelopes and $10 plastic boxes the material would be stored in.

[†] A comprehensive and detailed listing and description of the items in the collection, with verification status when available.

[‡] An article, book, paper, thesis, or dissertation based on the contents of the Collection.

"Dr. Durand," Moe said as the meeting broke up, "call my office for an appointment this week, please?"

I left the meeting smiling outwardly, but inside; Meli was right. This would take much of my mind and time for a while.

And . . . what's Moe want . . .?

At dinner with the family that evening . . . "I won my grant for the Steele Collection," I said simply.

"Congratulations, babe," "*Great*, Dad," "*Cool*, Pops," and "What's a grant?" was what I got from my family. I'll let you parse who said what.

As dinner proceeded, my lack of engagement with anyone became an object of curiosity for Maria. "Dad, something's wrong?"

"I have two months to inventory all that material. Then come up with a plan for a product, providing I can authenticate them."

"What's so hard about that, Pops?" Charlie asked, cutting sausages lengthwise before chopping them up. At eight, nothing looked hard.

"What's *authenticate* mean, Pops?" Jason asked, shoveling in some mashed potatoes.

"It means show to be true, Jason," Maria said. "Write it in your notebook and don't talk with your mouth full."

"What notebook?" Jason asked. "Don't *boss* me . . . "

"The notebooks you and Charlie are starting tonight," Maria declared. "Now eat up and I'm your big sister so I can boss you all I have to."

The ensuing exchanges were enough to distract me from my current woes, which, compared to my children's rivalry, were inconsequential.

And I wondered . . . authenticate how? The material, the content? Was this guy just a name-dropper? I could see the headlines: "Steele Collection: Piltdown Man* of American History."

And what *did* Moe want?

*   *   *

---

* The Piltdown Man was the best known fraud in archaeological history that took over forty years to expose.

After dinner, we would often retire to our respective after-dinner reposes as we would any July Monday if there wasn't to be a game in the backyard; it was raining pretty hard. Maria would go to her suite, the boys to TV in the living room for an hour before they retired to their rooms, I would withdraw to my den or wood shop, and Melanie to her sewing or baking or reading or whatever else she had a mind to do.

But *that* night, Maria corralled the boys into her suite. Meli and I listened from outside.

"Here," we heard Maria say. "Write your names on the cover . . . Now, write the date, July 1ˢᵗ, 1996, on the first page . . . now write 'authenticate; a-u-t-h . . . ' she spelled." We looked at each other, puzzled, before Maria called, "C'mon in; join the party."

The boys each had a little bound notebook in their laps, with pencils poised in their hands. "What's up?" Meli asked just as Midge led Smudge in a game of *catch me* down the stairs.

"I'm giving these two a lesson in journaling," Maria said. "Now, boys, after 'authenticate' write 'show to be true.' Now; what's that mean to you?"

"*I* dunno," Jason said quietly as a cat slammed into a cardboard box, then another.

"Um," Charlie started, "does it mean the difference between the truth and a lie?"

"In a way, yeah," Maria smiled. "But it's like how Jason knows where his Cosmos Rangers are, and *you* know what's in your Supertime card collection. You *authenticate* what's there by finding them wherever you last had them." A loud dispute between declawed opponents raged near the cold air return, judging by the way it resounded through the basement.

"And I've gotta make sure dumb old Megan dosen't bury 'em in *her* sandbox," Jason added. Megan, our six-year-old neighbor, was a frequent playmate/antagonist/buddy.

"Yeah, *that's* right," Maria nodded. "Now, write unfamiliar words, feelings, anything that comes to mind in these journals. Do it every day until next week and we'll talk about it. Now, go on and watch TV."

The boys dashed upstairs to watch whatever they could catch

in the living room, and Meli and I just watched as Smudge *blithely* followed them.

"Think it'll take, honey?" Meli asked as the boys settled in up-stairs.

"Find out in a week," Maria sighed. "I have homework, OK?" She bussed us both on the cheek.

"In *July?*" I asked as Midge circled a spot on the sofa.

"A workbook my Algebra teacher gave me."

And so, our daughter dismissed us just as Midge curled up.

"*Thanks* for coming, Curtis," Moe said when I entered his office for only the third time in my twenty-three years at Crest.

"Welcome . . ." I started.

"I knew Ned Steele slightly," Moe started. "He was a member of our Legion post in the '50s. I lost touch with him when I got this job and stopped going." He nodded, looked away. "I'm retiring, Curtis. Been at this far too long."

This surprised me, but didn't shock me; he'd been visibly aging for the past couple of years. "Who would take over as Chairman of the Regents?"

"Alan." He fingered a pile of files. "When I retire after next academic year, it would be my 35th. I hope to last that long. I was an Atomic Soldier.[*] If you know what that means, you know I've been doomed since 1956. Now have myeloid leukemia. It's gone unnoticed until recently."

"*Sorry,* Moe . . ." Personally, Moe was likable, if difficult to approach.

"I'd appreciate if you kept that to a small circle, Curtis." He smiled wanly. "Your *estimable* wife, of course . . ."

"Thanks . . . I'm *sorry.*" Until that time, I'd known no one with a fatal wasting disease. I wasn't sure what else to say.

"My wife may predecease me."

"Huh?"

---

[*] The men who went into atomic blast areas soon after the fireballs fell and the dust settled in the 1940s and '50s. Less than half survived twenty years; only a handful as long as Moe had.

The Persistent Past

"Her heart is failing fast, and she's too weak for a transplant."

"Oh . . . my . . ." I was running out of my very thin repertoire of sympathy sounds. "So sorry . . . "

"Yes; thank you." He looked back at me again. "If you weren't such an excellent teacher and researcher, I would have recommended you for the new Chancellor's position that the Corporation wants so badly."

"I hadn't heard," I said honestly. The administrative day-to-day of the school was not a matter for us lofty academics to gossip about; we had enough to concern us. Besides, the Regents did such a bang-up job running it . . . "Chancellor as in chief executive?"

"Yes; a single point-of-contact for the Corporation to complain to that they aren't getting enough cooperation from the rest of the school and Granite Ledge. At the moment, James is the leading candidate."

"I *believe* he's got good business sense," I said, wondering *why I was in this meeting other than bad news . . . and Ned Steele?* "Is the Corporation not working well?"

"Fits and starts, I'm afraid." Moe looked out the window again. "There are financial and administrative matters that may affect you and the other faculty, Curtis. We may have to weather a storm of administrative challenges." He looked back at me. "I just wanted you to know . . . all these things because I like you and your family a great deal. Just . . . prepare Melanie for my and Elizabeth's imminent passing, if you will."

"Hey, *thanks*, Dr. . . . *Curtis*," Mike said when I handed him his check that sticky-hot Thursday afternoon in my den. Connie and he were over for the traditional 4th of July cookout/get-together/fireworks viewing in our backyard.

"I got a grant to help pay for the preliminary work, so now those contents are owned by the Jenson Foundation."

"If I find anything else," he said, watching out the window at Connie playing Frisbee with the boys, "I'll let you know. Those medals are the real thing, according to a collector in town. The flags . . . he's never seen the like of that *big* one, but it seems to be for a unit called the 432nd Machine Gun Battalion."

"Good," I said as eight-months-pregnant Connie dove after the

Frisbee just as Meli emerged from the basement in her black two-piece, followed by Maria in a suit I hadn't seen before that seemed skimpy, even for her.*

Mike held his breath as Conne hit the ground, rolled, jumped to her feet, and shot the disc to Jason. "*Nothing* slows her down . . ." he sighed.

"Nope," I grinned as Melanie fielded a stray throw. "She did a *handstand* when her water broke with Johnnie . . . "

"Yeah; she said that." Meli spun around and fired it at Charlie.

"Is that development up by Camp Penobscot still . . .?" Camp Penobscot—a state installation—had been in irregular use for decades. When I saw the camp on my freshman tour of the area, it was barely being used, but the high-end housing development nearby was well underway.†

"Not a development anymore; a community with a strip mall and everything." Maria tried to snatch the disc away from Charlie, who tackled his sister, giggling.

"You ever been in the camp?" I asked. The disc rolled on the ground, where Jason grabbed it.

"Yeah. I've been tempted to go to the Visitor's Center." Jason shot the disc at Connie, who spun around and launched it at Melanie before falling on her knees by her giggling siblings, soon joined by Jason, when a tickle-fight began in the grass.

"That's new," I said, smiling as Meli joined the squirming, laughing pile. I saw in the news that the camp got a renovation in the '80s and became the state's Officer Candidate School in '89.

"Still a kid . . . can't slow her down." Mike said, smiling at the scene.

"We should join them," I declared.

"*Tickle my bikini-clad mother-in-law?*"

"*You* tickle *your* wife, and *I'll* tickle *mine*."

*   *   *

---

* Maria was thirteen, but even so, she was . . . small.
† Starting prices in the mid-six-figures were a dead giveaway, and the "luxury single-family condominiums" sign was another.

"Thanks for the check, Dad," Connie said that night as we watched the fireworks over the river. "We can use it."

"Thank the Jenson Foundation," I said. "Money can't be that tight." We were closer to the house than everyone else; she because she was going to the bathroom every fifteen minutes, and I because she said she wanted a chat.

"Cash-poor this month," she sighed as another starburst flashed overhead. "One of our front loaders blew an engine and our heavy lift crane needs major mast repairs; had to lease another one to keep going."[*] Our house was about a half-mile from the river as the crow flies, but high above. Our back lawn sloped down towards the river; we were just high enough that we could see the show and avoid the traffic jams at the riverfront.

"How about you? Are you feeling OK? You seem to have a lot more energy than Melanie did with any . . . "

"You know *me*, Dad," she sighed, shifting her weight. "It's just a matter of staying active."

"The same at 26 with twins as it was at 17 with just one?"

"Pretty much." She grabbed my arm. "Maria told me about that stuff. Kinda gruesome."

"Some of it." I glanced down at her belly surreptitiously. "You still aren't showing a lot." Even with her top pushed above her shorts in our pile, she only showed a slight bump.

"The doctors call me a medical phenom. Healthy twins, and I only put on fifteen pounds at eight months." She nudged my shoulder. "Most of it in my *boobs*, I swear."[†]

"Ah," I grimaced. We watched a succession of starbursts in silence. "Not *much* longer."

Smaller fireworks exploded up and down the river . . . "Good thing before we get eaten alive." She swatted a mosquito on her arm. "Maria's gonna get paid to work that stuff?"

"Yeah; she's a contractor to the Steele Collection."

---

[*] Connie invested her mother's legacy in heavy equipment (which she leased out), real estate, and other ventures.

[†] She said the same thing in the same way with Johnnie . . . often.

Crackling, crackling . . . the traditional signal that the grand finale was on its way. "I think she'll love it."

There was a rattling of minor explosions . . . "She says she likes history these days. Not like you did . . . "

"For now." She bumped my hip. "We'll see."

"What does she say about Ted? Meli says she draws a line at second base."

She breathed deep. "She says they sometimes go that far." A mine* and brilliant starbursts detonated over the river, sparking *oohs* and *ahs*. "Just so you know, Ted arrived just after me that Saturday. We all watched TV for a while, then I put the boys in the bath and then to bed. I came back to the living room as Ted was leaving a half-hour later." She shrugged. "No clothing removed that *I* saw; lights dimmed. There was lipstick on Ted. But she's worried about you guys."

"Worried about . . .?" A great machine-gun-like rattle sounded over the river as a wafting breeze brought whiffs of powder smoke.

"She knows where you guys went that weekend and is worried about why." The first of the finale's ground displays—a soldier in uniform—appeared.

"Worried . . . what . . .?" The second—a woman's figure in a star-spangled costume—appeared.

"Allison's parents are on the rocks, and they went up there for a kid-free weekend." Then, for the finale, the first flag lit up . . .

"But Meli and I are fine . . ." The second . . .

"Yes; you may know that, but . . ." Third . . .

"But, nothing! We . . ." Fourth . . . .

Fifth and biggest . . . . "*Curtis*, she's thirteen, and she thinks the most important grownups in her life are in trouble." Connie called me *Curtis* only when she needed to get my attention. "You need to say something so her anxiety dosen't spill over to the boys."

The flags were so bright I swear you could read in the backyard by their momentary light. "Did you tell her that Mike proposed to you up there?"

"How did you . . .? Mom!" She bumped my hip again. "No, I

---

* The loudest of fireworks, also called a *pot á feu.*

The Persistent Past

didn't." One more spectacular barrage of brightly changing stars . . .

"Maybe you should . . . "

"Yeah; I'll tell her now. Let's go inside."

"Last one in's a rotten egg!" Jason yelled, sprinting for the water. We celebrated his sixth birthday, a milestone in every kid's life, at the beach on the river.

So we charged for the river . . . and the last in was Maria, who, preoccupied, lagged everyone because she had just transcribed* a version of Dante.

We splashed and played—Maria tried very hard—all that Friday afternoon. Then Meli, in a modest one-piece, joined us after work for hot dogs, ice cream and cake, and Maria gave up and sat on a towel in the sand, watching as Meli and the boys kicked a beach ball around.

"Tired, sweetie?" I asked, sitting down beside her.

"Can't get that image out of my head, Dad," she sighed. "The dirt, the smoke, the stench, the . . . body parts. He called it 'Deadly Hill.'" She hugged her knees. "Didn't think it was going to be like that."

23rd November, Colline Mortelle.
I have seen the Inferno from the edge of
Purgatory, an extraordinary view. My Post of
Command (PC) is an elaborate bunker with a
periscope that I am to use to direct fire. I look
through it and see mud, wire, holes, water,
and the remains of man, beast, and
civilization. There is no sadder sight than a
ruined town. I saw that little village a mile
and a half off, behind the Hun lines, destroyed
by artillery and everything else. They use it
for a mess and dressing station.
No training can get anyone ready for this,
with [expletive] *rats the size of muskrats, bold as*

---

* We were transcribing these entries because they seemed compelling, neglecting the inventory for the moment.

brass, chattering in your face in broad daylight.

I could never have imagined what a howitzer shell landing so close could have felt like. It was as if an immense weight suddenly descended on me and then was gone. But machine-gun bullets hum like giant bees and sound like meat hooks hitting a side of [expletive] *beef when they hit earth. It was only a momentary barrage, but I felt as if it were days on end.*

Sgt. Thorsten and I went down to the front line with Talbott. Not trenches, but a string of connected holes. How could anyone live like this? We saw men in cubbyholes sleeping, smoking, eating, shaving without water or mirrors, cleaning their weapons. They live like [expletive] *animals in unbelievable filth and indescribable stink. Every sap forward, every communications trench got worse and worse. Talbott shoved my head into a trench wall so I wouldn't sneeze out loud, as we were so close to a Hun listening post they might hear. While we were in the forward posts, we endured a small bombing raid.* They handed us Mills bombs to throw; I failed to pull my pin but threw it, anyway. Don't think I've ever been so* [expletive] *humiliated in my life, but the fellows were good about it, called me a "colt."*

"Might just be worse than that, sweetheart," I sighed, watching Charlie and Meli chase Jason into the water. "You want to quit?"

"No," she answered quickly. "I just need to get used to it."

"If it helps," I offered, "think of these people as they are to us: long gone now, phantoms of a long-gone past. That vision of Hell Ned saw was cleaned up before even I was born."

---

* Hand grenades thrown by several men simultanieously.

The Persistent Past

She looked sly. "I know how old you are, Dad."

"I've got a decade on a rock."

"No, you don't; you just turned 41 in April.* I've been think-ing . . . "

"Dangerous in this line of work . . . "

She ignored me. "What if WWI isn't that popular in this coun-try because we entered it so late."

"That's one explanation I've heard. It wasn't popular when it was going on, either. Not as unpopular as Vietnam, but . . . "

"Maybe they associated it with that flu."

"That's possible, too."

"From what I've read, the British and French think little of our participation, either." She grabbed a handful of sand. "This sand might have been a mountain a billion years ago. It might be one again a billion years from now." She let it run through her fingers. "You and I and everyone here will be long gone, with nothing to remember most of us. But Ned and Angie left those diaries."

"Yeah, they did."

"It's our job to make people aware of them."

"Yeah."

"And it's your job to . . ." she jumped up, "beat me to the river!"

Eh, she had a three-stride head start on me.

"Dr. Durand?" the voice on the phone asked the next Monday. "I'm Mildred Sachenhausen with the Granite Ledge Historical So-ciety. Do you have a moment?"

"I do, ma'am," I answered. "About the Steele place?"

"The farm, yes," Mildred answered. "Mr. Ridgeway was most effusive in his praises of your scholarship."

"Thank you," I answered, not knowing if Colin ever heard me teach. "What can I do for you?"

"You told Mr. Ridgeway that Mr. Steele was a war hero? How did you know this? I'd been out there several times for picnics as a young woman, and . . . "

---

* It feels a little odd when your kids know exactly how old you are.

"When was this?"

"Last time was 1988 with my family, but I remember going out there as a girl in the '60s. But how . . .?"

"I have his diaries from WWI, and I have medal citations from the US Army, the British Army and the French. He may have been well acquainted with General Pershing."

"That is breathtaking, Dr. Durand. I never imagined . . . is he still with us?"

"He's not on that short list of WWI vets. The American Legion post here only has a record of ten years of membership for him, but he might have been a founder; in Paris . . . "

"So we missed that opportunity. Would you mind, Dr. Durand, helping us if we put together a spot for public television, publicizing the farm? We'd need thousands in donations to purchase it, and the best way . . . "

"I'd be proud to, ma'am . . ." I said, trailing off. I drifted away from reality as I sometimes did when things I never expected happened . . . an offhand reference at Connie's wedding two months ago . . . and I suddenly remembered I was on the phone. "Yes, of course," I said. "Please, tell me when your plans solidify."

The persistence of the past struck again.

"Well, I'll be damned," I sighed, reading the letter I'd got a week later.

> 27 Jul 96
> Dear Dr. Durand,
> This is to verify that Lieutenant Colonel (National Army) Edmund Archer Steele, commanding the 432nd Machine Gun Battalion, received the Army Distinguished Service Cross on 15 May 1919 for his actions from November 1917 to December 1918. The citation you have was the awardee copy. I have attached a copy of the award application, descriptions of the specific actions cited, and the endorsements.

Good luck with your project. The
Department is always interested in such
endeavors, and I have an especial interest
in the Great War. Please feel free to send
future inquiries about your project
directly to me.
    Stephen A. March,
    Chief Archivist, Department of the Army.

While it was a verification of who Ned was, it raised as many questions in my mind as it answered.

And there was all that name-dropping.

I walked the letter and *The Brownshoe Army* over to the Military History Department in the Brick Building,* hoping to catch Norm there, but . . .

"Sorry; not in today, Curtis," Olive Rinaldo, the department's secretary, said. "I believe Dr. Geohegan is in, though. I'll try her office . . . Doctor, Dr. Durand would like a word . . . I'll tell him," she said into the phone. "She's back there."

"Olive, how long have you worked at Crest?" I asked, suddenly curious. She'd had several jobs at Crest over the years I'd been there.

"Since you were ten, Curtis," she smiled thinly. "Don't ask how old I was . . . "

"Sixteen," I guessed.

She made a surprised grin. "Go on back, whelp."

The Military History Department used its space efficiently. Books on the shelves along the corridor were orderly; boxes on the shelves flush against the wall; pictures straight and aligned, almost as if they were in a formation.

I didn't know Jadwiga W. Geohegan well; I'd met her at school functions, not much more. Norm grabbed her up in '90 from King's College, Oxford, because he needed a scholar who knew European military history.

"Dr. Geohegan," I said, gently knocking on her door. "Curtis Durand."

---

* Often called The Barracks, because it was the home of the Military History Department. It had been completed with a donation from the Brick family of Long Island, New York.

"*Da, Virac* . . . ah, *yes*, Doctor," she waved me in while writing. "I shall be . . . right . . . with . . . you . . . *there*." She turned in her chair and smiled, offering her hand. "Best I finish my Russian thoughts before I turn them to English in my head."

"Doctor," I answered, shaking her hand. "Being multi-lingual has its confusions and drawbacks, I would imagine." She had a most charming smile and a firm grip.

"Yes, and when you have four tongues, it is even worse," she sighed, rolling lovely brown eyes.

"Four," I smiled slightly, "English, Polish, Russian, and . . .?"

"German; fluently. I also have some French, Czech, Hungarian, and Serbo-Croat."

"Always admired facility with languages," I admitted. "I barely got through French and Latin here. Doctor . . . "

"Please, Curtis, my Irish husband calls me Wickie. How may I help you?" I handed her the letter, explaining the context behind it as she read. "So, I have heard of your find like everyone else," she said as she laid the letter down, "and I am terribly jealous."

"Jealous?"

"It is quite the find, yes? And for a 19th Century economic historian a, ah, puzzlement?"

"Well, yeah; out of my range. There's plenty of work to do to put this material into some kind of context. We need . . . "

"Who is 'we,' Curtis?" She sounded somewhat like those black-clad *femme fatales* with indeterminate accents in low-budget movies.

"My daughter is helping me with it." I resisted the temptation to think I was being interrogated.

"Your Constance?"

"Maria."

"Maria? She swims, yes, with my Erica and Eric in the Crest league? Pretty girl; brown eyes and long face; braids her hair; no bangs."

"Um . . . yes."

"Yes, I know her to see her." She smiled widely. "Because I spoke languages, I was in Army intelligence. With such training, you remember many little things that otherwise mean nothing."

"You were drafted?"

"I *had* to serve so I could go to university in the '70s. Now, Curtis, what can I do for you?"

"That letter talks about things I know nothing of, such as the National Army and machine gun battalion. Diary entries speak of such things, but . . . "

"Yes, it can be confusing," Wickie nodded, reading. "The American National Army was where the Army formed new units and promoted men beginning in 1917. The Regular Army was far more rigid about promotions and new organizations, and it was easier to create new units and promote men in the National Army."

"I see," I said, nodding in near-comprehension.

"Such complexities are why there are military historians, my friend." Wickie smiled and stood—six foot and muscular—stepped lightly to a shelf, perused the spines for a moment, and pulled out a large volume that she handed to me. "This may explain in more detail. As for machine gun battalions, they existed in many armies until the 1950s. Their purpose evolved, but in WWI it was easier to put the specialists machine guns required in their own units."

"I see," I frowned, paging through the book she handed me, still not quite understanding. "We've been skipping around right now, but he talks about things we . . . "

"Curtis, my friend," Wickie smiled, sitting again, "I will be proud to help you on your project, providing it is not too much." She rapped her knuckles on her desk. "My especial interest is in the US Army in the 20th Century. Unusual for a Pole, eh?"

"It is, that, Wickie. How did you come by it?"

"Like many things, by accident," she grinned. "At Kings, my auditor assigned me a research essay on the impact of the Marshall reforms on the American Army in the '30s. I found that this one officer had more influence on the American Army than most others had on any other army. I did my first dissertation on the US Army's changes between the wars."

 "So the Great War, for you, is . . .?"

"Still a special interest, despite my second dissertation on artillery-direction development. I visited places like Gumbinnen and

Tannenberg, Verdun and . . . ." She stopped, looked away. "In Belgium, near Ypres, there is a memorial called the Menin Gate. It is for the over fifty thousand dead that the British Empire suffered on the Menin Road Ridge, including both my husband's grandfathers, in just five days. It is a most moving sight to see, especially at sunrise on a clear day." She looked back at me. "My friend, military history is a study of the need of such monuments as that one. I expect, if these diaries describe a man in a machine gun battalion, that he saw many horrors, was responsible for some, and having survived, he . . . "

I handed her *The Brownshoe Army* from under my arm. "His farm is out by Camp Penobscot. This came from there."

Wickie scanned the first page of the typescript and smiled beatifically. "My dear Curtis," she tapped a finger on her chin, "he is a local hero who wrote a memoir. He lived here; perhaps died here." She waited. "Think, my friend . . . "

"Funding," I nodded, suddenly seeing her point.[*]

"Granite Ledge's other local hero," she nodded. "My husband, Ian, is a television producer." She grinned. "I will speak to him."

I could become a TV star and a Great War scholar.

Verification," I told my grad students the next day. "The Department of the Army confirms that Edmund Archer Steele was a Lieutenant Colonel in 1919 and in command of the 432nd Machine Gun Battalion, awarded the Distinguished Service Cross in 1919." This graduate summer seminar on other forms of research than archives knew of my project.

"Congratulations," Beverly declared distractedly, flipping through her notes. Her area was camp followers in the early 19th Century.

"Machine gun battalion?" Sharon asked. She was a legal history student, concentrating on the early Supreme Court. "Never heard of them."

---

[*] While $25,000 may seem like a great deal, it is a drop in the bucket for a collection such as this, because getting it known ain't cheap. With *The Brownshoe Army*, the project grew bigger.

"They were around in the US Army until the Korean conflict," Larry said. He was an older military historian, working on the transitional elements from militias to Continentals during the Revolution. "Machine guns were specialist weapons in WWI. The British had a Machine Gun Corps," he added. "I can look into it."

"Just find me some sources, Larry," I said. "You have your *own* work to do."

"So, what's next for your project, sir?" Max asked. He was researching the financing of the War of 1812.

"Well, how would you approach authentication knowing that this mass of material isn't an elaborate forgery, but may not be historically accurate?"

"Perhaps using a time line?" Bayard asked. Bay was a German researching Hessian soldiers in America during the Revolution.

Bev stopped flipping, looked up at me disdainfully. "Use it to align diary dates with other sources."

"A timeline is a sound organizing tool," Sharon added. "It sounds like there are lots of names and dates."

"True," I said, then turned on the overhead projector. "From Ned's Volume VI, in 1910."

> 20ᵗʰ December, Dearborn, Mich.
> Five of us have chickenpox: Francine first, then Diane, then Helen, then Irving and George, now me. The older kids are staying with Uncle Moriss and Aunt Phoebe, but they had it already. This will be a miserable Christmas.
> I used a telephone for the first time to talk to Betty and Al and Charlie. It only took a few minutes to make the connection.

"We may know where to put this on a timeline, but what else does this tell us?"

"How old is he?" Larry asked.

"He would have been fourteen."

---

* Probably in his thirties.

"Chickenpox at fourteen?" Bay asked. "I had them at five."

"I never had them," Sharon said.

"My mother said I had chickenpox when I was in diapers," I said. "Our youngest daughter had 'em at two; our sons have never had 'em, and they may never have 'em since they were vaccinated. What else?"

"He was fourteen before he used a telephone?" Bev sighed. "Good God . . . "

"Though the telephone had been around for decades," I said, "it was new in homes in the early 20th Century. I remember my first glimpse of a color television in 1966. It was a candy bar commercial . . . "

"Just imagine what he would have thought about men walking on the Moon," Max said, shaking his head.

"He may have written about that somewhere we haven't found yet." I added.

"You first saw a color TV in 1966?" Larry asked. "Five years before I was born . . . "

"Yes," I sighed, "and I saw the Moon landing on TV, like nearly everyone else on Earth did, three years later."

"It's like he lived in a world completely removed from ours," Sharon said softly, grinning at me. "So did you."

"My point exactly," I said. "When we study the past, we have to remember that their world isn't ours. Now, look at this:"

8th May 1915, Jefferson Barracks, Misso.
The news of the Lusitania is devastating. We wonder if Congress will entertain war. We are ready if it comes, but we do not welcome it. Baseball again this afternoon, after a class on machine guns. This one is a Benet-Mercier, a version of the Hotchkiss made in France. This [expletive] thing fires 8 millimeter Lebel ammunition at a rate of 450 rounds a minute out to 3,800 meters, which is a little over 4,100 yards. I will study the manual until I know everything about it. Scientific American is just full of machine guns these

days. A rumor going around has us becoming
a machine gun company.

"*Lusitania?*" Bev asked. "That boat was torpedoed . . . "

"It was indeed," Larry agreed. "In 1915. Caused quite a ruckus in the US, too."

"Jefferson Barracks," Max said. "In 1915?"

"Yep. Ned had joined the Army a year before." I waited. "What about the machine guns?"

"Is this his earliest mention of them?" Larry asked.

"Not sure," I said. "I think so. What else?"

"He's showing an interest in machine guns," Sharon said. "Wonder why?"

"Another excellent question." I waited. "Any ideas?"

"He'd command an MG battalion later," Larry said.

"But why the interest *now?*" I asked again.

"He likes machines," Bev suggested.

"Could be as simple as that," I nodded. "Could be he sees that rumor—if true—could create an opportunity. This is from Volume X."

15ᵗʰ April. Fort Wayne, Mich.
Yesterday, Dad said that he failed to get me
an appointment to West Point, so today I
enlisted in the Army, nine days after I turned
eighteen. I <u>had</u> to get out of that overcrowded
house.
Mom and Dad understand, I think, but Mom
still cried when I went through the gates into
the camp. Little George saluted me. I know he
wants to join the Navy, and Dad will strive to
get him an appointment to Annapolis. I hope
he is successful. George is thirteen now, so he
won't be old enough to start until next year.

I never saw a classroom with five students so quiet, even during exams.

Larry said, "he couldn't get into West Point so he enlisted. How desperate would you have to be to get out of the house?"

"Overcrowded house," Sharon said. "How overcrowded?"

"We know of four brothers and four sisters," I said. "But I think his family was affluent. There are hints that Ned's father had been in the state militia for some time. In those days, that meant influence . . . "

"That kind of life-changing decision would not be easy for any young man," Bay added. "My father joined the *Bundeswehr** when he was seventeen to get away from his family situation." He smiled slightly. "It has given him a splendid career, but it was not a simple decision to make for Berliners in the '60s."

"Not when the Americans and Russians were ready to fight it out to the last German," Larry said.

"Annapolis at fourteen?" Sharon asked. "I don't . . . "

"The minimum age for Army and Navy cadets was fourteen until the MacArthur reforms in the 1930s. Then there's this," I sighed, putting up a transparency of *The Brownshoe Army.*

> After the Machine Gun Department moved to Ft. Benning, I attended the Command and General Staff School (then called the School of the Line) with Dwight Eisenhower and Terry Allen. Because the Army was still a Good-Old-Boy's Club, and Summerall and MacArthur held grudges against me, even the Senator couldn't get me a troop command. But Gen. Pershing got me a post command in New England. While what I was doing was important, they were not what I needed for advancement. My big break came when Charlie Willoughby, knowing I spoke French well and German passably, wrangled me an assistant attaché posting in Paris in '31.

"Sounds like he's got an axe to grind," Larry mused. "He did some stuff in WWI that pissed off some important people, even though he served with lots of others after. There might be a story in that, but . . . "

---

* West German Army.

"That would take too much time to research, Doc," Bev said. "Your grant's got a short leash. Inventory and authenticate by time-line and go from there."

Then that was a plan . . . but for what product? Was there one? Could we just announce the existence of the diaries? Yes, that TV spot would help us do that, but that could be months or years off. But justifying that money and any interest the Historical Society had would take more.

A popular history product. But where in New England did he get a command?

"Maria, we have a plan to create the inventory." We were in the Holding Room again; she wore more appropriate shoes for the dry, chilly air. "We'll start with a timeline."

To begin, we ran out a sheet of paper for a full three-table lengths; twenty-one feet. "Volume I *here*, II *here*, III *here*, and so on." We placed the volumes we had (up to XX, April 1925–April 1926) in order. I put the loose sheets in place of what he probably called Volume XIVA, which would have been the first three months of 1919, followed by Volume XV (April 1919–April 1920). Volume XA (January–April 1915?) was missing; we only knew of *it* from the catalog list in Volume XI (April 1915–April 1916).*

"Think *The Brownshoe Army* just an overlong diary en-try . . .?" I asked Maria.

"Dad, we don't even know *when* he wrote that," she sighed, "or if he just had a bad day and pounded that out. Let's keep it out for now."

Great instincts my Maria had.

After the diaries, there were stacks of notes, notebooks, sketches, and maps among the orders, letters, and oddities like a typed memo.

---

* Ned started cataloging his diaries at the back of Volume X, 1914–1915 and then recapped in every volume after. We guessed it was because he'd left some behind somewhere, or just wanted to keep track.

15th March 1917, Ft. Bliss, Tx.
From: General J. J. Pershing, Comdg 8th
  Brig.
To: Commander, 89th Infantry Regt.
  Sir:
It has come to my attention that Corporal
Steele of your command has the technical
expertise and leadership potential to make
a useful officer in the coming conflict,
especially in the field of machine guns.
Your headquarters is to afford him every
assistance in his commissioning. Orders to
that effect shall be forthcoming and acted
upon at once.
  Pershing

"How would he know Pershing before the war?" I asked.

"The Army was small then; they must have met somewhere. But Pershing was very senior, and Ned very junior. This suggests that they'd not only met, but . . . "*

"Somehow interacted."

"But when . . . and where? And how? And their association somehow extended beyond mere acquaintance. All stuff we've gotta figure out, Dad," Maria nodded, laying the memo down.

After hours of sorting and guessing at dates, we put the trunk receipt at last in with Volume XV and stopped, reflecting. "*Twenty years* of a man's life," I mumbled. "He would have been twenty-eight here," I pointed to the Volume XXI space, which contained, among other things, a First Communion certificate for Corrine Millicent Steele.

"Yeah," Maria agreed. "Where will I be at twenty-eight?" She looked up. "Where were you?"

"Here. You were two."

"His life in Volume XIV seemed so different from the others."

"That was his first wartime volume," I said. Then . . . there are moments in your life when you see everything so clearly that what you just said or did changed everything. "That's it," I breathed.

---

* I'd seen Maria reading about the Great War; she knew a few things.

"*The Great War Diaries of Ned Steele.*"

"Or," Maria smiled, "*Steele's Battalion: The Great War Diaries.*"

Thinking up that title gave us the product to justify that grant, and would be a Big (unique) Thing. But the goal was the same: We would concentrate on transcribing, validating, and publishing Ned's WWI diaries.

"Now," I said authoritatively, "the inventory."

Maria looked puzzled. "Isn't that just a list?"

"It would be easy if it were, yes. But, it's more. I'll show you." I took the Pershing memo to a magnifying table, pressed it gently on a felt pad, and switched on the white light. "C'mere. Look."

She looked through the big magnifying lens at the memo. "O . . . K," she mumbled, "what . . .?"

"Watch." I turned off the white light and turned on the black. The paper looked like a dry riverbed in a desert. "See? The paper's falling apart. That means high-acid pulp stock. I'll wager that most of this old loose paper is disintegrating like this is. That's when an inventory is important because it lists the type of paper and the condition, and what's on it." I pulled a paper-weight caliper off the wall and measured it. "And it's about 0.013 inch thick, so . . . 25 pound paper."* Grabbing an inventory blank pad from the box near the magnifying table, I handed it to her. "Fill this out. Then . . ." I waved my hand at the timeline. "The *rest.*"

That was the first of the 495 items in the Steele Collection Inventory that Maria and I would create. Each would take about fifteen minutes . . . or something over 120 hours.

To start.

"Oh, fabulous," I grinned, opening that first letter from Ned's family.

> *10 July 96*
> *Bridgeport, CT*
> *Dear Dr. Durand:*
> *I learned about you and your project from*
> *my nephew, Carl. It appears he sold the farm*

---

* Not an exact measure, but a ballpark.

*to a careful owner. I am intrigued by your
project involving my brother's voluminous diaries and am glad to learn they are in excellent hands. That said, I would like to learn
more about what you intend with them. Allow
me to point out that Ned was the last surviving flag officer from WWI, and as such, the
shabby sendoff he got in Korea was an embarrassment to the entire country, regardless of
the revenge he got on MacArthur in the end.
I hope to hear from you again soon.
Yours,
George Steele,
VADM, USN, Ret.*

Last flag officer from WWI? Shabby sendoff in Korea? Revenge on MacArthur? Some answers just asked more questions.

The next day, I got another:

*July 10th, 1996
West Allis, Wisconsin
My Dear Dr. Durand:
It was with gratitude and pleasure to hear
from Carl that such a worthy as yourself has
Dad's diaries in his hands. Of all the institutions and trash heaps that those journals
could have landed in, yours is probably the
best. We knew of them, of course, but Dad
didn't think they had any value at the end.
My family would appreciate knowing what
you intend with the diaries, as some things in
them are intimate, some funny, and some
downright embarrassing. I remember reading some of them, finding great amusement
in Dad's youth and horror in some of his ex-
periences. I realize that, as a historian, it is
your duty to speak the truth about the past.
But not all truths of the past have the same effect on the present. I shall reach my 76th year*

soon, and some truths of my and my brothers growing up are just not historical.

I have one request. If you find any entries about Mom and Dad's first wedding—the one in France—I'd appreciate knowing about them. I have a dim recollection of a wedding when I was about four and my brother Charlie was about two: 1924 or so. We have trouble reconciling that with Mom telling us about her marriage in France before that, even if Uncle George says it happened just that way. Just curious because after all these years, it hardly matters.

Yours Sincerely,
Corrine Steele Maxon

I mailed Corrine an image of the page from what I believed was Ned's Volume XIVA (1919).

29th January, Paris, France.
~~I am~~ We are wed. The ceremony was so brief I barely knew it took place. We just signed the papers, and it was done. Mike, Harriet, the Senator, and Millicent were there. General Pershing, Colonel Marshall and Angie's other friends from the hospital joined us at the luncheon.
The hotel put on a magnificent spread. Rodgers and his workmates provided champagne, caviar, sweet strawberries (where they came from at this time of year, I shall never know), fresh bread, butter and dozens of flowers in our room.
Jack Willis and Doc Miller made the luncheon. Chaplain Haldane gave a lovely benediction. Talbott sent a telegram. So did Lucas, who's a full Colonel now. I wonder how they knew?

And this, from Volume XX (1924–25):

1ˢᵗ May, Ft. Levenworth.
This morning Angie and I wed again, this time in a church (At least the license didn't cost me anything). Mike and Charlie sent regrets from the PI; Al and Betty and their families all made it; Francie had sent her regrets because of her pregnancy. The Senator, Millie, Margaret and Edgar made the trip from the East Coast with George, his wife and children. Corky and Charlie met most of their cousins. Corey stood up for me. Jack Willis in Ft Vancouver arranged for a dozen rose arrangements.
All the fellows from the School of the Line kicked in a few bucks for the party at the Preston Hotel downtown. All had a great time; I left sober despite all the bathtub gin passed around.
I am to get a post command as a wedding present from Gen. Pershing.

Sending that letter and her baptismal certificate off was, somehow, satisfying, and correlated with *Brownshoe Army*. Ned and Angie's daughter was perhaps finding out something she had wondered about much of her life. Had she dared ask her parents about the two-wedding conundrum? It *was* puzzling until I saw a TV movie where a French couple who first married in a church stopped off at the registrar's office for a civil ceremony on the way to their reception as required by French law since their Revolution.

The past just kept coming back . . . and back . . . when I got this one:

14ᵗʰ Jul 96
Bismarck, SD.
Dear Dr. Durand,
My sister contacted you, and I thought I should.

Dad's diaries are a historical gold mine I never wanted to dig into. As a historian (Emeritus Prof. 19ᵗʰ Century Europe, USD), I know the value of such sources. I congratulate you on your find.

Mother always had some trepidation about Dad's diaries, although she didn't interfere as writing them was so important to Dad. We lost some volumes in various moves, and my brother masticated one. Some sources just remain imperfect.

I am glad to learn that someone might want to preserve the farm. After my Air Force career ended in '56, I lived there with Carl and the folks for a year. I found Granite Ledge to be a pleasant yet placid little village, and I wanted more excitement, so despite the attractions of Crest's history program, I attended NYU for undergrad and Columbia for grad school.

Please don't hesitate to contact me if you think I can provide anything. I look forward to seeing your work.

Yours,
Charles Steele

So, now we knew what happened to Volume XIVA that Maria and I got a whiff of: a very young Carl Steele chewed it and spit up on it.

The evidence of that very persistent past just kept coming back . . . as they did with this tantalizing entry fragment I found in Volume XX.

[Unknown date; stain] . . . *we found a farm cottage near the camp.* [Stain] *is a charming little burg next to* [Stain] *I understand it's an excellent school. I shall go down there, perhaps take some classes.*

"Same shit, different day, Curtis," Polly said, swinging her purse and jacket onto my office sofa that late July afternoon. "The TA contracts we reviewed at the beginning of the meeting didn't change more than a few words and commas from those you and I signed."

"That's good to know," I answered. "So what was the meeting for?" I tried not to be distracted as she flapped her t-shirt and skirt* in my fan's breeze in my stuffy office. The high at the airport that day was 98 degrees, with humidity at nearly 50% and no wind. I imagined someone walking by my hall window, seeing Polly with her shirt and skirt flapping and me trying not to see.

"This legal beagle started rambling on about how 'good-faith in the contracting process won't work,' so when the TAs get here and they get hired, the contracts can't just be there, waiting for them."

"Why the hell not?" I asked, puzzled. "They've been . . . "

"This lawyer said something like, 'doing that may be simple and convenient, but legally questionable as to applicability' or some *bullshit* like that. Murray† about had a fit." She shuffled out of her sandals.

"I can imagine," I said, seeing in my mind's eye the dark Native American rage at the imprecision of such language. "He'd want case examples or cites of some kind."

"Yeah, he did. 'What's legally questionable about convenience?' Murray asked. 'One size may not fit all,' this other lawyer says. 'TAs are all the same size,' Murray says. 'Nothing different about this one or that one or every other one.'" She pulled the stick out of her barrette and shook her hair loose before she sat on my sofa.

"They're peas in a pod," I agreed. "But this guy . . .?"

"He acted surprised, asked something like 'each department and school uses the same hours, the same conditions, the same . . .?' We all said, 'yeah. Who says different?' 'Our research

---

* *Sans brassiere;* she was about as well-endowed as Maria. At least she wore underwear
† Murray Walking Elk, the head of our Law school.

suggested that schools and departments had different working conditions.' 'Quarry science and English TAs and all the rest are under the same hours, the same rate of compensation, the same . . . ' Murray says. 'Ah,' this lawyer says, 'working conditions are far different for those different departments. State labor standards . . . .'"

"Don't apply for student labor in this state," I interrupted. "He didn't know that? Besides, all the TA contracts cover is compensation for their labor: X sections for Y money."

"You and I know that," Polly sighed, "but this guy didn't. This guy had the crazy idea that they had to spell out hours of labor and safety requirements for different time periods and departments."

"That's nuts," I said. "TAs can spend fifty hours this week and five next, depending on exams. What's this guy . . .?"

"He started waving this ten-page, fine-print thing with all kinds of blanks, saying 'these are much easier to defend in court.' Murray said we'd never faced a lawsuit over a TA contract because they're so simple, and this yokel says '*yet.*' So, we started into him like he was out of his mind, and he finally says, 'very well; I shall take it up with the Corporate counsel.' 'That's not you?' damn near everybody screams. 'No; my firm was contracted to draw up these contracts that the Corporate counsel is studying, pending approval.'"

"So, we're nowhere," I said.

"We're sticking with the old contracts for now, I guess." She lay down on my sofa, her skirt and t-shirt flapping almost indecently, hair cascading off my sofa. "Nobody said different." She yawned widely. "I need a nap, sugar. Wake me before you leave, will ya? Thanks."

THE TWINS ARRIVE

I remember that halcyon-if-steamy day *so* well. The weather was as clear—but much warmer—as that June day in '82, when Melanie and I made our momentous decision . . .

I was perusing TA resumes in my office. Even if I let my professors hire their own TAs and all the adjuncts they'd need, I still had to hire mine . . . then the phone rang. "Curtis," Meli said. "Connie's water broke; she's on her way to Allen.* *She's* fine; *Mike's* not . . . "

"His first trip to the fair," I sighed. "I'll come hold his hand."

I carried several resumes in a battered little canvas portfolio I slung over my shoulder. Connie's labor would be about, oh, anywhere between four hours, like Melanie's average, and twenty hours, like Connie was with Johnnie. However long it was, I resigned myself to sitting in uncomfortable hospital waiting rooms for a while.

"Mike," I said, meeting him outside the Maternity Suites, a newer, fancier place to have babies.†

"Curtis," he nodded. We chatted for a few minutes: he nervously answering simple questions; I trying to be casual. "They could at least try to make us more comfortable."

"Yeah." Jenny Hoffmeir (nee Rizzo), an intimate friend of Connie's, and Meli were Connie's coaches, and Connie didn't want any

---

* Allen-Frobisher Medical Center, the regional hospital across the river.
† Women had been squatting behind trees for this since time immemorial, so why all the fuss?

rubbernecking interlopers in the Birthing Studio.* We knew what could go wrong—we'd seen it on all those doctor shows on TV. It normally didn't, of course, but . . . "This could take a while."

"Should I call *Mother-Dear?*" Mike asked, with his usual ominous emphasis.

"It's her grandkids, too."

"She won't *deign* to put in an *appearance*, of course, but she might dispatch an aunt so they can *complain* about the *delay*. They treat me like an errant peasant on their estate." He stopped. "I *should* call Gramma Devota."

"Sun's over a yardarm *some*where, Mike; call Devota and let's go get a drink."

Izzy's, the first saloon we saw across the street, sported chrome-legged vinyl-covered stools, brass foot rails, oak curbs on the bar's edge, and peanuts in wicker baskets. Boxes of cigars, bottles of the five whites† and scores of browns‡ and pickles the size of a baby's leg in a jar lined the mirrors behind the bar. Fans blowing over mounds of ice provided cool-ish relief from the humid 90 degree heat outside.

We sat on stools near the door, a fan at my elbow, and ordered a couple of ponies.§ The barkeep, made in the same mold as the bar with his apron hitched up around his chest, tapped our beer silently, taking the offered $20 and putting back $15, adding a basket of peanuts-in-salted-shells and two pickles. *Two and a half bucks for two ponies and pickles?* I dimly thought we'd gone back in time twenty years.

We were halfway through our beers before Mike said anything. "I *love* my family, but sometimes . . . "

"They're like that, ain't they?" I agreed, chomping a pickle. "Drive ya nuts if you let 'em. Mine isn't very large and much of it's distant. I've got cousins I've never met. I . . . "

---

* Delivery room
† Vodka, tequila, gin, peppermint schnapps (or triple sec), and light rums.
‡ Whiskeys, dark rums, and everything else.
§ A small glass; about four ounces at Izzy's.

"Yeah." Mike finished his beer; signaled for another. "And two of those Monte Cristos, please."

OK; not talkative. So we wait.

We sat in the not-busy saloon, barely comfortable, sipping our little beers and eating while the barkeep chatted with patrons at the other end. I glanced at the clock too often . . . before I thought out loud, "Joanie died nine years ago today." *

"Connie's mom?"

"Yep."

"Huh." Mike sniffed his cigars, munched peanuts and pickles . . . waiting . . . "Is it always like this?" he asked at length.

"Waiting for kids? Yeah, kinda. It's that unknown stuff that's the hardest part. Maria was my hardest . . . "

"Connie wants more . . . "

"Do you?"

"I dunno . . . "

We waited, exchanging a few syllables between the silences, refills, and potty stops . . . †

"Connie is my world," he finally said. "I don't know what I'd do without her."

"She's special, all right," I agreed. "Now you'll have . . . "

"When Jenny and me were at FOB Cobra,‡ we talked about *back here* a lot. She knew Connie and Jerry were together; she tried not to think about it; told herself it didn't mean nothin'. I thought the whole damn§ thing was *nuts*. I mean, they were all friends, yeah, but what the *hell?* Shit, I dated Connie before the war . . . ."

His next pause was very . . . very long . . . "One night off-shift we were talking about *back here* behind the fuel bladders and next thing I know her pants are off and mine are around my knees and she's on top of me and it was over so fast and she said, 'this didn't happen' over and over while she climbed off me and hitched up

---

* 7 August 1987. It's the nature of historians to make those kinds of correlations out loud at all the wrong times.

† I never knew where those hours went.

‡ Forward Operating Base built behind enemy lines in Iraq.

§ He didn't say *damn*. Mike's story, like Ned's diaries, has the vulgarities cleaned up.

her pants. But we told Jerry and Connie at the same time; figured they deserved to know." He stared at me. "I told nobody that story before. Why you?"

"*Hell* if *I* know."

"Did you tell Melanie about all the women you slept with?"

"There weren't that many, but, yeah. She knew about all of 'em at Crest before we got together, and there were only two before that, and one was . . . "

"Connie's mom. You thought Connie could have been yours."

"Yep; the thought crossed my mind." I finished another pony, signaled for another. "Your generation has different attitudes between the sexes than ours did—does."

"You grew up in the '60s," he said, surprised. "I thought . . . "

I sighed. "Yeah, everybody thinks that." The barkeep took the cash left on the bar, and I pulled another double sawbuck out of my pocket.* "I saw my sister's skirts shoot up from mid-calf to mid-thigh in '67. Mom got a shorter skirt—like two inches above her knees. Dad eventually got used to it." I shook my head. "Karen wanted to go to a drive-in with a friend and her older sister. 'Car date?' Dad said. 'How do you think you got here?' Mom talked him into it since there were no boys involved." I stopped, thought . . . "Mom was barely twenty when Karen was born." *I never did that math before . . . huh.* "The Sexual Revolution wasn't what the movies and TV said it was, though it was . . . something. We're just the walking wounded from that little fracas."

"How so?"

"Well . . ." I thought for a moment. "My *first* reaction to what you just told me about you and Jenny . . . surprise is one way to say it, but . . ." I thought back to that January night, when Connie and Jerry . . . in the suite. "When you cross that bridge with someone, you can't cross back; your relationship changes for good.† When Meli and I were that age, crossing it meant more than it does to your generation, and it'll mean less to both our kids." I stopped.

---

* We'd had how many? The cigars . . . ? There was a candy wrapper there, and a couple of jerky wrappers . . . How much had we spent?
† Polly was still my friend. We never *did it* after the next morning.

"And more's the pity. Sex might be natural and safe and all that these days, but it gets cheaper when it's just . . . "

"Screwing, yeah."

"Yeah. Connie was very vulnerable for a long time, and Jerry loved her deeply as a friend . . . "

"Still does; so does she."

"I'd believe it. Meli and I knew how they felt. But Jerry feared what Jenny might think if he acted on his feelings with Connie, and Connie . . . "

"Was looking to come back from her assault with a guy she could trust implicitly. Yeah." He was quiet. "That's the way Jenny put it, what they both told her." He finished another pony; signaled again, put his own sawbuck on the bar. "That's another difference between our generations, I guess. She and Jerry told both Jenny and I at the same time. Then *we* unloaded on them and had a good laugh." He chuckled, half to himself. "Abstinence," he mumbled. "That's what I'll teach my . . . "

"Not a good idea; won't work anymore. That's the one thing from the '60s that's had any permanent effects. I've been teaching young adults long enough to know that, especially in a town full of seasonal residents from all over. The mysteries of sex are often too tantalizing not to explore. Teach self-respect; respect for others." I reflected on my next words. "There's going to be challenges when they get older. The biggest challenge is knowing when to tell a son about how babies are made. Girls are easy because . . . "

"Yeah, *then,*" Mike sighed, putting the cigars in his shirt pocket once more, glancing at the clock: five in the afternoon. "I need to call the unit, tell 'em we won't make the drill this weekend." He made to get up. "I need more than bar chow."

I finished my pony and left another $5 on the bar. The barkeep waved as we left.

Not many saloons like Izzy's anymore.

The lights were dim. Mike and I were still in the ungodly hospital waiting area chairs amid the wreckage of vending machine sandwiches, chips, candy bars, and way too many cups of machine coffee that had been our late supper around 10.

John D. Beatty

111

I had gone over all the resumes I'd brought, decided on two promising scholars to interview; a political historian from Brooklyn and a social historian from Mississippi who I believed had what I was looking for. I was thinking about my choices when . . .

"Babe," Meli whispered in my ear . . . and I realized I'd fallen asleep.

"Huh," I jolted awake, the back of my neck and left foot numb. I looked over at Mike, sacked out on a couch-like thing across the room. "Is *she* . . .?"

"The nurse gave her morphine so she can rest. Jenny's in there." She stood up, held out her hand. "I need to eat; barely had any lunch."

"OK, honey." I stomped my foot and craned my neck awake as we walked down the corridor, watching for any signs that might mean food as I realized I was hungry again. The cafeteria was closed, the deli shop shuttered, the vending machines rejected, and the employee cafeteria only open to them. "I wonder why they don't think about overnight visitors?"

"Planners don't think about the planned-for until the planned-for complain convincingly," Meli said absently. "Trust me: urban planning is for the builders and the taxing authorities, not the people who live there. That leaves the people who manage their wonderful plans to fix the issues. I don't imagine hospital planning is much different."

"You've been working in urban management for how long?"

"Too long."

I noticed foot traffic at the end of another corridor. "Something may be promising." We shuffled down that corridor to find an odd sort of convenience store; odd because the prices were on a whiteboard behind a woman with a cash box. Employees and others of all descriptions lounged at folding tables and chairs in the bigger room outside. The woman took our money for our cellophane-wrapped cold sandwiches, bagged chips and soft drinks in plastic bottles, and we sat at a folding table.

"I called Maria at about nine," Meli said after the first half of her tuna salad was gone. "This is fresh."

"Yeah," I said, after gobbling down half a corned beef-and-provolone on rye. "She's managing the boys OK?"

"They're excited about the babies."

"How's she doing?"

"She's fine; progressing well, they said. She'll be fully dilated by sunup."

"I meant Maria . . . "

"Oh, yeah; she's fine. Her buddies are there."

"Which?"

She took a bite. "Ted and Allison." She glanced at me. "Don't think that, babe." She shook her head. "This labor business is sure different from when we last did this."

"How?"

"The idea of walking away from a woman in labor by jolting her with dope and expecting everything to just stop for a few hours. Not with Johnnie; *that* was a day and a half marathon."

"Different generations, honey."

"Just nine years, though."

"Took less than that to develop the A-bomb."

She *eyeballed*[*] me. "From babies to bombs?"

"Long night."

"Yeah."

We finished our meals with only a little more discussion and walked back to Connie's suite. Meli pointed to a slightly open door just off the suite entrance. "There's a little *accommodation* we can use over *there*." It had two beds with a curtained window over them, a sink, and a stall shower in a corner. "*You* go ahead; get some sleep; take a shower. *I'll* go back in with Connie."[†]

"*Curtis*," a familiar-yet-not-familiar voice roused me while shaking the bed, "Curtis, get up."

"Huh?" I grunted, looking up at Jenny, frowsy and red-eyed. "What . . .?"

---

[*] Brother, you know when you've been eyeballed.

[†] Then the Maternity Suite idea made sense.

"The first baby's a girl." She shook me again. "C'mon, Curtis, up and out. I need a shower and we're not *that* good friends."

"Uh," I grunted, swinging my feet down. Her Army experience accustomed her, I suppose, to seeing men in and being seen by men in underwear; she was shirtless and shorts-less* by the time I pulled my pants and shirt on, grabbed my shoes and socks and shuffled out.

Still trying to gather what wits I could, the morning sun through the waiting room windows was dazzling. Helen and Devota Klein stepped into Connie's suite just as I stepped out of the accommodation. I was not expecting to see Maria and the boys there. While Maria chatted with Mike, looking like he'd slept in his clothes (he had), the boys played with the generic toys stacked in the corner for just such visitors.

"A girl," I sighed, stretching my back before extending my hand. "Congratulations, Mike."

"Yes, thanks: her name's Joan Melanie," Mike declared, handing me a cigar. "For both her maternal grammas."

"Well, good," I declared. "I'm sure Meli is proud . . . "

"If the next is a boy, we wanted . . ." he glanced at Maria, "Curtis Charles."

"I . . ." I stumbled. What could I say? "I'll be proud to share my name with my grandson: it was my father's father's name, too. I'm sure Dad will . . . "

"My father was Charles, Curtis," Mike mumbled. "So we cover both maternal and paternal sides."

"Leave it to Connie to have the perfect solution," I declared, watching Jerry Hoffmeir coming down the corridor. "Jerry," I called, "leave the girls at home?"

"With my folks," he said, extending his hand first to Mike, then to me. "Congratulations, gents. What's the score?"

"A girl twenty minutes ago," Mike nodded, handing him the other cigar. "Connie's taking a break before . . . "

"That cost me five bucks," Jerry grinned. "I had a boy first in the betting pool."

Meli stepped out of Connie's suite. The boys flocked to her,

---

* I didn't look. Honest! I just kinda saw, out of the corner of my eye.

and, as worn as I could see she was, she still did a motherly embrace. "She's OK; tired, but OK," Meli sighed. "I need a break myself. Mom and Devota are taking over."

"Gents: we should fetch coffee for the ladies."

"And ourselves," Mike said. "C'mon, Maria," he added, hooking her arm. "You can hold me up." Maria was nearly Mike's height (he wasn't a big guy), and she came up to my nose and Meli's chin.

The hospital was busier than the night before, and the coffee bar was open. We got coffee for ourselves and, knowing our respective spouse's preferences, for them. Maria ordered a decaf.

We shuffled back to the waiting room, where Jenny, wrapped in a hospital gown with her hair still damp, took her coffee from Jerry. While Maria took Connie's coffee in, I took Meli's to the little room where she was taking her turn in the shower. I closed the door just as Meli stepped out in a towel. "Coffee, honey."

"*Ooh*," Meli sighed. "Just what I need." She sat on one of the two beds, letting one towel drop, her hair still wrapped in another as she sipped her coffee, her back to me.

"You're gorgeous," I said, sipping mine.

"You say that to all the naked girls."

"That would be you for the last fourteen years."

"It was Jenny a few minutes ago."

"She wasn't naked, and I didn't look."

She sipped. "Didn't look, huh?"

"Not really, no."

"She said you're surprisingly well-preserved for an older man." Even with her back to me, I could see her grin. "Just underwear, anyway." She put her coffee down and lay down on the bed. "Rub my back?"

"Older man?" I mock-asked, moving to her bed. "Surprisingly well-preserved?" I started massaging her upper back and shoulders. "Should I be insulted or grateful?"

"Whatever floats your boat, babe," she groaned. "If a twenty-something woman says a forty-something man looks good in *any way*, shape or form, he should take it as a compliment." I kept massaging, trying to loosen the knots in her back. "Mmm," she sighed as I continued, ever-so-gently. It was several minutes before I realized she'd fallen asleep. I threw a sheet over her, took my coffee, and left.

"Beautiful, honey," I gushed as I bussed Connie's forehead six hours later. She delivered Curtis Charles an hour before that instant. It took that long to get her presentable and both babies in their little tubs. "Congratulations."

"Six pounds each," Connie sighed. "Felt like *sixty.*"

I blanched at that, but Mike and Jerry just held her hands and smiled. Maria acted like she didn't hear, staring out the window; Meli looked a little peaked, standing behind the boys, clicking away with her camera. My boys, fascinated, looked at the little bundles of joy. Jenny was on the phone, talking to Jerry's parents about her girls.

Helen watched the entire scene with a look of some satisfaction. "*Four generations* of us here," she sighed.

"Ye *gods,* Helen," Devota said, patting her friend's arm, "how far have we come?"

Helen smiled sadly and shook her head. "Devota, if not for our children, and now our great-grandchildren, where would we be?"

Knowing what I knew then about Mike and Jenny and Jerry and Connie, the difference in attitudes about relationships between the sexes again struck me. OK, Jerry and Connie had been intimate on one occasion, at least.* Mike and Jenny had their tryst, though I wouldn't call it that by Mike's description; more like consensual rape. They all knew of these liaisons, yet they were still good friends. *I wonder how Dad might have acted if one of Darla's friends had caught him in his boxers.†*

While the great-grandmothers marveled at their longevity.

Sure, Meli knew about my liaisons; she'd talked about hers. Neither of us was so naïve as to think we wouldn't look at or think of other people as long as we didn't act on it. We were children of the '60s, and Helen and Devota survived not just the Depression,

---

* I was never so boorish as to ask if they *did it.*
† One of them was fond of flashing me. Would she have dared flash Dad?

but a world war and, between them, five children and two husbands.

Then I thought of Ned and Angie, their "courtship" in a hospital surrounded by the dying and the maimed. And their first liaison, as rushed and dark and wonderful as Ned described it, and the sweet memories he carried with him into the Hell of 1918 France.

Five completely different worlds; societies constrained in one way and unconstrained in others.

Yet . . . *Jenny thinks I'm well-preserved?*

"So, Mr. Bergin," I said to the well-dressed young man in my office the next day, "you have an interest in financing the Civil War?"

"I do, yessir." Elias Bergin had a nasty scar across a discolored eye. "Long interest in . . . "

"Excuse me, but I have to ask: your eye."

"It's OK; everybody gets to it eventually. Subway accident when I was eleven."

"Ah. Now, this is important, and I have to know for safety reasons. Is it sensitive to dust? Archives can be . . . "*

"It's glass, sir. I patch it in dirty environments because it is a little like an open wound."

"All right. Had to ask."

"I understand. I also have trouble with depth perception, and I don't know if this state will allow me to drive."

"Is that important?"

"I'd like to at least ride my scooter legally."

"Last I looked, twenty years ago, motor vehicles under ten horsepower didn't require a driver's licence. Has the registrar's office gotten around to you yet?"

"They have, sir. My registration depends on this interview."†

"OK, let's get to it." We discussed approaches and commitment to teaching, depths and styles of research, ability to handle multiple sections of different topics and periods, and the like. Then, I asked the most important (to me at that moment) question. "I'm in the early stages of an archival project to do with WWI. It

---

* Paper archives age messily.
† The grad student seat Elias was interviewing for required a TA job.

will take much of my time. How are you at being ignored for perhaps days?"

Elias blinked. "I thought you were 19th Century economics?"

"This fell into my lap."

"WWI," he made a most curious face. "I, ah, wouldn't have a problem unless I needed some interaction in case of an actual emergency."

"Like?"

"My father's not well. If—*when*—he passes . . . "

"An e-mail would do it for me as long as you also find someone to cover your sections." I waited for a pace. "If you don't mind my asking . . . "

"Two packs a day, working the steam tunnels in Manhattan for thirty years and living in Flatbush for fifty, and COPD happens."

"OK, sorry." I leaned forward. "You know much about the Great War?"

"I did a paper at CCNY on the shifting of the center of the economic universe from London to New York during that war." He shrugged. "Got me interested in economic history; got me here."

"Have any interest in working on my project as a volunteer?"

"If I have the time."

"Can you find out how much 200 French Francs were worth in 1919, and if that was a lot?"

"In a few hours, but I can also recommend a reference for that kind of thing."

"Good. Got a dissertation topic yet?"

He stared at me hard and long, shifting from side to side.* "I think I just got an idea for one: paying the bills; a contrast between 1865 and 1918."

"I'll e-mail the registrar to have your contract ready . . . how about tomorrow?"

"Soon enough." He extended his hand. "Thanks, Professor. I think I'll like it here. And congratulations."

"Thanks . . . for . . .?"

---

* Many people with only one eye do that to aid depth perception.

"Your grandkids. I heard about them this morning. You're about the youngest grampa I ever saw."

"Ah, well, yes, thank you."

"What's that mean?" I asked the voice on the phone the next day. "TA contracts are with the school . . ." Elias emailed me that morning that someone was holding up his and other TA contracts and thus registrations.

"They are with the Corporation starting in September," the voice answered, as if to a child asking to play hooky.

"These people need to make plans . . . "

"The Corporation is well aware of that, Dr. Durand. However, the new contracts have to pass review through the Corporate Counsel, and that will take . . . "

"School starts in three weeks," I said patiently. "The new TAs have to be oriented. I thought this was already worked out . . .?"

"Sorry, but the legal review should be concluded on August 23rd."

"That's the Friday before classes start; way too late for the TAs to register, get oriented . . . "

"Cannot be helped. Is there anything *else?*"

"This is unacceptable, but I have a suggestion," I said patiently. "Sign them up with the old contracts now so they can at least get registered . . . "

"*Registered?*" the voice sounded . . . surprised, dumbfounded?

"Yes; Our TAs need contracts just to register. Requirement in their first year."

"I was . . . we were not aware of that, Dr. Durand. Let me get back to you."

You were not aware . . .

"Curtis, this is getting to be . . ." Polly started, storming into my office the next afternoon.

"This . . . what," I asked, all innocent.

"These Goddamn TA contracts, *that's* what," she spat at me, slinging her bag onto my sofa again, standing defiantly in front of me, hands on hips. It was hard to take a woman in a crop-halter top and micro-shorts as serious, but . . . "I've got three TAs I need registered now, and they can't get signed up. One wants to go back to State, for the love of . . . "

"I talked to the registrar yesterday," I said. "I sent you all an email about it. They said . . . "

"Whatever it was they said yesterday, they ain't saying it now. We're three weeks from classes and I can't get . . . "

"Hold on," I sighed, reaching for my phone. After several minutes, I said, "Yes, this is Dr. Durand on speaker with Dr. Winfield. We spoke yesterday about the TA contracts . . . "

"Yes," the woman answered smoothly. "What about them?"

"Well, we need to get our TA contracts or they can't register . . . "

"That's not a legal concern," the voice answered. "Corporate counsel has assured us it is school policies that must change to suit the legal requirements of . . . "

"*Who the Hell is the Corporation working for?*" Polly yelled. "Why couldn't you have brought this up . . .?"

"The Corporation works for the good of the school," the voice replied loudly. "The school must act according to . . . "

"Crest University pays the Crest Corporation, yes?" I asked, holding up a hand to stop Polly from screaming again as a small crowd gathered outside my office. "The Corporation does the school's bidding, yes?"

"Yes, but the Corporation has to ensure the school complies with the law, Dr. Durand," the voice answered. "Corporate counsel has determined that the old contracts cannot be defended in the event of litigation. Therefore, the new contracts will not be made available until . . . "

"Too late for my TAs to go to other schools to complete their degrees," Polly declared. "You have any idea how *catastrophic* this is for . . .?"

"Once again, the Corporation acts in the best interests of the school, *missy.*" The woman with the tart voice sighed. "It's simply a matter of the law. Those young people will have to be made to understand . . . ."

"*Missy,*" Polly cried, "I'm *Dr. Pauline Winfield,* you . . . "

The Persistent Past

"Excuse me . . . *Doctor*," the voice replied smoothly. "But those children have to . . . "

"One of 'em ain't a child," Polly answered. "Disabled Gulf War vet, got a wife and two kids. Just moved here from Iowa. What do I tell him now?"

"That is unfortunate, but . . . "

I hung up, dejected and concerned that Polly might make a mess when she exploded . . . as, by her livid face, it appeared she might. "*Polly*, buddy, calm down," I said softly. "We'll have to take another tack."

"*Calm down?*" she shouted. "I've got some of the *best* new scholars in the American history field waiting for this *Goddamn cockamamie Corporation to get its head out of its ass* and . . ." She stopped. "By the way, congrats on the grandkids."

"Thanks. You've got a vet for a TA?"

"Yeah. A solid performer; lost his foot in the desert." She sat heavily on my sofa. "What do we do *now?*"

"I wish I knew, buddy."

"So the corporation didn't know your new TAs needed jobs to register?" Meli asked that night.

"Apparently not," I sighed. "And they don't seem to care."

"What's the Corporation supposed to be for, anyway?"

"The physical plant, the grounds, buildings and the non-academic staff, as I understand it. The Foundations want to distance themselves from the messy labor and contract stuff for . . ." While the Crest and the Jenson Foundations, the Regents and several trusts owned the school, the Crest University Corporation was (allegedly) going to improve the maintenance of the buildings, the grounds, and the labor conditions of the staff—60% its employees. Which made the new contract issues with the graduate teaching assistants that much more baffling. They were students, and they were learning to teach. And they paid for credits and books, but not . . .

"Maybe that's it."

"What?"

"They don't pay tuition, which makes them look like non-academic staff to a non-academic."

"Makes sense to a corporate bureaucrat. You've never had to deal with that kind of mess, though."

"Well, no, but how much different is it than academic bureaucracy and money and . . . "

"Corporations exist to make money, babe. The school's happy when it's only slightly in the hole. A corporation can't afford to be."

"But it's private, not public."

"Still has stockholders."

"That's so, even if the stock isn't publicly traded." Members of the Regents and the scores of officers in the Trusts (that included several Kleins) owned everything, including the Corporation. And they didn't sell it to anyone outside their little circle. Which made some of what happened later a little baffling.

That persistent past . . .

"*What?*" I asked, incredulous.

"There was an assault last night, near the Cubes," Larry said. "Girl got away, but it scared the bejesus out of her."

"And the night before," Sharon agreed. "Same guy, the cops think."

"And Campus Security's been disbanded?" I asked, still finding it hard to believe.

"As of the first of August," Bay said. "The policeman I spoke with, who told me this, said there simply aren't enough of their people to patrol the campus more than once every three hours."

"This I believe," I said.* "OK; I have some phone calls to make, folks. We'll meet again Friday."

My first call was to Moe Hardin, who was thunderstruck by the news. Then I called James Jenson, whose reaction was similar, except . . . "The Corporation took over contract responsibility for the Campus Security team when the Corporation was formed . . . "

"Well, apparently, the Corporation disbanded Security while telling no one at the school, though they were kind enough to tell Granite Ledge PD," I said, trying not to sound *too* . . . yeah.

---

* The Crest campus was a third larger than the City of Granite Ledge, whose police department was less than fifty sworn officers.

"What the *Hell* is going on here?" James asked.

"I think our Corporation is . . ." I started, then . . . "Murray?" I wondered.

"Do you know him well, Curtis?" James asked.

"Well enough."

"Uh-huh," Murray nodded sagely when I told him about both the contract nightmare and the Campus Security disaster. I'd gone to his campus office as soon as I hung up with James, hoping to catch him there . . . and I got lucky. "I'm due in court this afternoon," he frowned.

"It's kinda urgent, Murray," I sighed. "Two days more and these people . . . "

"I've got to have the same problems, Curtis," he said. "Just no one's told me yet."

"You are a busy guy, Murray," I said. *And scary . . . .*

"Mmm," he grunted. "Sometimes I think too busy." He dialed the phone. "Grace, send today's calender to Judge Palmeri, will you?* Give her my apologies and tell her I'll take up her cases for two days next week, but this matter requires my immediate attention." He glanced at me, phone on his shoulder. "Curtis, you are about to take part in a session of the Granite Valley District Court . . . Grace, how soon can you get a court recorder here? . . . Ask him to hurry. And ask Michelle to come up here, quickly." He hung up. "I'd better get dressed for this." He got up, stepped to a clothes pole, and pulled a judge's robe off a hanger. "These people have to learn they can't just run roughshod over us up here. I *think* I know what this is . . . "

"New York vs. our state law?"† I guessed. "Maybe they don't know the TAs are students for the contracts, but the security?"

"Yeah, it's those things, too," he said. "It's that this Corporation has an *agenda,* and it isn't a pleasant one." He gazed at me placidly. "Tina Klein's said she'd rather sell off this school piecemeal than lift a finger to make it more efficient." We passed the time in similar discussions for another few minutes until a woman in a Sheriff's

---

* Murray *was* also a district judge.
† The Corporation was based in New York.

Deputy's uniform came in. "Deputy Reisener, as bailiff for this court, swear in our plaintiff, please," he pointed at me. I'd just finished my oath as a man with a transcription machine entered. "David, Dr. Durand was sworn in as plaintiff in the matter of Crest University vs. Crest Corporation. The Granite Valley District Court Number Two is now in session; Judge Murray Walking Elk is presiding," he added as he pulled his robe on and punched his phone again. "Penny; please call the Crest Corporation counsel in New York. Tell 'em it's *Judge* Walking Elk on the phone for the *chief* counsel and the *Judge* will get him on the line and not one of his subordinates or the chief counsel *and* the Corporation will be held in contempt of the Granite Valley District Court." He sat down, straightened his tie.

"Chief corporate counsel on line *two,* your honor," Penny's voice said on the intercom after a few minutes.

"Thanks, Penny," Murray said, punching his phone again. "Mr. Brighton, you are on speaker with Judge Walking Elk and Dr. Curtis Durand, the plaintiff in the matter of Crest University vs. Crest Corporation. The first question before this court is *why* did the Corporation disband the school's security?"

"Murray, I . . ." Mr. Brighton began.

" *Your honor*, Mr. Brighton," Murray said emphatically. "Court is in session and demands an explanation."

"I'll look *into* it, your honor," Mr. Brighton said. "I'll get back to . . . "

"You'll get the responsible party on the phone *this instant,*" Murray declared. "Hang up on this court and it'll cost your Corporation a $500 contempt citation."

"I'll put you on hold, your honor," Mr. Brighton squeaked. There followed a long pause as Murray stared out his window. "Your *honor,*" Mr. Brighton came back in a few minutes, "I have Ms. Tallebuch from accounting on the line. She'll explain . . . "

" *Mr.* Walking Elk," a stern female voice said, rather like a school principal, "we reviewed the contracts for school security and . . . "

"Judge Walking Elk, or your honor, Ms. Tallebuch," Murray growled. "You are addressing the court."

The Persistent Past

"Very *well*," the voice said, as if indulging in a child's fantasy. "We've reviewed the contracts and determined the cost/benefit rato was . . . "

"We've had two assaults up here in the last two nights," Murray said. "Where's *that* in your cost/benefit analysis, Ms. Tallebuch? The Granite Ledge Police lack the manpower . . . and who informed the school that Security disbanded?"

"Our numbers showed that for the number of security incidents reported, the cost of private security was simply too high," she answered tartly. "We informed the Granite Ledge authorities. We saw no need to inform the school, since those services were rarely used."

Murray and I looked at each other blankly; Michelle and David were impassive, like the court fixtures they were. "How many incidents would have to be reported to be worth the cost, Ms. Tallebuch?" I asked quietly.

"By our figures, at least three times what we've been seeing over the course of the surveyed five years . . . "

"Ever heard of *deterrence*, Ms. Tallenbuch?" Murray asked in a way that sounded like a threat.

"Why, *I* . . . "

"What's the body of a young woman worth, Ms. Tallenbuch?" I asked. "How about her peace of mind?"

"The school has *Courtesy Patrols*, whoever *you* are," the voice snapped. "They . . . "

"*Not* during summer break," I answered.

"The court demands an answer to the question, Ms. Tallenbuch," Murray said. "Have you ever heard of *deterrence?*"

Silence. "We didn't . . . "

"The court didn't think you did, Ms. Tallenbuch. This court finds that the Crest Corporation has been negligent. It shall reinstate the Campus Security organization by the close of business tomorrow," Murray said breezily.

"You lack the . . . " Mr. Brighton began.

"The Granite Valley District Court has the authority to fine your Corporation $500 a day beginning tomorrow until they are reinstated, Mr. Brighton," Murray snapped. "And while we're discussing fines, the Teacher's Assistant contracts shall be instituted as written last semester. There is no legal reason for student labor—for they are students—in this or any other state, to be subject to New York State wage labor regulations."

"Student labor," Mr. Brighton answered. "They're . . . ah, yes, they would be, wouldn't they? Yes, your honor, we'll . . . "

"Inform the registrar forthwith," Murray snapped. "The court shall wait."

"But . . ." Mr. Brighton sputtered.

"Forthwith means *now*, Mr. Brighton. The court shall wait upon the registrar's call to my office at the school within ten minutes."

"You're going on hold again, your honor," Mr. Brighton declared.

Problems solved. But why were they problems in the first place? Was Mike's mother really that vindictive or greedy?

"Well, Ms. Durand," I asked a week later, "where are we on the inventory?" I had left Maria to start the inventory on her own, hoping she'd move on from just reading and start the actual work of history.*

She took a deep breath. "I have started an inventory card for every item through 1918. They are mostly . . ." She spoke about a sense of what the items meant, how they fit into the puzzle of Ned's early life. "But there's *this* pile," she pointed to an untidy stack of paper, "which don't really fit anywhere. I don't believe they're Ned's."

"Well, then, where should we put them?" This was key to a researcher's skill: what to do with that which you cannot account for?

"Leave them for later," she blinked. "Inventory them, but do not investigate them. Concentrate on that which we might verify." She swept her arm along our timeline. "There's enough work we have to do."

---

* It always starts with "what the Hell is this?"

Norm Hammond, a professor in another department working on another line of tables in the Holding Room, softly applauded. "Very good, young lady," he grinned. "First thing to do is decide what you don't need to do."

"What are you working on, Norm?" I asked. "What have you got there?"

"I needed to talk to you eventually," Norm said. "This seems to be a very early Franklin sketchbook. I got it because it's in my period and I wrote about Franklin in France."

I changed gloves* and walked over to look; Maria followed me. "It looks like Franklin's work," Norm said. "The paper looks authentic . . . "

"Needs a Franklin expert," I said. "How'd you get it?"

"Alan Jenson sent it to me," Norm sighed. "His boy found it."

Maria looked closely at the first page, then at the binding. "We might research the watermark," she said authoritatively, "and the stitching in the binding." She wiped off a pica stick† (one of many around) and held it to a page. "Between crown and demy in height . . . "‡

Norm and I looked at each other. "You, ah, have looked into paper and bindings, have you?"

"I study it in your library, Dr. Durand, as you instructed," she answered, leafing through the book, not looking up but grinning. "You have quite the collection on paper and bindings for a professor of history."

"I'm also an archivist, Ms. Durand," I said. "I had to learn about paper and inks and pens because of my research . . . as you well know."

She looked up. "Uh-huh. I'm finding this work to be fascinating."

"You have the advantage of me, Miss," Norm said, sticking out his hand. "We have not been introduced. Dr. Norman Hammond,

---

* Cross-contamination is a potentially catastrophic problem.
† A hooked ruler used for measuring on paper, so called because one scale is in picas (1/6th inch) once common in the print industry.
‡ Crown=16¾ inches; demy=17¾ inches

Early Modern* Atlantic Rim† History."

Maria smiled and took Norm's hand. "Ms. Maria Durand, researcher and transcriber for the Steele Collection."

"Pleased to meet you, Ms. Durand," Norm smiled mischievously. "I just got this item, and I recommend we send it to a Franklin expert, as Dr. Durand has suggested. What say you?"

Maria cocked her head and shrugged her shoulders. "Dr. Durand is the archivist and curator of this facility. My knowledge of this material is . . . I dunno."

Norm and I chuckled. "That's what I say," I finished. "We wouldn't have a place for this. I don't think we have any Franklin documents at all. So I'd say, 'I dunno' and send it to Philadelphia."

"I was just getting there, Curtis," Norm admitted. "It looks like it could be kosher, but what would we do with it? Should we spend the extra time figuring it out, or just let someone who knows Franklin better do it?"

"It's always better to admit you don't know something important than just bluffing," Maria said. "But you might document the odd paper size."

"I'm sure someone will, Ms. Durand," Norm said.

"You can call me Maria, Dr. Hammond," she smiled her winning grin. "Dad calls me 'Ms. Durand' when he wants to make a point."

"Then please call me Norm, Maria," Norm said. "We should all get back to work. We only have two weeks until school starts, and we now have TA contracts . . . ."

"How can I help you, Ms. Cooper?" I asked Kensie Cooper, my other newly hired TA, sitting in my office.

"First," Kensie said, "I have to express the thanks of *all* the teaching assistants for your clearing up that contract logjam."

"Thank my wife and Judge Walking Elk," I nodded. "She pointed to the problem, and he fixed it."

"Whatever," Kensie declared. "But I need your advice on how

---

* Roughly1500–1800, but that window is hotly debated.
† Also hotly debated; Norm worked on technological interactions.

to avoid the student groups trying to pull me in." Like any university, Crest had an array of student groups with activities, newsletters, meetings, signs, petitions, and occasional demonstrations.

"Official or unofficial?" I asked. The school couldn't easily stop the unofficial ones, but we could corral the official ones that received segregated fees, the part of tuition set aside for such groups.

"Both. I told the CAAU* I didn't have time for their politics, or the patience, and they backed off. Censorship of language in the name of racial grievance is bullshit. It's those AMN† and NMM‡ assholes that follow me around like some lonely dog."

"My advice is to join the ACSU.§ They get their fees based on how many members they have, and they can intervene . . . "

"Join one outfit to discourage two others? Doc, I ain't much of a joiner in the first place, but how does that make sense?"

"ACSU members stick together. If you don't want those other outfits bothering you . . . "

"Just because of the color of my skin," she sighed. "Sick and tired of this race bullshit."

"I noticed you didn't check the box on your application, and I wondered at that. I take it neither you nor your family were the victims of prejudicial behavior in Biloxi."

"Oh, sure, we was. Still are, sometimes. My granny and her sister were at the Pettus Bridge in '65. They got hosed down good, too. But black folks can be as racist as white folks: *you* know that. I'm not cool with race politics. Wastes time and energy. In my family, we take Dr. King's words to heart; content of character, not color of skin. Do the job and ignore those fools burning shit. You can't tell me you ain't been sneered at for walking into a black bar."

"No, I can't." There were a few in Granite Ledge,** and there were more in Cicero, where I grew up.

---

* Crest Afro-American Union, the largest group for African-Americans.
† Any Means Necessary, an unofficial group.
‡ New Mau-Mau, banned for their militant, arsonistic tactics.
§ All-Crest Student Union, the largest of the official groups.
** Izzy's barkeep and all the patrons but Mike and I were African-Americans.

"I didn't think so. So far, my experience here has been positive. Nobody's tried to brace me for walking across the Quad at night like they did at Columbia."

"Good to know. I want you to come to me with any concerns at all. How is your program shaping up?"

"My interests are well in hand, thanks."

"Tell me: do you have any interest in WWI?"

"No more or less than any history major. I understood from our interview you weren't gonna use us as your scut puppies like every other . . . "

"I won't, but I wondered if you wouldn't want to do the occasional little research on something that pops up in our documents. Just for variety's sake, if you've got the time."

"Like what?"

"Right now, I've got a question about when the metric system reached America. How common was it in practice before that metrication boom in the 1970s? Did schools teach it?"

"Now that's an interesting question. I know those wooden rulers with millimeters on one side predated the Second World War, because my granny had one in her school box."

"Really?" I scratched down a note. "When did she . . .?"

"She was born in 1920, attended Biloxi schools, had my father in 1940, so right in there."

"So, it's possible it was widespread enough to make its way to school rulers before 1920. She's still with us?"

"Granny will outlive us all." Kensie shook her head. "She was just out roller-skating to celebrate her 76th birthday." She made to stand. "I'll give the ACSU a shout, see what they want from me other than my name."

"Before you go, if I might ask," I said, "what's your father do? This place ain't cheap, and neither's Columbia."

"Daddy has a couple of gas stations and a string of dry cleaners. Mama's where our money came from: she patented an automated cleaning process for leather that revolutionized the industry. We get royalties from it. I'm also in a Mississippi state grant program for grad students in the liberal arts."[*]

Ask the right question in the right place, provided you know where that place *is*.

> *17ᵗʰ May, Jefferson Barracks, Misso.*
> *Charlie received a promotion to Sergeant in the 2ⁿᵈ Field Artillery in the Philippine Department. He's been in for seven years and he says that's pretty fair. He has no school beyond grammar school.*
> *Because I have completed four years at the Normal School, I will be a Corporal soon. Charlie will be green with envy. I wonder if I will go to the Philippines like Charlie? Will I get to fight in a war? After the* [expletive] *Heinies sank the Lusitania, the fellows here are sure we are about to ship out for France soon.*

"Where to start?" I puzzled over that entry, certain that the answer would come to me soon enough. It was the last week in August, and classes would start the next day. And Maria would go back to school the week after, cutting her time down.

"What do you mean?" Maria asked. "Inventory's mostly done . . . isn't it?" She had started her inventory at the beginning; I started a week later at the end. In between, we'd grab a diary and read some random pages just to keep interested—inventory can be incredibly dull. I showed her how to input the inventory data into the computer's inventory system—a new thing for everyone, only started six months before.[†]

"Yeah, but no; we need to research the transcriptions.[‡] We'll finish the inventory next week or the week after." Maria had actually done most of the work up to 1919. My inventory starting in 1926 was pretty straightforward. But some documents were objects of

---

[*] There were many such grants our Financial Aid department found.

[†] Out of caution, we kept the paper forms.

[‡] While we had been transcribing, we'd done very little research into the entries.

mystery, like the backs of "Dear Georgia" letters never sent, but repurposed. Is this the "G" in his diaries? Was paper that scarce? Was Ned absent-minded? It would take time to figure stuff like that out. "Do we start when the US entered the war, or when the war began? Ned barely mentioned the beginning of the war in 1914."

"What will people want to read?" she asked.

"More important, what will they buy?" I asked. "Tony's right: diaries of enlisted men before WWI are not only rare, but practically unheard of. But *who cares?*"

"Well," she said, reaching for a diary she'd just inventoried, "There are entries like this one, from Volume XI (1915–1916):"

> 17ᵗʰ September, Jefferson Barracks, Misso.
> Diane's wedding day and I can't be there. It is to a fellow named Theodore Morgan; never heard of him until Di wrote to me about him last month. Even though they are to wed today, something tells me that Di isn't sure. [Expletive], I have to wonder if she's in trouble. Once again, we train on machine guns. We have a Chauchat auto rifle which, I think, is too delicate to take to the field and the Lebel ammo is the wrong shape for a box magazine. We also have a Lewis gun, which is far more robust. The big, heavy, water-cooled Vickers gun is more like a cannon, and elaborate. Still, it puts out a steady fire and the British rely on it in Europe.
> Just heard they want to turn us into a machine gun unit. [Expletive], I'm ready.

"Vulgar profanities aside, entries like this make Ned Steele a person, not just a soldier," she continued.

"Yeah," I mused. We could fill in the blanks between diary entries with other archives (once we got responses to our letters and e-mails), and other information as we found it.*

"And we could try to contact more of his family," she added.

---

* Maria posted queries on internet bulletin boards that I knew little of.

The Persistent Past

"Between all his surviving brothers and sisters, it's likely that at least one had children of their own. Getting in touch with them might fill in some blanks."

"Yeah, but WWI is not my period." Like my TAs and everyone I spoke to except Wickie and maybe Tony, I knew the basics.[*] My eager assistant and I faced a very steep learning curve, and I had my teaching and administrative duties, and perhaps something more on the Barbary Wars, since I was the resident expert, since the bicentennial of my period was coming up like gangbusters. "Then again, diaries are very fashionable these days, which makes Ned's diaries very marketable. We have to produce something that could sell."

"That said," Maria said, turning to another page in Volume XI, "there's this:"

31ˢᵗ August, Jefferson Barracks, Misso.
That explosion in New Jersey last month that blew up all that ammunition has got people thinking. It looked like an accidental fire, like Pres. Wilson said, but there's this Slav who said he'd worked for German agents transporting suitcases. What if the [expletive] *Heinies sabotaged the place? And what if they fired up the Irish last Easter? It seems to a lot of people that the Germans are just too conveniently taking advantage of so much bad* [expletive] *luck.*

"Know what he's talking about?"

"Yeah, the Black Tom explosion that July. If memory serves, investigations after the war showed it to have been an act of German sabotage. And the Germans didn't incite the Easter Rising in Ireland in 1916 even if they supported it: the Irish didn't need any outside encouragement."

"Yeah? Ned thought enough of it . . . "

---

[*] Which, for any trained historian, was usually somewhat more than the average layman, but not as much as a specialist.

"Yeah . . . all right. I say we start the transcription research at Volume XI, so we can catch his reaction to the Lusitania. Plan on publishing the interesting entries after May 1915."

"Then we can capture his whole Great War experience," she beamed with some pride in helping me reach such a momentous decision.

"We make a good team, honey," I said finally. "Are you sure you want to . . .?"

"*Sure* I'm sure, Dad. Now," she started for the door, stripping off her sweatshirt as she went. "I'm meeting the guys at Kool-Js. Can I get a ride?"

"You can't be serious," I said, hearing the news.

"Yep," Polly declared, smoothing her longer skirt than she'd worn all summer as she sat down. "Dr. Anthony Zane shall be the Chancellor of the Crest University as of the third of September 1996."

"And here he's been saying he wants to retire . . . "

"He is. Says he'll be emeritus on the first of January 1997."

"And now we need to replace him," I sighed. "Can we find one like him?"

"An Early Modern historian who wants to come to the Icebox* in January? Nowhere short of a loony bin. We'll have two feet of snow by Thanksgiving. We *always* do."

"Well . . . you and Sam can cull that stack of resumes," I said, pointing to the small mountain of paper.† "There's bound to be *some*body suitable who's desperate enough to want to work here."

> *24ᵗʰ November, Hill 90, Flanders.*
> *I have brought 190 men this far and hope to take ninety Per. Cent. of them back. Rain as we moved in, making the mud deeper and wetter, sticking to everything.*
> *Our HQ and vehicles are miles behind the*

---

* Local slang for Granite Ledge.
† We kept about twenty at a time of the hundred or so we received every year.

hill, but they say we are on the 'front.' That word means very little here.

It is an odd thing, this horizontal fortress. Part is well-constructed, part is falling down. I find old trench saps collapsing, new ones being dug. This little [expletive] hill is an insignificant mound on a long ridge blasted barren by artillery and transformed into a bastion of dugouts, trenches, and bunkers. Tunnels below us are for keeping the Huns from tunneling. Those fellows from the Iron Range dig and dig and dig. They haul the spoil out at night to avoid detection by the Hun balloons and aeroplanes.

We moved into the positions in complete darkness and cold, soaking rain, taking the range cards and positions of a battery of the 1st CMMGB* as if we knew what the [expletive] we were doing. I got a briefing with Mike Brick and McTee from the outgoing 'battery' commander, a little fellow with a rambling speech who looks haunted.

To our left, on Hill 84 four miles to the north, another CMMGB battery backs up another Canadian battalion; to our right, another CMMGB battery backs up the battalion on Hill 85. The CMMGB is less a brigade than it is a five-company (that they call batteries) battalion with odd-looking Armored Autocars (that they use very little), plus mortars, motorcycles, and bicycles. I know the Autocar firm makes good trucks. I hope to get close enough to inspect one. These positions have been here for a little over a year, moving only a few yards of the front at a time, mostly of barbed wire entanglements in 'no-man's-land'. We are best thought of as an

---

* Canadian Motorized Machine Gun Brigade.

annoyance to the Huns on Hill 92 that the
Huns hold just three and a half miles
southeast of us.

I stared at Maria's transcription, putting it all into my mind's eye. A mechanized unit in the British Army in 1917? A little research showed that it was the first of its kind.

Ned's outfit had both trucks and mules and knew enough to relieve veterans. So many questions to answer. So little time to do it.

Something stuck in my head. Hill 90, huh?

FROM: POLLY
TO: CURTIS
RE: REPLACING TONY
FIVE MAYBE CANDIDATES AVAILABLE . . . .

I read Polly's e-mail with mild interest, scanning their qualifications, contract terms desired, titles of increasingly dull dissertations . . . until I hit . . .

S. BRIDGELY PHD UKAN 93: WE CAN KILL THEM BUT WE CANNOT STOP THEM: GERMAN PERSPECTIVES ON AMERICAN PARTICIPATION IN WWI.

I snatched up the phone, punched in her number, and waited impatiently until she picked up on the third ring. "Hey, Curtis. Thought you'd . . . "

"Who is this S. Bridgely, Polly?"

"*Susan* Bridgely is an Modern American historian who researched her German kin in the US Army during the war and wrote using their postwar letters and other material from their families in Germany. She's been an adjunct in Virginia . . . "

"Publications?"

"Two; an article in a journal and her dissertation's turning into a book."

"Let's talk to her and you can pick four of the other eight. Set up conference calls . . . "

"On it, boss."

THE STEELE INVENTORY

I was in my den a week after school started when the phone rang, which was odd for three in the afternoon; the deluge of peddler calls usually waited for dinnertime. "Hello?"

"Dr. Durand?" the vaguely familiar voice asked. "This is Anna McKendrick at Granite Ledge Middle School. We met last year at the parent-teacher conference; I was Maria's English teacher."

"*Yes*, Ms. McKendrick." I remembered an older* woman with interesting gray eyes. "What can I do for you?" I dimly hoped she was asking about some program at the school where I might . . . "Call me Curtis; saves time."

"Very well, Curtis; I'm Anna. I've got Maria for English Lit. this year. As we always do the first week, we ask for an essay on what students did on their summer vacation because we want to find out how rusty they've gotten since June. She handed in her essay yesterday, and . . . it's very unusual. Now, we expect some fibbing because most kids' summers are pretty dull, but Maria wrote she was—um, is—a contractor . . . let's see . . . 'inventorying, transcribing, and researching the Steele Collection.' She says, 'the diaries are over 80 years old, written by an officer in the National Army in WWI.'"

"Did she say how much the Collection is paying her to do her work?"

"You mean . . . ?"

---

* 50's maybe.

137

"She's down to working the Archive five hours a week during school. Ask her to show you her credentials for the Archive Building. She might take them to school; I told her not to lose them because the security people are very sensitive about that."

"She . . . huh." Anna cleared her throat. "Thanks for clearing that up, Dr. . . . uh, Curtis. We'll see you at the next conference?"

"Certainly, Anna."

My only dilemma after I hung up was whether I would tell Maria about the call before or after she brought her graded essay home. I would certainly tell Melanie; she'd get a good laugh.

Maybe . . . if . . . Maria's teacher didn't trust her veracity. That, for me as a parent and an educator, was a problem.

"Do I remember this woman?" Meli asked that evening after dinner.

"Older; gray eyes." I was still thinking about the trust issue. Without trust between teacher and pupil and vice versa, what teacher could ever impart any real wisdom?

"Peasant skirt and blouse; old-fashioned French twist."

"You say so."

"And . . . you've got more to say . . . "

"Ms. McKendrick didn't trust Maria."

Meli glanced at me, a little stunned, made her *I'm thinking* face, and turned to her reading.

For about an hour, that included a snack break and putting the boys to bed, we didn't speak. After I checked on Maria and we sat on the sofa for some TV, Meli came closer, took my hand, and said, "well, as she said, they expect some truth-stretching, but this would be so far outside what an 8th Grade teacher would expect. She might have expected a story about aliens abducting us before she bought the truth about her helping her father on a major historical project."

"There's the matter of trust, honey," I mumbled. "I wouldn't mind getting a call about an alien abduction essay, but . . . "

"This one hit closer to home?"

"Well . . . yes . . ." It was an issue. These diaries were the only ones of their kind that scholars had ever heard of. The Steele Collection needed to be micro-formed and publicized, and that took far more money than our research grant could afford.

We had to go public, and soon, somehow.*

I scanned the greenbar printout of the inventory as it came out of the printer, looking for obvious errors or omissions. Each item had its own index number based on its location in the Steele Collection. For instance, Item S-421 was the receipt for, we believed, the trunk that Ned may have purchased on 6 April 1919.

The printer hammered away for perhaps twenty minutes before that last inventory item came up. I stared at the thirty-odd pages of paper, neatly anonymous in its robot-like precision, that summed what we believed was twenty years of a man's life.

This inventory was one part of the business of history, which can be incredibly callous. Each item had been at one time handled by a human being, often in great peril, and sometimes in great joy.

But this list of things was merely a cold roster. It was my job and Maria's to make it live.

I looked again at that last inventory listing . . . and once again, inspiration struck. I grabbed the diary Volume XIV (1919–1920) and opened to the first entry where, after Ned's usual cataloging . . .

> 6th April, 1919, Hotel Deluxe, Paris.
> I am We are wed nearly three months now;
> 29th January 1919. It will be easy to remember
> that anniversary; it was Mother's birthday.
> Angie still works, and I still have duties with
> the battalion.
> As this was a pleasant Sunday, and Angie was
> working, I took a walk down the Rue de
> Flaubert, not expecting to find or see
> anything, just to reminisce about my life as I
> do every birthday. I exchanged pleasantries
> with a man in a French soldier's greatcoat
> with a pretty girl on his arm, admired the

---

* That didn't mean tomorrow, but . . .

flowers everywhere, and stopped in front of a
luggage shop, Le Baggage avec Benoit.
I learned the word "anvil" in French from him;
the name the French gave me after the Germans
did, I guess. M. Benoit, missing his left arm,
had the coarse hint of the lingering effects of
green cross gas* in his voice. Since neither
Angie nor I had any serviceable luggage that
we could call our own, I bought an oversized
steamer trunk for about $30. I'm given to
understand that's about a fortnight's wages
for a French workman these days.

By emphasizing this side of Ned Steele, we would make him and Angie more than this pile of paper and ink.

"What do we make of this?" I asked my 800-level class for dissertations, flashing that diary entry on the overhead projector.

"This is out of one of those diaries?" Brandy asked. She was working on the development and evolution of tank towns[†] in New England.

"Yes." This course had an enrollment of twenty, but I didn't expect to see over ten in a class session, which met twice a week. But here were seventeen students . . . .

"He was what rank here?" David asked. He studied the Cherokee removal in the 1830s.

"A Lieutenant Colonel in the National Army." This course taught dissertation thinking. As their faculty auditor—our code for form-checker—it was up to me to critique their dissertation outlines and early drafts.

"He sure covers a great deal of ground in one diary entry," Phil said. A quasi-military historian, his field was the social and economic impacts of military recruiting in the 19th Century.

"He does that." Enrollees had to attend at least half of the sessions, or their committees would not accept their dissertations. But

---

* Phosgene.
† So called because they built up around the railroad water tanks.

I had nearly all my enrollees in most classes.

"Was his mother alive here?" Brandy asked.

"No; she'd died of the influenza the previous October."

"Remarkably profanity-free," Brandy observed.

"Hadn't noticed that," I said. "Thanks. Maybe after so long being away from the troops all the time, such usage wears off."

"The way he talks about the luggage salesman; the writer had been around," David mused.

"Indeed. How would you know?"

"He knows the salesman had been gassed by the sound of his voice," David answered.

"Yes."

"It would be cool to find out if that luggage shop is still there," Phil said.

"But unnecessary," Brandy declared. "Has nothing to do with this . . . what did he mean by 'the name the French gave me after the Germans did, I guess?' How would he . . .?"

"Now, there's a good question. How might he know?"

"Users assign nicknames for something," Phil said. "This guy was known for doing something big if both the French and the Germans used the same nickname."

"And somehow he found out," Brandy said, puffing her cheeks.

"Such things have a tendency to proliferate," David said.

"They do, indeed," I said, clearing my throat. "This shall be one of the *last* entries—postscripts, if you will—in *Steele's Battalion: The Great War Diaries.*" I stopped; they all stared at me. "This project will contain *selected* transcriptions from Ned Steele's WWI diaries. My daughter and I . . . "

"Connie?" Phil asked.

"Maria. Anyway, we plan to have this project ready for publication by 2004, the ninetieth anniversary of the beginning of WWI."

"How much volume are we talking about?" Brandy asked.

"Between 6 April 1915 and 6 April 1919 is 1,462 days. He didn't make an entry every day, but for at least 80% of them. Some entries are just a line or two; some are several pages. We figure about fifteen hundred diary pages, with footnotes."

"Footnotes," Phil said, shaking his head. "What for?"

"Explanations," I said. "For instance, the questions you had about this entry alone; all those kinds of things have to be explained somewhere. This is an entirely different world from ours. How many of you guys had to ask a girl's father for permission just to write to her? How many write letters to anyone? And you, Brandy, have you ever had to make underwear out of your shirt sleeves? Ever thought of having to do it?"

"I'd have to go without," Brandy admitted. "I don't sew that well."

"Young women of Angie's time all sewed a little, regardless of how well. And they wrote, because, well, Ned didn't use a telephone until he was ten. E-mail would have been like magic to him."

"Doc," Brandy said softly, "let's get together after class."

"Sounds like an ambitious project, Doc," Brandy said as we walked to my office. "That's a lot of pages to check."

"And we have some ancillary documents, and a memoir, and we need to research all those tidbits in those entries."

"Quite something," Brandy answered as I let her in the door of my office. "Will you go on the record with this story? The *Intelligencer** will sure want this one about a local unsung hero."

"Certainly," I nodded.[†]

"How did you find these diaries?" Brandy asked. And we were off to the races. We talked for perhaps half an hour when the phone rang.

"Curtis: Mike. Listen, this thing's got a false lid that I just got open."

"And?"

"You'd better come look."

I glanced at Brandy. "Want an exclusive and some hands-on historical research?"

*   *   *

---

* Granite Ledge's only daily paper; I knew Brandy was a stringer for them.
† Since the Historical Society was trying to drum up interest in the farm, I tried hit two birds with one stone. Call it rope-a-reporter.

"Wow," was the only thing I could think to say, looking at the stacks of more notebooks, more documents and, to top it all off, a pair of dog tags that read, "STEELE, ED A 4_____9 O POS C" "Now we know his blood type, his service number, and that the Army truncated his name to 'Ed.'"

"There's also *this*." Mike held a black box in his hands—a camera. "I believe this is an original Kodak Brownie."*

I gazed at the object in some wonder. "Is it intact? There might be film in it . . . "

He looked it over carefully. "If there is, I got a guy who *might* be able to develop it." He grabbed a cloth off the shelf, wrapping the camera carefully. "See what he can do."

"Yeah," I said softly. "Money's no object." *Eighty-year-old imagery?*

Brandy, having fetched her own camera from her apartment on the way, clicked away at the trunk and the material Mike found. "This is fabulous," She could barely contain her excitement. "Mike Klein: any relation to Tina Klein, socialite?"

I left Mike to respond to Brandy's questions about his family while I perused the new hoard. I counted fifteen notebooks that looked like Ned's style of diary. I flipped the cover of Volume XXIII (1927–1928) open and stopped.

> 6ᵗʰ April 1926, Camp Penobscott.
> Corkie lost another tooth yesterday, so this
> Tooth Fairy had to come up with another
> silver dollar, and on my birthday. Georgie
> will start losing his teeth soon, too. Kids will
> drive me bankrupt on a Major's pay.
> After today's inspection of horses, the men
> gave me a fine silver-handled riding crop for
> my birthday. National Guardsmen care for
> their Regular mentors.
> After Gen. Summerall becomes CoS this fall, I
> shall not get another good assignment; he
> will never forget that meeting before

---

* Circa 1900.

Cantigny, nor forgive me for being right and showing him up. If Gen. MacArthur succeeds him, and he should, I may never get promoted again because I was the other Boy General in the war, younger yet than he was, and he won't forgive it.

I shall prepare for my final examinations at Crest with as much diligence as I can muster, for I may have to find work after the Army shows me the door, and a degree in Liberal Arts should take me far. Perhaps I should pursue the law like Pershing did.

"Brandy," I said, showing her the page. "The Army posted him up at Camp Penobscott."

"Let me get that," she said, clicking away. "As soon as the prices come down, I'm gonna get one of those digitals."

"The Archive has one; have to reserve time on it a year in advance, and then it's only a week."

"Doc," Brandy declared. "I'm calling Nancy, see if she can get someone down here with a real camera and not this cheap-ass thing. This is huge!"

While we waited for Brandy to call her editor, Mike and I studied the old steamer trunk, thumping the sides and hoping for even more revelations. "Never saw the like," Mike sighed.

"Nor I," I agreed. "How's the twins?"

"Sleeping this morning when I left. They were up half the night. The nanny has them this afternoon, so Connie can get some of her business work done."

"Just so you know, babies in the house and a full night's sleep are mutually incompatible."

"So I gather," Mike agreed. "Hasn't been that bad yet, though."

"Wait until they're teething," I sighed.

"I heard."

I studied the upper compartment of the trunk, perhaps twelve inches deep. Little bits of paper stuck to the inside. "Someone made this thing for . . . what, do you think?"

"I've been trying to work that out. The luggage collectors I've communicated with say false bottoms are common but never heard of a false lid. But the lid's so heavy I just figured . . . "

Brandy was speaking most effusively, from what we could hear, about Mike's business, the trunk, and the spectacular finds within. Then we heard, "thanks, Nancy; I'll tell them. See you in a few minutes." She came back into the showroom wearing an enormous grin. "They'll send a photographer down tomorrow to get some shots of this place and that trunk. I'll come back if I have any followup, OK?"

"Sure," Mike nodded. "They gonna run the . . .?"

"I think so," Brandy said, jotting down more notes. "The city desk said it sounds like a big one." She shrugged. "I just hope they let *me* by-line it."

"There's a chance they won't?"

"I'm a stringer, and not even a journalism student," she answered wanly. "A story this big they might hand off to a regular reporter using my notes and give *them* the by-line and most of the money."

"How many are there?" I asked.

"Two cover the city desk and pick stories off the wire services; one does statewide and one covers the school. Us stringers write whatever we can to make a couple of bucks and a little credit at the end."

"Huh. Let's pack this stuff up and get it in my car."

"Dr. Durand," the woman said, shaking my hand in my office the next day. "It's an honor to meet you."

"Ms. Flack," I smiled, "pleasure's mine." Nancy Flack introduced herself as the Editor-in-Chief of the *Granite Ledge Intelligencer.*

"And Brandy brought us a story."

"Quite a story, too." I gave Nancy the outline of the trunk, the contents, and the historical community's reaction to it. "I believe these diaries and other papers will be the nucleus of a major biography of an important former resident of Granite Ledge who . . . "

"How important was he?" Nancy asked. "I've never *heard* of him."

"He apparently knew General Pershing personally, and several other officers from WWI. He was also in the second war, and Korea. I've just started my research . . . "

"The Historical Society mentioned something about that farm up by Penobscot," Nancy said.

"If we can preserve the farm, it would be a real boost to tourism. And . . . ."

I had to stop because, at that very instant, I realized how much work on this project I'd been neglecting, how far off track I was getting. I was so excited about each new discovery I hadn't had time to authenticate most of it. OK, Ned's DSC was genuine, but the rest?

On top of that, I was publicizing discoveries, not authentication. That I'd finally found the One Big Thing my career needed distracted me. I was neglecting what the ever persistent past needed: completeness. Or at least something that looked like completeness. Yes, the project needed money; yes; the farm was possibly important. But there were so many other questions that needed answers before we went public, especially with the diaries.

"Nancy, I'm just going to say that the Steele project is still in progress. Now, I'd . . . "

"Can we get back to you on this in, say, six months?"

"Please."

But the inventory had to be turned in to the Committee this month, and now there were scores of items to add to it.

"Maria, I need your help," I said that night. "I need it this weekend."

"I've only got an hour to go for this week, Dad," she said, her brows knitted in concern. "I've got a soccer game Friday, and I was planning on . . . "

"Honey, I've gotta get that new material into the inventory, and I need to turn it in by Monday."

"Well," she put on her *I've got an idea* face. "How about if I ask Ted to help?"

"Ted?" I asked, surprised. "How long would it take to get him up to speed?"

"He's been up there with me, Dad. We've talked about what I've been doing 'cause we meet at the coffee shop after his services on Saturday mornings. He thinks it's interesting."

That's where she's been going. "Services?"

"He's Jewish, Dad, remember?"

"Oh, yeah. Well, OK . . . "

"Ted," I said as he and Maria arrived at the Archives Saturday afternoon. "Good sabbath?"

"Yessir," Ted answered, a little surprised.

"Just a curiosity: where are your services held? I didn't think there was a synagogue around here."

"At St. Barbara's church, sir," he said, nodding with a grimace. "We've heard it before."

"Heard . . . what?"

"All the jokes about Christians hosting Jews, sir."

I shrugged. "St. Barb's hosts everyone, even Wiccans. Now, let's be clear, here. Maria and I have a deadline we have to meet. We've got to get these new items in the inventory today so the computer can digest it. That means no . . . ."

"Yessir," Ted answered solemnly.

"Dad, I *told* him all that," Maria sighed. "Now, I'll do the data entry, and you and Ted can fill out the forms. Here," she handed Ted an inventory form pad and a pair of gloves. "Take any of these." She picked up a piece of paper from the many spread out. "Add today's date, 28 September 96, and describe this as a loose, typewritten 8½- by 11-inch mimeograph copy of military orders, dated 15th September 1931, ordering Major Steele to report to the US Embassy in Paris for duties as assistant military attaché. After you fill the slip out I'll create the item number when I stroke it in."

"I think I've got it," Ted said.

"Good," I said. "You start on *that* end, Ted, I'll keep working on *this* end and we'll meet in the middle."

To my grateful surprise, that's exactly what happened. Ted and I handed Maria our slips about every five to ten minutes. He had some questions, like what to do with items with no date, and how to categorize a document with no date, title or signatures.

After a couple of hours, we went to the lobby to warm up. The sunbeams streaming through the birches in the courtyard made a colorful show as we gazed through the windows.

"Dr. Durand," Ted blurted suddenly, "I'd like to go out with Maria, just the two of us."

"As in on a date?"

"Yessir."

"Well, there she is: ask her."

"But, sir, I . . . "

"*Ted*," Maria groaned, "I *told* you . . . "

"Go on," I prodded.

Ted turned to Maria, bowed slightly, and cleared his throat loudly. "Maria, since we couldn't go with the gang this afternoon, will you please go with me tonight for dinner at Mercer's* and a movie . . .?"

"*Yes*," she snapped, rolling her eyes. "We'll . . . "

"OK," I said.

They both looked at me, surprised, then at each other, then back at me.

"We wanted to see *Twister,* now that it finally got here," Ted said. "I asked Red to get tickets for the last show at 7:10."

"Should I pick you up after, or do you want to take the shuttle home?" I asked.

"It's a two-hour movie," Maria said.

"You *have* a 10:00 curfew . . ." I started.

"I *do?*" Maria asked in semi-panic.

"You're thirteen, Maria. Ten is plenty late."

"Then the shuttle back would be too late . . ." she sighed.[†]

"Red said he'd bring us home, but he gets off *work* at ten," Ted said, deflated.

The next few moments were vital to Maria's social development and to my marriage. Say her wrong things and her life as she knew it would be over. Say the other wrong things and Meli would brain me. "Have her home by 10:30, then." I glanced at my watch. "We've

_____

* A popular family restaurant in New Town.

† The weekend shuttles ran every *other* hour between 6 PM and 6 AM.

got about two hour's worth of work left to do. Let's finish up."

We finished in about an hour and 45 minutes, logging a penciled list of names on the back of the last of three "Dear Georgia" notes at 5:50 that afternoon. I set the computer to compile an inventory by item number, loaded the bins back in their vacuum racks, and left just in time so Ted and Maria could grab the shuttle.

It would take about half a day for the system to compile and print the new inventory. And it would take me a while to explain to Melanie how I'd decided on a curfew and then given permission to violate said curfew on our daughter's first proper date all on my own.

"Hello?" We had just got the boys in bed when the phone rang. Like all parents of teenagers out on their own for the first time, I answered the phone with some trepidation.

"Curtis? Colin Ridgeway. I found something out at the farm you'll want to see."

"Like ... *what?*" I asked with even more trepidation. *More stuff to add to the heap?*

"Six headstones in a clearing out behind the pole barn."

My heart briefly stopped; I stopped breathing. "Any . . . .?" I looked into the living room, where Meli was hearing half the conversation; her face etched with dread said it all. I quickly shook my head.

"They appear to be that Steele fella, his wife and some others."

"How accessible are they?"

"Not that bad. The brush is cleared under the trees, but the grass needs cutting. It looks like they used the area for picnics because there's tables, benches and a grill out there."

"OK, Colin," I sighed. "You gonna be out there tomorrow?"

At 10:16 that night, Ted and Maria started saying goodnight on the front sidewalk, just out of range of the porch light. At 10:27, she came in the front door.[*]

---

[*] Meli marked the times.

"Hi, baby," Meli called as we turned on the sofa. "How was the movie?"

"It's . . . really something," Maria sighed, not looking at us but staring blankly at the police procedural we'd been watching on the TV.

"Did you see . . .?" I started; Meli swatted my leg," . . . anyone you knew?" I finished, swatting her.

"We hung out at Kool-Js after with Allison and Jamie until Red picked us up."

"Who's Jamie?" Meli asked.

"New boy." Maria slowly took her jacket off. "A transfer." She hung her jacket on a peg by the door.

"Ah. Want to go out to the Steele Farm tomorrow? They found some headstones out there."

"Sure . . . I'm . . . going to bed." Maria was two steps down the stairs when she turned around, came back up, grabbed her jacket,* then took off downstairs again at twice the speed, with Midge in hot pursuit.

We turned around on the sofa again, watching the TV for a few minutes, listening for . . . there it was: the phone call to her dearest friend.

"Think it went well?" I asked.

"It was *perfect*," Meli answered, patting my leg. "So perfect she is stunned by its sheer magnificence." She bussed my cheek. "You did so good she didn't register about the headstones."

"That's not what you said four hours ago." A knock-down, drag-out fight it was not, but a disagreement it was when I got back from taking them downtown.†

"That was for the boys," she shrugged. "They needed to know that we have to set curfews, that they need to be followed, and that their dates will have them, too." She sighed. "She will be the envy of the 8ᵗʰ Grade for a week."

"Why?"

---

* She had her own pegs outside her suite.
† We were always careful not to have disagreements in front of the kids; we rarely had anything more than that, anyway.

"First solo date in her class."

"That's a big thing?"

"That's huge. Don't you remember?"

"Um . . . no, not in my neighborhood."

We listened to Maria drone excitedly on for another few minutes as the show finished. "C'mon, big guy," Meli tapped my arm. "Let's finish our date."

"There," Colin pointed to a low iron fence surrounding several headstones. It had been a pleasant walk on that early fall Sunday afternoon. We followed a narrow trail through a magnificent stand of red oaks, down a small hill, through a dry gulley, and up another slight hill to a small stand of birch trees that neatly bracketed a picnic bench in the twenty-yard square clearing in the tall pines, quaking aspens and old oaks.

"Edmund Archer Steele," I read. "Born April 6th, 1896. Died 1st April, 1994." I lingered on that stone for some time before going on to the next. "Angela Corinne Gibson Steele. Born April 10th, 1896. Died April 3rd, 1994." I blinked.

"Is it . . . them?" Maria asked quietly.

"I think so," Colin sighed.

I looked around at four other headstones with *Steele* in their names. "Ned's mother, two sisters and a brother, all died of flu and cremated in Michigan in 1918 while he was in France; marked nowhere else, probably," I sighed; Maria took my hand, wiped an eye with her sleeve.

"I wondered what *they* were," Colin said.

"That's what they are," Maria sighed, kneeling in front of Helen's stone. "She was my age when she died of something I've survived a half-dozen times."

I gazed at the picnic bench, only barely able to imagine Ned and Angie sharing a meal or a glass of wine there. Then I imagined them like Meli and me in that *diversion*, serene in the forest and oh, so loving.

"The others all died the same day," Colin mumbled.

I snapped back to now. "Flu? Yeah, that makes sense."

"I wonder what his diary read when every other October came

around?" Maria said. "Wonder if he marked it at all?"

"Might be worth looking into, sweetie," I said, gazing around the clearing, imagining a crowd of friends and neighbors, laughing and eating together, even paying respects to strangers.

"This complicates anything I'd want to do with the property, that's for sure," Colin said. "Stops those wolves cold, though."

"Wolves?" I asked.

"The Penobscot Estates developers want the joint for an expansion. Moving graves is an expensive and complicated business in this state, especially on private land not zoned for a cemetery. Makes the buyer pool a lot smaller."

"Are we sure they're buried there?" Maria asked off-handedly. Brilliant instincts. But . . . *why here?*

"Yes, they are," Corrine said over the phone two hours later. "Mom and Dad loved that meadow; took us out there in pleasant weather when we were in town, held neighborhood picnics, put those other markers there."

"You go there often?" I asked.

"We took the kids out there every few years, then when they left we'd go ourselves. He marked his family because they're marked nowhere else, said that's where he wanted to be laid out. Dad wanted nothing fancy, nothing big. He didn't want to share a cemetery with General Summerall at Arlington, who Dad thought held him back from promotion. We were all there for the internment that May."

"I'm told there is a state permit required . . . "

"We had a time getting that straitened out, too . . . "

"Not something your parents could have started before . . .?"

"Oh, they started it, all right. But the permits they started were for single graves, and we were asking for two. Bureaucrats at the capital couldn't just issue one permit because a dual plot is a whole other form . . . "

"Sounds . . . "

"It gets worse. The inspector came out, pointed to the other stones—Dad placed them in the '70s—and started asking about the permits for *them.* Uncle George said there was no one there; the remains were in mass graves in Michigan." She chuckled. "The inspector actually asked for death certificates. Uncle George finally made a phone call and suddenly . . . here was the permit."

"I suppose a retired Vice Admiral knows people who know people. When was the funeral?"

"Saturday before Memorial Day in '92. Getting a flight out took some doing that Monday." There was a pause. "A lovely chapel your school has, Dr. Durand."

"Curtis, please. Yeah, we like it. Been around since before the Civil War."

"Your Dr. Bentley did a fabulous job. He said Dad started going to church for a couple of years before he passed, got to know him pretty well."

"Yes, indeed; a fine man."*

"Does anyone have any idea what's becoming of the farm? I never lived there, but Charlie did for a while, and Carl was in and out for a good decade and a half."

I explained the interest of the Historical Society, enhanced now by the graves. "There will be fund-raising efforts that, if you want, you can take part in."

"Feels a little ironic, though, dosen't it? We sold the place to Ridgeway, and now . . . "

"Your brother was the sole owner . . .?"

"The will left it to Carl, but we split the proceeds."

"Ah. Yeah, a little ironic. Maybe we can prevail on Colin Ridgeway to donate it for . . . for . . ." I stopped.

"My husband is a retired tax attorney, Curtis. Maybe you'd like to talk to him."

"We, ah, have some of our own, Corrine . . . "

"Corky, please."

"So, all this was in that magic trunk, Curtis?" Moe asked, flipping through the pages.

"That's everything we got out of it, yes, *and* a typescript of a

---

* Norris Bentley, DD, was a wise and gentle man who had passed a year before. I'd had him in my undergrad years; he hitched Meli and I.

memoir he had in his desk. I have two correlations for the trunk: one in a diary and a receipt for two hundred Francs with the same date. I'm still waiting to see if there's anything useful in the camera. Delicate work, century-old film . . . "

"Well, that's something, anyway." He pushed the pile of paper away. "Are you well on your way, Curtis?"

"We've barely begun, Moe."

"Yeah." He drummed his fingers softly. "Have you ever thought about filling a seat on the Committee of Regents?"

My mouth went dry. "They own the joint, don't they?" *What on Earth is he talking . . .?*

"Members have traditionally had an ownership stake, but Regent's shares also pay a dividend annually. Your extraordinary daughter Constance is going to buy Christian Fisk's Regent's shares; he has money trouble. She wants to put *you* on the Regents; said it would be more appropriate."

"*Me* on the Committee of Regents? I had no idea I . . . I . . ." If lightning had struck me at that moment, I would not have felt it.

"No one else does, either," Moe said heavily, "not even Melanie, and we need to keep it that way for now. The Regents are inclined to allow it, and because Constance married a Klein, and Michael's father was a Crest kinsman on his mother's side. no one's objecting. Our bylaws allow it, and Christian has . . . "

"Wouldn't that take a great deal of money? Has Connie got that . . .?"*

"That and *more*, according to our accountants. She's a very shrewd investor."

"Well, she didn't learn that from us," I sighed, suddenly feeling out-of-place in Moe's office, talking about my adopted daughter who, unbeknownst to me, had amassed a fortune large enough to buy an interest in my employer. "She was complaining about money trouble in July."

"A cash shortfall; it happens." Moe reached into a desk drawer and pulled out a bottle of something brown and two glasses. "Here,"

---

* I knew the shares in the Regent's seats were worth money; it was in the Crest Employee Handbook.

he poured a glass. "You look like you need this." I took the glass and downed the contents; Moe did the same, wincing. "Alan has the acumen to take my place." He poured another drink. "My children do not want any part of the Regents; ownership shares of the school are separate." He drank his shot; I sipped mine. He stared at me for a very long time, then looked away. "Curtis, it is my belief that you and Melanie's family have a greater concern for this institution than anyone else who is not an owner." He produced a blue-backed document. "Read this."

I read . . . and in my entire life . . . Upon his death, Morris Hardin bequeathed Melanie and me with his family shares of the Regents. There were twenty-four Committee of Regents shares held in seven blocks: Moe Hardin's family held five shares because of their direct blood connection to the oldest son of Tiberias Jenson, who started quarrying the clear Jenson granite nodules that put Granite Ledge on the map; the other families held three shares each. If Connie bought Christian Jenson's shares, between us we would hold eight shares and two seats on the Committee of Regents.

"We would own more control of the school." I sighed. By now, I was running out of thoughts. "Why us?"

"Curtis, your wife cared for my family the summer before you got here, and we are so grateful for that. My boy, you have been here all your adult life.* You dedicated your teen years to getting here.† You are the *warp* and *woof* of this institution's greatest asset: the Archives. Your work on the Truxton is a shining light of the school. Not a month goes by when some scholar somewhere does not have a 'eureka' moment over one of your discoveries."

"I try," I said, trying modesty. Most of those discoveries weren't spectacular; just pieces of historical puzzles.

"And your leadership of the American History Department, as such a young scholar when you took over, has been nothing short of . . ." He stopped, searching for the words.

"*Moe*," I cleared my throat. "The Steele Collection has met its obligation. Will the Jenson release the next part of its grant?"

---

* I arrived four months after I turned eighteen.

† I started preparing to be a Jenson Scholar when I was thirteen.

"Yes, Dr. Durand. Thank you for your punctuality."

And I wanted words with Connie . . .

"Hi, Dad," she chirped when I called. I could hear a baby squalling in the background. "Glad you called; get me away from the smell of . . . "

"Connie, honey, I just spoke to Moe Hardin. He mentioned that you're buying . . . "

"Not here; not now, Dad," she answered quietly. "Meet me at your office in an hour."

That was possibly the second-longest sixty minutes of my life, comparable only to that drive from State after Connie repeated those fateful words on the phone . . . *

Connie appeared at my door nearly 58 minutes after we hung up, looking tired, wan, cheerful and concerned all at the same time. She was the only person I ever knew who could do that. After a quick hug, she sat in one of my overstuffed chairs; I sat on the sofa. "You haven't told Mom . . .?"

"I'm not supposed to," I said. "But I needed to talk to you. Just what . . . how . . .?"

"Chris lost his burger chain franchise because of vendor fraud, and now he's facing bankruptcy. And his second wife is taking him to the cleaners in their divorce. His only remaining assets, specifically excluded in their prenup, is his shares of the Regents and his share of the school. Gramma Devota approached me just before the wedding." She shrugged, cocked her head in that curious way she had. "I can *finance* the seat, but *you* would *occupy* it."

"We're talking about millions," I said, still incredulous. "Where would that have come from?"

"Somewhere near two million a share for the seat." She looked dimly uncomfortable momentarily. "Remember when Schuyler[†] said she still had some liquidating to do in '89?" I nodded, recalling a seemingly trivial throwaway *mention* of a few things left of Joan's

---

* "No matter what you do, you can be both right and wrong." That phrase proved she was Joan's daughter.

† Schuyler Colfax, executrix of Joan's estate.

estate. Last I knew, Schuyler liquidated those few things before Connie turned 21 and gained complete control of her trust.

"Yeah, well, Mama's preferred shares in the North Texas Stockman's Petroleum Company were tied up in two acquisitions when she passed. Their board begged Schuyler to hold on to Mama's shares until their common shares split after the last acquisition was completed. She held, and two years ago January, they offered us $50 million for Mama's shares . . . shares she won in a poker game with a *pair* of *tens.*"

My daughter, the millionaire. "Congratulations, honey," I said, feeling . . . left out was one way to put it. But she was an adult and I, no longer her guardian, no longer had any reason to know. "But money was still tight in July . . .?"

"It's not in cash anymore, Dad," Connie said, knowing I knew very little about business or money. "I invested it as soon as I got it. When that engine blew and that mast failed, Mike was down to five weeks' operating capital, Submerged Stone was down to four, and I was shorting stock to cover million and a quarter for that loader engine and repair the mast and lease another while we're waiting, and that crane ain't even paid off yet. Your check kept Mike liquid for another month, so that was off my plate. Dad, just . . ." she grinned.[*]

"I trust you, honey, but I . . . I hate to ask, but have you looked at the school's financials? Are we in good shape?"

"I've had a quick look, yeah, because of the dividends," she nodded, suddenly more serious. "The school's OK; the Corporation, for its function, I think is under-capitalized. And, it's letting contracts that are . . ." she grimaced, "unwise, engaging out-of-state firms to do work that it could easily develop or buy here. The Regents still own the Corporation, even if Tina . . . "

"When you buy that seat, does that mean that much of the school is . . . ours . . .?"

"Our families would control *shares* on the *Regents*, Daddy,"[†] she said softly, winking with her winning smile. "The Regents might

---

[*] This was all Martian to me, and she knew it.
[†] She called me "Daddy" less often than she called me "Curtis."

make the rules and the Corporation might service the joint, but the Crest and Jenson family descendents still divide ownership. The dividends from the Regents shares are a bonus: low five figures per share every year on average."

"That means you and Mike . . .?"

"Would control Chris's Regent seat, not his share of ownership."

"Moe said his kids . . . "

"They want nothing to do with the Regents."

"How much would the school be worth?"

She breathed deep. "Well into ten figures." She looked away, then back at me. "Much of the school's cash value to another institution is in the Archives, Dad; your Archives. If it were sold tomorrow, we could get about a *billion*."

Heart . . . beat . . . again . . . "Is anyone looking to buy it?"

"There have been rumors, but since the Foundations own it, it's going nowhere." She looked uncomfortable again, took my hand gently. "One rumor involved, as I understand it, lock, stock, barrel, and you." She looked into my eyes. "But it was just a rumor, Daddy." *I was worth that much money?* "You look tired; why don't you guys plan a vacation at Christmas? You could stand to get out of town for a while."

"Yeah, maybe." I was still trying to get my head around the ideas of me being on the Regents, my daughter being that wealthy, and the prospect of an annual family bonus of . . . maybe a million a year, or so.

All this while remembering that, for most of my college years, I had to work as a finish carpenter in whatever spare time I could scrape together just to get enough to go on a date once a month.

Wow!

"Happy day, honey," I murmured into her ear, spent. Meli still loved morning sex, though not as frequently as the years passed.

"Happy 41, yeah," she answered breathlessly, waiting to hear kids and perhaps cats outside the door. "They'll be in here any minute."

"Should we at least pull the covers up?" We had stripped for our indulgence; the covers were on the floor.

"I don't want to give our children a show when they bolt in. It might alarm the boys."

"Nothing they haven't seen before."*

"Nothing they need to see again." She got up.

Just then, we heard a soft knock on the door. "Don't . . ." I said, imagining a herd of feet, arms, and fur charging into the bedroom, knocking their naked mother over.

"Hey," Maria called softly. "The boys have something for Mom."

"Just a minute, baby," Meli called, reaching for her robe. Turning to me, she grinned, "they remembered from last year."†

"Maria did, anyway." I pulled on my shorts and loose shirt.

"OK, now," Meli said, opening her arms wide to receive her children's adoration. As it wasn't quite six on a Monday morning, the boys were still in their pajamas; Maria was in sweats for her morning run.

But the boisterous greetings, the handmade card (that Maria helped with), and the many, many kisses and hugs and happy birthday songs . . . who cared what we wore?

> 25th November, Hill 90.
> Rain. Tried to [Illegible].
> Men work much of the night building,
> repairing. Talbott and Dona in the rear.
> We should simply pull this shift as if the
> duration is of no consequence because it isn't
> a matter of [expletive] choice.
> Gen. Pershing thinks too highly of me. His
> proposal for the battalion's structure is, to say
> the least, generous. Five MG companies, a
> support company, an infantry company. I
> have to wonder if we would ever see all of it.
> And somehow, he imagines me to be some

---

* It happens in families.

† We were commemorating her natal when all *five* of them burst in *just* as we reached . . . .

kind of [expletive] *military genius. Still, McTee*
and I made our suggestions and returned his
plan to the same dispatch rider.

I contemplated the diary entry while I gently tried to discern (under the magnifier and black light, with distilled water on a cotton swab) what he'd either blotched out or what rain had destroyed. It was nearly a third of a page, and it would have been nice to know what he tried to do.

Once again, what was there raised more questions. He was in direct touch with Pershing? Pershing asked him about the unit structure? I thought unit organization was determined at the top levels. Name-dropping again? Or does he really have a direct line to the future General of the Armies?

Once again, despite nagging questions, my idea came back . . .

"Dr. Durand," the pleasant-looking young woman smiled, "so honored to meet you." Susan Bridgely was the second of two candidates we invited to the campus.

"Dr. Bridgely," I said, shaking her hand. "Thanks for coming to meet with us." We'd met the other candidate, a solid performer who worked on the American Civil War, the day before.

"She got in last night, Curtis," Polly said. "She leaves *tonight*, so . . ." We gave Susan a quick tour, then went to lunch.

"Yes, of course," I waved to a chair in the faculty lounge. "This will be a rush job, Doctor, so . . . "

"I understand," Susan said, "but transportation up here . . . ." She was maybe thirty and athletic in appearance.

"Yes. Let's get started." The interview that followed—about two hours of academic blather and jargon—would bore anyone not associated with academia, so I won't repeat it. At the end, I asked, "do you have questions for us?"

"Just one: how's the skiing here?"

"My husband really likes it," Polly said, "but he's from here."

"I couldn't say," I said. "Tried it once or twice and never took to it. You ski much?"

"Whenever I can. My husband was a downhill Olympian who's

been following me from one flatland to another for ten years—we're both from Idaho."

"What does he do?" I asked.

"Freelance photographer; travels a lot, but we're looking to settle somewhere we can start a family before I run out of time."

"Well," I glanced at Polly; she winked. "How about here?"

"Oh, my goodness," Meli smiled, holding up a red and gold floral brocade vest from Connie and Mike. "How did you know?"*

"Little birds," Connie said, trying to soothe Joanie, who'd been fussing since we got to their condo.

"Little birds named Maria and Curtis, no doubt," Meli sighed, placing her gift back in the bag. Meli saw the vest advertized in a newspaper flyer and gushed over it . . . repeatedly.

"And oh, *my*, babe," Meli grinned at me, opening the box containing my gift. "I absolutely adore it!" It wasn't the first gold chain I'd bought her, but that was the only jewelry she wore, other than her wedding ring and stud earrings. Arrayed around her were her favorite cologne (from Maria), a certificate for a spa day (from Helen), and handmade pot holders (from the boys).

"Everyone, I love it all," Meli cried. "Let's finish the cake and get you guys home." Despite what the reader might think, she was not insincere: Meli wasn't like that.

And as *there* as I was; *present* I was not. She was right: those diaries had gotten into my head.

The ideas, the questions kept rolling around my head . . .

---

* Meli's favorite fabric and her favorite top.

EDMUND ARCHER STEELE, CLASS OF 1928

I mused, "there might be something to this internet thing after all." I'd put queries about the makers of the notebooks on internet chat rooms and had sent letters both near and far. By the first week in October, I received five replies. Three of them were of the "we're sorry, but our records don't . . ." variety. One said, "we've been making them since 1919," and little more. But one was an elegant, hand-written letter response from the makers of four of them.

> 1ˢᵗ September 1996
> Brixford Court, London
> My Dear Dr. Durand:
> I hope this letter is acceptable as I do not trust this inter-net. I have been informed of your query about our journal products and am intrigued by your diary project. As a devotee of the Great War, I am most interested in your researches into these diaries.
> Two of the journal books you describe (three stitched 8 x 10 inch, 48-sheet blue-lined signatures* bound in black dyed buckram leather with our seal on the back cover)

---

* Sheets of paper bound in the middle. Here, with four sides per sheet, there would be 192 writable sides per signature.

are from a line that began in 1910 and discontinued in 1915, selling for 2s, 6p in Britain.

The third (four stitched 48-sheet blue-lined signatures bound in cardstock and leatherette with our seal on the back cover) was in a line that began in 1915 and discontinued in 1932, selling for 3s, 2p in Britain.

Brixford Court Stationers has been in our trade since 1790. In the course of our business, we have compiled an extensive body of data on paper, booklets, forms, and journal books manufactured the world around, which we have combined into a single database. I have forwarded a copy of this data in a print-off by parcel post, since it is quite voluminous. I hope you find it useful in your endeavours.

Please feel free to contact me by any means in the future if you have any further needs.

Your obedient servant,
Charles Westley-Hammersley,
OBE

The journals I asked about were Volumes XIII (April–December 1918), XIIIA (January–April 1918), and XV (April 1919–April 1920), I had *reason* to believe Ned got *them* in the US.

"*Now,* I covert shillings and pence to dollars and cents," I sighed. Checking the reference Elias provided . . . $3.18 to the Pound in 1917 . . . two shillings and sixpence . . . my long division came up with . . . a buck and a half for two, three for the third; three and four bucks for overseas pricing.

Now, I had verified the maker of those volumes. I knew what they cost Ned when he bought them, where he likely got them, and when. And when I got that printout, maybe I'd find out where the rest of the journals came from.

And you thought historians just read archives.

*　　*　　*

The Jenson Granite of the Alumni Court's walls holds the chiseled names of all Crest's graduates. The class reached the Class of 1928 slab—perhaps a hundred yards from the Freedom Arch that memorialized alumni and staff who perished in military service—and looked up to see Edmund Archer Steele, halfway up the wall.

"He *is* an alumnus," I sighed. "One diary said he was preparing for exams on his birthday, but I haven't found out anything more. I should look . . . "

"Doc," Larry asked, "why?"

"Yeah," Max said. "Focus on something achievable. A full-blown biography of this obscure guy should wait until you can get just one part of his life nailed down, and someone shows interest in the work."

"All the research you've already handed off to us is still a lot, Doc," Bayard said. "Even if it is just . . . trivia." I had been asking for little fact-finding favors of my grad students: currency values, pay rates, weights of machine guns, ammunition and other equipment, gear for mules and horses and the location of geographical features I couldn't find on current maps.

As we looked towards authenticating the 1917–1918 diaries, we knew there would be so much more to work. But *all* the wartime diaries would have to wait. We needed a shorter period to concentrate on to see if there was any interest.

That same idea kept coming back . . .

"Mr. Clark," I said, shaking Jason's teacher's hand. "Pleased to meet you."

"Dr. Durand; Mrs. Durand," he nodded, gripping mine hardly at all and barely wiping Melanie's. He had 25 1ˢᵗ Grade students' parents to talk to that night, so I understood why he wasn't that enthusiastic.* "Have a seat."

We settled on two folding chairs by his desk while he found Jason's file. The usual 1ˢᵗ Grade drawings, letter samples (including cursive), maps, and the like lined the room. "Jason is doing well in nearly everything," Mr. Clark declared. "He has a little trouble with

---

* He would be doing it for a little over six hours . . . poor bugger.

arithmetic, but he's diligent and dosen't give up."

"I didn't do well with math," I admitted. "Just didn't much care what *x* was, because it could be anything."

"His sisters taught him not to quit," Melanie interrupted. "He keeps pushing his brother."

"Yes, Jason is aggressive," Mr. Clark said. "Sometimes a little too aggressive, but not to the point of bullying." He pulled a drawing out of his folder. "But *this* is a little disturbing, if interesting."

Mr. Clark showed us a drawing that wasn't what one would expect a six-year-old to produce. Instead, it was an amazingly detailed, down to the cross-belts, sketch of a dying soldier that looked familiar. "He must have seen one of my books on WWI," I sighed. "There's a painting with that detail in it."

"That would explain it," Mr. Clark said. "Jason says you and his sister are copying books about this." I explained the Steele project. "I thought you were an economic historian, sir." Mr. Clark said. I explained how I happened upon the Steele material and why we hung onto it, rather than selling or just archiving[*] it. "Dr. Durand," he said at last, "if you have to bring this work home, try to talk to him about what it is, what it means. Beyond the subject matter, he is a gifted artist. However . . . "

"We will encourage him, *not* treat him as gifted." I said. Crest Teacher Program students got a required seminar called "The Curse of the Gifted." It told of the agonies many "gifted" students suffered by being sped up too fast by a well-meaning but misguided system that drove them into an adult world of achievement while denying them a typical childhood of learning and growing. The education system demanded much more of the "gifted," and those kids rarely have the maturity to know they could say *no,* nor do the parents always have the courage to slam on the brakes, either. That system would label six-year-old Jason as "gifted" in a heartbeat.[†]

We shook hands again and moved on.

*　　*　　*

---

[*] Producing an inventory and forgetting all about it.

[†] Which was also probably why he pushed Charlie into mischief; it was a common response with boys.

Charlie's 5th Grade teacher was a large man with huge hands and bull-like shoulders and the uncharacteristic name of Mr. Flowers. We sat on the offered folding chairs as Mr. Flowers picked Charlie's file out of a rack. "Charlie Durand," he started, but then he said, "you don't remember me, do you, Curtis?"

"*Cut* Flowers?"

"That's me: Kurt 'Cut' Flowers." He turned to Meli. "We were in elementary education class together. You work for the city?"

"Yes, I do," she answered. "Now about Charlie . . . "

"Yep, good ol' Charlie," Kurt said. "I can always rely on Charlie to do what no one else in the class can do: behave when everyone around him is goofing off."

Meli and I looked at each other, then at Kurt. "We're talking about Charlie *Durand?*" I asked. At home, Charlie and Jason were always getting into something, often involving (or annoying) Maria.

"He's all about self-discipline," he said. I half-expected him to break into rib-splitting laughter, but . . . "Yeah. He's doing well. Fact is, I have to give him very high marks on behavior and deportment, besides his extraordinary musical talent."

"He's got some voice,"* I agreed. "I can't hit a note with a hammer, but Charlie's got my mother's singing talent."

"Nothing musical on my side, I'm afraid," Meli added.

"And he seems to lead the Life Skills lessons," Kurt continued. "He knows about banks and credit cards and says his big sister's boyfriend is a nice guy. And he has a nephew in Michigan who's older than he is?"

"Yeah, by three weeks," Meli said.

"He talked about his bigger sister's wedding and her babies all in one summer," Kurt said. "Made me recast *that* part of Life Skills this year."

"Sorry," I grinned.

"Eh, it happens. I wasn't going to talk about out-of-wedlock until later in the year, but," he shrugged.

---

* He soloed Wagner's "Bridal Chorus" and Shubert's "Ave Maria" at Connie's wedding; people wept hearing him.

"Um," I grimaced, glancing at Meli, "do you talk about the actual birds-and-bees details?"

"No; just that when two people care for each other very specially, babies happen." He grimaced. "That part of Life Skills is delicate with 5th Graders, but half of 'em already know. I had a student last year whose aunt did an in-vitro procedure for her mom using her dead dad's frozen sperm she talked about in Show and Tell. That was complicated to explain to nine- and ten-year-olds."

"Yeah," Meli grinned, standing up, "explain it to *us* first."

"Um, just one thing," Kurt said, holding up a hand to the next parents trying to come in. "A mean bully put his nephew in his bigger sister's stomach?"

"Yeah," I said simply, turning away.

The boys were in bed by the time we got home; Maria was doing homework. We both descended to her suite; Meli knocked on her door. "Honey; your father and I want to . . . "

"Just a minute," Maria said through the door. "Hi," she opened the door in gym shorts and a t-shirt a half minute later, "c'mon in." She pointed us to her sofa, a small stack of stuffed animals precariously balanced on one arm as Midge marched in. "How were the meetings?"

"Fine; the boys are doing great," Meli led. "Jason's kinda pushy; Charlie's the opposite."

"Yeah, I see that," Maria sighed, sitting in her ancient wing chair, her hair hanging in her face as Midge jumped into her lap. "Charlie tears up around here, especially around me, but Jason's driving it."

"Nothing surprising, then," I said, glancing at her trophy shelf, where she also stored scrunchies and a few photos. "How about Jason drawing war pictures?"

"In class?" Maria said, surprised. Midge batted and wrestled with her hair as Maria teased him with it.

"Yep," Melanie nodded. "His teacher showed us."

"From the stuff we work on, Dad?" Maria threw her hair over her shoulder; Midge jumped up after it.

"It looked like a painting from one book, yeah."

"We need to take better care where we leave that stuff around." She pulled her hair together, stacking it on top of her head; Midge watched from the chair back.

"Yes," Meli agreed. "And we need to be careful when talking about all the facts of life."

"Yeah, we talked about that before; the mean bully," I said.

"Right. Jason saw a picture with guns and death and replicated it. Charlie heard your simple explanation of rape and repeated it," Meli said. "And Charlie thinks Ted is a nice guy."

"He *does?*" Maria looked surprised again; Midge jumped down to the floor and dashed out.

"Yeah," I said, glancing at Meli, who winked. "So do we."

Maria grinned, looked down. "I do too." She looked up, cocked her head. "We OK, then? I've got a biology lab report to finish."

26ᵗʰ *November, Hill 90, Flanders.*
Have to admire Prussian consistency. Their artillery barrages, while not on a schedule, usually come in when our guns change positions at night, no matter how we try to stagger them. I'm not sure how they know in advance, because they are a mix of heavy and light guns and rum jars, [expletive] *and the heavies need more than a few minutes to ready even a* [expletive] *harassment mission. Night plus minor trench raid, gas and shelling adds up to a major attack in the next day, two at most. I do not look forward to a ground attack, but at least then we can see the* [expletive] *Heinie soldiers. I'm ordering up all the ammunition we can get hauled up here in preparation.*
The [expletive] *clouds here are fickle, almost like Michigan's changeable weather, but the rain has stopped for now. As weary as I am at night, I must learn to sleep during the day*

---

* Large caliber, crude mortars, called "coal buckets" by the French.

because night is for work and day is for rest,
unless you are new. We are new, so we have to
learn or be weary all the time.

"*This*," I told my class, "is the face of war in Flanders in the winter of 1917."

"A lot of waiting," Larry nodded. "Long periods of inactivity and back-breaking work interspersed with short periods of sheer panic."

"What work?" Sherry asked. "What do they do all night? And why the reversal?"

"German balloons and observation planes, for two reasons," I answered. "They were under constant observation."

"The work is hauling ammunition and rations forward," Larry said, "and trench repairs."

"And getting rid of the tunnel spoils," I added. "There were tunnelers all under the lines."

"Didn't the allies have balloons and planes, too?" Max asked.

"Sure," Phil answered. "I just saw a documentary on the balloon war in WWI."

"Both sides tried to shoot down each other's balloons," Larry added. "Big air battles over observers over the front, especially during major offensives."

"Tunnels," Patty wondered. "With all that rain?"

"Tricky business, draining those tunnels, I understand," I sighed, speaking only from what I'd just read in a magazine. I waited. "What do we understand about the diarist here?"

"He's pretty worn out," Patty declared.

"He's that," I agreed. "What else?"

"He's new to this," Larry observed. "And he knows he's new."

"He's in charge," Sherry ventured. "Talks like it's his responsibility to know all this."

"New or not," Max agreed.

"He sees this as inevitable," Larry said. "He either has to do everything he talks about or people die."

"OK," I agreed. "Does this look like reliable source material?"

"It's not how WWI is usually depicted," Sherry murmured.

"We expect to see the ol' over the top or a gas attack."

"This is the day-by-day," Max declared. "As Larry said, boredom or panic."

"That's what it was like on Hill 90, yes," I agreed. "This kind of thing goes on for eleven days."

"That all?" Patty asked. "I thought they were there for weeks."

"Normal shift on the front line was four days, but Ned's outfit is stuck up there for eleven. No one to replace them because of what was going on elsewhere."

"What was going on?" Sherry asked.

"Paashendaele," I sighed. "Half a million casualties in three months and nothing changed."

And the idea came back . . .

"Hey, Pops," Jason said, plopping into the armchair in my den that evening. "Mom said you wanted to talk to me."

"Yeah, I did," I started.

"I didn't do it," he blurted.

"Do what?"

"Whatever *Dummo* or *Stinky* say I did." Dummo was Charlie; Stinky was Maria.

"They didn't say you did anything," I sighed. "No, this is about something else . . . "

"Megan, then," he blurted, looking out my window.

"Not her, either," I said loudly. "Now, Mr. Clark showed us a drawing you did that looked like it came from one of these books; pictures of some not-so-nice stuff; war stuff." I pulled the book I believed Charlie saw off a shelf. "This one?"*

"Uh-huh."

"You like this kind of book?"

"I like the stories pictures tell."

"Can you read the captions?"

"Huh?"

"The descriptions under the pictures."

---

* I know, all the parenting books say don't let them see those, but that just increases curiosity.

"Some of 'em, yeah. Some of 'em have funny words."

"They're French, some of 'em. Others might be German. Know what those are?"

"Different countries?"

"Yeah, that's right. They have their own languages, so their pictures have captions in their language. What about the captions you *can* read?" I opened the book on my lap, with Frank Schoonover's iconic painting of Marines; Jason's drawing in school was a detail of it.

"Wheat Field."

"You saw this one?"

"Yeah."

"What story does it tell you?"

"They're getting shot; killed." He cocked his head. "They're mighty brave." He looked at me. "That guy in the middle, the one I drew, he dead?"

"I don't know. What do *you* think?"

"Well, there's dead guys all around him, so . . . yeah. I like pictures that tell real stories, not comic books with make-believe stuff."

I turned the page to John Singer Sargent's "Gassed." "How about *this* one?"

He studied the picture for a long moment. "Are they blind?"

"By gas, yeah."

"Poor guys."

I turned to Arthur Bastien's "Cavalry and Tanks at Arras." "This one?"

"Yeah! Tanks and horses . . . wait; that one's dead."

"Yeah, probably." I closed the book, put it back on my shelf. "Jason, when you see these, remember that the artists who made them saw these things, saw these guys getting shot, gassed, charging so bravely."

"They *did?*" He looked at me as if it were a revelation.

"Yeah. They were being shot at while they were looking for scenes to paint."

"Yeah?" He looked thoughtful. "Pop, I want to show you something." I followed him into his room; he looked behind me and closed the door before he reached behind his dresser for a spiral pad, handing it to me.

I flipped the cover and saw respectable and recognizable sketches of Megan; the next page of Charlie; the next of Maria, then Connie's twins in their tubs (one with Connie in bed), a bust of Meli, my face, many landscapes, street scenes, and the cats in various poses—even eating. "Jason," I whispered, "these are incredible."

"I saw a book in the library at school." He handed me another pad. "This is what I did first." These images were 3-D exercises one would expect from an art student, but not from a 6-year-old.

"How long have you been drawing like this?" He shrugged. "Let me show Mom . . . "

"*No*, Dad," he blurted. "Don't."

"Why not?"

He looked away. "I like to tell stories, not be told about."

"What?"

"Megan's big brother was one of those kids. Drew like this." He looked back at me. "Now he dosen't come out of the basement except to eat. Megan says he went crazy one day, tore up all his stuff. I saw his stuff, all torn up; it was . . . like *this*."

"My son," I said gently, "I won't let that happen to you. Mom will just want to see what you can do." As predicted, Meli handed Jason his pads back, kissed him gently, and told him to go play with Charlie . . . which he did.

We didn't even think about calling him gifted, or displaying his art, unless he said it was OK.

"OK," I said, pulling on gloves like everyone else, "since it's Wednesday night and school is in session, this must be the Truxton Committee."

"Get a new joke, Curtis," Lew Carmody sighed. "You've been using that one for years." Lew was a physicist who analyzed documents for their composition and age, and had been doing so since I started the Truxton project. He was also an amateur historian.

"I haven't heard it before," Sam sighed. "It's OK, Boss."

"This is your second meeting, Sam," Nina Hirschfeld nodded. "It'll grow on ya like a fungus." Nina was an assistant professor of history who, like Lew, had been on the Truxton project since the beginning. "Old business: T-1021, unsigned note fragment to J.

Ewing, dated December 18th 1776."

*I must commend you and your men on
your most impressive raids upon the enemy's
outposts. It is most imperative that the enemy
not know of our intentions. This . . .*

"The rest is torn off. James Ewing of Pennsylvania commanded a brigade in Washington's army and conducted several raids on Hessian positions around Trenton before the battle, but didn't make it across the river for the battle on the 26th. So, the context fits as long as we knew who the author might be. Lew?"

"The ink is iron gall, the water it was made with is certainly river, given the diatom shells in it. It's written on hemp paper, then rolled for some time after the tear, then pressed flat. Given the broad strokes, it looks like the writer used a hard-surface pen, like wood or reed," Lew said.

"How common is that?" Sam asked.

"Not too unusual," I said, "especially in those kinds of conditions. I looked at the handwriting, and I believe it to be Washington."

"Washington used a reed pen?" Nina asked.

"It would be the first *I'd* seen," I answered. "We could check with Mount Vernon and see if they've anything like it." I put the note in the middle of the table. "Questions?"

"Washington didn't write too many commendatory notes during the war," Nina said.

"Few are known, yes," I agreed.

"Would be nice to know whose signature was on it," Sam said. "Might make this easier."

"Not necessarily." I shook my head. "Even with a well-forged signature, we'd be in the dark about contexts and dates. That Washington didn't write that many casual commendations, the unusual pen . . . this one stays in Category C until we hear from Mount Vernon on the pen."

"The *why*, though, Curtis," Lew added. "Why would anyone forge such an innocuous thing?" It was this kind of question that made our Truxton work so frustrating. Devoid of provenance, the twenty-thousand-odd documents in the Truxton Archive were both a gold mine and a pyrite pit. Without going through every document, we couldn't know, and it was often foggy even after the research.

"Forgery is expensive," I agreed. While it made sense to forge documents of importance, like contracts or court decisions or letters with controversial contents, casual notes like this weren't worth the effort. "OK: Category B, then." And thirteen years later, we were still at it, having reviewed about 10% of them.

We looked at three other documents with similar, ambiguous results until I asked, "what've you got in your bag, there, Sam?"

"I ran into this some time ago and forgot all about it until the other day," Sam said, reaching into a paper bag. "Item T-24,561, dated 1928, entitled 'With The AEF.' Author E. Steele, 290 pages, typescript . . . "

"Steele," I repeated, donning another glove. "Let me see it." I placed the stack of yellowing bond paper on the table, noticing the flying capital *A*. "I can't believe *this*," I mumbled, opening the stack randomly.

```
     By the end of October, we had trained
up as far as we could, given our
ammunition shortages. Maj. Dona had given
everyone at least one dose of white cross*
before we got orders for Flanders and the
Iroquois line on the 1st of November . . .
```

"This will move to the Steele Collection," I declared.

"Is this that guy, Curtis?" Sam asked as I flipped ahead about a hundred pages.

```
     They planned the Cantigny attack well,
but I knew that the German counterattack
would have an easy time of it, hitting
their northern flank. I proposed to attack
five miles west of Cantigny and seize the
Chateau le Aisne Sud, four miles behind
the German outpost line, thus cutting the
roads the Germans would have to use to get
```

---

* Tear gas.

```
to Cantigny. Gen. Summerall was apoplectic
at the idea, but Gen. Bullard said go
ahead. We captured a German artillery
battalion almost intact, took nearly 500
prisoners.
```

"It is that guy, yeah," I sighed. "He's an alumnus; he was stationed up at Penobscot and he's buried up by his farm." I went back to the title page for several moments, then turned to the dedication. "John McTee, who he dedicated this manuscript to, was First Sergeant of his machine gun company, killed on Hill 90 in Flanders in December 1917."

And sometimes, that persistent past just keeps coming back.

"Hey, Charlie," I said that evening after dinner. "Wanna come to the store with me? I need stain for Maria's door."

"Sure, Pops." An upstairs bathroom water leak had damaged Maria's bedroom door early in the summer, but I was just getting to the door after fixing the leak* and the other damage it did to the drywall, carpeting and trim.

It was about a ten-minute drive to the monstrous version of the neighborhood hardware store/lumberyard called a home center that sold everything a handyman and homeowner needed in volumes only a contractor bought. But they also had pints of the red oak stain I'd used for the rest of the woodwork in the house that no one else had.

"Dad," Charlie asked as we got back to my SUV, "do you like girls?"

"I love your mother, Maria and Connie . . . "

"No, I mean other girls. Girls like . . . well, like Jenny or Allison or. . . ."

"There are different ways to like girls, Charlie. Do you like girls?"

"Like 'em like *kissy-kissy*? That's gross. No, I mean, *like* 'em to play baseball and swim with 'em and stuff."

---

* By calling a plumber. My marriage vows forbade me to touch pipes with tools.

"I've played baseball and swam with girls. They're just . . . "

"They're different."

" *Vive la différence*," I grinned.

"What's that?"

"Hurray for the difference in French. It's a good thing girls are different . . . "

"They have babies; boys make 'em do it."

"That's true. Remember what Maria said about what that mean bully did to Connie?"

"Yeah."

"You repeated it in school."

"Yeah."

"Connie didn't want that mean bully to do it; he *hurt* her doing it."

He looked out the side window. "*Kissy-kissy* is supposed to be nice."

"When you want to do it, it is. When you don't, it's very mean; terrible. You can't force anyone to do anything they don't want to do. And most of all, you can't talk about stuff like that with anyone. It's a secret." I inhaled deeply. "One day soon, you'll . . . "

As we pulled into the driveway, he said, "Betty's nice, plays baseball.* Sandy—I swim with her. She's funny, pretty; *likes* me, I think."[†]

"Just come talk to me about *kissy-kissy* when you might *like* a girl that way . . . "

"Sure, Dad."

I gazed out my den window as the first blizzard of the season reached full force; it looked to be a two-footer. We knew what that meant in mid-October: it'd be gone down here in the valley in a week, but it would stay up in the mountains until at least April.

We knew better than to venture out; the TV weather lady was calling for at least 18 inches before noon, and the schools were closed. But the upside was the staff meeting probably wouldn't happen that afternoon. The downside was we'd have to move the small

---

* A neigbor two houses down.

† Polly's daughter.

mountain of snow on the driveway, and prepare for the bigger mountain the county would block the driveway with, but they wouldn't get to us until at least mid-afternoon. I spent the morning reading *With the AEF.*

At about noon, I got a phone call from Elias. "Doc, what's the story on snow removal around here?"

"Maintenance hasn't started yet?"

"Nope. We've got a foot on the sidewalks and it's still coming down."

"Huh. They should be out doing the walks, anyway."

"Yeah; I asked the maintenance guy here, and he said 'not our job anymore.'"

I knew the head of maintenance, sort of. I called him at his office . . . no answer. Huh. I had his number in town . . .

"Yeah, Doc," he said. "The Corporation contracted another outfit to do snow removal, said our medical bills were too high from that work,"

"That I get," I said, "but when's this other outfit supposed to start? Students still have to eat."

"Got me, Doc," he said.

Another Corporation responsibility . . . *now what?*

"Need to inventory another memoir, Maria," I said that night when I checked on her at bedtime. We'd spent most of the afternoon and evening moving snow. The blizzard died out just after nightfall, leaving 28 inches at the airport. We destroyed the five-foot drift that the city left in the driveway just before that.

"He sure wrote a lot." She ran her fingers through her hair, looking up from her reading. "Old habits die hard."

"That's what Helen says." Our snowsuits, suspended on hangars around the furnace, dripped loudly.

"Gramma's studying our transcriptions pretty closely." Snow, for New England homeowners, meant both fun and work. Our fun—a brief snowball fight, where the boys and I overwhelmed Meli and Maria—came after our work, with everyone wielding shovels or snowblowers.

"I asked her to check for linguistic inconsistencies. And she seems more than willing now she's Emeritus."

As she stood up from her desk chair and stretched, Midge did the same on the sofa. "She calls it dialect work." While she reached for a scrunchie, Midge started a bath. "She asked Mike to find her a second or third edition of Webster's Collegiate dictionary."

"You in touch with her often?" I ducked as her hair flailed at me when she threw it in front of her as she bent forward.

"Sorry, Dad. She posts on my AmericaWeb bulletin board. And I get emails . . ." She wound a scrunchie into her hair. "You don't?"

"You should show me how to get in that thing," I sighed.[*]

"Sure, Dad." She pecked me on the cheek and headed for her bathroom. "I gotta knock off. Clear weather means class tomorrow."

"Yes, Maria Durand," Anna McKendrick smiled, probably for the 200th time that night. "Such a talented girl." The maintenance crew, unwilling to sit on their hands, had moved the snow on the Crest campus all day.

"She's pretty smart, all right," I agreed. "Only you . . ." About mid-morning, four snowplows and a dozen shovelers and snow-blowers from an out-of-state company arrived and grumbled about the work many hands had already done, since they got paid by the hour.

"How is she doing in your class?" Meli asked gently, elbowing me in the ribs. Unlike grade school, middle school made the parents stand in front of their teachers for the few minutes it took to get their appraisals.

"Just fine," Anna said, her coiffured hair barely moving. "Her work is on time, and her class participation is more outgoing than most of her peers . . . "

"Can she write well?" I asked, trying to get off the 'your above-average child' spiel that we were getting from nearly every teacher, save her Algebra teacher, where she was faring 'better than last year's grades would have predicted.'

---

[*] I just never had gotten onto that big network, though I used smaller, academic ones and the school's.

"From what essays I've seen," Anna answered, "she can compose her thoughts very well, yes. That first essay . . . "

"*About* that . . ." I started, getting another jab.

"Well, as I said on the phone, it is most extraordinary. I would have been satisfied with just her excitement over her sister's children, but she wrote extensively about her work with you." She handed us the essay.[*] "I wanted to make sure you saw it and she didn't stash it away."

> . . . Before that [her description of Connie's kids] I started working with my father on the diaries of Edmund Archer Steele, an officer in the National Army during the First World War. We are transcribing his diaries and researching his life and career.

"I've never seen such eloquence in an 8th Grader," Anna added, but I barely heard her.

> Before last year, I was not very interested in the past or my father's work as an archivist and historian that always seemed dry and abstract. But last year I understood: America's past is interesting, meaningful, and impactful in our lives today. Now, I often dream of reading, transcribing, researching the next entry, the paper the documents are on, and what he wrote with. Now I feel as if I have a connection to the past and Dad's work as I've never had before. I get excited about making our next discovery, and authenticating what he wrote . . .

When I looked at the front page of the paper again, at the enormous A+, I said, "why would she hide . . .?" and got another elbow in the ribs.

"Thank you, Mrs. McKendrick," Meli said, leading me away,

---

[*] I was expecting to see it weeks before.

The Persistent Past

putting Maria's essay in her purse. There were two more teachers—her stocky PE teacher and her vest-wearing French teacher named *Monsieur* Wirtz—but I barely remember what they said.

It was later that night, when I was going to take Maria's paper down to her when I checked her in, but . . . "I'll do it tonight," Melanie said.

She joined me on the couch later, watching the news, before I asked, "Why did you . . .?"

"She'd be embarrassed."

"About what?"

"She's bared her soul and her father read it." She rested her head on my shoulder. "Teenage girl thing."

"Did you tell her I read it?"

"And that you were immensely proud of her." Silence. "She's a young woman and you're her most important male role model, babe. You can't imagine what she feels, even if it's admiration, a connection. Leave it at that."

"But . . ."

"Because she doesn't know what to do about what she feels. I'm frankly stunned that she wrote that much." She switched the TV off when the sports started. "C'mon."

As was her habit, Meli opened the bedroom window for a few minutes when the A/C wasn't running. In the fresh, chill night air, we cuddled, listening to the house sounds.

It was the middle of the night; too early for the kids or, normally, for us. "This is gonna sound weird," I whispered, my head on Meli's shoulder, "but . . . Ned's diary, his other writings. He meets Angela on a train, then dreams about her before he sees her again." I reached for her hand, resting it softly on my belly. "I'm thinking it was some kind of . . . of . . . "

"Souls reaching out to each other?"

"Yeah; like that. I'm trying to understand how his mind worked. The horrors he'd been through in France . . . "

"You're thinking about horrors with your head on my shoulder before sunrise? You're right; weird."

"I want to understand this guy. He lived in an entirely different time. The first time he saw anything like a naked girl was his six-teenth birthday, when his father took him to a burlesque show."

"Huh."

"But the next time they met, he'd got a dose of typhus and was in her hospital in France. They courted there. Just hours before he left . . . he didn't see Angie when they . . . "

"Did the dirty?"

"Yeah, but he barely knew it was happening and didn't know if he'd see her again when he caught a truck for Flanders."

She kissed my head. "Sounds like *my* first."

"Reynold-something?"

"Yeah. He was more sober than I was. We *did it* in his dorm room. Didn't have another date . . . didn't have *that* date; just . . . *that.*" She pushed me over and slid on top. "Were you aware of what was happening with Joan that night?"

"Oh, yeah," I said, my hands resting on her hips. "At fourteen, we had to be careful I didn't get *too* close."

She shifted her hips, and me, gently. "Didn't do *this* . . . "

"Uh . . . uh . . . *oh* . . . "

Then I awoke with an image in my mind . . .

I'd barely pulled my underwear on before I was studying the Polaroids of the Steele family in my den. Ned had a little scar on the end of his nose; I wondered how it got there. His face was an-gular, yet soft. His brown eyes seemed to see everything around him. He stood behind his family.

The older boy, Charles, looked more like his mother than his father. Corrine had her father's face and her mother's eyes. The younger boy, Carl, had his mother's coloring but his father's jaw.

Angela sat to the right of the picture, behind her kneeling chil-dren, and wore a proud smile below her haunting hazel eyes. Her red hair hung down to her shoulders.

It was *Angie's* face I saw in my mind . . . .

Melanie, in her morning sweatsuit, came up behind me, placed her hands on my shoulders, and whispered, "now what?"

"Good morning to you, too," I whispered back. "I dreamed of her as I woke up."

"Huh," she feigned indignity. "Even after our amazing . . .?"

"She reminds me of you."

"Huh." She studied the photo, then patted my shoulder. "Get some pants on, babe."

11ᵗʰ November, Overlooking the Moselle River near Neuville, Luxembourg.
They told us to stop shooting at 11 this morning, and I never heard a silence so profound, even if it is raining. Standing up outside a hole or a trench with no need to duck is a liberating experience.
I have by God survived and I cannot weep properly or as much as I feel a need to. The men caper in No-man's-land and I know there are unexploded shells out there, but I cannot find it in my heart to stop them for they are celebrating being alive after this horror; I wish to join them, but I dare not as their commander.
I must stop being so profane. Just because I hear it all the time does not mean I need to write it down.

"Gimmie your best thoughts on this," I asked the class.

"We cannot imagine his feelings," Bay said slowly. "They have survived all of that, and they dance around deadly shells."

"Glad to be alive," Larry said. "Not that hard to . . . "

"I was in a near-head-on collision," Patty added. "I was nine; a truck tore our car in half. Dad got out with a busted arm and leg. Mom got a few scratches from the glass; suffered from whiplash later. My brother and I strapped into car seats; glass but not much more."

"Sorry," someone said.

"I was scared but, when we got out of the car, Mom laughed, told us an angel was watching over us . . . then did a little dance, and Bobby and I joined her, firemen and cops and paramedics all clapping and grinning. So, I get it. You're just happy to be alive."

"But he cannot weep," Bay said. "He cannot express what he

has wanted to express for himself and himself alone."

"Would he weep for himself or for public consumption?" Larry asked.

"Good question," I said. "Any thoughts, anyone?"

"Emotional freeze," the woman next to Larry added. "Comes with PTSD and combat stress reaction, or CSR, which is related but different."

"Yeah," Larry agreed. "Shell-shock . . . "

"Or just weariness from the stress," she interrupted. "PTSD; shell-shock; whatever you call that, lasts longer, but it dosen't go away with a week's sound sleep like CSR does."

"Excuse me," I said, "but are you auditing this class?"

"Visiting, Doc," Larry said. "My *sensei* from Michigan. She's an . . . "

"NP squared, sir; neuropsychiatric nurse-practitioner," she interrupted. "I work in the neuro-psych ward in the VA hospital in Hazel Park near Detroit."

"Thanks for your insight, Miss . . .?"

"Mrs. Donna Paulson, sir." She was older than any student and had a decade, at least, on Larry.

"Just *Sensei* Blondie, Doc," Larry declared. "Like I . . . "

"Donna's fine, Doctor," Donna said, elbowing Larry swiftly. "Pay no attention to my insolent former pupil."

Blonde, she was, with blue eyes and looked like that cartoon character. "If you will call me Curtis, OK; can we talk after class, in a professional capacity?"

"If you wish," she smiled, her arms across her ample chest.

"Mrs., er, Donna," I shook her hand; she had a powerful grip. "My office is across the Quad."

"Well, let's go, then." She had an attractive, winning grin.

We reached my office in a few minutes as I pointed out the buildings and features of interest. She was mostly quiet, with the occasional "uh-huh," to a building or statue.

She stopped in front of the Star of David Memorial in the Quad. "For our alumni Sons of Abraham who served their countries," I read the English inscription. "the Hebrew I can't make out."

"'Doing what is righteous and just is more acceptable to the Lord than sacrifice,'* she said. "That's what it says. It refers to persecution, and resistance to persecution. A popular saying around the 1948 War of Independence." We walked on, not speaking. "They taught us that in Hebrew school, Curtis," she smiled as I opened the door.

"My office is down here." I led her to my door. "Your coat?" She handed it to me without hesitation. She had the muscular physique of an athlete and some pretty impressive legs under a longer skirt. I pointed to the sofa; she sat easily. "So, Donna, what can you tell me about this CSR?"

She folded her hands in her lap with an enigmatic smile. "You really *want* to know, don't you?"

"Um . . . yes?" I answered. "Why else would I . . .?"

"You wouldn't be the first university professor who asked me for one thing and wanted another, Curtis."

"Not me. Happily, contentedly, and safely married with two daughters and two sons."

"Me, too, but three young sons," she sighed, crossing her legs. "This is my first trip away from them since the youngest was born in '91. What, exactly, do you want to know?"

I told her about the diaries, about how Ned tried to weep several times during the war, to break down after all he'd been through, but could only do it after he'd heard about his family after all the shooting was over, and in the arms of a woman he loved. Donna listened quietly, her eyes occasionally darting around the room, shifting her weight. "I just need to explain, somehow, just what was going on in his head," I finished.

"That's the thing," Donna said with a brief grin. "Nothing. He locked his brain up while he . . . how old was he?"

"He was twenty-one when he got to France; twenty-two when the war was over."

"Social conditioning of boys early in the 20th Century would have helped him a great deal, but I can tell you from experience that young adults of the '60s and '70s didn't have the same social

---

* Proverbs 21:3.

expectations as your guy did."

"Change that much?"

"Oh, yes." She smiled indulgently. "Curtis, you and I both grew up in the '60s; you saw what was happening in the streets then, at the beaches and the clubs . . . our *hemlines.*" She hoisted her skirt above her knees briefly. "But that kind of liberation, though there was some then, was unthinkable—even for women—in your Ned's time."

"He has one entry about his teenage sister's bathing skirts and stockings."

"Would that my Dad could have put me in those," she chuckled, shook her head. "Some suits I wore . . ." she smiled.

"I could imagine," I grinned. "My sisters . . . "

"I'd guess," she said. "But, back to CSR. If I remember, the medical profession wasn't talking about shell-shock then, or even combat exhaustion—what we used to call CSR."

"You've looked into the history of . . .?"

"I have; NPs are new to neuro-psych, so we're sensitive to our lack of track record. Anyway, as a younger man, he could literally turn it off, but forgot where that switch was because of lack of use. Young people do it now without thinking so they can be promiscuous about sex. That's why our generation is more susceptible to PTSD, because it was harder for us to turn it back on again because we forget where the switch is."

"Life experience," I said. "Ned's life experience before then was . . . he joined the Army at eighteen. His first physical romantic encounter, that we can tell, was when he was nearly twenty-two . . . "

"Don't confuse sex with life experience, Curtis," Donna said with a wry grin. "He'd been living with hardship for three years before he got to France, before he first *did it* with a woman—I'm guessing—and been living in the company of men most of the time?" I nodded. "That set him up for one helluva switch. Sex made his exterior life—the one beyond the military—bearable, providing escape in emotional and physical passion. The life in his head—that included both the Army and everything else—had to be controlled to keep the two from smashing each other. And there's battle rage, too . . . "

"That's . . .?" I asked. While Donna was physically stunning, her scholarship truly fascinated me.

"A theory-cum-diagnosis," she answered. "Some call it berserker rage, but I'm not that sure that it's simply that because, I believe, there are degrees of it like everything else in our panoply of diagnoses and syndromes."

"Excuse me, but you sound very scholarly for a nurse."

"Thanks; I teach nurses now," she said, fussing with her hair casually. "Finished my degree in psychology last June. Need to know all the theories behind the theories so I can teach the next generation of NP squareds. But I . . . "

Then the phone rang. "Excuse me, please," I got up, walked to my desk, and glanced at the caller ID window, not expecting much because so often it read UNKN . . . like now.

"Hello?"

"Dr. Durand?" the voice asked.

"Yes?"

"This is Carl Steele, Dr. Durand. I'm in town and thought I'd touch bases . . . "

"You're . . ." I stopped, glanced at Donna, who'd gotten up and was perusing my diplomas, plaques, and pictures. "You're Ned Steele's son?"

"Youngest and the apple of Mother's eye, yessir."

"Um . . . how long are you . . .?"

"I'm taking off again tomorrow afternoon."

I found out what brain-freeze meant then and there. Here was this gorgeous blonde telling me how Ned's mind might have worked, and here's his son who might tell me the same thing differently. But I realized that neither would be available for as long as perhaps I'd like. And there was our family dinner in a couple of hours.

"Are you free for dinner?"

"Hi," Meli smiled, shaking Donna's hand. My hurried conversation with her, explaining how I had two very important short-term visitors who Maria and I really needed to . . .

"Thanks for having us on such short notice," Donna smiled. "I know what a pain . . ." Meli really didn't sound that irritated when

I called her, told her the import of my two guests.

"Breaks up the week, keeps me young," Meli said, shaking Carl's hand and conducting them both into the living room. "Maria will be here in a few minutes; the boys are in the backyard.* Dinner will be a beef butt in about an hour. Can I offer you refreshments? We have little liquor, but more wine . . . "

I fetched the Steele family pictures from my den while Meli poured wine. "Handsome family," Donna said. "When was the photo taken?"

"The pictures that painting was based on was taken in 1937 in Washington when I was seven." Carl, in his late fifties, studied my Polaroids wistfully. "Corky was about to start nurse's school in Detroit and live with Aunt Francie. Dad already had orders for the Philippine Department after he finished the War College." He sat down with his wine. "Grampa Branch had it made while we were in the Philippines. None of us saw it until after the war."

"You and your brother went to the Philippines in '37?" I asked.

"I did, but Charlie attended a boarding school in Detroit, spent holidays and summers by Aunt Betty. In the summer of '40 we all sailed to Hawaii and met with *Uncle* Charlie. That was the last I saw my brother or sister until 1946; only time I ever met *Uncle* Charlie or his daughters."

"So, you were where when the war started . . .?" Donna asked softly. Just then, Maria walked in, still in muddy shorts and leggings.

Carl told us his story . . .

"Thanks for indulging us, honey," I sighed as we got into bed.

"Hey; anytime we can have guests like them during the week," Meli said. "Breaks up the monotony."

"That's true," I agreed, listening to the night sounds.

"Donna's a what, besides a black belt in karate and some kind of official?" She asked, adding, "and the beautiful woman the boys are in love with?"

---

* The snow from the previous week was mostly gone, as that from October blizzards often did.

"Neuropsychiatric nurse-practitioner; works with PTSD patients at the VA. She *is* beautiful, yes, visiting a former student and officiating in a karate tournament here this weekend."

"Didn't think there were that many karate types around here."

"It's a regional tourney. She gave me tickets if we want to go."

"Something different." We listened to the furnace start again. "Get any insights on your people tonight?"

"I got a few, yeah. Carl helped personalize them; Donna helped explain some of Ned's more cryptic diary entries, like why he couldn't weep for so long, even after all he saw, his dead friends . . ."

"He couldn't cry because Angela or someone like her wasn't around."

"Yes," I said, surprised. "How did . . .?"

"She made it safe for him to express how he felt, despite or because of his diary."

"I should have asked you, because that's what Donna said."

"Yes, you should have. Any woman who loves a man could have told you that."

"Maria didn't; none of the women in my class . . . "

"They haven't let men weep." She held my hand. "Remember when Connie talked about Joan, right after she got here?"

"We cried *with* her . . . "

"And *for* Joanie . . . "

I remembered.

CAMP PENOBSCOT

I t took no persuading at all to pile the kids into Meli's minivan and go up to Camp Penobscot after both Jason's and Maria's last soccer games of the season.*

"Can I try karate, Dad?" Charlie asked, still full of the tournament we'd watched the weekend before. At the end of the tourney, Donna squared off against another black-belt in a demonstration. They moved so fast their hands and feet were blurs, but the kids all loved it.

"Remember what Donna said, Charlie," Meli answered for me. "Karate is not for trying; only for doing. But we'll see† after Christmas, when the next class starts." There was one *dojo* in Granite Ledge, teaching all ages and skill levels of judo and karate; Larry taught there for pocket money. The owner, a PE instructor at the Academy, also taught *tai chi.*

That Saturday morning broke chilly, the brilliant colors of the birches and elms, oaks and maples fading into their winter sleep after that first blizzard. Vehicles containing people in uniform crowded the road on the road up the river, and we soon learned why: the first weekend of every month (except federal holidays) is a Guard/Reserve drill weekend.

We pulled into the gate, where a young woman in uniform wearing an MP brassard stopped us. "May I help you?" she asked.

---

* Maria's school team broke even for the season, 4–4. Jason's Crest squad had the best record in the three-team league at 2–1.

† The one parental answer kids dread.

191

"We just wanted to look around if we can." I answered.

"The Visitor's Center is right over there." She pointed to an elegant Victorian revival brick structure fifty yards down the road. "You can't go past that gate," she pointed to another gatehouse a hundred yards away, "without a valid military ID."

The sign over the Visitor's Center entrance read *Welcome to Historic Camp Penobscot.* A smaller sign beneath read *Upper New England's Oldest Military Camp Site.* Just inside the doors, a painting of militiamen illustrated the site's first establishment in 1680.* A small counter with an elderly man behind it lined one wall. "Hello," he said. "Welcome to Camp Penobscot. Your first time?"

"Yes, indeed," I answered as the kids scattered to the glass display cases. Scenes of ages gone by, from before the Revolution to the Gulf War, lined the walls.

"Lived here all my life," Melanie declared, "never been in here."

"This center was built out of the old camp HQ in 1990," he said, "so there has been little for civilians to see."

"Ah," I nodded, scanning the photos of past camp commandants until I reached *Major Edmund A. Steele, 1925–1931; 1937.* "I've got some papers of his," I pointed to Ned's picture. "Many diaries . . ."

"*Really?*" our interlocutor smiled, came out from behind the counter and offered his hand. "Mickey Parnell; I was the General's junior enlisted aide in Germany. I came up here in '52, and I stayed on."

"Yeah?" I asked, shaking his hand. "Did you live on the farm?"

"For a while," Mickey said. "The General and Miss Angie loved their privacy after everything that happened."

"Mickey, I think you'd appreciate this." I showed him a copy of the "meeting Angela" diary entry out of my inside coat pocket. "He wrote this in . . ." I started.[†]

"1917," Mickey smiled. "Miss Angie often spoke of their first

---

* I'd never known white men had penetrated this wilderness that early.

† I brought it hoping someone at the farm might be interested on the way back.

The Persistent Past

meeting, especially near the end of their lives." He was suddenly wistful. "The General wasn't speaking much after his stroke in '89."

"I wasn't aware of . . ." I started.

"You found the Great Ugly Beast?" Mickey suddenly asked, as if he'd just heard me say it.

"The steamer trunk full of . . .?" I asked.

"That's what Miss Angie called it, yeah." I told him who I was, and about the trunk and the Steele Collection that was coming out of it. "Well," he sighed, "someone found it who can do something with it; what the General wanted." He looked off into space, speaking slowly. "I remember well the day he stuffed the Great Ugly Beast full of his diaries and other stuff. He couldn't interest anyone in them, so he . . . "

"He didn't know about the Crest/Jenson Archives?" I asked, surprised. "We would have snapped it up in . . . "

"The what?" Mickey asked, blinking.

I explained the Archives, ending with, "anyone with such a treasure-trove of material *with* provenance would have been welcomed with open arms."

Mickey stared at me, incredulous. "Sorry, no; never heard of it."

"You said you remember when he stuffed the trunk? When was that?"

"March, 1989. He'd just been turned down by the Marshall Foundation and he'd just heard about General Brick's passing."

I chuckled. "They have offered a tidy sum for it from us."

"Is that right? He offered it to them for nothing. 'Take it off my hands,' he said. They just said they weren't interested." He shook his head and smiled wistfully.

"What did you do for General Steele?"

"Mostly I dealt with the farmers who worked the fields, and the people who wanted their cars and equipment fixed. I also did a lot of the upkeep on this camp as long as the state wasn't doing it. That's how I got this job."

"What did he need the farm equipment for if he didn't work on the farm?"

"He added about ten acres to the fields with that equipment.

When he wasn't doing that, he was repairing everything in sight. Cars, trucks, bulldozers, cranes . . . practically anything. He did it so cheap the construction contractors brought their equipment up here and other shops rose a stink. Even the quarries brought equipment up here."

"Where did you live? There's a cottage on the farm . . . "

"I lived there until I got a house downriver in '53. Raised my family there; wife and I still live there."

"Parnell," Melanie mused. "*Geoff* Parnell is your son?" She'd been listening to us with her enigmatic face, but I heard her gears grinding.

"Yes, ma'am."

"We dated in high school."

Mickey looked hard and long at her. "Yes . . . Meli? Junior promenade? Pretty girl in a gorgeous gown that looked like it was cold."

Meli shook his hand. "Yeah, that was me, and it *was* cold; there wasn't much to it. Where is Geoff these days?"

"Works for TV in New York now, married with three kids. Remember Sue, his older sister? She married . . . "

"Stan Ridgeman," Meli interrupted. "They were together since grade school."

"Yep. Got three kids in Vermont. My little girl Mary . . . "

"Would be in her thirties now," Meli declared.

"Yes; she teaches grade school, lives with another woman in New Town."

"Small world," I interrupted, sighing at that ever persistent past, knowing that his son was the first boy to feel . . .*

"Tell Stan I'll see him at our 25th reunion in '99," Meli said.

"I'll surely do that. *Sir,*" Mickey came to attention, "would you like to see his *field desks?*"

"*Field* desks?"

"Come with me." We followed Mickey back behind the counter, and through a door. "The camp's archives," he explained, waving his arms at several shelves, filing cabinets, and tables loaded with

---

* Yes, Meli; you said so.

old paper files, boxes, and the odd wooden crate. "I took this stuff out of the farm myself." He perused the shelves, then reached up with both arms, coming down with several journal books. "Here's these," he sighed, setting them on a table and reaching again, "and these," setting more on the table. "I have the rest . . . ."

I stared at the journals, speechless. "Why are these . . .?"

"They're what I could find around the farm after Miss Angie passed and me and the kids were cleaning out. Over there," he pointed to a small, magnificent hardwood secretary* and three forlorn green boxes in a corner. "The secretary is from the first war; two of the new ones are from the second, the third from his stint in Korea."

"Who owns all this material?" I asked, scanning the tables, shelves, filing cabinets . . . and eyeing the field desks.

"Well," Mickey sighed, looking around. "The stuff *in* these cabinets belongs to the camp, so that's the state's. Some of the rest belongs to them, too. The rest the kids let me keep but I ran out of room at home. Why?"

"Because the Steele Collection wants to buy it all."

"Well," Mickey said, knitting his brows. "Nobody's ever asked about the General before." He shook his head briefly. "Got a buck a piece?"

"How about two bucks each?"

"OK."

"The field desks. How about them?"

"You might want to look inside first, babe," Meli said. "Might be empty."

"They ain't, but have a look, Doc," Mickey said.

I first ran a hand over the secretary, with its patinaed brass fittings. An old-fashioned key unlocked the fold-down desk board, which unlatched the four drawers beneath. I pulled the desk supports out of their niches and beheld five document slots half-full of rolled-up paper. I pulled out the small center drawer, which contained a candle, matches, and toiletries. A steel mirror wrapped in a towel sat in the slot atop the drawer. The four drawers under the

---

* A high drawer cabinet with a desk board.

desk table contained more, smaller notebooks, ring binders, maps and . . . "This must have been Angela's," I said, pulling a Red Cross apron out of the bottom drawer.

"It would have been Miss Angie's, yeah," Mickey agreed.

I held it out to Meli. "See if it fits."

She held it in front of her. "Way too small on me. Might fit Maria."

"We'll . . ." I stopped, realizing that these were three-dimensional, personal objects of real people I was getting to know through real archives. "Maybe the Visitor's Center should display these."

"Good idea," Mickey agreed. "But I know nothing about that kind of thing."

"Well, I know people who do," I said. "I've gotten letters from his children and his brother, George. Carl was here just . . . "

"Couple weeks ago, yeah; he stopped in for a chat. His family send us Christmas cards. The General's oldest brother and sister are gone; older brother was killed at Pearl Harbor. His younger sister—the doctor—I think passed a couple years before he did. His brother George . . . "

Sometimes you find a pearl among the oyster shells.

"More inventory, Maria," I said on our way back home. I'd put all the journal books and a handful of papers into cardboard boxes and paper bags to haul back to the Archives. Angie's Red Cross apron fit Maria but we left it with Mickey.

She made a face. "Yeah. Can I . . .?"

"How many hours have you got this week?" She was filling her quota every week with the transcription and filling in details in the inventory.

"Not the problem; I've got a date tonight." I had planned to just drop the new material in Holding until Monday, anyway.

"Ted?" Meli asked.

"Yeah."

"Who else?" Charlie mocked. "Betcha he'll pop the question tonight . . . "

"*Shaddap*, Weird-o," Maria sighed, slapping him softly in the head.

"So grab a piece out of the bag and see what it is," I said, pointing to the bag between her knees.

She did, frowning. "A map on one side," Maria said, holding a piece of paper, "and another Georgia letter."

"Huh," I said. "What's the date?"

"1918, so . . . it goes . . . ?"

"After Hill 90 somewhere."

Our family listened, curious, all during this exchange. "That's what you guys do all the time?" Charlie asked.

"Pretty much," Maria said, putting the paper back.

"That sounds *boring*," Jason sighed.

"New word, Nasty?" Maria asked, bopping him upside the head.

And we were off again . . .

```
. . . [A] single French soldier could have
stopped and reversed the German
reoccupation of the Rhineland in
1936 . . . A German officer of my
acquaintance from the war, Col Ivan
Gordecki, told me then, in no uncertain
terms, that the German Army was in no
condition to resist any show of force from
France or Britain, and all the German
generals knew it. Personal conversations
with several other German and French
officers confirmed this. This would no
doubt have caused Hitler's downfall. But
Hitler's orders were to be obeyed without
question, as he had a gambler's luck so
often.
It is this soldier's belief that his next
move will be Austria.
```

"What do we make of this?" I asked my class the next week.

"Diary again?" Larry asked.

"Nope. Ned Steele's Master's thesis in history right here at Crest, submitted in January 1937."

"That was . . ." Bayard started.

"A year before the *Anschluss*. Steele's thesis was on postwar

Germany's antithetical Weimar republic and the historical causes of its failure."

"His personal observation?" Larry asked.

"He was in the Rhineland when the Germans crossed into it. I have orders placing him in Paris as assistant military attaché before then, and his diary corroborates this. He may have drafted his thesis while he was there."

"I'd have to say this guy is a living history lesson," Bay nodded.

"Something to that. But, how often do we see personal observations in a Master's thesis in history?"

"Never?" Bay asked.

"Right. Why?"

"History isn't current events," Larry said.

"Who says?" Nobody answered.

"Did he ever get his Master's?" Larry asked.

"The School of Liberal Arts conferred him a Master's in history in 1949, after he wrote a letter asking for it. But that was an exception they make for veterans. They made a few for the Reservists and Guardsmen called up for both Korea and the Gulf, so only serving in a war will get you one like that."

> 27th November, Hill 90.
> Gas attack last night. Could feel myself
> breathe in the smoke hood as we heard the
> gas shells pop all around us and the Hun MG
> bullets hit the ground with their buzz-thut-
> buzz-thut.
> When the shelling let up a bit, Dona said we
> should move to my forward PC, as gas always
> means they're attacking. We ran and
> stumbled up the hill, dodging more shells
> and MG bullets, tripping over signal wire.
> Running in that getup was hard in camp
> and training, but doing it in combat was
> pure [expletive] hell. Trenches at night are
> disorienting, especially during an attack. We
> made our way forward and into the
> communications saps, dodging the ammo

parties and the litter bearers. I am ashamed
to say I stepped on more than one man, but I
don't know if they were alive or dead.
[Expletive] *me.*
The attack started in earnest not long after I
reached the PC. I switched and called for
barrages for a good three hours; our MGs
pounded away all night. I don't know how
many [expletive] *rounds we fired, but we'll*
figure that [expletive] *shit out later.*
Twenty-eight casualties, including Grimes.
Not that bad for an evening in a [expletive]
charnel house. The dead included Dent and
Hallie, men I met in the chow line, and
Grunhalt from the Machine-Gun Section in
Mexico. I wonder how many of them are left?

Maria, reading her transcription again, wiped another tear from her cheek. "Men he knew," she whispered. "Some he'd just met."

"That seems to be right. Grimes was one of his officers . . . "

"Killed?"

"No; he's in later diaries." I waited. "Honey, are you still OK with this?"

"I'm more OK with this shit than I was before we went to that damn farm, Dad," she said flatly. "Those lonely headstones are who we're doing this shit for."*

"These diaries are coarsening your language," I said. "You're sounding like . . . "

"Yeah; sorry, Dad. Ned cleaned up his act, gradually." Silence. "Huh."

"Huh, what?"

"If his diaries help him think, his language doing it must reflect the environment he has to think in; about."

Like I said; brilliant instincts.

*   *   *

---

* She was more coarse than I have here, but I [expletive] cut the real bad stuff.

John D. Beatty   199

"How's the twins these days?" I asked Mike as we surveyed Ned's field desks. "Haven't seen them for weeks. They're teething?"

"Doc says it's way early, but yeah. Melanie's teething solution got it under control."*

I nodded, knowing that teething lasted between a lifetime and forever.† "My mother used peppermint schnapps. What can you tell me about these desks?"

We studied the hand-cut dovetail drawer joinery and fine oak cabinet and drawer fronts on Ned's WWI desk. "English, late 19th Century, a custom-made job, certainly; the five-pound cut‡ finish is well-worn but still got some sheen. Got a maker's brand here I'll look up. Where'd this guy get it?"

"His supply Sergeant was good at acquiring things."

"He probably traded this for that. Supply guys do that. The other three are common GI issue; same pattern still used today." These were square wood boxes covered with dented sheet tin, painted pale OD greenish. The latched front cover of each came off and hung on the case to form a surface like a single-pedestal desk. A folding stool clipped onto the lid. The five drawers came out of the case. All the components were remarkably intact. Papers, maps, ration cans and boxes, cigars, and toiletries, including toilet paper, filled most of the drawers. "Find anything interesting in any of them?"

"I did indeed," I sighed. "Each desk is a treasure-trove of personal, semi-personal and official correspondence. I'm getting to know more about this guy all the time."

"Yeah? He's a good guy?"

"I would have liked to have known him in the flesh." I looked at him wistfully. "But he's buried over at that farm; died four years ago."

"Curtis," Mike said softly, "let's go get a drink."

The nearest saloon was the Class VI store at Camp Penobscot. We drove through the inner gate using Mike's ID and to the pole-barn with a sign that read "Mike's Place: Class VI IDs Only."

The "bar" was nothing more than a counter with a cash register.

---

* Three parts honey, two parts whiskey, and one part water.
† It seemed that long, anyway.
‡ Five pounds of shellac flakes to a gallon of alcohol.

Beer came in bottles out of a cooler with plastic cups; liquor out of a locked cabinet and not sold by the drink. Mike flashed his ID, pointed to me and said, "my father-in-law," took our beers and sat at a table.

"Who's Mike?" I wondered. This place was crudely modest. Stacking chairs, square Formica tables, tin ashtrays and recruiting posters were the most prominent features.

"Dunno who that one was," Mike answered, "but this one's a little worried about you and your family." Since it was mid-afternoon on a Tuesday, there were only a few patrons.

"Why?"

"When was the last time you took the family on a real vacation? A weekend at a local resort with my beautiful mother-in-law doesn't count."

I looked at him long and hard, wondering what I should say, where he got that idea. "Mike, I appreciate . . . "

"Connie sees it, too, pal. You've been going through the motions with your family. Sunday, at the baptism, you looked and acted as if nothing was wrong, but," he shrugged. "Even Helen and Gramma Devota saw it. Your head's here with us, but your heart ain't."

The baptismal feast at our place was a gathering of Durands, Hubbards, Kleins, Fullers (Meli's sister), and Valencias (Meli's other sister). My sister Darla dragged her boyfriend from Ohio along; my folks and other sister, Karen, and her family came from Cicero. I thought it was a fabulous get-together engineered so everyone could see the twins. "Um . . ." I started.

"Your body was there, Curtis," Mike said, swirling his beer, "but your heart was off somewhere in France."

"Camiers," I said absently, "near the North Sea coast and the Machine Gun Corps depot in the British sector of . . . "

"See? I don't even have to prompt you."

"It's where I am in the research," I said defensively. "It's pretty detailed work."

"You get too involved."

What Meli said when we took that magnificent long weekend back in June came back to me. "Because you need this Big Thing, babe," she said . . . and I absently repeated aloud.

"Call me 'babe' again and we'll have a problem, pal," Mike sighed, finishing his beer.

"I was just . . . something Meli said." I sighed deeply and sucked down my beer. "This could be the crowning achievement of my career, Mike," I mumbled. "It takes a great deal of . . . "

"Yours and Maria's time, yeah," he said. "More beer?"

"One more." I looked around the gradually-filling bar, noticing more civilians than uniformed military people. "What do I do about it?" I asked the air as Mike came back and handed me another bottle.

"Try to think of the past in more cosmic terms."

"What do you mean?"

"OK: for you this is a big Goddamn deal. For Maria, it's an interesting project she makes a few bucks off of, and maybe some more for a while. For history, it's a significant contribution. But to the cosmos, it's really just a blip on the scale of time." He sighed. "Gramma has a saying: the best most of us can hope for, a century from now, is to be a trivia question at a family reunion. Maybe this guy is more important than that, but," he shrugged. "Your family's *here* now. *You* need to be."

I stared at him for a moment. "The past is what I do; what I've done since I was thirteen . . . "

"And you do it well, Curtis. You're the best history teacher I've ever had. You're a brilliant writer, too, from what I've seen. But ask yourself if it's *what* you are. You must do all the other stuff well, too, or at that family reunion you'll be remembered as a 'yeah . . . *him*,' instead of a '*YEAH, HIM!*'"

I looked at my son-in-law, astonished at his grasp of the historical profession.* "It's a priesthood . . . "

"But it's not a monastery. At least, with two kids of your own, you don't live in one and have not taken a vow of celibacy." He tilted his beer at me before he set his bottle down. "So, when was the last time you took your family on a real vacation? One where you could forget all about any history, and this Steele character and

---

* That I suddenly saw quite clearly.

The Persistent Past

his family and what he did before you were born? And what's the place of the past in the cosmos of your life that includes your family?"

Good. Question.

I opened the envelope from the Ministry of Defense eagerly.

9th October
Whitehall, London
My Dear Doctor Durand
    This reply is tardy because it took some time for it to be forwarded to my desk, and your request subsequently caused a great stir in the MOD.
    The Ministry of War gazetted a Military Medal for Captain Edmund Steele of the American Army for actions between 22nd November and 4th December 1917 on 9th February 1919, and presented said medal to Lieutentant Colonel Steele on 20th May 1919. However, the Ministry never awarded a second gazette from 15th September 1918, made to the same officer for his actions between 25th and 27th March 1918.
    The Crown Honours and Appointments Secretariat created a pennant declaring the 432nd Machine Gun Battalion to be the 'Prince of Wales' Own Americans,' awarded on 20th May 1919. The Secretariat also forwarded Colonel Steele's name for a Commander of the British Empire in 1954, as he was responsible for saving Her Majesty's uncle—then the Prince of Wales—from captivity in March 1918. This honour received royal assent on 19th December 1955, but has never been presented.
    I have attached the citations for both the MM awards and the CBE. In due course, an Army officer will contact you directly to determine who should officially accept them.
    Your obedient servant,
    Rodger Blakely-Stuart,
    MOD Archivist

PS: "Gazetting" was the term used during
the 1914-18 war by the Ministry of War
when it approved awards, a throwback to
the days of the Horse Guards.

He saved the future King of England. It was hard for me to
breathe for several moments after I read the letter.

"We should do it," I said Thanksgiving night. "Mike and Connie
are right; we need a serious break."

"I don't know." Meli sighed. Silence, listening to the night
sounds and the rising wind.

"We need to get our current lives out of our heads. You're getting too cynical about your job, honey. I need to lose Ned and Angie for a while; so does Maria. We can afford it."*

"You're right, babe." She sighed, curled up beside me. "We
shall. A good long vacation; someplace warm and sunny . . . "

> *28th November, Hill 90.*
> *Quiet night. No more*[Blotches of ink] *bn. from*
> *Prince Edward Island relieved the*
> *Newfoundlanders. Met senior Capt. as Col.*
> *and Maj. are casualties. He has 367 men in a*
> *bn. that should have 600.* [Expletive]
> *Passchendaele has used them up.*
> *Tomorrow would be Thanksgiving. We won't*
> *get any* [expletive] *turkey up here; even Willis*
> *isn't that good.*
> *I resist calling this place a Golgotha, but it*
> *certainly is a place of suffering and skulls.*
> *Canucks mounted heads on sandbags, left*
> *them on a parapet as bait for a Hun they've*
> *been trying to get for days.*
>
> *29th November*
> *[No entry; pen date]*

---

* With our two salaries totalling nearly $300k annually and the house paid
for, money was never much of an issue for us.

"What to do with them?" I asked Maria, showing me her latest transcription.* On that last Saturday afternoon in November, Maria was just reading.

"Are the blanks important?" I only allowed her to transcribe when I was with her.

"In that entries like this show he tried to be diligent in his diary writings in trying circumstances, yes." I set her transcription aside. "Sweetie, we need to talk."

"This another one of those father/daughter talks, Dad?" she rolled her eyes. "Ted hasn't . . . "

"No; not about that." I sat down beside her, trying to feel my way ahead because this was uncharted territory. "We're going on a vacation over Christmas."

"OK, great," she smiled, then asked, "where?"

"That dosen't matter. What matters is, when we go, we won't talk about this project or anything like it at all."

She cocked her head curiously, frowned, then asked, "why?"

"We need perspective. We need to get Ned out of our heads for a while."

"I get it," she smiled, patting my hand. "Might be a good idea."

"Everyone take one and pass 'em around," Meli said the next Monday night before dinner. She'd stopped at Granite Ledge Travel and grabbed all the brochures she could for west and south coast destinations.

"Pick a place," I sighed. "Anywhere warmer than here."

"How soon would we have to book?" Meli asked, perusing a Tampa flyer. We had gone on family vacations up and down the east coast—all with some US history connections—but now a place we've never been and I had no interest in, beckoned.

"Soon as possible," I answered, looking at a brochure for Orlando, shocked by the prices.

-----

* Draft transcriptions were in bound books we could carry for research. Final transcriptions were stored on computer disks in my office, owned by the Steele Collection.

"We're not going down there . . . are we?" Maria asked, passing the brochure for Miami to Charlie.

"I want us to think about lots of places," I said, glancing at a Santa Catalina brochure from Jason.

"How about Texas?" Meli asked, studying a pamphlet for Galveston Island.

"This place looks cool," Charlie declared, looking over a New Orleans brochure.

"I don't like this one," Jason added, passing a Puerto Rico pamphlet to me.

We looked at the entire stack that took us everywhere sunny and maybe warm in December that, I hoped, wouldn't be too crowded at Christmastime.

"I like this one," Maria finally said, having gone through all of them. "Looks real sunny."

"I wanna try that," Charlie grinned, pointing at a skin diver on the back.

"They got sharks I can see?" Jason asked.

"Maybe," Meli said with her little smile of satisfaction. "We'll have to go down there and see."

So we settled on Key West, Florida.

"Hey, Boss," Polly waved when I walked into her office. In cold weather, she dressed more like an Eskimo, complete with mukluks.

"Polly, I need another favor."

"What ya need, pal?"

"Can you take up evaluations in the last week?"

"Sure." She looked at me curiously. "Going somewhere?"

"Key West," I sighed casually.

A broad smile covered her face as she jotted down a note. "Here: Call this number and tell Harriet *I* want you to have the *Super-Duper-Deluxe Beach Suite* package." I read the note: Gulfstream Motel and Suites. "It's just across the island from the airport; ya can't miss it. And tell her *I* said *the works plus*."

"You *know* Key West?"

"I grew up there, sugar," she winked. "Just take every swimsuit you've got and lots of tanning lotion." She reached into her purse and pulled out her wallet, handing me a card with a map and address. "Take *this*. You need the card to get in . . . *if* you go."

"In . . . where?" She told me, then smiled enigmatically. "Go get sane there. I do it once a year, at least . . . and tell *Mom* we can't get down there until Spring Break this year."

"Mom?"

"Harriet."

"Hello, this is Harriet. How may I help you?" I took a chance and called that night. Booking commercial flights was surprisingly easy since we were willing to fly in the middle of the night. I resisted the temptation of chartering a plane since price was no object; didn't know how, anyway.

"Yes, *Polly* wants me to have the Super-Duper-Deluxe Beach Suite package for my family, and *the works plus*."

"How do you know Polly?"

"She works for me."

"You're Professor Durand, then?"

"Yes, ma'am."

"Did she give you a card with an address and map?"

"Yes. She says she can't get down there until Spring Break this year."

"Ah, well . . . glad she let *me* know. Do you know what's that card is for?"

"She told me."

"Good. When will you be arriving?"

"Flying in early morning on Saturday, 14 December."*

"Excellent; I'll have a rental waiting for you at the airport. Will a mini-van do?"

Waiting? "Ah, yeah . . .?"

"How long will you be staying with us?"

"Our flight out is on Friday 27 December. Now . . . "

"Two weeks; excellent. Now, the package is our three-bedroom balcony suite overlooking the water. The suite also has three full

---

* The tickets were available on dates we could make by pulling the kids out of school a week early.

bedrooms with bathrooms, and a kitchenette, washer and dryer in the great room joining the three. One door only for the suite, but one for each bedroom and bath, of course. How many key cards will you need?"

"Two adults, a teenager, two preteen boys."

"How old's the teenager?"

"She'll be fourteen in February."

"Old enough for her own key, if that's . . . "

"Yes . . .? Now, *wait* a *minute*," I said desperately. "*How much is this gonna cost me?*" I imagined somewhere in the mid-five figures.* She named her price, which wasn't anywhere near . . . "Say that again?" Same number. "Ma'am, how much of the price is *Polly . . .?*"

"None." Her voice dropped an octave. "Only for friends of our family if she gave you that card."

Before she wakes up or changes her mind. "*Done*, Mrs. Newman."

"See you soon, Dr. Durand. And tell Polly to do her own dirty work next time."

"We'll take the *kids* out of school early." I said.

"We'll sleep late." She reached for me.

"Yeah." I reached for her.

"You'll forget about history. I'll forget about municipal management, and we'll make love every morning." She pushed my pants down.

"Yeah?" I lifted her nightie.

"I'll wear my blue bikini and you'll wear that *thong-*thing." She pulled me on top of her. "I'll stay naked in the hotel; frolic with my children and best-ever lover on sunny beaches."

Yeah . . . sure . . . and I've got a bridge for ya . . . .

*   *   *

---

* Money wasn't an object, but it was a concern.

The Persistent Past

"They *what?*" I asked into the speakerphone. As another blizzard of dense snow fell on Granite Ledge, we were trying to get our snow removal company to just show up.

"We have priority jobs here," the voice declared. "Your contract is . . ." The Vermont snow removal firm the Corporation hired promised they'd get here by sundown . . . tomorrow.

"We've got *sixteen inches and counting,*" I said.

"We've never seen the contract," Chancellor Tony announced. "I believe we have a right to . . . "

"I'll speak with the Corporation," the voice said. "If they wanted you to have a copy, they would have furnished you with . . . "

"If they wanted us to . . .?" I said loudly. "Your contract with us is . . . "

"With the Corporation, *not* your institution," the voice said.

Then, that was the real problem: the Corporation.

"All right," Chancellor Tony sighed after he hung up. "We can't live like this." This was two days after we'd got fifteen inches, and the snow removal company had just left.

"No," I agreed. "What can we . . .?"

"There's a local firm, Masters Services, that has been sniffing around," Tony said. "They'll do an adequate job faster than the Corporation's firm in Vermont . . . fer *Crissakes,*" he sighed. "I thought the Corporation was supposed to help us . . . "

"Can we shake that much money loose from the Regents?" I asked.

"Find out." Tony punched some numbers into the phone.

"Jenson Stone; Alan Jenson's office. How may I help you?"

"Chancellor Zane for Mr. Jenson; it's urgent."

"Hello; this is Alan."

"Mr. Jenson," Tony started.

"Alan, this is Curtis." I interrupted. "We need money for snow removal."

"*This* bullshit again, Curtis?"

"*This* bullshit again, Alan."

He made a nasty noise. "I'll *send* someone, get a contract through Stone for this season. They should start in a few hours."

"You can do that, sir?" Tony asked.

"I own *enough* of that place, Dr. Zane, I can do what the *Hell* I want, and call me Alan."

"Master's Services, Alan," I said. "They've been . . . "

"Great idea; they'll do," Alan said.

That last week in Granite Ledge was not *quite chaos, but close* to bedlam, compounded by the snow. The kids were in an all-schools Christmas pageant held at the high school—Charlie sang a solo of "O Holy Night" that got wild applause, and Jason's slide-projected illustrations of the Three Wise Men and the manger got rave reviews; no one but his family knew who drew it. A combined school choir chanted "Ring Christmas Bells" *rondo*; *very* entertaining. The grade schoolers sang a medley of Christmas carols through a succession of hasty costume changes that had us all in stitches.

At the end came a student from each of the three schools read a sentence at a time from Ned's diary as our transcription flashed on a screen.

> 25th December, Camp Steele, Etaples, France.
> Another Christmas away from home. The boys
> have found a tree, decorated it with shell
> casings, ammo box paper and ammo strips.
> They scrounged a piano from somewhere.
> Someone had a squeezebox; another a fiddle;
> another a guitar; others played the spoons
> and harmonicas. The YWCA and Red Cross
> gals joined us for the party, sang hymns and
> carols and dance hall tunes all night. The
> cooks prepared goose, found bitter berries
> and made stuffing with some sort of sausage.
> I couldn't have had a better Christmas
> anywhere.
> They had a new verse to "Mademoiselle from
> Armentières."

All the kids and teachers in the auditorium stood up and joined in the song as a piano played.

The Persistent Past

"Mademoiselle from Armentières, parley-vous!
Mademoiselle from Armentières, parley-vous!
You might forget the gas and shell
But you'll never forget the Mademoiselle!
Hinky-dinky parley-vous!""

A teacher finished with:

I only hope we won't still be doing <u>this</u> next
Christmas.

All the kids and teachers shouted, "and they weren't!"
And we were ready for our vacation.

OUR VACATION

S triding along the sandy beach at the Gulfstream Motel, Maria
yelled at us, "this place is *awesome.*" She wore a strapless top
that covered no more that it needed to, and bottoms that . . .
*whew.**

"Brilliant choice, babe," Meli said in her blue bikini, sitting on
a towel.

"You and the kids made it," I sighed, watching the boys splashing in the water.†

"Your idea." We frolicked on the Gulfstream beach's sand and
water part of our first morning.‡

"Is it me or is our daughter somewhat . . .?" During those first
hours, a five-minute sprinkle amid the dazzling bright sunshine almost torpedoed our pleasures, but we never saw a cloud all day.

"Bold; yes," Despite the non-cloudburst, we got our first motel-
provided skin diving lessons that day. "She wanted to show more."

"And she is." Maria yukked it up with two boys—fellow students. "I'm still not clear about what prompted this," she sighed,
watching the boys capering in the sand and water with three girls
and a boy about their age.

"I have been too absent from you all for a while. Mike and
Connie pointed it out." We watched Maria and her new friends-
who-were-boys plunge face-first into the water.

---

* I was surprised Meli let her leave the suite with it on.
† No thong-thing; I was in a Speedo.
‡ Since we got to the Gulfstream at 3 that morning, we had to get some sleep.

213

"Uh, huh," Meli murmured. After a while, she whispered, "I love you."

"Cozy little museum you've got here," I told the docent/cashier of the Key West History Museum.

"Thanks; we try." On our second and third days, we went museum-hopping to get that out of my system. That, and it was raining and thundering most of those days.

"I'm a connoisseur of museums," I declared, as Jason gaped at a shark's mouth that could swallow him whole. "I teach history." Other museums down there included Fort Zachary Taylor (a state park that had been an active Army fort), and a pirate museum that was nothing more than a lot of skull-and-crossbones flags, skeletons, swords, hats, stuffed parrots, and made-up ship names in a tourist trap/big gift *shoppe* called Pirate's Alley.

"Oh? Where?" The woman/docent/clerk asked. She was probably about my age.

"Crest University."

"Oh, my sister works there. Said it was too cold most of the time."

"It *is* in New England," I nodded. "Known for harsh winters. Who's your sister?"

"Polly . . . "

"She works for me."

"Oh. *Mom* said you were coming. Cold down here this winter, too," she said, holding herself.

I gazed at other tourists in shorts, t-shirts, halters, and tube tops. "Only the natives think so."

"We call ourselves Conches; citizens of the Conch Republic," she declared. "At least you guys brought some rain."

"I noticed it has rained down here every day," I said, wondering at that title—Conch Republic.

"It's not all rain," she declared, grinning at a customer buying some trinkets off the rack. "Most days it's our *liquid sunshine.*"*

---

* An earth scientist explained it to me, but I still have trouble understanding that sudden tropical rainfalls can originate hundreds of miles away from where it comes down.

The Persistent Past

"This was such a fantastic idea," Meli said that night. We left Maria and the boys with cable TV and pizza and enjoyed a grown-up dinner and drinks at the Gulfstream Lounge in the motel.

"Right up there with marrying you."

"Key West wasn't yours; it was the kid's."

"So was marrying you."

"That was Maria's, in a way." She stirred her drink—a rare for her scotch-and-soda—with a straw.

"I sometimes think your life didn't turn out as you planned."

"Well, I had a different plan that June than I had that January. Babies do that." She took a swallow of her lingering drink, the ice long gone. "Municipal planning and management has always been an interest of mine. But . . . "

"But what?"

"I just don't feel inspired to haggle with engineers and unions and politicians and lobbyists for a year just to redirect one storm intercept that takes about six months of work and saves businesses and residents thousands every time it rains."

"Yeah, I get it." I glanced at my watch and remembered I wasn't wearing it. "Think we should check in with the children?"

She glanced out the window. "I see neither smoke, nor fire trucks, nor police cars. They're fine." She stood up, smoothing her short (for her) skirt. "I will take a walk."

We walked along the beach in the glow of a sliver of new moon as the waves lapped soothingly up the hard sand. Other walkers stayed an unobtrusive distance away from each other, most hand-in-hand or arm-in-arm in the soft, salty breeze coming off the warm water. "I wanna go skinny dipping."

"Ever been?"

"No. You?"

"Once, with some buddies."

"Boys or girls?"

"Both." I waited. "There's a clothing-optional, private beach on one of these little islands."

"And how would you know?"

"I got a card from Polly; says she goes there to get sane."

She breathed deep, as she often did when she was going to say Something Important. "Sounds like Polly." Silence as we walked on. "Ya think Maria and the boys would be up for it?"

"The boys, maybe. Maria, unlikely."

We strolled along, watching the waves, the shadows roiling in the shallow water. "The boys would." She grabbed my arm. "Maria says she wants to be more open to new things." Meli had many voices, but this one was new to me: more reflective. "That reading was her idea she sold to the schools; this morning's suit she borrowed from Allison . . . those boys she barely knew . . . "

"They're more interested in what's under that suit than in the rest of Maria," I sighed.

"She wore it for that reason."

"That's why you allowed her to . . . "

"I noticed you didn't object to your daughter's costume."

"I leave that kind of thing to her mother."

"Coward."

"*Buck-buck bacaw.*" Somehow, I did not think my almost-fourteen daughter became an exhibitionist overnight. *Or was it overnight?* "I'm fairly confident no teenage girl would want to go naked in front of her brothers and father in broad daylight, let alone complete strangers," I declared confidently. "Go she might; strip, she will not."

"Think about you and your buddies, babe. Why did you . . .?"

"It was dark; we were on one end of the beach and the girls were on the other end. We could only hear them and see shadows."

"And you were blitzed . . . "

"Very."

"Well, I'll *bet* you Maria will be interested in going just to see . . . "

"That, she might, but strip?"

"With that top, what difference does it make?* OK; we'll make a bet. If she poops out altogether, you and I will take the boys and she can fend for herself. If she goes at least, you carry the towels and a cooler down to the beach. But if she does not at least take that little top off, you'll carry it back, too."

---

* I have wider rubber bands in my desk drawer.

The Persistent Past

"And when she *doesn't* at least take *that* off?"

"I'll carry it *all* back."

"Remember, you guys," Meli admonished as we pulled onto the long road with two hairpin turns that morning, "you don't have to go bare-butt, and this is a secret from everyone."

"Sure," "OK, Mom," "Uh, huh," were the replies.

The sign at the entrance read, OPENS ONE HOUR AFTER DAWN. CLOSES ONE HOUR BEFORE DUSK. About a dozen cars, three vans, nine motorcycles and a *host* of bicycles parked along the shipping-container-walls enclosing the half-full parking lot and part of the road. A burly guy in shorts and a polo shirt who sat at a gap in the containers looked at both sides of the card with a black light, *eyeballed* us, and collected $10 a head for plastic wristbands.

A banner over the entrance read ABSOLUTELY NO CAMERAS BEYOND THIS POINT. STRICTLY ENFORCED. NO UNACCOMPANIED MINORS OR MEN WITHOUT WOMEN OR CHILDREN. ONLY APPROPRIATE ATTIRE ALLOWED.*

Since I lost our bet as to Maria's level of interest,† she helped me shoulder a foam cooler filled with ice and water, two beach bags, and ten beach towels. We followed the kids through the dogleg entrance, expecting . . .

I didn't see what I had been expecting. There were thirty-odd people of all ages on the beach in various states of undress in the brilliant sun. More women were topless than completely *in dishabille*; more men were starkers than suited; many of both sexes wore nothing but a hat or sunglasses. A couple of tents, a dozen cabana domes and scores of towels edged the grass line ten feet inside the wall and fifty feet from the pale-blue-changing-to-azure water that lapped the 300 yard long beach of golden sand. Some wise souls had placed portable toilets and rain barrels with filter systems un-

---

* The card also read: We reserve the right to determine what is appropriate.
† After the boys' glee came her surprised excitement.

obtrusively along the container wall. Notices on every other container declared ABSOLUTELY NO OVERT SEXUAL ACTIVITY ALLOWED ON BEACH OR WITHIN TEN FEET OF TIDE LINE.

"Encouraging," Meli said, following the boys along the grass; Maria walked with me. I dropped the towels in a heap on an open spot, setting the foam cooler down as we stretched five big towels out on the grass before the boys shucked their shorts and shirts and charged for the water. Meli and I took off our shorts and coverups and sat on towels. Maria shed her shirt, ditched her skirt, and sauntered away, looking around curiously.

"We got her here," I sighed. "Kinda wonder why." Two floats fifty yards out from the beach had banner screens flapping from their canopy posts, reading TWO ADULTS ONE HOUR ZERO MINORS.

"Curiosity," Meli mumbled. "She wants to . . . just be." Two women in one-piece suits climbed onto a float, flailing their hair and laughing before rolling up a banner. "I wonder how many people go wild out there?"

"Watch and . . ." The boys joined two naked girls and a naked boy playing with a Frisbee. Next thing we knew, they were running up to their towels and shedding their trunks as fast as they could. An *au naturel* couple ten yards away nodded at us. I nodded genially, and Meli waved. "Jason's idea," Meli mumbled, casually taking *her* top off before donning her coverup again.

"You gonna join the party?" I asked.

"*Ma*ybe." A formidable-looking woman dressed like the gatekeeper—one of several people walking around, twirling nightsticks—stopped two naked boys without wristbands and unceremoniously escorted them to the gate.

Out of the corner of my eye,* I saw Maria giggling with a boy. "That's interesting."

"He's about her age," Meli sighed, keeping an eye on the boys' game, now joined by two more boys-in-the-buff, three half-unclad girls, and another Frisbee.

---

* I was distracted by two women strolling by wearing only wristbands.

The Persistent Past

"Look at them, will ya?" I sighed, watching them splash and play, launching at least three discs, skipping them off the water and sand.

Four women started playing volleyball with an enormous beach ball not far away; two were topless, two were in a state of nature. Four *sans apparel* men they clearly knew joined them.

Maria and the boy parted; she walked towards us, he to our neighbors. "And . . . here she comes." Meli said. On her way, Maria chatted up an older (18 or 19) girl who was tossing her everything away with abandon before she sauntered nonchalantly to another group of young people, waving and calling, "it won't hurt."

"Having fun, honey?" Meli asked Maria.

"He's nice, Mom; his name's Bill," she grinned, donning a dorm shirt with the Crest logo that came down to her knees. She turned, looked at the boy, who smiled and donned a similar garment with a school logo I couldn't identify. "*Well,*" she sighed, "here *goes . . . ours!*" She pushed her bottoms off as he dropped his trunks, pulled the string on her top and dropped it, and rejoined the boy along the water.

"Mutual decision to go that far," Meli loudly observed, pulling the strings on her bottom.

"Yeah, it was," our woman neighbor said. "Bill's fourteen. I'm Dawn Collie;* this is my husband Ed."

"Melanie and Curtis Durand," Meli grinned. "Maria's fourteen in February; two of those boys are Charlie and Jason."

"Three of them are Dolly, Mitch and Florida: ten, nine and six," Ed said, looking around Dawn.

"Charlie's ten; Jason's six," I declared, watching Maria laughing about something with Bill, water lapping around their thighs, their shirts getting wet from the waves.

"Bill hasn't stripped for years," Dawn grinned. The two women dove off the float, now without a stitch on.

"And you didn't think Maria would be interested," Meli mumbled to me.

"Maybe it's the anonymity." Our keyed-up boys came back to our towels as the Collie kids did theirs. Maria and Bill sashayed up

---

* That's what we *heard.*

the beach, giggling.

"Boy, this is fun, Mom," Jason declared, swigging water from a bottle. "Why aren't you . . .?"

"Maybe soon," Meli said, stretching her legs, pulling her bottom out from under her.

"This was your idea." I nudged Meli's shoulder.

"My idea was different."

"Different how, Mom?" Charlie asked after glugging water.

"Different . . . different," she sighed. "I wanted different."

Maria sauntered up to our towels. "You guys having fun?"

"You bet," Jason yelled, running back to join their friends.

"C'mon, Stinky," Charlie shouted at Maria, dashing after him.

"Folks," Maria grinned, "here . . . goes," grabbing the hem of her shirt and turning to look at Bill before saying, "*OK*," and yanked her shirt over her head just as he did, tossed it away, then sprinted to the water.

"Yep," Meli declared as she stood, pulling her top off before jogging to the sea. I shucked my little thong-thing and followed her. Ed and Dawn were right behind me.

I did not feel self-conscious after the first few moments, nor did I get libidinous despite all those beautiful women, and they all were beautiful . . .

But I only saw people. It was liberating because I thought of nothing else for the rest of the day.

We stayed at that beach until it closed, playing Frisbee and volleyball and sunning, necking with Meli on one float while the Collies were on the other, and swimming with family and new friends in all stages of undress.

And we shared in hauling the stuff back to the car.

"Did you mind my going leafless like that, in broad daylight, with strangers?" Meli asked. The boys were in bed finally; our outing wound them up like clock springs. Maria, ebullient, was hanging out with clothed friends at the pool—curfew suspended.

"Too busy thinking about nothing." We sipped wine on our little porch overlooking a little bay.

"Me, too; even while we were making out out there. So tired of the pressures of fashion and decorum." She wore a towel around her neck; I sat on a towel. *

She poured more wine. "The boys were utterly shameless; glad to throw off their inhibitions and their clothes with those other kids."

"The boys didn't surprise me; Maria did."

"She had someone to do it with; a dare." She arched her back.

"That other girl?"

"Bill; the girl was doing it anyway." We sipped. "She can swim like a fish." She topped off our wine glasses. "Not everyone was naked, either . . . I *love* it, babe."

"Me, too, honey." We sipped.

"Clear your head?" She finished her glass and drained the bottle into our glasses.

"Mostly. Wanna go back?"

"Absolutely . . . after a decent interval." Silence. "Bill gave Maria his phone number."

"They're not in a motel?"

"His grandfather's house." We heard a fish jump in the bay and watched a boat cross the mouth of the bay. "We should get together with them again." She drained her glass, stood up, held out her hand. "C'mon."

I chugged my wine down, took her hand, and . . . well, what do you think we did?

"Look at those pilings out there," I said. "There were railroad tracks on 'em once." We spent our fifth day driving to Marathon, an hour up US 1, where we stopped for the best seafood I'd ever had and discovered Key Lime pie.

"Really?" Maria asked, staring out the minivan's window. At a beachwear store in Islamorada, Meli and Maria modeled swimwear for our approval. Meli's piercing gaze and Maria's raised eyebrows convinced the boys and me to do the same for them. Our laughter soon drowned out the rattling hum of the air conditioner.

---

* True to her pre-vacation pledge, Meli spent most of our time while in the motel room together disrobed. I, of course, in solidarity . . .

"What happened to the trains?" Jason asked. All the way up and back, I found it fascinating how those little islands with a single building, many marked *private*, seemed to thrive without trade or industry.

"A hurricane in 1935 wiped 'em out," Meli answered, reading from a guidebook. I decided that many of those little places were commuter homes, vacation rentals, or retirement residences. "*Some* pilings were used to support these bridges between the keys."

"Why are they called 'keys?'" Charlie asked.

"Spanish for 'small island,'" Maria sighed. "Did you bring your journals?"

"Yeah;" "sure," came the responses.

"Here?" she persisted. Charlie reached into his beach bag and produced it; Jason's was on his knee. "Then write 'key' and . . . "

"Look." Jason showed her his journal.

Maria looked. "That's great, Nasty," she said softly, "but we'd rather you didn't draw people at *that* beach, especially with nothing on."

"But you're *pretty* . . ." Jason protested.

"Let's see, Jason," Meli said, reaching back. "It's OK; you're not in trouble." He handed it over; Meli paged through it. "Absolutely beautiful, honey," she smiled, glancing at me. "But nobody needs to see these but us, OK?"

"Can I see?" Charlie asked. Meli handed it to him; Jason just stared out the window. After several minutes, Charlie said, "Maybe you can draw, but you can't spell."

"Why do you say that, Charlie?" I asked.

"He spells 'Dawn' with an O," came the answer.

Mid-afternoon, we pulled over at one of the many ice-and-bait shops for a breather; on that cloudless day, the sun off the ocean was *brutally* hot and bright. "Can I see your journal, Jason?" I asked.

There were winter scenes in Granite Ledge, an image of an airport gate we'd passed through, of shark jaws and fish in the water and cannons. There was naked Meli lying on the sand, Maria and Bill playing volley-Frisbee, a 3/4 bust of Dawn, Charlie and I swimming, and other children and adults on *that* beach and elsewhere in the Keys. All stunningly accurate for any artist, let alone a six-year-old.

And no one sat still for them.

"These are fantastic, Jason," I said, grinning at him. Maria and Meli handed out snow-cones. "But Maria and Mom are right; you shouldn't show some of these to anyone else."

"Know what, Nasty?" Maria said, her hand on his shoulder. "I want *that* one on my dresser at home."

"And I'll keep *that* one on my mirror," Meli smiled.

Jason tore out the pages before he pocketed his journal and slurped his snow-cone.

"Sweetheart, I need to know," I said on our sixth evening in Key West, "why'd you decide you want to strip to the skin in front of your family and a bunch of strangers?" We'd spent that day on an excursion boat going around a couple of Keys, a relaxing if dull time. Maria and I grabbed burgers so Meli and the boys could see a movie we scholars weren't interested in.

She smiled slyly, then gave her *it's OK, Daddy,* face with her clear, brown eyes, and whispered, "I wanted to feel as free as the little kids did."

"Free?"

"Yeah." She shrugged. "I wanted a guy to look at me that way, once, see what it felt like. Bill said he liked my suit. I said it's right next to being naked 'cause it barely covers anything."

"Ted dosen't look at you like that?"

"Not . . . really, no. We make out and stuff, but . . ." She shrugged.

"Then why did you strip?"

"He said he hadn't gone Full Monty for a while. I said I'd take mine off if he'd take his off." She gobbled some fries. "He's got scars from an accident a few years ago; broke him up pretty bad. He said the scars are ugly, but I said I'd read about a lot worse than he could have in Ned's stuff. Then he said we should not think about sex no matter what, so that pressure was off. Thought you'd want to know."

"Thanks for that."

"We started with shirts on, then we got all wet, and we finally said . . . then . . . naked *there* wasn't . . . it's like . . . without clothes or sex, we could see each other as we really are and not worry about how weird our bodies look or how fashionable we are or what we might want to . . . "

"That's . . . is he still self-conscious?"

She smiled a little. "Not anymore. Why did you guys run around naked in front of your family and a bunch of strangers?"

"Your mother's always been more open about that, but I didn't expect . . . now Bill's seen more of you than Ted has. Just remember . . . "

"Yeah; third degree." She looked out the window. "Some second degree with Ted." She grinned widely. "You take me to a nudie beach, go crazy on a raft in broad daylight, then remind me about degrees of exposure?"

I shrugged. "Ted, sweetie, is more possible. You and Bill took sex off the table. You two were hanging off the floats while we . . . "

"We were *not* snooping on you guys *doing it.*"

"We were *not* full crazy . . . "*

"Bill said his parents were, and it wasn't the first time, according to him." She smiled. We finished our dinners, not saying much more until we headed back to the Gulfstream. "Did you love Connie's mom?"

"Still do. Your first, you've got nothing to compare it to—especially if they love you back. You always remember your first with great fondness. I certainly do."

"When did you know you loved Mom?"

"Think? The winter before we got married. Know? When I first heard your heartbeat inside her; you were about twelve weeks." We crossed the street; the Gulfstream was a hundred yards away. Cars were pulling in, unloading. "You love Ted?"

"I dunno," she sighed. "I think about him a lot." We climbed the stairs (it was quite stuffy and smelly in the elevator) but lingered, elbows on the railing, outside our suite.

"Did you think about Ted when you were naked with Bill?"

---

* Close, but . . .

More guests arrived, hustling past us.

"I wasn't thinking about anything. But, um . . . "

"What?"

"You're in pretty good shape for a man of your age, Dad."

"Ah, well . . . thanks."

"Do you think I'm pretty? As a guy, not my Dad?"

"I think you're beautiful, honey."

"I wasn't supposed to ask that, was I?" she asked quietly after several moments.

"It's impossible to separate the man from the dad."

"Even though you're not my bio-dad?"

"I never make that distinction, honey. I'm the only one you've ever had. What do you think of your mother as a woman, not a daughter?"

"She keeps herself in good shape, too."

"Glad you think your parents are fit for your company."

"I think you've been a great dad." She kissed my cheek, whispered, "night, Daddy, love you," and walked into the suite.

"This is heaven," she whispered as we disentangled ourselves just before dawn on our eighth morning in Key West. Maria had taken the boys to an arcade just down the street the night before while we ran loads of laundry. We had heard them come in at about midnight and knew they would sleep for hours. Knowing this, we'd just made love with the sliding door open, the fresh salt breeze wafting in.

"Sure is." We'd spent our seventh day with the Collie's on the Gulfstream's beach,* trying to touch fish while cruising the shallow bottom in diving masks and flippers.

"Gotta admit, you made me love it in the fresh air."

"Especially in the morning," she grinned, arching her back.

"Yeah."

"What do you feel right now?"

"A great deal of love, dear." I glanced out at the sea, the bright morning sun kissing the waves in the distance.

"Serious."

_____

* We finally shook their hands; we were all wearing suits.

"Gratitude. And love. And affection."

Silence for several moments. I heard the chintzy clock radio hands click. "Yeah." It was just before six. She reached for me eagerly . . .

"Wait . . ." We heard Maria start the washer . . .

Gratitude for everything, even when kids interrupt.

"Why do girls smell funny sometimes?" We'd just come back from the shrimp docks, splitting up again for the afternoon. Charlie and I went back to Pirate's Alley for Cuban-seed cigars for Mike and were walking back to the car. We'd watched the cigar rollers make them by hand, one after the other.

"Boys smell funny sometimes, too." Meli and Jason went to an aquarium so he could look at the real sharks—again. "And girls wear perfume."

"Yeah, but . . . girls . . . sometimes . . . smell real bad." Maria and her Gulfstream friends went with a motel excursion group on an island tour and to watch the sunset at Land's End. "Like the bathroom wastebaskets when I empty 'em sometimes."

"Yeah . . . that smell means they're not having a baby."

"Oh." I thought of options for dinner, then . . .

"Did you put a baby in Mom this morning?"

"What makes you think that?" Charlie would be ten in three months; this felt a little early. Though there was that *mean bully* thing, and there were Dolly and Flo and the other women and girls on *that* beach . . .

"We heard you and Mom *kissy-kissy* this morning."

"OK, ah, first," I answered with remarkable calm, "I can't put babies in Mom anymore. I had an operation that keeps me from doing that. Second: that's very impolite to ask, so don't; not anybody. Third: that's really none of anyone's business but Mom's and mine. OK?" *

"OK . . . *sorry.*" We drove towards the aquarium, passing more tourists in tropical costumes and residents bundled up against the

---

* As an academic, I wanted to give my son a complete answer. As a father and husband, I wanted him to know everything his question meant.

The Persistent Past

brutal 75 degree temperatures.* "Do you think Maria's pretty?"

"All fathers think their children are . . . "

"Dolly said you'd say that. Mitch said Maria was beautiful after she took her shirt off."

"What did you think when he said that?"

"I think Maria's pretty with clothes or without, stinky or not." We dodged more traffic, coming in sight of the aquarium.

"Why do you think she took her shirt off?"

"It was fun."

"Is that why you did?"

"Because Jason was gonna. Then it was fun to be bare-butt, especially with girls." We saw Meli and Jason waiting on a bench by the road.

"You know," I said as Meli and Jason got in, "places like that are the only places you should go bare-butt."

"Flo kept saying that," Jason said. "She said she only does it there, too."

"Mitch says Dolly does it at home a lot," Charlie added. "Can we go back?"

"We'll see," Meli answered, winking at me.

"He said what?" We all went to the pool after dinner while we waited for Maria, then bundled the boys into bed.

"They heard us this morning." After Maria got back, Meli and I retired ourselves and Maria dove into the pool with her friends.

"And he asked about . . .?"

"Yep."

"Feels early."

"That's what I thought."

"He likes girls at nine."

"Maybe."

Silence, listening to the night sounds of late check-ins, a loud TV below us. "This was the best idea you've ever had."

"Next to marrying you."

---

* Though it never went below 70 when we were there, nights were chilly because of the humidity.

"Damn right. Let's just cuddle, OK?" I spooned behind her. The loud discussion below our room was only slightly distracting. "This is nice," she whispered.

"This is beautiful."

"Our children are growing up so fast."

"Keep feeding 'em and they do that."

"When did you know about sex?"

"Thirteen. Between Karen, Joanie, and the neighborhood, I got a synthesis of The Talk that summer." The discussion in the other room got slightly louder. "You?"

"My first period; so, thirteen. Maria started at twelve."

"And you gave it to her . . . "

"Connie did most of it before." Silence. "I just wanted to skinny-dip with you, so we might *kissy-kissy* in the open air." The discussion ended; they switched off the TV. She placed my hand on her breast. "That feels better."

"Are we going to do more than cuddle?"

She wiggled her hips. "Part of you wants to . . . "

"Hard to resist such a sensuous . . . "

"*Shaddap.*" She reached down. "Nothing fancy . . . "

Not fancy, but it was splendid.

"Like fishing much?" I asked Meli, sitting on our little porch sipping wine on the evening of our eleventh day in Key West, a full-moon Christmas Eve.

"Never did it much. The boys took to it right away." The Collies invited us on a big fishing boat on Christmas Eve. We'd spent our ninth day doing laundry, sightseeing, watching Navy planes take off and land on Boca Chica to the north, and recreational shopping.

"And Maria, too," I answered. On our tenth day, we ran into the Collies at *that* beach, when they invited us to go fishing.[*]

"That was because of Bill."

"Maybe." Jason, Florida and Mitch looked for dorsal fins on the boat, claiming every fifth wave could have been an approaching

---

[*] I checked the hotel bill later; a local call was made from Maria's room the day before.

shark. Charlie and Dolly held poles while sitting in the "fighting chairs" as we trolled, occasionally hooking red snappers, dolphins and bonita that the boat's captain and mate took off the hooks. "They like the freedom of no sex between them. Said they wouldn't think about it on *that* beach. . . . "

She looked over at me, knitting her brows. "She said that?" Maria and Bill sat on what was called the flying bridge, trolling, catching fish sometimes, but mostly just chatting.

"Yep." The adults sipped watery cocktails on the bow deck, where we found Ed taught history and genealogy at a small Michigan college, and Dawn was an insurance adjuster.

Silence for a long time before she whispered, "Freedom. Yeah; that's it. Don't have to worry about how saggy my boobs and butt are getting."

"They're fine, dear," I answered.

"Don't tell me you don't notice . . . "

"I don't look, dear, unless you tell me to."[*]

"Uh, huh." Silence; she sipped her wine. "You looked at Dawn."

"Yeah, then decided it was rude." I finished my wine.

"Well, I feel no shame in telling you I looked at Ed and Dawn and you and my children and theirs and decided that we are in great shape as a family."

"But that beach is the only place we'll ever go naked together: absolutely no . . . "

"No. Tried a group grope once. Creepy."

"That's one word for it."[†]

Though we didn't make love to seal our agreement—it was getting wearing—we cuddled for a while before we drifted off.

"Oh," I nodded, looking at the family crest in the *Colloloys'* great room on Christmas Day. "That's how it's spelled . . . "

"Yeah," Ed nodded. "Colloloy *was* a mining village in north-

---

[*] Absolutely true; I swear.
[†] Another is confusing. One snowed-in weekend in the dorms . . . .

western Wales; long gone, now. Pronounced *collie* in Welsh; everybody else wants to pronounce it *col-o-loy*."

We met Ed's father, who owned the big four-bedroom house, and enjoyed their company for most of the day. The grownups watched the kids chase balls and Frisbees around the backyard of pounded dirt and patches of grass. Maria and Dawn dominated the all-family volleyball game before dinner, but I can't remember if we kept score.

"Dawn," I asked her during the feast that followed, "you said you've been going to *that* beach for a while . . . "

"Beaches like it," she answered. "I've been coming to them since I was Flo's age. Met Ed at one." She looked at Ed, who was chatting with Meli. "Ed and I grew up down here."

"I got my card from a friend at work."

"Ed's Dad's still a member of the Association. So was my family when we lived here, but my folks are in Tampa now."

"What 'association?'"

She looked . . . sly? Coy? "You're cute dressed and not." She smiled. "It dosen't have a name. Only county residents can get one of those cards." She touched my arm. "What's your friend's name?"

"Polly *Newman's* her maiden name . . . "

"Polly Newman baby-sat for my brothers. She got some scholarship . . . "

"A Jenson Grant in '68. She teaches at the same school *I* do now."

"Huh," she nodded. "Small world. Tell her Dawn and Ed said 'hi.'"

"Um," I mumbled, "is there a place where a couple could take an *adult* night swim?"

"That was different for a Christmas dinner," she sighed, casually stepping out of her panties and depositing them on a towel with the rest of her clothes on Christmas night. "This is the first Christmas I've ever spent away from Granite Ledge."

"It was good," I said, doffing my briefs, listening to the lolling surf twenty yards away.

"How are the boys, really?" The kids had a sleepover at the Colloloy's that night. She stood at the water's edge, gazing out at the dark sea, the tide lapping around her feet. "Are they gonna brag about . . . ?"

"I don't know," I said, stepping behind her. "I doubt it. Besides, who'd believe them?"

"We'll talk to them tomorrow." She sauntered into the water; I followed.

Later, in the waning, glowing full moon, making love on the beach, she whispered, "*this* was what I wanted."

"A brilliant end to a fabulous vacation, babe," Meli sighed, lying on a towel. "This cabana was even more brilliant."

"Yeah." The Colloloy's had three folding cabanas; this one was about four feet high and about seven in diameter. They were in another not far away. "Maria knows why we borrowed it."

"All the kids know why they're out here." We listened to the sounds of the beach, the ocean waves, the kids doing what kids do when bare-ass on a beach with scores of others. "Do you find me as physically desirable as you did?"

"We just spent thirteen days . . . "

"That's mechanics, Curtis, and habit." She put on her *get serious now* face. "Habit can mask feelings."

"If any other woman offered herself to me right now, I'd tell them I already have the most sensuous, responsive and generous lover I could ever imagine, and who I find more desirable, physically and emotionally, than all the rest I've ever known save *one.*"

"Joanie." She stared at me for a long moment. "The first genuine love is always the most memorable."

"Yep."

"And this is brilliant." She shifted and pressed herself against me. We made long, languid, sweet, ever-memorable love before snoozing side-by-side as the world cavorted outside.

"I'll send Charlie in first," Meli sighed as she left.

Charlie, damp and red, sat down swiftly in the cabana's 2/3rds closed shade a few minutes later as Meli kept Jason and Maria busy in the water. "Mom and I want you to understand you really *can't* talk about . . ." I started.

"Being naked with girls," he said. "Yeah; Dolly and Flo and Maria keep saying that."

"What do you feel about seeing naked girls here?"

He looked thoughtful in his almost-ten-year-old way. "I kinda knew what girls looked like; just smaller Moms without *hair* down there." He knitted his brow. "Most girls are pretty. I don't feel about Maria's like I do Dolly or Flo or any of the other girls; she's my sister, even if she's not your kid."* He looked at me earnestly. "She feels like a sister should, I guess, *half*-sister or not."

"That's good. Just remember: we can't talk about *here*. OK?"

"OK. Can I go?"

Jason, even more reluctantly, sat down with me, panting. "Mom and I want to remind you . . ." I started. Meli played beach-ball volleyball with Charlie and three other people.

"I'm not supposed to talk about seeing naked girl parts here."

"That's right. How do you feel about that?"

He shrugged. "I don't talk about where I hide my Rangers from dumb ol' Megan, either."

"Do you like seeing naked girl parts?"

He looked out at everyone playing outside. "I like . . . naked is different." He looked back at me. "Naked means I don't have to hide."

"Hide . . . what?"

"Hide *me*." He shifted from sitting to kneeling. "When I'm dressed, I have to get kids moving. When we're all bare-butt, they move anyway."

"So, naked kids are . . .?"

"Just people. So are naked grownups. With clothes on, they're kids and grownups." He concentrated oddly. "I see their girl parts when we're naked, but they don't matter. I like that."

"Maria said kind of the same thing."

---

* Maria's birth-family sent cards, photos, and visited occasionally. We needed to tell the boys something, and went with truth.

"Yeah?" I nodded. "She's pretty smart for a stinky girl."

"Girls are smart, too."

"I guess." He looked out at the crowd; Maria and Charlie, Meli and Bill teamed up at volleyball. "Even if she's not your kid, she's Mom's and I love her, anyway." He looked back at me. "You gonna have her in here, too?"

"I'll talk to her outside. Ask her to join me?"

"You wanted to talk to me, Dad?"

"Yeah, honey. Just wanted to make sure you and the boys get the same message: we can't talk about this beach . . . "

"Yeah, I know." She shook out her hair, rubbed her scalp.

"Are you gonna tell Ted?" The boys didn't have Significant Others they confided in; Maria did.

"About Bill, sure, and the other guys I've met, but nothing happened. I won't tell him about *here* . . . yet." She turned away and whipped her hair, then turned to me and suddenly transformed into a stunningly beautiful and mature young woman. "What's this vacation done for you and Mom?"

"We've *been* good, honey."

"But are you *better?*" She put her hand on the cabana; I thought she'd say something Very Grown Up, but she gave me a sly wink and an upturned corner of her mouth just as Dawn crawled out of their cabana and dashed for the water; Ed was right behind her.

"We've been OK, honey."

"And . . . your . . . perspective?"

"The past has moved behind you guys in the cosmos of my life."

She winked . . . slowly. "Good" She turned away again, then back to me, becoming my about-to-be-fourteen-year-old daughter once again. "That it?"

"How about you? Have you gained perspective, gotten Ned and Angie out of your head for a while?"

She blinked, looked over my shoulder and waved at a new friend. "Mine's been better than it *was* ever since I took my shirt off two weeks ago, Pops . . . That . . .?" She waved at another friend.

"What would you say to turning the Hill 90 entries into an article?" What I'd been thinking of for months *just* came out.

"We said we weren't going to . . . ." She planted her hands on her hips, then gave a thoughtful look. "Article?"

"There are magazines that concentrate on WWI, and more than a few on military history. If we could interest one of them, we might drum up interest, find a publisher for the entire Great War diary in time for the centennial."

Distracted as Bill grabbed a bottle of water, she stretched her arms out, craning her neck. "Those eleven days . . . transcribe, verify . . . the whole enchilada?" She shrugged. "I can see that." She stretched out a hand. "We're done, now! Come swim with us, Dad! Bill: come on! Race ya to the floats!"

History was so far from my mind, I couldn't even remember how I got there. But, I shall long remember my slow jog to the sea, side-by-side with Maria and Bill, followed by Meli and the boys, how *serene* that tepid and salty water was, in the altogether with my loved ones and friends.

The profession of the past transformed from being my life to being my livelihood on *that* beach.

The Memoirs

I showed two entries we transcribed for our proposed article on the overhead. "OK, now, what might we make of this?"

30ᵗʰ November. Hill 90. [Pencil date and entry]
Pen became a casualty yesterday.
It is absolutely still on most days between about three in the afternoon and full dark; the Canucks call it Toilet Time, when we can dump without too much interference from shrapnel, gas, or bullets.
Ground attack last night; they were in the outpost line behind a rolling barrage with green cross minutes after it started. My only reaction was, oh, [expletive]. *There was no time to lose; moved a hundred yards down the hill to my forward PC. Saw hundreds of ghostly lumps, Huns moving, crossing the OP, moving in flare after flare, both ours and theirs. One minute they're there, the next they're . . .*
[Illegible; scratched out] *remember who was down there. Our casualties were not heavy, but we feel them no less. Canucks lost more than we did, of course, but they have more to lose.*

1ˢᵗ December, Hill 90. [Pencil date only]

"What year is this?" Sharon asked.
"1917," I said. This class, Sources as Questions, was a graduate

elective that, much to everyone's surprise, enrolled nearly 100 students in three sections.

"Where's this?" Elias asked.

"Hill 90 was barely in Flanders, on the border with France," I answered. I was admittedly the only instructor for the class, now in its second run.*

"What's with the brackets?" Phil asked.

"Our transcription will preserve a disintegrating and often very profane record," I sighed, "and we feel it's important to keep as much of the feel of the original as possible without his explicit vulgarities."

"What's an OP?" Max asked.

"Outpost line," I answered. "Everyone's impression of the front lines in WWI was a trench. Well, they are wrong." Since I had started this class years before, I had used Truxton documents as examples. But Ned's diaries seemed to be more useful.

"That's true," Larry mused. "The front was less well defined on the ground than it was on the maps."

"What's green cross?" a voice asked.

"Chlorine, phosgene and diphosgene gas; pulmonary agents," a voice in the back answered. "The Germans started marking their artillery rounds with colored crosses in 1917."

"Thank you," I called. "Your name?"

"Vihaan Tagore, sir," the voice answered. "Just call me . . . "

"Vinnie," a young woman's voice called, followed by some chuckles.

"The day-after-day impression most people have is wrong." I switched off the projector. "You'll be seeing more of these diary entries over this course, besides other material. The basis of this course is to familiarize you with the kinds of questions you need to be asking when you evaluate sources. One question none of you asked was . . . "

"Who wrote this?" Vinnie said loudly.

"That one, yes," I answered. I told them about Ned Steele and his diaries (though many already knew), all the work Maria and I

_____

* It was also the only class I was teaching that semester.

had already done. But the one question I was not ready for was . . .

"Who transcribed this?" It came from way in the back of the room, where only a few questions had originated.

"This one was done by my daughter, Maria."

"The kid?" Someone else asked off to the side.

"She'll be fourteen next month."

"I thought she was a student . . ." the side voice replied.

"Middle school. Why?"

"Been seeing her in the Holding Room all summer, then on the 3ʳᵈ Floor this fall,[*] is all," the voice answered. "We talked about the school; I asked about her major, thinking it had to be history, and she said 'undeclared.'"

I blinked momentarily nonplussed. "Middle school dosen't require a declared major," I said in a measured tone, but met with some chuckles. "Has anyone else seen her in Archives?" Several hands shot up. "When we're done here today, I'd like to speak to all of you with your hands up. Nothing bad, just a dad's concern for his child."

Fifteen minutes later, three men and four women gathered near the podium. "Now, like I said, I just want to know about her interactions with you. Did she start them or . . .?"

"I never talked to her," an older student said. "She didn't look up from whatever she was reading."

"She sounded smart," a Hispanic woman said. "I asked what she was doing, said she was helping her father and learning a great deal about WWI. Said she wanted to know more. We talked about it for a while."

"I didn't try to pick her up or anything, Doc," an older[†] student declared. "Too young for me. But I gave her a sweatshirt for her shoulders one Saturday afternoon 'cause she was shivering. The kid she was with . . . "

"That'd be her boyfriend, Ted," I said.

"Anyway, he'd already wrapped his sweatshirt around her feet."

---

[*] The Steele Collection started moving out of Holding and up to a 3rd Floor space in October.

[†] Possibly as old as 28.

"I grabbed a pica stick from her," another woman said. "She said she was done with it. I thought she was too young to be in college . . . "

You're right.

"Hey, Boss," Polly smiled when I came to her office that afternoon. "How was your vacation?"

"Fabulous," I answered, handing her the card back. "Ed and Dawn and your mom and sister say 'hi.' Your mom says . . . "

She looked surprised, then puzzled, then amused. "Yeah, I got my earful when I called on Christmas. Ed and Dawn are still together? Dawn and Ed *Collie* by now?"

"Yeah, they've got four kids, live in Michigan, but Ed's father's still in Key West. Met them at *that* beach." I briefly described our interaction.

She chuckled. "Yeah, that's them, all right; haven't seen them since I left for the Jenson, but I've been down there nearly every year since '76." She smiled enigmatically. "Feel the magic?"

"Yep."

She looked more thoughtful. "My first time was wondrous; I was twelve. Took Simon on our honeymoon. At first, he didn't want to . . . "

"Strip in front of strangers?"

"Right; thought I was nuts. Then, after about a half hour, he just jumped up and . . . "

"Right there before God and everybody. So did Meli, after Maria."

"That's how it happens." She looked out the window at the snow-covered yews. "We go down at least once a year just to get right in our heads, make everything else disappear. Conceived Sandy in a tent there one morning; we ran into the sea knowing I was pregnant. I was carrying Neil when I lay in the tide, my enormous belly awash, stretch marks and all, Sandy giggling next to me, thinking of nothing, feeling nothing, not even those guys in Somalia." She grinned. "It was wonderful."

"I'll bet. Do your kids talk about . . .?"

"Nope. They feel the magic, too. Know if they talked about it, they couldn't go anymore." She tapped the card on her desk, put on her hungry, *take-me-now* look I'd seen before our sexathon. "Spring break?"

We'll see . . .

"Hi, honey," I knocked on Maria's door that night. "Got a minute?" Midge gazed up at me from the sofa, then looked down at Smudge in alarm as she invaded his space.

"Sure, Dad; c'mon in." She dropped a long sweatshirt on as Smudge strolled into her kitchenette.

"So, how's this semester going?"

"First week, it's hard to tell." Midge ascended the sofa back, watching Smudge.

"I guess." I told her about the brief session after class. "You're taking Ted up there a lot?"

"He's interested, and it's lonely work." Smudge padded into the bedroom, jumped up on the bed.

"It is that," I agreed. "Are you working more hours than the project pays you?"

"Working, no. Reading?" She looked embarrassed. "Yeah."

"We told you, your schoolwork comes first." Midge prepared to leap.

"It does, Dad, but . . ." She looked . . . contented? "We do homework during the week, then we go up there on weekends. That stuff really interests me."

"A student loaned you a sweatshirt . . . "

"One of your students?" I nodded. "That was late last summer. He's a nice guy." Midge did a skillful double-jump onto the bed and the chase was on.

"I'm sure he was. Just limit the hours, OK, honey?"

"OK, Dad," she grinned. Two furry blurs dashed out the door, pounded up the steps.

I glanced around, seeing Jason's sketch of her taped to the wall. "So, that's . . . "

"The best image of me anywhere." She sighed. "Looks like freedom." She shook her hair out of a scrunchie. "Ted thinks it's magnificent." Hoofbeats in the living room, the kitchen, all the way into our room at the far end of the house.

"He's seen it?"

"Yep." She blushed slightly. "Felt, *not* seen, the model."

Good, honey.*

"She told you, on her own?" Meli asked, holding my hand.

"Yep." With everyone in bed and the wind off the mountains howling a -34 wind-chill, we were close together. The cats huddled by the heat vent next to the fireplace in the living room.

"Like Sarah and I thought."

"Yep."

"So much for degrees of exposure."

"I tried that down there."

"She probably laughed."

"Called me on it; 'take us to a nudie beach and talk about degrees of exposure,' she said." Silence. "Her birthday's Friday. Do we think a mature young woman of fourteen as sensible and openly honest as our Maria Helen really wants dinner at a cafeteria with her family on a Friday night?"

"One who's made a platonic-by-agreement boyfriend on a clothing-optional beach yet still limits her makeout boyfriend to second base? No; Let's give her a real present."

"Happy birthday, baby," Meli smiled at Maria that morning.

"Thanks, Mom," Maria sighed, sitting at the breakfast table. "Wish it was Monday after next and I could be off school."

"Happy birthday to you," the boys sing-song-chorused in grade-school fashion, "you live in a zoo! You look like a monkey! And you smell like one, too!" as they dashed into the kitchen carrying a pasteboard banner they put together the night before,

Maria, nonplussed, smooched each of her brother's cheeks. "Thanks, Nasty; Weird-o," she murmured.

I leaned down, pecked her cheek, and said. "Happy day, honey."

"Thanks, Dad," she smiled.

---

* Yeah, I know, my parents would have murdered my sisters if they'd known. But atitudes change.

The Persistent Past

"Where's dinner tonight?" I asked Meli.

"That cafeteria in Old Town," Meli said, on cue, "with Connie and them."*

"Yeah, but," I interrupted, "I think Maria and her friends might like something . . . else."

Meli gazed at me, then at Maria, then finished giving the boys their cereal. "Suggestions?"

"This year, how about they get Fiorelli's Pizza† here while *we* go out for dinner? It's not chateaubriand at the Ledge House,‡ but . . . "

Meli said, "yeah, you can handle that, Maria," winking at me. "We'll do presents and cake when the boys get home after school."

"Just like we planned, right?" I agreed, nodding at Meli.

"Right." Meli agreed. We both saw Maria's ebullient response out of the corner of our eyes; the boys were too intent on their breakfast to notice.

"Hey, Mike," I called, walking into his shop the next week. "You called?"

"Curtis," he yelled from somewhere in the back. "I'll be there in a minute."

Looking around, I saw that a dual pedestal desk had replaced the spinning wheel in his display window. A highboy dresser in the same cherry finish stood next to it. After a few minutes of browsing, Mike emerged, wiping his hands. "I found this at another auction." He held out a framed photo, sepia with age, of several soldiers posed in a group. "This is your guy."

A sign in the middle of the line read, "Camp Penobscot Staff, 1928." I looked where he pointed and, despite the scale . . . it was Ned, all right, with a dozen other men in uniform. "Nice find, Mike."

He handed me a yellowed, crumbling paper. "This was taped to the back; came off when I unpacked it."

----

* It was also Mike's 27th birthday; we'd be meeting them.
† The best in town, bar none.
‡ The only restaurant in Granite Ledge with no the prices on the menus.

L to R: Maj. E. Steele, Cmdt.; Cpt. M.
Brick, Adjt.; Cpt. J. Willis, Supply; Cpt.
C. Isham, Personnel . . .

"Well, now," I grinned, ignoring the other names. "Now I know what Mike Brick, Jack Willis and Corey Isham looked like."

"They important?" Mike asked.

"Brick and Isham met Ned in OCS; Ned was Brick's pallbearer in '89. Willis' nickname was 'Pirate;' a real scrounger. Isham was reassigned out of the 432nd in '18."

"If your outfit wants this photo, it's $50," Mike said.

"I'll get you a check. It's material like this that helps to give their story life beyond all that paper. Anything on the Great War secretary?"

"Yeah; I found the maker, Dutton & Sons of Manchester—an English firm like I thought. They made several of one requested pattern, thinking if one sold, they could sell more of the same thing. Did that for nearly a hundred years. They made as many as a hundred of this pattern; it got as far afield as India. Dutton went out of business in 1941."

I breathed deep of the old wax, musty material and other smells in his shop. "How's your business doing, Mike?"

"It ain't bad, really," he answered. "My turnover's gotten better after the first of the year. I can sell musical instruments better earlier in the semester, buy 'em later when the kids give up. Artwork, I can move better now when I go on-line with it. Invested in a digital camera so I can . . . "

I liked Mike, even if he had a tendency to chatter too much about not a lot.[*] As long as he was good to Connie and my grandchildren, he was OK. I suppose I was much the same when I got started on some historical subject or another, and I was on that track in my head when I suddenly realized he'd asked me" . . . so we're still on for dinner at your place Saturday?"

"Far as I know, yeah. See you then."

*   *   *

---

[*] In my opinion, anyway.

"Gotta tell you guys something," Mike said after our meatloaf. While they hadn't been cool, neither had they been warm during dinner.

"OK," Meli said, glancing at the boys. The cats watched from their perches in the living room. Midge did a sniff test of the babies in their carriers every time they came over; Smudge did it the first time, and not since.

"Some buddies and I crashed a dorm party at State in '86 and this girl . . . she got pregnant and . . . ."

"You were sixteen?" Meli asked, glancing at the boys and Maria.

"Barely," Mike said.

"Can the boys . . .?" Maria asked in semi-panic, glancing at Connie and Meli.

"Up to you, Mom," Connie said. "Like we talked about, they need to know actions have consequences." Meli nodded. "Go on, Mike."

"She had a girl, Antoinette, in '87," Mike said heavily. "She'd filched my brand-new driver's licence that night, figured out the connections to the family fortune."

"Should I take . . .?" Maria gulped.

"No," Meli said evenly. "They can listen and learn. So, a daughter, Mike; when did you find out?"

"*Mother-dear* found out almost as soon as she was born because Leslie—the mother—knew about the family from the society columns and went to New York looking for money."

"Yeah; no doubt," I said, watching the boys, who looked puzzled. Butter would not have melted in Connie's mouth.

"I couldn't even remember what Les looked like before I saw her on my 18th birthday in '89, when *Mother-dear* brought her and Toni around and handed Dad a bill for the child support she'd been paying." Mike sighed.

"*What . . .?*" Meli asked.

"You don't want to know the politics of my family and their bucks, Melanie," Mike answered. "Old money gets moldy. I've never tried to hide her since I've known; couldn't if I wanted to. I'd been paying Les *some* since '91."

"When did you tell Connie . . .?" I asked.

"First date, before we finished our salads." Connie answered. "We pay more support now. I called Toni Mike's youthful indiscretion before the wedding. Now she's my step-daughter."

"Why are you telling us this now, Mike?" Meli asked.

"Tell 'em the rest of it, Mike," Connie said quietly.

"Yeah. *Mother-dear* wants her Corporation to take a more active role in the school's governance, and claims she deserves a seat on the Regents because . . . "

"Her daughter-in-law is soon to be the proud owner of a Regent's seat." I sighed, glancing at a suddenly confused Meli. The boys were beyond puzzled. Maria looked alarmed.

"Mom dosen't know?" Connie asked, glancing at her, then me.

"No." I gave her a capsule rendition of the Regents situation, but leaving out the Hardin shares we would inherit sooner than later.

"The rest, Mike," Connie prompted.

"She'll be demanding a restructuring. She wants all seats to be equal. And . . ." he paused, "the Corporation claims the school is broke, and is eyeballing the grounds and the Archives . . . "

"She wants to sell us off in pieces, Dad," Connie sighed.

"How *can* she . . .?" Meli started, surprised. "*Her* Corporation? *What . . .?*"

"When all that started," I said, knowing I'd never pondered the consequences, "we heard about the Klein's saying they were finally getting their feet under the school's table; we thought little of it because there's so many of 'em."

"They never owned enough to have much say," Connie added. "Now . . ." she shrugged. "If they can restructure the Regents, and the Corporation pleads poverty by looking at the books *just* the wrong way . . . "

"They can sell the school," I finished.

"And they can cook those books," Mike says. "*Mother-dear* is an expert at finding people who can do that kind of shady work for the right money. She's done it before . . . "

"So we wanted you to hear about this unholy mess before it hit the newspapers, which it will, sometime," Connie sighed before

The Persistent Past

grinning at the kids. "You have a thirteen-year-old niece named An-toinette—Toni—living in New York City."

"Tell 'em the rest, Connie," Mike said.

"Yeah, well," Connie took a deep breath. "Toni's mother says she'll have everything taken care of if . . ." she bit a lip, "I sell them Submerged Stone."

"*You will not do it,*" Meli declared, staring at Connie so hard it probably hurt.

"It's worth a good deal less than the school, Mom," Connie said, not looking at her. "Without the school, Granite Ledge is just . . . "

"The quarries," I said.

"And I love this place the way it is," Connie finished.

"So who's this Leslie who's got this much influence?" I asked, not quite seeing the connections.

"The way the law and public opinion are in New York nowa-days," Mike severely intoned, "she can say all kinds of *shit* that ain't true and get away with it. This woman who is the mother of my other daughter can charge me with rape now."

I glanced at the kids; I believe they'd gone numb.

"But if we sell Stone," Mike said, "*Mother-dear* says she'll back off the school and me, not demand a seat on the Regents or try to auction off the place. And all just to hurt Dad's family."

"Animosity there?" I asked.

"They hadn't spoken for fifteen years before Dad died," Mike answered. "Didn't even send me a card after he passed, but she con-tested his will long enough to soak a few thousand out of his estate."

"Well," I said, "boys, what did you learn here today?"

Charlie blinked. "Girls can be mean?"

"OK; Jason?"

"Not all of 'em are mean. Connie and Maria and Mom are still girls, yeah?"

"Maria, get the boys to bed," I said. "Enough excitement for one night."

As Connie and Mike packed the babies up, Meli and I finished in the kitchen silently. "I couldn't tell you about the Regents, honey," I mumbled as they left.

"Yeah," Meli nodded, heading off to the boy's rooms.

I stood in the living room, trying not to think about these revelations, wondering dimly about our future. *I don't know many of the Regents well. If I became one of them . . . I'm not a politician or a manager; I teach history . . . what can I bring to the Regents?*

"Daddy," Maria said softly as I gazed out her window later. "Mama's sad."

"I know, sweetheart," I sighed. "Because I kept it from her . . ."

"I don't think that's it," she said. "I've got midnight oil to burn." She kissed my cheek. "Night."

"You'd be a member of the Committee of Regents?" We were in the living room, fully dressed and wrapped in a blanket. The steady wind outside howled; it had been howling since mid-morning. The weather report said it was -16 at the airport with a -41 wind chill.

"You heard right," I sighed. "Connie buys Christian's seat . . ." I wondered if any of the kids grasped Tina Klein's threatening consequences, though I was pretty sure the boys understood about their niece.

"Yeah . . . how could you have kept all this from me for so long?"

"They asked me to," I said again. "This is a big deal, obviously."

"Yeah, obviously. I'm not clear on where Connie got that kind of money." I explained Joanie's last legacy. "For an old girlfriend, pal, she sure did well enough for us."

"She did it for Connie . . . "

"And she handed* Connie to us."

"Almost ten years ago, now."

"That long?" Silence. "Yeah, I guess."

"I think I can effect constructive changes in how this outfit works."

"You could also be a bull in a china shop."

"The other Regents would stop me from doing too much damage."

"Yeah." She rested her head on my shoulder. "Connie showing

---

* Joan awarded me custody of Connie using a peculiarly Texan, handwritten document of a kind often used to bequeath cattle.

up on our doorstep bonded us, I think, even more than Maria did."

"Yeah?"

"A pregnant teenager knocks on the door, looking for you. Says she's the daughter of your first girlfriend . . . "

"And your first thought was . . .?"

"Same as yours. But she said no, and I believed her."

"Before I got home?"

"She volunteered it, yeah." We lay silent, listening to the night sounds. "Then came Charlie, then Jason, and Connie was still *so* . . . "

"Yeah." Connie was like a live-in nanny/maid/chauffeur/cook while she went to school for the duration of both of Meli's pregnancies, with nary a peep of demur.*

"Connie bonded your past to mine, babe."

"Yeah?"

"Yeah. Let's go to bed."

"Let's."

On Monday, I called . . . "Hello, Alan Jenson," wanting to get ahead of what I believed was an oncoming disaster.

"Alan, Curtis Durand."

"Curtis, how are ya, pal?"

"I've been better. I wanted to give you a heads-up . . . "

But he interrupted before I got too far. "Let's meet for lunch in the Exec at—say one?"

"Sure."

When I got to the unadorned anteroom of the Executive Dining Room, the *maitre d'affaires* smiled, said, "good afternoon, Dr. Durand," genially, and invited me in. I wasn't sure what to do with myself[†] for those long minutes other than drinking coffee before Alan arrived.

The Exec—what everyone called it—had space for a hundred people, and setups for four at each of four small tables that afternoon. Three window walls looked out on the Quad, most of the

---

* She did take time out to deliver Johnnie in February of '88, though.
† Other than wonder *he knows my name?*

school, and, in the distance, the Gray Mountains, and Granite Ledge—the domains of the owners of Crest University. "Glad we could talk on such short notice, Curtis," Alan said, sitting down. "We could do this anywhere, but here is safer."

"Secrets and more secrets, Alan?" I asked while the *maitre d'* poured his coffee; he nodded. "So as I was saying . . ." I told him what I understood from Connie and Mike's revelations of Saturday night, not embellishing anything with my probably faulty understanding of what was happening.

"Curtis, from the moment I met that Connie, I knew she was special," Alan said when I finished. "But she's not gonna sell, is she?"

"She's inclined to, Alan, because she wants to save the school and Granite Ledge . . . "

"Yeah," he grunted. "I'll talk to her."

"You'll . . .?" I started.

" *We* lease equipment from her firm, too. Tina Klein's understanding of how to make a takeover of this place work is way off, buddy," he said, nodding to the *maitre d'*, standing by an open door in the paneled wall. "What'll ya have for lunch, Curtis?"

"Ah, what can I . . . I haven't seen a menu . . .?"

"What would you *like*, sir?" the *maitre d'* asked with a small grin. My earlier visits to the Exec offered small buffets.

"Ask for what you want," Alan said breezily. "See what they can make of it."

"Ham sandwich on rye?" I asked timidly.

"Virgina baked or Black Forest uncured, sir?" *the maitre d'* asked *ever* so politely.

"Um . . . Virginia?"

"Hot or cold, sir?"

"Hot?"

"Light or dark rye, or pumpernickel, sir?"

"Light? With hot mustard?"

"Lettuce? Tomato? Fennel? Olive oil? Onions?

"Ah, a little lettuce?"

"Chips? Fries?"

"Fruit salad on the side?"

"And to drink?"

"Just coffee, thanks."

"Excellent choices, sir. Mr. Jenson?"

"Chicken strips lightly breaded, please, David; three onion rings and a side salad with bleu cheese; hold the cucumbers and tomatoes."

"Excellent, sir," David glided away.

"So, Curtis, get used to this place." Alan steepled his hands, elbows on the table. "When you join the Regents, it is yours to use from five A to seven P any day without a reservation for up to four people; anytime and any number of people *with* a reservation."

I dimly wondered if I had just ordered a $200 lunch. "Expensive?" Most of the places we dined out didn't have tablecloths or linen napkins or glass water goblets, let alone this spectacular view.

"It's one perquisite of the Regents. That and better parking; few other things. But," he sighed, "Tina's rattling her one saber."

"If you mean a teenage girl in New York, yeah," I said. "Got my family kinda . . . "

"You didn't tell anyone about Moe's shares, did you?"

"No; not even Meli. Moe said . . . "

"He's right; not yet."

I cleared my throat. "Where are the Klein's in the founding story?" Everyone knew about the pirate/privateer Captain Crest, who started the town and the school to attract families to the area, and Tiberias Jenson, and the marriage that fused the families together. People said the Kleins also played a part, but it was unclear what that was.

"They helped fund the school's expansion into a university. The Klein money was simply too little and too late to have a major seat at the ownership table."

"That might help explain the Klein's attitudes at Connie's wedding," I mused.

"No doubt. Devota still holds their family strings, but her mother was old Jacob's third wife, so her bloodline is pretty thin in the school." Alan gazed out the window at the mountains in the distance. "Curtis, we may not know each other very well, but the

Regents trust you." He sipped his coffee. "Angelina* was very impressed with you back in '87. John,† not as much, but he respected your integrity. Now, Adam‡ has a different take on you personally, as do James and Judy§, but we all think you'll be an asset to the Regents."

"You've discussed . . . ?" I asked almost timidly.

"A great deal," he smiled. "But to business . . . and Tina Klein. Christina Jenson Klein has been a pain in this school's backside for a quarter century. We voted to allow her to own part of the Crest Corporation as a sop. I'm not sure why Chuck married her, anyway." He shrugged. "She was never happy here, and we grew up with her. She didn't even try to fit into the social milieu; the queen without a court, we called her. But she was a Klein and had some money. She didn't think our buildings were big enough, and the mountains weren't as impressive as Times Square. She loves the money the quarries bring, but she hates where it comes from."

"What was her problem with Mike's dad?" I asked.

"Chuck Klein loved the mountains, the school—even though he didn't attend—and his profession as a dealer in New England furniture and local art he built from nothing. Chuck was a gifted artist, like Mike is, and a fabulous restorer. But he was a haunted man, really. His days in Vietnam always . . . "

"I wasn't aware," I said. "Mike dosen't . . . "

"I doubt Mike knows 'cause Chuck didn't talk about it. He was a Marine RTO. His tour started at Khe Sanh at the beginning of the siege and ended when the Army lifted it and the last casualty got out; he was one of 'em, with shrapnel in his back." Alan clucked his tongue. "I don't think Chuck ever got over it. He came home, married Tina Klein because she was gorgeous, willing and had Klein money and influence . . . you get it."

"Yeah. Tina's a Jenson, too, though . . . "

---

* Angelina Silver Crest was the widow of Captain Crest's great-great-grandson Mordechai.
† John Davidson was a great-great-great-grandson of Captain Crest.
‡ Adam Jenson-Rall was a great-great-great nephew of Tiberias Jenson.
§ Judith Jenson-Wyman was the great-great-great-granddaughter of Tiberias Jenson and a shrewd businesswoman involved in retailing Connie's slabs.

"A impoverished branch compared to the rest of us, one of Tiberias' brothers, who drank and whored too much. When Mike was born in . . . um . . . "

"1970."

"Right. I don't think Tina ever picked Mike up till after they left the hospital; Chuck had to take the boy in his lap on the way home. Tina was furious that Chuck wouldn't hire a full-time nanny; hired one herself and left for Manhattan when the boy was still in diapers." I must have looked puzzled (I was), because Alan smiled and said, "I was Chuck's best friend since junior high, his best man, and one of his pallbearers."

Our lunch arrived in a few minutes. My sandwich was much as I expected, which, without a menu, was . . . then it hit me. "You knew about the girl?"

"We stumbled into her while we looked into Connie's background in '87. The school's investigators look into everything."

"Connie's . . .?" I asked, not sure if I should have been enraged or . . . what.

"Because the money she got from her mother raised some flags; not her assault, though we looked into that, too," Alan answered. "Due institutional diligence. Now," he bit into a chicken strip, "since your family will hold eight shares of the Regents when Moe passes—soon, I understand—Tina's Corporation would have to round up four Regents to outvote our combined eleven shares, and I know James and Judy will tell her to take a flying leap at a rolling doughnut out of habit. Nobody wants to dismantle this place; too prestigious. But Tina would as soon burn it to the ground as she would make it a success."

"The snow problems, the TA contracts, the security," I said. "Didn't make the connection."

"Murray put the kibosh on those shenanigans, didn't he? Whatever Tina's got cooked up, buddy, we can handle it. How's that project of yours going?"

We spoke of Ned Steele and his papers for the rest of our very pleasant luncheon.

As we left, Alan shook my hand, grinned and said. "Carl dropped in on me on his way out of town."

"Yeah," I answered, somewhat surprised. "You know him well?"

"Not well, but we've done some business together." He paused. "Tell Melanie . . . tell her not to be concerned about all this shit. Tell her we've got it under control." He paused. "Tell her about Moe's shares, too, but *only* her. Your kids—bright as they are—don't need to know yet."

"How well do you know my wife?" I asked suddenly curious.

"She was a freshman cheerleader when I was a senior running back in high school, so not well, but I knew her to talk to her." He sighed. "Always thought she was a pretty girl." He smiled. "Now she's a beautiful woman."

She is that . . .

"*Alan* said that?" Meli asked. The kids were in bed, and the house was quiet except for the furnace firing up every five or six minutes.

"Yep." We were in bed, bundled under two blankets and a quilt. The outside temperature rested at -25, with a steady twenty-knot wind.

"I barely knew him in school, *or* Tina Jenson, *or* Chuck Klein. All seniors when I was a freshman." Silence. "He said I was pretty?"

"Yeah, and now he says you're beautiful."

"What do you say?"

"I say you're the most beautiful woman in the county."

"What else would you say?" Silence. "I always wondered why there's been no faculty representation on the Regents. The faculty, not the owners, make the school what it is . . . "

Now, there's a good question . . .

The fat envelope from Baltimore was a surprise.

> *Dear Curtis:*
> *My wife found this some time back among some old family papers; I'd forgotten about it, frankly. It's Dad's last attempt at a memoir; the title's misleading because it goes all the way past his Congressional hearing in Washington after he left Korea under a cloud.*

The Persistent Past

*Charlie and Corky know about this mem-
oir, but they don't know what's in it. If you
can use it in your work, I believe I can speak
for his estate and us kids and say, 'go ahead.'
My business brings me to Granite Ledge about
twice a year. I'll call in when I do.
Yours,
Carl Steele
PS: Third time may be the charm, because I
know Dad wasn't happy with the other two at-
tempts, but he felt better about this one. He
may have forgotten about it.*

"Huh," I grunted, examining the 400-odd pages of typed, marked-up and hand-edited typescript entitled *From Corporal to Lieutenant General,* dated "written in the blizzard of '76–'77." Reading one page at random . . .

> . . . I could never have imagined the devastation I saw on that road. Twenty-four machine guns turned 640 men (I found out later) into dog food along a 600-yard space . . . .

"1918." Then I found . . .

> I sometimes looked at my kids and think "You wouldn't be here if I hadn't got typhus in 1918." Then I remember seeing them with Charlie, his wife and grown daughters in Honolulu in 1940, and I wonder how any of us survived that war, because Charlie died on that first day. His wife died three days later from her wounds. I never knew what happened to his girls.

"Oh," I said softly. "Charlie was killed at Pearl Harbor, and his wife was too. Carl talked about the daughters . . . wonder if I can find them?"

That jogged my brain: *Ned's siblings probably had children who might have little tidbits. Maybe Ned's kids are in touch with their cousins . . .* I fanned ahead.

> My appearance before the Congressional Armed Services Committee on 20 September 1951, came after I'd retired and MacArthur gave his swan song that April. Most of what they wanted to know was how MacArthur's policies in Korea affected the conduct of the conflict, since he'd wanted to cross the Yalu and attack China directly. Senator Gibson, in one of his last acts on Earth, chaired the committee when I was testifying.
>
> I had to tell them the truth: from where I sat in Japan, before I got to Korea, MacArthur was again guilty of criminal hubris. One night in early November of '50, Willoughby came by our house, got drunk and told me that Dugout Doug simply refused to hear bad news, so he downplayed the growing Chinese presence along the border until it was too late. I was never sure why the Committee didn't call for Willoughby, too; he <u>was</u> in the country.
>
> My War College classmate Joe Collins, who was Army Chief of Staff during that time, told me MacArthur had written so many poison pen memos to put in my DC file the clerks had to put them in a separate box. He and another classmate, Bedell Smith, burned them before the hearing.
>
> The Senator, 89 and a great admirer of MacArthur, passed away in his sleep three days after my testimony. At least we were in town for his funeral; we'd missed Millie's funeral in December of '41.

Another mystery solved. Ned had complained in his diary that Summerall and MacArthur impeded his advancement, but there was little evidence of it. Now, a backhand conversation with an old friend revealed that what evidence there had been of MacArthur's connivance went up in well-meaning smoke.

"So," I asked my class the next day, "what can we make of this?"

They studied the transparency quietly for several minutes before a voice said, "sour grapes."

"We might start there," I agreed. "But this correlates not only with his diaries, but with his career. A guy who was a rising star in WWI is suddenly frozen in rank for some time . . . "

"Eisenhower was a Major for thirteen years, postwar," Larry said. "Ned's case is neither sudden nor unique, really."

"Perhaps not, but," I said, "but what of the poison pen memos? Do we imagine Ned would say that about his friends Collins and Smith if it weren't true?"

"When was this written?" Bay asked.

"Winter of 1976–77, a hard winter around here; I remember it well. We had nearly five feet of snow in this valley in one week; we dug tunnels in the drifts to get to the cafeteria and the library.* He may not have been able to leave his house for a week or more."

"So he wrote this," someone else asked. "based it on his diaries?"

"Likely," I said. "And some other papers we're still evaluating. There's a trove of material in his field desks up at Camp Penobscot."

"Let's say we publish this finding in our bio of your Ned," Sharon said. "Then say some MacArthur fan or scholar says 'bullshit' and 'prove it, bud.' Then what? The only proof is . . . "

"Many historical claims are made based on a single piece of evidence," Max mused. "Many on less than this."

"Let's look at the provenance of this text," I said. "I got it from the youngest son of the purported author. What would he have to gain by forging it? We can't date the paper; it's too new. We could match the typewriter, but the estate agents have auctioned off half the household furnishings at the farm."

"And who's to say the family didn't pick up this very typewriter when their folks passed and write it themselves?" Vinnie agreed. "But like you said, Doc, there's no profit in making this up, and too many liabilities."

"OK, fine," I said. "That makes it possible to use. But . . . how?

_____

* And some of us got naked after four days, and . . . yeah.

How do we couch this source? How do we present it to the consumers?"

"Tell 'em the truth," Max said. "Nothing baffles 'em like the truth."

"OK." I changed the transparency. "This is one way."

```
    For much of Steele's post-WWI career,
he felt, but did not know, that Generals
Summerall and MacArthur stymied him. In
1951, a former War College classmate told
Steele that he and another classmate had
destroyed many unflattering memos in his
Washington file before his congressional
hearing.
```

"Simple, accurate, and vague enough to allow for all kinds of inferences," Sharon said.

"Bedell Smith was in the War College at the same time as Steele and Collins," I nodded. "In 1951, Smith was the head of the CIA. Either Collins or Smith could help an old classmate. Adds to the vagueness."

"Dosen't that seem . . . dishonest?" Phil asked. "I know it's accurate, but . . . "

"It's how we have to write about the past sometimes," I answered. "We have this piece here, and that one there, but we can't always make the connections. So, we put these pieces together and say 'that's what I think,' and let the next guy figure it out."

"Part legend, part fact," Larry said.

"But mostly interpretation of those who have gone before us," I finished.

"Historians repeat each other," Max said.

14ᵗʰ June, Ft. Leavenworth.
Got a very nice note from Rogers, offering his condolences for Dad and congratulations for Charlie. He's still working for the Senator, married, has a son, and is a First Sergeant in the DC Guard.
Why am I not surprised?

"What do we make of this?" I asked the class. Ned's diary entry was intriguing, because it suggested a far more intimate relationship with Sergeant Cedric Rogers than we'd been seeing in his earlier diaries, though he was there often.

"Rogers was mentioned earlier, wasn't he?" Brenda asked.

"Yep." I waited. "This is 1922." Still waited. "Why would a Sergeant keep tabs on his Colonel?"

"Respect," someone said. "He's looking for work?" another asked.

"Something more," I said. "Found this in *Corporal to Lieutenant General.*"

```
It is rare to find a man like Cedric
Rogers in uniform, and more's the pity. As
an aide and secretary, he was invaluable;
as a friend and soldier, dependable and
deadly. After meeting Pershing in
Manchuria in '05, his British master
showed him a part of life that took him
beyond his imagination and encouraged him
to enlist in '12. He could keep tabs on me
because he went to work for the Senator
after 1919. I sent his son my condolences
when he passed in '72, since Cedric sent
me his condolences for Dad in '22.
```

"Interesting," Sharon said. "This was written in '77?"

"Yep," I said . . . waiting. "This is about process, people. Pulling all these pieces together is hard work, but ultimately rewarding because it suggested pathways of research that . . ." I went on . . . and on . . .

This is the really dull part of my work as a teacher, where I have to explain how to follow all these breadcrumbs. I finished with, "we can tie these to other diary entries, to other texts, outside sources, perhaps find his son somewhere . . . and on and on and on. Then we write it all up into a neat package, and hope a line editor will appreciate when we send it off to a publisher, because it's the line editors who work manuscripts to death. The acquisitions editors say 'marketable;' the general editors say 'readable;' and the line editors say 'accurate.' *Maybe.* But that's the way all this works: pulling the pieces together and making these guys more than just names on a page."

But that was the product Maria and I had to make. We enhanced the Hill 90 entries with Rogers in them because Ned took the time to know and remember him.

Can this really go on forever?

"And the over-watch of the blah-blah academic outlook blah-blah blather boo-boo-boo and on and on and on . . ." our dean rambled, projector slides splashing on the screen like shutters in a windstorm. The third Tuesday morning of every month was for those indispensable yet interminable wastes of everyone's time called *staff meetings.*

The Crest deans handled department money and room assignments, course loads in terms of hours, degree programs in terms of financial benefits, dormitory and housing non-maintenance management, student life, and other non-academic matters for the four colleges/schools. *

Finally, our estimable Dean of the Jenson Endowment College of History concluded his remarks with, "and now, I turn this meeting over to the American History Department head, *Dr.* Durand."†

"Thanks, Dean," I said, striding boldly to the front of my own classroom. "OK, how was the break?"

"Great," "Fabulous," "Just the usual," "Went to Vegas and lost my shirt," were among the replies I got.

"OK," I steeled myself a bit. "I'm looking for archival help. Gotta face it: can't be the archivist, curator, *and* a department head *and* a teacher *and* a father *and* a grandfather *and* a husband *and* a homeowner *and* a researcher into WWI all at once, even at a young and vigorous 41."

"What ya mean 'help,' Boss?" Polly asked, genuinely curious.

---

* Surface Geological Engineering, Liberal Arts and Education, History, and Law.

† He'd put that odd emphasis on my title ever since I took charge of the Department. I never knew why.

"I'm going to ask the Regents to form a separate position of Chief Curator and Archivist. And in the meantime," I continued, amid groans and grins of derision, "I'm going to hire an assistant who will become the Chief, because an assistant is within my discretion."[*]

"So why are you telling us, Boss?" Sam asked.

"I want you to enquire seriously, find suitable candidates for the position of Assistant who could step up to Chief." The very best sources of archivists were other archives, where someone might want to move up, on, or out. The best way to find them was to work with them in their archives, which was what these people did.[†]

"We can do that, sir," one of Polly's adjuncts declared.

> On my furlough before I went to France, I met Georgia Pamplin, who attended the same church as my family. She was fun to be with, but she took our association too seriously. She asked me to find her brother Stanley, inducted in the first wave.

"Well, that answers that." I was working in my office while waiting for the '93 Jenson Scholar, who was struggling with Latin badly enough he might fail, which would lose him his grant.

> I said I would look for him if I could and asked Jack Willis to use his connections to find him. She kept asking about him in her letters and had a much different recollection of our few hours together than I—she even got my eye color wrong in one letter. She mostly wrote of inconsequential (to me) things that I could not understand or relate to.
>
> In her next-to-last letter, she stated Stanley had died of a ruptured appendix at Camp Custer before Christmas 1917 and that she was joining Ford's peace ship movement

---

[*] A separate chief archivist position needed Regent OK.

[†] Yes, it's poaching, but in academia, it's called cross-hiring.

and never wanted to hear from me again. Her last letter dated the day after, declaring everlasting affection, and please, would I <u>not</u> read that letter? Because I had grown so much closer to Angie by then, I stopped corresponding with her. I later learned that she and her entire family died in the influenza.

"So, I wonder," I mumbled, looking through the inventory and finding several of Georgia's letters, one dated August 1917, from Ned's WWI secretary.

> *My Dearest Ned,*
> *The more I think of our brief association, the more I believe I am losing my heart. I cannot imagine my life without you. You are my soul, my life.*
> *I went to the late-summer cotillion with your brother George, who was a perfect young gentleman but was not you, my dear. Your father was most gracious in allowing such a young man to escort me. I wore a pink lace and crinoline dress with my white shoes and a funny little pink hat. The band was competent, but kept changing time; hard to dance to.*
> *There is a Red Cross function your sister Betty wants me to take part in; dancing for tickets. I find such a thing crass, crude and demeaning for all concerned. I have far better uses of my time; rolling bandages while imagining your men using them.*
> *Write to me as soon as you can, dear heart.*
> *Your loving,*
> *Georgia*

It took me some time, but I found an unsent "Dear Georgia" letter he'd repurposed.

Just got back from the front, lost a little more than a hundred men killed and hurt and found out what vomit, gunpowder, blood, rotting corpses, rat droppings and green cross all at once smell like.

"No, Ned," I mumbled, "sending that reply to a letter like this would have baffled Georgia Pamplin; she probably wouldn't understand a word you said."

But I wanted to know what a woman who waited for her soldier to come home would think.

"I wish she was unique," Helen said, reading my research in my office that afternoon. "In the second war, sentiments like that weren't unusual. Probably common in the first, too."

That surprised me a little. "You mean it wasn't like the movies?"

"The wartime flag-wavers?" She shook her head. "Those were just for that. Turkel's 'good war' was an illusion created to boost morale and bond sales; he even admitted that in that documentary. I had to beg for a tire on my way here; got to the point when I thought about prostituting myself. I knew women who did, just to keep food on the table and gas in the tank."

"OK, Helen," I said, steering her back on track. "Would it have been common to reject the idea of dancing with servicemen?"

"Not all women are the same, Curtis. But, based on her letters* she might have felt it was beneath her station to be so common."

"You didn't know the Pamplins of Troy?"

"No, but I know her type. Her family was just wealthy enough she did not have to work. She was looking for a husband to take care of her and so she could be a socialite forever, and Ned fit her bill."

"Figured he'd inherit the family fortune?" I asked.

"That, and," she shrugged. "My guess is that she was getting desperate. She might have been stood up or jilted one too many

---

* We had several others from the secretary.

times. Women over twenty-one with no prospects were already considered old maids then." She sipped her tea. She looked out my window. "The day I got his proposal letter . . . the happiest day of my life. Still I had to wait another two months before he came home." She grinned. "Our wedding day came sixteen days after he got back. My father gave me away practically at the hotel doorstep. We spent seven days in that room, and after he left I didn't see him for another thirty months."

"You know what that kind of waiting is like, Curtis? I waited for Bert longer than we'd been together. It's a big, empty, roaring-silent hole in your heart; your soul."

"And they told you he was dead . . ." I mumbled.

"I knew he wasn't," she snapped. "I never thought he was, even after his GI insurance check came. But I cashed it because I owed everyone in Granite Ledge money. And I waited, got wild with everyone else on VJ Day, kissed a few guys and . . . yeah, more because I was so lonely."

We sat quietly, as if waiting. "When I told Bert that, he said nothing either, Curtis. We never spoke of it again, but I know he forgave me." She patted my arm. "You're the only person I've ever told that story to."

"So," I cleared my throat, "are you comfortable with your earlier evaluation of the diaries?"

She shifted in her chair, rolled her shoulders. "They're linguistically consistent with the other papers. His master's thesis, of course, is couched in a different grammar. It's not every scholar who uses his own direct, eyewitness evidence in a history thesis, but it's not unheard of, and the pacing and timing are consistent with his diaries and memoirs." She winked. "It's a miraculous find, Curtis. Congradulations."

It was My Big Thing.

"Dr. Durand, *hallo*, this is *Colonel* Paul-Luc Remaude of the French Embassy in Washington . . . "

When I got to my office the next day, that message was on my phone.

"My Ministry has instructed me to contact you regarding your inquiry of last June. Excuse my tardy reply, but *Paris* didn't inform me of this until last week and the press of other business . . . "

As I listened, I had to think that all military bureaucracies are the same, as Mike suggested more than once: hurry up and wait.

"If you will please call me at . . . at your earliest convenience, I have information that you may be glad to have. Until you call, I shall wait."

I thought about that on the way home, not quite knowing what to make of it. I guessed this Colonel was an attaché of some sort; he might be quite senior. What little I knew of that kind of business told me that much.

I called him back the next morning at the entirely decent hour of 9:21 AM and got no further than the receptionist. "I am sorry," the young man said. "*Mon* Colonel does not get to the office before the noon hour. Shall I ask him to call you? Or may someone else help you?"

"I'm Dr. Curtis Durand at Crest University. Colonel Remaude called me yesterday . . . "

"Oh, *mai oui, mon* Dr. Durand. *One* moment." I heard a series of clicks before . . . "*Hallo*, Dr. Durand? This is *Colonel* Remaude. Thank you for returning my call."

"Yes; I got your message yesterday. I'm not getting you out of bed?"

"*Mai non,* Dr. Durand. I screen my calls before noon or I would get no work done at all."

"I see," I said, wishing I had someone to screen my calls before 7 or 9 or noon. "So, something about . . .?"

"Yes, indeed, Dr. Durand. Your query excited a great deal of interest in Paris, and I must admit more than a little in my office. We know *General* Steele quite well. I have a copy of an extensive file here that I must give you. But," he said, dropping his voice, "is *mon General* still with us?"

"He is not; passed away in April 1994." I resisted the temptation to render a French-ish pronunciation.

"I am sorry to hear that; *France* shall mourn him. Does he have any living family?"

"He does . . . ."

"Do you have information for them?"

"I do, but . . . what's this about?"

"Dr. Durand, the National Order of the Legion of Honor created *General* Steele a *chevalier** in 1954, but he was not interested in *la cérémonie.*" Silence. "Do you know where he is buried? I must think Arlington . . . "

"No, he's buried here in Granite Ledge."

"Granite Ledge . . . an hour by plane from Boston, four hours by train. There is an airport . . . *bon.* Dr. Durand, may I call you after we have made our arrangements?"

"Certainly."

Arrangements? For . . .?

Snow skidded across the runways of Granite Ledge Regional Airport/Holman Field as I waited for Colonel Remaude's flight. A chain *burned* coffee shop opened in the small terminal a month before; getting a cup there at least took up a few minutes.

Holman was not one of those big airports with jetways attached to the terminal. It relied on the aircraft's built-in stairs or, in the extreme, small platform ladders to board and disembark passengers into whatever weather there was that day.

Which compelled me to stand in the terminal, which kept me out of the cold and wind,[†] waiting for *Colonel* Remaude's plane to unload. It gave me time to reflect on what the Colonel said he wanted to *do* in Granite Ledge. The Colonel was not terribly specific—a ceremony he had to perform. It sounded a little like *mon Colonel* was making a pilgrimage.

There would be cameras involved. A French film crew had contacted me the day before, having arrived that very day, wanting directions—or a guide—to Steele Farm. I contacted Wickie, who informed her husband at WGL-TV[‡] to coordinate the technical details of the coverage at the farm, and send another crew of their own.

The plane's ladder descended to the tarmac, one of only a half-

---

* Knight; the lowest order *and* the order *non*-French citizens recieve.

† It was -4 for a high that day, with an average 10-knot wind.

‡ Granite Ledge was only big enough for one broadcast station.

dozen scheduled flights on an average day coming in. *Colonel*[*] Remaude, in a military uniform, strode surely across the tarmac. A French Captain walked with him, her long skirt flapping in the wind. I extended my hand when they entered the terminal, shaking their gloved hands. "*Mon Colonel,*" I smiled, "*Mon Capitaine, bienvenu* Granite Ledge. I'm Curtis Durand."

"*Merci beaucoup, mon professeur,*" the Colonel grinned, "pleased to meet you, and to be here. May I introduce *Capitaine* Marianne Grant, assistant liaison?"

"*Capitaine,*" I nodded. "So, *mon* Colonel," I started, "you said you're getting a rental car?"

"Yes," the Colonel answered, "and *please* call me Paul-Luc."

"I'm Curtis."

And all the rest of that day, as I showed them some sights around Granite Ledge, and gave a brief tour of the campus, and after they checked into the hotel, I wondered . . . *what are they here for?*

"*Enchante,*" Paul-Luc smiled, meeting Meli and my family at the hotel restaurant that night. They had asked if they might dine with my family, and I had trouble saying no, but the why puzzled me.

"So good of you to meet us," Meli answered, amused when Paul-Luc made to kiss her hand, and Maria's.[†]

"We wanted to meet some genuine Americans," Marianne smiled. She was a charming woman whose English was not as good as her boss's, but who held a slow French conversation with Maria during dinner.[‡]

"We're as genuine as they come," Charlie answered loudly.

"Yeah," Jason joined in. "American as baseball," much to our guest's amusement.

"So, what brings you to Granite Ledge, Paul-Luc?" Meli asked, unprompted.

"I must perform a ceremony at General Steele's gravesite," he answered. "My father served with *mon General* in Korea, and, as

---

[*] I recognized French rank insignia by then, part of our research.

[†] Between strangers, it's less a *kiss* than a *chin.*

[‡] Maria's French had improved since she first translated that receipt.

my assignment in the United States is ending this year, I wished to ensure I honored *General* Steele."

"Is your father still . . .?" Meli started.

"He is, Melanie," he smiled slightly. "A *pensionné de guerre*—an *Armee* pensioner, eh? He lives now in Eu, the small town in Normandy where we are from."

"And," Marianne added, "we are exhausted of American officials. You are a very kind people, but in Washington, everyone seems to work for some function of your government. It is wearying."

"Sorry to disappoint," Meli shook her head, "but I work for the City of Granite Ledge."

"But she's not elected, if that helps," I added.

"What is it you *do*, madame?" Marianne asked.

"Municipal planning," Meli said, "storm and sanitary systems . . . "

Our guests spoke to each other in French. "*Mon frère* is in that business in Vaux." Marianne smiled.

"Her brother," Maria added.

"*Mai oui, ma chérie*," Marianne smiled. "You are *très rapide.*"

"*Merci beaucoup*," Maria grinned. "I hope Mom's job dosen't disappoint you."

"With such a charming family, you cannot disappoint us, *ma chérie*," Paul-Luc declared.

"And . . . got it," the *Intelligencer*'s photographer called two days later at the gravesite. We also met news crews from WGL, France's TF1, and the school's cable channel, Crest U TV, who were all still setting up.

Paul-Luc and Marianne, resplendent in dress uniforms, stood at attention while the sash of a *Chevalier* of the Legion of Honor, draped over Ned's tombstone, flapped in the lazy -5 degree breeze.

"We have only come to honor our late comrade-in-arms, *General* Edmund Steele," Marianne told Brandy, who *was* writing a *series* on Steele for the paper,* the wind whipping both their hair around.

---

* With a by-line, that the wire services picked up.

"*General* Steele is a hero to three generations of Frenchmen," Paul-Luc declared. "During the First and Second World War, and in Korea, *General* Steele served with courage and skill unmatched by any other American officer leading French soldiers."

"Why haven't we heard more about him, then, Colonel?" Brandy asked.

"You must ask your own history that question." Paul-Luc shook his head. "It is there that you must look. France feels great shame for the way he was treated in Korea."

"How *was* he treated?" Brandy asked; the TV crews were suddenly interested and started filming.

"When *Colonel* Monclar of *Le Battalion Francais* learned *General* Steele was in Japan, seeking a duty, he asked *le General* if he would help him," Paul-Luc explained. "*General* Steele, then a, ah, *Lieutenant-General,* did not *hesitate* and joined *le battalion* just before the crucial fighting for Hill 247. He stayed with *le battalion,* suffering all its travails, making so many, ah, *make-shifts* that kept the Chinese guessing while *le battalion* helped stabilize the United Nations line at Chipyong-ni. It was then that your *General* MacArthur ordered *General* Steele out of Korea and ordered all mention of him removed from reports." He grinned at the camera conspiratorially. "Soon after, *General* MacArthur was relieved of his command and ordered to Washington. Cannot be a coincidence, eh?"[*]

"And how do you know this?" the WGL reporter asked; the French reporter was silent.

"My father was chief of staff to *Colonel* Monclar in Korea," Paul-Luc declared. "He wrote of it all. I have his day-by-day accounts, and copies of *le battalion* reports to Paris that were unaltered by General MacArthur's decree. It is for this and his conduct in the World Wars that France honors him now."

"He led French soldiers in WWI?" the Crest U TV reporter asked.

"His *bataillon de mitrailleuses*[†] had a *compagnie* of *La Legion*

---

[*] Ned wrote about all that in his *Corporal to Lieutenant General* memoir. Here was confirmation.

[†] Machine gun battalion.

*Etrangere** attached in France and Flanders, yes."

"*Et pendant la Seconde Guerre mondiale?*"[†] the TF1 reporter asked.

"Once more, he led Legionnaires as part of his task force in North Africa and Sardinia." Paul-Luc answered in English.

What a career; what a story no one had ever heard before, but I'd read about it in *From Corporal to Lieutenant General.*

```
    That winter in Japan, a French officer
I'd known before the last war approached
me and asked if I'd help him and the
French battalion joining the UN force in
Korea. Since I had little else to do, and
nobody would stop me, I rustled up a field
desk, packed my duffel bag, and caught a
plane to Kimpo. Nobody was going to stop a
three-star.
```

Behold! My Big Thing!

* * *

"Now you're off to Wisconsin," I said the next day at the airport.

"Yes," Paul-Luc answered. "I will privately meet his daughter and oldest son there tomorrow. I shall meet his brother and youngest son in Baltimore next week."

"We have enjoyed our stay here, Curtis," Marianne said, lightly kissing my cheek. "Your family, your *village*, are charming, but *very* cold."

"Yeah, but we like the place," I smiled.

"This fall, I shall return to my home for good," Paul-Luc said. "*Au revoir,* Curtis. *Bon chance* with the diaries."

And good luck to you both . . . and to me, telling Ned's story.

---

* Foreign Legion.
† "And in WWII?"

THE STEELE PROJECT

I opened my presentation with, "ladies and gents, meet *Captain* Edmund Archer Steele of the 1ˢᵗ Machine Gun Instructor Company, American Expeditionary Forces." I switched on the projector with a most dramatic diary entry, one of those that ran more than one page:

> 2ⁿᵈ December, Hill 90.
> [Illegible; unknown stain] . . . *we were in a standing barrage that cut and hit everything. We hunkered down most of the day and half the night between MG and 77s, and then we heard the iron ringing, then the klaxons screaming: GAS. In our hoods, we can barely* [expletive] *breathe, but had to fight for our lives.*
> *I looked through the periscope and realized another ground attack was in the making. McTee went to some emergency. I cannot fathom what it was or how he knew to go, but he knew and went. And here they were, once again in the OP line. We fought with bayonet and grenade, blackjack and shovel, club and bare hands, our gunners hitting targets they could touch. I lost track of how many* [expletive] *Mills bombs I threw.*
> *How glorious the sunrise after a night in a smoke hood, thin like every other on this God-damned hill but so welcome.*

*We were told last night was a "minor attack."
That "minor attack" cost twenty dead and
thirty wounded, so for them it was hardly
"minor."
A 77 hit the mule pens, killed or wounded
nearly all of them. But the hot food those
beasts provided will restore the soul better
than a million* [expletive] *sermons. McTee and I
slurped up the long-ear-stew and biscuits as
fast as everyone else. We fed everyone a hot
meal who showed up, even the villagers.
The Newfoundlanders came back in last
night during all the festivities, lost ten men
doing it. You would think they could wait
another day to get on this Godforsaken*
[expletive] *rock.*

"Oh, my," Judy said softly. "What a *story.*"

"It's right up there, Dr. Durand," Alan agreed. With Moe in-disposed, he was chairing this meeting of the Regents. "Wish I had a nickel for every grenade I pitched in the Rung Sat zone."[*]

"We didn't see many grenades in the Air Force," James sighed. "Hoods?"

"Smoke hoods; early gas masks," I explained. "Can't say about iron ringing . . . "

"Gas alarms," Alan explained. "Metal on metal's the expedient sound signal for gas attacks."

"Ah," I nodded. "First-hand experience is always best. Thanks, Mr. Jenson."

"Those trenches must have been horrible," Judy sighed. "Long-ear stew: they ate mules?"

"Fresh meat," I said, "scarce up in the trenches. Maconochie stew in a can was the best they got most of the time, and it was mostly turnips. He reported scurvy among the Canadians."

"Quite the education, Dr. Durand," Norm said. The Regents

---

[*] The Mekong River delta south of Saigon.

invited him and several other professors to this meeting as consultants on the project. "I understand you're *staging* this project?"

"Yes, we are, Dr. Hammond," I answered. "The Steele project will comprise three parts. The first will be the hopeful publication of an article based on eleven days of entries in late 1917, when Ned was the machine-gun officer on Hill 90 in Flanders; this is one of those entries."

"Do you have a publisher in mind?" Wickie asked.

"I have feelers out to several; haven't got replies, Dr. Geohegan . . . "

"Wouldn't the British market be more interested?" Tony asked. He'd been Emeritus* since January, but he had an interest in our venture, aside from his new duties as Chancellor.

"Probably, Dr. Zane. There's the new Western Front Society in England, which is promoting their new magazine, *Duckboards*. I've sent them a query . . . "

"You said 'we,' Dr. Durand," Judy said. "Who's the other?"

"My daughter, Maria, has been contracted to transcribe and research . . . "

"Quite the scholar herself," Norm declared.

"Indeed, she must be," James said.

"She just turned fourteen, Dr. Durand?" Wickie asked. "My children said something about a little party at school."

"Indeed, yes, Dr. Geohegan," I answered. "Thanks for remembering."

"Your, ah, selective censoring, Dr. Durand," Wickie said. "I gather it is . . .?"

"Primarily vulgarisms," I answered. "References to . . . ."

"Female body parts and rather private activities," Wickie replied. "You leave the milder profanities in your transcriptions. Excellent."

"Continue, Dr. Durand," Alan sighed. "After the article . . .?"

"*Steele's Battalion: The Great War Diaries* will be the second phase. We believe he was in Mexico in late 1916, when he was a Corporal; we haven't located that diary yet . . . "

---

* Academic-speak for retired.

"And his medal citations call him a *Lieutenant-Colonel*..." Norm said.

"Corporal to Lieutenant-Colonel in less than two years," Alan nodded. "Quite the feat."

"He was quite the officer," I answered. "Quite the man, from all I've seen." I paused for effect. "He's buried up by Camp Penobscot on his farm, the contents of which is now being auctioned off."

Silence. "Wow," James said.

"And by 1951, he was a Lieutenant-General in Korea..." I started.

"*What?*" Norm asked loudly. "Never heard of a *Steele* in Korea." he added.

"I haven't either," Tony mused. "You sure, Dr. Durand?"

"Well, if you wait until this evening," I answered, "you'll hopefully see a news story about why France made him a *Chevalier* of the Legion of Honor. The story should also be in the *Intelligencer* this evening.* And," I added, "he's also an alumnus; received both BA and MA degrees here when he was stationed at Camp Penobscot between the wars."

"James," Alan glanced over. "Are you thinking what I'm thinking?"

"A museum, Alan," James said.

"The Historical Society is looking for funding to buy his farm..." I started.

"I'll talk to them," James declared. "Your third stage, Dr. Durand?"

"The whole diaries, which go through..." I started ... again.

"In microform, I'm guessing," Wickie said.

"Well, World War Two and Korea might be worth another book..." I started a third time.

"Brilliant plan, Dr. Durand," Alan declared. "We'll decide on how the project will be funded at a later time, but funded it shall be."

"One question, though," James said. "His relationship with Pershing: real or grandstanding?"

---

* I had just that morning been informed of both.

"I don't know for certain, since there are very few documents that verify any kind of personal relationship . . . "

"He could have fudged his diaries," Alan nodded.

"That might discredit the entire project," Norm declared.

"Another Hitler Diaries," Tony frowned. "Unlikely with that volume of material, but he might have been a fabulist."

"Eh," Wickie sighed. "His rapid promotion, that he kept his unit together and got new men while the rest of the AEF was scrambling for replacements? Un*likely*. He *had* to have known someone close to Pershing, or Pershing himself."

"Well," James said, "I'd be more comfortable with some kind of proof of his relationship with Pershing and . . . Dr. Durand, you say he knew other officers, like Patton and Marshall?"

"His diary says so, so do his memoirs," I agreed. "And you're right: without something more concrete, we just have his word on it."

Alan cleared his throat. "If our guests would please step out." The stenographer put her hands in her lap as my fellow professors left. "Curtis," he glanced around, all nods, if hesitant. "On Moe's death, we want to invite you to join the Committee of Regents after James assumes the chairmanship. How do you feel about it?"

"Ah, Moe mentioned it would be you," I said.

"When I retire from Stone, it'll be to somewhere a lot warmer than here."* Alan answered. There were murmurs of agreement. "Well?"

"I've thought about it a great deal," I said, "discussed it with no one but Connie and Melanie." I paused. "But how much time would it take up?"

"It varies," Christian said. "Anywhere from an hour a month to a week."

"It depends on issues," James said. "Our bylaws require the Regents form a quorum at least quarterly; we usually quorum every month during the school year. The meetings you've attended have been special. *This* meeting," he waved his hands at the door the professors used, "has been the only one of its kind. But Christian's right; it varies."

---

* The *high* temperature at the airport that day was -18.

I blinked, thinking. *Not that much more time for a lot more control over my life.* "What about my professorship?"

"That's . . ." Alan stopped; looked around; nods were all I saw. "You'd still have the income you have now, *plus* the dividends and non-cash perquisites."

"Can we create a separate *Chief* archival curator, please?" I asked. "It's just gotten to be too much. I'd stay on as a consultant, but if they are sold, Connie says they'd sell me with the Archives because they want me . . . "

Alan glanced at James and nodded to the stenographer. "Done. But selling the Archives isn't an option, *ever,*" James declared. "You'll become Curator Emeritus of the Archives." He paused. "Dr. Curtis Durand," he intoned solemnly as the stenographer handed me a letter. "Are you prepared to become a member of the Committee of Regents of Crest University?"

"After consultation with my wife, I shall formally respond."

"We should expect nothing less, Dr. Durand."

"And, one more thing," I said . . .

"It wasn't just a matter of laying track with Chinese on one end and Irishmen on the other," Polly declared, glancing at me in the back of her classroom as she was holding forth on some finer point of 19ᵗʰ Century railroad construction. "There were leveling crews, tie-setting crews, ballasting crews, then came the track-laying crews and the Hell on Wheels towns that followed them from both directions. Now that Dr. Durand has graced us with his presence, I believe that's enough for today."

I came forward as she was picking up her notes. "Polly; how would you feel if I were to fill a seat on the Regents . . . and you, another one?"

She looked aghast. " *What* in the *name* of the *living Christ* are you *talking* about?"

"Look," I said calmly, "for now, I'll just say I've got the power to make some serious changes in this place."

"Yeah? Like what?"

"I can change the Regents bylaws to make at least one perma-nent faculty seat. The number of owners is diminishing . . . "

"True . . . Huh."

I explained as much as I could about the seats, ending with, "and with seats on the Regents, the faculty can renovate not just the conduct codes that got excellent teachers fired,* we can liberate the student body from the more draconian strictures."†

"Wow," she shook her head before she whispered, "*holy shit,* sugar. I heard rumors of a shakeup. But if I were to take a seat I will not support taking government money." That had been an issue since 1972, one that cost many admissions. If we accepted government-backed student loans we would be subject to the strictures of Title IX, a well-meaning but ambiguous federal regulation that set up the US Department of Education as the arbiter of all aspects of co-educational higher education.‡

"*I* won't advocate it, either." We followed the spirit of the regulation, but would not allow the Federal government to tell us our athletic teams had too few women and had to close. Besides student loans and athletics, our biggest enrollments were in surface mining engineering, and there were only a handful of women interested in quarrying. This would compel us to get more women into other programs, which was a lot harder than it sounded.

She made a stern face before she transformed into . . . "why me, sugar?"

"Because, lover, you have as much invested in this institution as I do. And you've been here five years longer."

She crossed her arms across her chest. "I'd have to talk it over with Simon."

"Just . . . quietly . . . "

She looked away, knitted her brows, and drummed her fingers briefly. "I love this place."

"Me, too."

"Sugar," she winked slowly, "we can make this joint sing and dance."

*   *   *

---

* These codes were one reason Meli and I got married so fast in '82.

† Unmarried pregnant women were still asked to sit classes out.

‡ Crest was one of few private universities that had never been single-sex.

"Real thing, huh," Melanie said. "No BS, no bureaucratic obfuscation, just . . . "

"Yep. I get another office in the Executive Building, passkeys and parking permits for everywhere on campus, another email box to look at . . . "

"And a partridge in a pear tree," she sighed. "Then we fight with Mike's mom about . . . "

"No. She's got zero pull." Silence. "I think James wants to pull the contracts from the firms she's using now."

"And move them where?"

That was another story.

"Connie's paid Christian," James said, "so that's done." He had moved into Moe's old office; Moe had moved into a hospice after resigning his post.

"That's it?" I asked, surprised. James seemed to me to be more genial than Moe had been, eschewing his desk chair and sitting in an armchair in front of me after pouring a drink. "No secret ceremonies, no animal sacrifices, no swearing in?"

"Until now, the members have all been part owners as well, so we've been more or less born into it. But times change, and our bylaws didn't have to, remarkably. Now," James handed me a small ring binder from a side table. "Read this: our bylaws and charter. Common sense, most of it." He cleared his throat. "Those TV segments and newspaper article," he sighed. "The French seem to think more of your General than the Americans do."

"It sure looks that way."

"Any idea why MacArthur did that?"

"Not yet. It might have something to do with WWI, but I don't know. I'm working on it."

"Since you know more about that farm and your Ned Steele than the rest of us do," he smiled thinly.

"If we want to buy it, I get to do the heavy lifting?"

"Now you're getting the gist of it. I'll coordinate with the Historical Society—they should have at *least* a third interest—but you should lead this project for the school. You up to it?"

"Um," I started, "I spoke with Polly Winfield and, when Moe

passes I'll fill *his* seat and *she'll* fill Connie's."

"A sound choice, Curtis. The farm?"

Like I had a choice?

"Your pseudo-daughter bought a seat on the Regents and put *you* into it," the voice on the phone said that evening without introduction. "Are you ready to follow instructions?"

"What instructions are those, Ms. Klein?" I answered, knowing who it was with no need for an introduction. Meli, listening in the kitchen, frowned, puzzled.

"The Corporation's instructions for reshaping the Regents, *Curtis*," Tina answered, my name bitter in her mouth. "The institution must change with the times, and . . . "

"I agree, but I see no need to . . ." I rolled my eyes, shook my head.

"If you are not *willing* to follow the Corporation's instructions, *Curtis*, the Corporation shall have to take *steps* to *make* you *willing*," she spat. "Now, first, the Corporation requires . . . "

"Now, just what gives you the idea I'll do what you want? There's nothing I . . ." Meli made a face.

"*Curtis*, it will be incumbent on you to comply with Corporate wishes if you want your school to see another year in operation. Now, listen carefully: the Corporation requires . . . "

"*My* school?" I asked. "Isn't the Corporation acting in the best interests of *our* school, Ms. Klein?"

"That mausoleum with do as the Corporation wishes or it will not *be* anymore . . . *Curtis*," she fired back. "Now listen to what I . . . "

I hung up and called Alan. "Yeah, she called James and me, made the same threats. Ignore her."

"What could she do?" I asked. Meli joined me on the sofa.

"Stupid mischief," Alan sighed. "We took security, utilities and snow removal out of her hands last month, so she can't turn the lights off or bury us. The staff are all on Corporate contracts, but even if she fires 'em all—which she'd have to have cause to do in this state and they know it—we can rehire them ourselves like we did before."

"We'd need a bigger HR department for that, wouldn't we?" Meli shook her head.

"We'd use a temp agency until we got one up and running." Alan said. "It'd take a few days, but not much more."

"Well, then, what *could* she do?"

Meli sat next to me. "I'm not sure, but . . ." Alan started . . .

Meli yanked the phone from me and started talking. "Alan, hi; It's Melanie . . . long time, yeah. The city wants to have a role here . . . the Head City Planner mentioned it to me the other day . . . the Mayor will do what's needed for the City . . . yes . . . I can have them call, sure. The County Board probably, too . . . so, how's Barb these days? I haven't seen her in an age . . . she baby-sat for Al sometimes . . . yeah, we need to get together. So, you thought I was pretty in school? Well, you were kinda cute in those tight football pants . . . yeah, Alan; my best to Barb; I'll call her . . . OK."* She handed me back the phone and got up.

"Um," I said into the phone, "didn't know you two were acquainted . . . "

"Not . . . well . . ." Alan said slowly. "Does she do that a lot?"

Often enough.

"Dr. Durand," the woman smiled, shaking my hand with some vigor. "So glad to meet you at last. I've followed your researches into the Truxton Archive with envy." The interview room in the Crest/Jenson Archive Building was austere but comfortable.

"Dr. Palgrave," I smiled back, "I've heard nothing but good things about *you*." Elizabeth Palgrave was probably ten years older than I and had the most impressive resume of all the archivists that crossed my desk. "Hope you had a pleasant trip."

"I did, Doctor, though *New* England is considerably colder than *Olde* England." She had flown to the US for this interview.

"The worst thing about New England is the weather, that's true." Of the five candidates who we interviewed (by phone, then in-person), Dr. Palgrave was the most distant and, as far as the

---

* Another reminder that Melanie called Granite Ledge home all her life.

school was concerned, the cheapest and therefore the best qualified. "Your accommodations are comfortable?"

"Indeed, yes," Dr. Palgrave nodded. "Most comfortable. My husband is most enthralled with central heating." Wickie Geohegan had contacted Dr. Palgrave at the Bodleian Libraries,[*] knowing she was looking to move.

"Good. He's touring the campus, I gather?"

"With Dickie and Ollie in tow, yes." The school flew her immediate family across the pond. "They're of an age to enter a university in Britain."

"Ah, I see. May I offer you coffee? Tea? Water?"

"Thank you, no, Doctor."

"Very well. What do you know about the Crest/Jenson Archive?" The next twenty minutes focused on the minutiae of an archivist's and curator's life, descriptions of archives around the world, and other details that would bore the average reader—and many history professionals—to tears.

She ended with, "Frankly, my keen interests are in the Truxton Archive and your new Great War material."

"You heard about that, did you?"

"Of course." She winked conspiratorially and laid a finger along her nose. "In our trade we should, should we not?"[+]

"Handy to know what others hold."

"Scholarship isn't a competition, but for publishing."

"Yes, that's so." I drummed my fingers lightly for a moment, then stood. "Care to have a look at some Archives? Call me Curtis . . ."

"Lead *on*, Mac*duff!*" she said, rising to her feet. "I'm Bess to my chums."

"It feels a bit . . . strange," I told Meli after dinner. "Turning over the Archives to someone else."

"You'll be the Archivist Emeritus, too, right?" We were watching some nonsense on TV about the recent inaugural celebrations

---

[*] The 26 libraries serving the Oxford complex.
[+] It would have surprised me if she hadn't.

that seemed odd; we *re*-elected him last November.

"Whatever that means, but I still plan on running the Truxton project."

"What does her husband do?"

"He's a barrister . . . a lawyer."

"Two kids?"

"A seventeen-year-old boy, Richard, and sixteen-year-old girl named Olivia, both ready to go to college or university in Britain."

"Here?"

"They could be admitted. No minimum age in college."*

"Will they come with her?"

"She seems to think so." We watched the editorializing in mute contemplation. I wondered if Elizabeth would accept our offer.

"If someone in England offered you a job, would you take it?"

"Not now, no," I sighed, without even thinking about it.

"Because of those diaries?"

"And so much else." I slid the cable box switch to some rerun station. "Because I love this institution. I've lived here longer than I did in Cicero."

She slid across the sofa, putting her head in my lap. "Good."

I opened the envelope with the British stamp and the Ministry of Defense return address with interest.

```
Main Building,
Whitehall, London.
My Dear Dr. Durand,
I am contacting you to ask if you know
anything about how to contact Lieut. Gen.
E. Steele's family. On November 25, 1952,
the Crown awarded Gen. Steele the George
Cross for his actions in Europe and Korea
in three different conflicts, but Her
Majesty never had the pleasure of
presenting it to him.
```

---

* The youngest modern Crest undergrad was admitted in 1978, at four-teen. He graduated with a BA in Pre-Law the same year I got my Ph.D.

The Persistent Past

```
    Our military attaché in Washington
learned via a television programme that
the General had passed on. It has fallen
to me to follow Her Majesty's wishes in
this matter, which she conveyed to me
personally.
    If you would be so kind as to contact
me directly with any information you have.
    Yours sincerely,
    F.M. Charles Guthrie, GCB,
    CIGS
```

There followed telephone numbers, e-mail addresses, fax numbers, and TELEX addresses, appropriate for a Field Marshal, Grand Commander of the Order of the Bath and the Chief of the Imperial General Staff.

I dropped him an e-mail with Carl's contact information, wondering once again why everyone seemed to honor Ned Steele but his own country . . . but wondered . . .

"A *George*," Wickie said that afternoon. "A *George* Cross? Good . . ." and she said something in what might have been Polish.

"That's good?" I asked, all innocent.

"It is the equal to the *Victoria Cross*, Curtis; the highest medal in Britain, equivalent to the *Medal of Honor* in America."

"Maybe we should have another TV spot. but I'll call the *Intelligencer.*"

"When the English come to call, another TV spot would not be amiss."

MOE HARDIN

A phone call at that hour was rarely good. "Hello . . . "

"Curtis; Alan. Moe's gone. I need to get down to the hospital so . . . "

"Why?"

"I'm his executor;[*] he's my cousin. Moe's great-great-grandfather and my great-great-grandfather were sons of Xerxes Jenson."

"Handy to have such genealogy."

"Well, in our case, it's vital. Can you do us a service or two?"

"Contact James, Amanda, and the Red Cross for Eric? Is there any point in contacting Florence?"

"I doubt it; she's been uncommunicative for months."

I retreated to my den, a little weary after such news, but now . . . "James Jenson, please," I said to James's answering service.[†] "It's Curtis Durand on an urgent school matter."

I hung up and called the Red Cross . . . . waiting . . . until the phone rang back. "James here, Curtis. Is Moe . . .?"

"He passed a few minutes ago, Mr. Chairman."

There was a deep pause. "Thank you. I've known Moe Hardin for, Hell, most of our lives."

"Friends?"

"Most of the time, yeah. We've had our differences. He went into the Army; I was in the Air Corps until it became the Air

---

[*] In our state, there could be *actual* and *legal* executors. Usually they were the same; sometimes not.

[†] It being Saturday and I did *not* have James' home number.

Force . . ." He cleared his throat. "Well, I should contact the rest of the Board . . . "

"I'll help," I offered.

"Thanks."

"Polly, Moe Hardin died about an hour ago." I'd called her at home after several more calls to other Regents and deans.

"I talked to Simon. After he stopped laughing, I convinced him I was serious." She paused. "His business won't be affected,[*] but he's complaining he'd have to get into a monkey suit for all the fundraisers."

"Well, there's that, but there's also the governance issues we get to solve around here."

"And you'll be everyone's boss with the biggest vote on the Regents."

"There's that. How about it?"

"If I say 'yes,' then what?"

"James Jenson will call you."

"*Yes.*"

"So, what do we make of this?" I projected a shorter entry on the overhead:

> 3rd *December, Hill 90.*
> [Illegible; unidentified stain covers the rest of the page.]
> *Watching the bodies in the zone like the song:*
> *If you want to find the old battalion,*
> *I know where they are,*
> *They're hanging on the old barbed wire*
> *I've seen 'em. I've seen 'em,*
> *Hanging on the old barbed wire,*
> *I've seen 'em,*
> *Hanging on the old barbed wire.*

"What song is he talking about?" Sharon asked.

---

[*] All I knew was that he was a general contractor in the area.

"I think it's a lyric based on 'I've Been Working On The Rail-road,'" I suggested.

It was several moments before someone said. "Dosen't work, Doc."

"Chumbawamba did a song like it," another voice declared. "In the "English Rebel Songs" album about ten years ago. I thought it was original to them."

"Chum-ba-*who?*" I asked.

"A punk band, Doc," the voice said. "After your time."

"And when would that be?" I asked.

"Post-Boomer, Doc," the voice answered. "After you graduated, got married, joined the rat race."

"Where you'll be soon enough," I answered.

And they all laughed . . . bitterly.

At the end of that class, I announced the death of Elizabeth Hardin that morning. Moe had been gone for just three days.

"*Dr.* Durand," the stranger at my front door intoned severely that cold Saturday afternoon, "I shall instruct you on your duties as a representative of the Corporation." He simply strode into my living room and sat on my sofa. "Be seated," he gestured to a chair.

"Just who the Hell do you think you are?" I asked, ignoring his 'request.' "Barging in here like you own the place? Who . . .?" The cats, uncharacteristically, watched from the hallway.

"I am Attorney Ridge," he said, in a manner that I interpreted as perhaps a threat. "NOW sit while I . . . "

"You're not the lawyer that Judge Walking Elk had on the phone," I said, ignoring his tone. The kids had gone swimming; Meli was in the basement, wrestling with her pile of mending that never seemed to get any smaller.

"No," Ridge said, taking a paper out of a valise. "Now, this *fraud* you have perpetrated on the state is punishable by a year in prison." He handed me a copy of Maria's birth certificate.

"What fraud?" I asked.

"Your name in the space that reads 'Father's Name.' You are not the biological father. If this fraud were to become known . . . "

"How would you . . .?"

"We know that the late Steve Wabrzeznoski was her father. Now . . . "

I grinned widely. "Just about everyone knows I'm not her biological father, sir. And, I adopted her in . . . "

"The Regents? What would they think?" His voice was completely flat; his face was expressionless. "We are prepared to relate this knowledge to the newspapers and the state's attorney, Dr. Durand, if you do not do as you are told."

"Again," I asked, "how would you know?"

"That is of little moment, Dr. Durand," Ridge said. "There is also the matter of your adopted daughter's attack on a young man in Texas, Jasper McCulloch, whose fledgling football career was destroyed. The family is prepared to sue . . . "

"The kid who raped her?" I asked. "Who are you trying to kid? And that was nearly ten years ago."

"Her allegations are completely unsubstantiated," Ridge declared. "And limitations be damned; the papers will know. Now sit down and listen to your instructions . . . "

"*Get! Out!*" Melanie declared, materializing out of the basement and wielding a baseball bat.*

Ridge seemed unfazed. "Mrs. Durand, your threatening behavior is noted and shall be documented. You are also responsible for your husband's fraud and . . . "

"The only way you can prove *intentional* fraud is with a time machine," she declared, with the bat resting on her shoulder. "Even I wasn't sure at the time who her father was,[†] and we never did a test."

"But who knows . . .?" Ridge started.

"Who *cares?*" Meli spat. "Our family all know. Beyond that, what difference does it make?"

"The girl knows?" Ridge said, his voice rising an octave.

"Yes," we both said. "She figured it out when she was eight," I added.

---

* Her sewing corner was right next to the furnace, and you could hear living room sounds quite well through the air return.

† Not so, but only she and I knew for some time.

"The attack on Jasper McCulloch," he spat, "that was . . . "

"That wasn't even her; it was her friend," I said.

"The newspapers won't see it that way," Ridge replied oleaginously. "Now, be seated and . . . "

"I can get Will Gerard of the Texas Rangers on the phone in a minute to disprove that, you jerk," Meli said. "And Connie will sue for defamation if you do anything like that." The cats crouched, watching Ridge as if he were a mouse in a hole.

Ridge stared at us hovering over him and blinked. "Clearly, other measures are required here," he sighed, standing up. "You would have been much better off if you had cooperated," he declared, heading for the door. "You have not heard the last . . . "

"Heard all we needed to," I said. After Ridge left, we stared at the door for several minutes before we packed our swim bags and joined the kids at the pool.

But I wondered . . . *what's next?*

"Happy birthday, Charlie!" Maria smiled, sweetly bussing his lips after Connie and Meli had pecked his cheeks.

"Thanks, Stinky," he grinned. That he allowed Maria's lip-smack* surprised me dimly, but there had been a transformation with our children. The boys were less aggressively obnoxious with Maria; she didn't snap at them as much. Though she didn't parade around nude, Maria was less self-conscious during her wrestling matches with her brothers—usually two-on-one. Once, after a day of snow-shoveling, she wore only a sweatshirt while grappling with them in her suite after allowing them to use her shower.†

Never would have happened before Key West.

Amid the cake and ice cream and trucks and wrapping paper and a new baseball mitt, Charlie's birthday party that last Saturday in March saw the first ball game of the year. Even if there was still some snow on the ground, which was normal, we threw a few pitches and shagged a few fly balls in our winter coats against the chilling wind coming off the river.

---

* And he puckered back.

† Only reason I knew about it was I looked in on the rukus.

That night, Connie buttonholed me in my den with, "*Charlie* said something bizarre . . . "

"Yeah?"

"It amounted to he'd gone skinny-dipping with girls."

"I told him not to . . ." I started.

"Not to what, Curtis?"

"Not to talk about the *clothing-optional* beach we . . . "

Connie gaped. "A nude beach?"

"*Clothing-optional.*"

She looked stunned. "The *boys* I can understand; even Mom and you, but *Maria nude in public?*" She blinked furiously, looked away, then giggled before she laughed out loud. "*That's* where she met Bill, naked . . . where was this?"

Of course, Connie's her pal, too. "I'm not supposed to say we were in Florida at the time . . . you know about Bill?"

"She talks about him, calls and emails and . . ." She glanced at me. "Naked boy on a nude beach with the family around changes a gal's perspectives about everything else to do with guys and her body." She grinned widely, crossing her arms. "It surely did mine at twelve . . . "

"You've done it?"

She put on her Texas drawl. "*Honey,* south Texas summer nights are *made* for *night-swimmin' au naturel.* Used to go with Mama all the time. The river at midnight in July; August . . ." She smiled. "Guys, gals, all ages and colors gettin' cool the way God meant: from everything *on* to everything *off.*" She looked wistful. "Makin' out, havin' your first with someone you really care about and not havin' ta worry about takin' it all off 'cause it's already off. Folks need ta do that up here. We need a naked beach 'round these parts. Ain't done that since . . . "

"Buy a lake," I said. "You've got the money." My imagination was going wild . . . wilder . . .

She gave a big grin. "Only 'cause you want to see my girl parts, Dad . . . "

"You wanna see my boy parts?"

"You're too eager," she chuckled. Suddenly, she got serious. "I

The Persistent Past

wasn't gonna bring this up but, Tina Klein's lawyers filed some papers the other day, claims Chris's shares are 'ancestral property' under state law. My lawyers say those laws were written to protect the reservations and the tribes." She gave me a sly look and a slow wink. "I know Mama's family had Sioux and Blackfoot ties from way back. Uncle Will found that out when he was doing his family tree. This way or that, Chris's shares are staying with us."

"Even if Tina's crew spread that false . . ." I started.

"That Ridge asshole came by our place the other day. Mike showed him the door before he got through it." She shook her head. "Dealt with his kind of shyster for years in construction."

"What do we make of this?" I asked, another transparency on the screen.

```
Date: 1 Apr 51
From: SCAP, Seoul
To: All Commands
Re: EA Steele
Edmond Steele has no orders to be in
this theater. Security personnel escorted
him from this command area. All subunits
of this command will remove all mention of
this unauthorized officer from all reports
and destroy all correspondence bearing his
name.
```

"Where'd that come from?" Larry asked. "Dosen't even look real . . ."

"From one of Ned Steele's friends," I answered. "General Brick commanded I Corps for about two weeks after General Milburn suffered a mild heart attack. It just so happened he sent this copy to Ned, but I don't know when."

"Who's it from?" Brenda asked.

"SCAP was an acronym for Supreme Commander Allied Powers, a title given General MacArthur during the Korean conflict," I said.

"The first two sentences may make sense," Vinnie said, "but the last one . . . nope."

"I didn't think so," I agreed. "And neither does the Army, according to this e-mail." I put the next transparency onto the projector.

```
To: C_Durand@crestu.edu
Subject: Steele material
I've studied the memo, the diary and
the memoir entries from General Steele
regarding General MacArthur, and I must
say I am dumbfounded at the memo, but not
surprised about the sender, who would have
been General MacArthur. He may have been
vindictive, and I now know how he felt
about General Steele, but we did not know
how that bitterness manifested itself
until you sent us your findings. I look
forward to any publications you may see
fit to create.
  Stephen March, Chief Archivist,
  Department of the Army
```

"Does anyone know why?" Sharon asked.

"My best guess is that Ned was a younger General at the end of WWI than the *Boy General* MacArthur was, and MacArthur wanted that title all to himself. Even if Congress never confirmed Ned's first star, he wore it to the end of the year, and I have copies of orders for General Steele to form the First Machine Gun Brigade and take it to Germany. Some people accused MacArthur of murdering a former neighbor during WWI by ordering the young man to go on a highly risky mission. He believed the neighbor had an affair with his wife, which was never proven. The accusation haunted him, as he feared losing his reputation. Same, maybe, the Boy General handle."

"It's as good a surmise as any, Doc," Larry nodded.

And it will have to do.

CONNECTING THE DOTS

A s we watched the kids skip across *that* beach at Spring Break, Meli sighed, "Fabulous."

"Yeah," Polly said, lying in the sand next to her. "Every year . . . fabulous." We stayed in a short-term condo, having flown a charter plane to Key West.*

"Just because you want to get naked with my husband again," Meli murmured. We were under the shade of a big awning that Harriet loaned us; there were also two empty cabanas nearby.

"You got naked with mine," Polly sighed. Of course, we were all in the altogether. Our boys and five other stark naked boys ran after soccer balls in the rolling surf, joined by a couple of topless girls.†

"Leave me out of this argument," Simon, on the other side of Polly, grunted. Maria played volley-Frisbee with a group of teenagers she'd just met—all in a state of nature.

"Why would you be exempt?" I asked on the other side of Meli. "What if Meli and I were to race you two out to those floats?"

"What's the stakes?" Polly asked, raising her head to look at me over Meli.

"Dinner . . ." Meli said, jumping up.

Though Simon and I reached our floats at about the same time,

---

* Polly knew how, had an account with a charter firm.
† At their age, one could barely tell they were topless girls except for their frilly bottoms.

Polly was a stronger swimmer than Meli, though they spent more time giggling than swimming.

That night, the four of us went to that *other* beach, strolling together before separating for an hour.

Neither Christmas nor Spring Break would ever be the same for us.

"Dr. Durand, what can you tell us about General Steele who lived on this farm from 1952 to his death?" Madeline Cornish, the young reporter from the public broadcasting station in the state capital I'd met just minutes before, came down to do this interview just after Spring Break.

"Well, from his diaries, memoirs and papers," I started, "and talking to a few people who knew him personally, I'd say he was a resourceful and energetic man who spent his health, wealth, and youth in the service of his country."

"And what was his service like, do you think?" Madeline was earnest enough, and talking to her briefly before the interview, I wanted to think she was asking these questions because she knew something about Ned.

"Well, near as I've been able to determine so far, he served in the Army from April 1914 to early 1951: about 38 years. He saw three major conflicts, and rose from Private to Lieutenant-General . . ." Somehow, her attitude during the interview suggested complete ignorance of him.

"Wow," she said earnestly. "Why have most people never heard of this guy?"

"The simplest explanation is that he didn't seek publicity like other senior officers did, and he took on the riskiest assignments with few resources that he completed with a minimum of fuss and fanfare. That, and one influential General—Douglas MacArthur—didn't like him."

"I see," she nodded to the camera. "He married a *senator's* daughter . . .?"

"Angela Gibson, in France in 1919, and again in Missouri in 1924 . . ." We continued in a similar vein, and I answered as many questions as I could, pausing at intervals for longer breaks.* During one break, Madeline came clean. "I've been doing research on Senator Gibson for some time," she said, "and finding material on his little-known son-in-law has been difficult. Can you explain that?"

"MacArthur didn't want to be shown up," I said, based on what I'd found out about Ned in Korea. "We haven't found his Korea diary, but . . . "

"You're still working on him, yes?"

"I am, but I understood this interview is supposed to publicize the Historical Society's effort to buy Steele Farm, and now Crest is trying to help raise . . . "

"Yes, I know, Dr. Durand," Madeline grinned, "but to do that, we want to start some controversy. Scandal sells." I showed her a recently transcribed, interim version of a diary entry from 1918, with the vulgarities intact:

11ᵗʰ November, Overlooking the Moselle River near Neuville, Luxembourg.
They told us to stop shooting at 11 this morning, and I never heard a silence so [expletive] *profound, even if it is* [expletive] *raining. Standing up outside a hole or a trench with no need to duck is a liberating experience. More than one of us wept; I have by God survived this shit, but I cannot weep properly no matter how I try.*
I must stop being so profane. I realize my diaries have become storehouses of profanity and vulgarity, but I resist the urge to edit or destroy them. If someone wants to know what a soldier sounded like, they can read the [expletive] *things, or not if they get their noses out of joint over my language. My only response to any future reader is that I have, by God, survived the worst, most hellish*

---

* The interview took most of that day in my office, and the next day at Steele Farm in a snowstorm. The run-time for the PBS broadcast was fifty minutes.

[expletive] experience anyone could imagine, and [expletive] you if you don't like how I recorded it.

"Scandalous enough?" I asked. "Not much salacious scandal here, I don't think."

Madeline read the entry with a slight smile. "In 1918, it might have been salacious, but I hear my husband yell worse at the top of his lungs while watching a football game."

We finished the office part of the interview that afternoon, and met the next day at the farm, where Millie Sachenhausen of the Historical Society laid out their plans to buy the farm from Ridgway, and I laid out Crest's plans.

"The financing is a matter of money, and of public support," I said into the camera, with Millie by my side and the Steele graves behind us. "We're hoping that public pledges to help us keep these treasures available to the public will put us over the top in financing." Asking for $100,000—a fraction of what Crest and the Historical Society had already pledged to Ridgeway—would make it look like "everyone" had a stake in the $10.2 million asking price for the farm.

The Regents planned for the school to lease the farmland to the farmers who were already working on it and sell off the most modern and working equipment that little interested us. Our accountants calculated we'd make profit enough to offset the property taxes for a decade, and pay for necessary changes to make the place a museum and a research center.

What surprised me was how easy it became once I was a Regent, even if Polly wasn't sure it was a sound investment.

Money talks, I guess.

"What's 'bells of hell' mean, Dad?" Maria asked, showing me the entry she was working on that Saturday.

4ʰ December, Hill 90.
Silence is strange here, even in the morning.
And so is the sunrise, peaceful and warm
through the smoke and gas. The Huns hit us

hard last night, once again, and yet, here we still are, despite their efforts to throw us the [expletive] off. I cannot imagine how these medicos do it, up to their elbows in blood and gore, day in and day out. We have suffered another nine dead and twenty-two wounded last night. [Illegible]

"Bells of Hell," Top.

The Huns killed five gunners and hurt two others; one with a bullet, three with shrapnel, one by gas, not a mark on him, but his mouth was foamy. Talbott, Buchalter and Isham are among the hurt, to be evacuated. Thirty-one in all. I should write letters, especially to McTee's brother in the Navy. Should I write to Gen. Pershing?

We are being relieved this evening, a Canuck MG company, newly formed, with sixteen MGs instead of the British twelve. They're getting the idea.

McTee's replacement has very big shoes to fill. Brick, Willis and I hauled his body down stuffed into a [expletive] mattress cover like a [expletive] sausage. Nagurski's next in line as top Sergeant in the company. He seems to know what to do, but he's no McTee.

My Canuck counterpart is a fragile-looking man with a ragged mustache who obviously knows his business. Never knew anyone could hang that many Mills bombs on himself; I counted twelve that I could see. Chain-smoking ready-roll coffin nails while I showed him around. He will have to move some MG positions as he has Vickers guns. We leave Hill 90 with no regrets, having learned more in eleven days than in the previous eleven weeks. Just told they found Dona's body buried in a [expletive] collapsed trench. Must have caught the same shell burst as got McTee. We lost the best First Sergeant in *the Army and we have lost a most helpful trainer who gave us valuable training that kept more of us alive than he will ever know. I asked McFadden to make sure his family knows he's buried up here with ours; said he will.*

"I know it was a British song," I answered. "the doughboys heard it, adopted it. It's in an earlier . . . "

"Yeah," she sighed, "I was just wondering where the title came from, and why do they say 'for you and not for me?'"

"I looked into that," I said. "Some think soldiers called machine-gun bullets 'bells of hell' for the sound they make when the charging handle on the gun is pulled back. Never heard it, so I can't say. But others think it's just an alliteration of 'hell's bells,' which is an older expression. As for the 'you and not me,' that should be self-explanatory."

"Yeah." She was quiet. "But Sergeant McTee got killed . . . "

"Yeah. That's sad . . . why would Ned write to Pershing about him?"

"I'm not sure, frankly."

"*Commandant* Dona was killed at the same time."

"Yes; all his American officers have been wounded up there except he and Brick."

"Yeah." She looked back at her work. "This is the last entry on Hill 90." She stopped. "When I get done figuring this out, I'm gonna take a break for a while, OK?" *

"Sure. Take till summer. It'll still be here."

"So will you, Dad. You should take a longer break from this stuff than a few weeks."

I regarded her seriously. Maria had grown about an inch taller since Connie's wedding and blossomed otherwise; I saw that at Spring Break. She was also thinking of herself as more of an adult than she should have . . . like now. "It's my trade, sweetheart."

---

* "Figure this out" was our shorthand for completing the research on names, dates, and other information in the entries as far as we could take it.

She blanched slightly. "*Ted* called me that the other night."

"Pretty common term of endearment."

"A little *creepy* hearing it from you and him."

"I can see that." I waited for a pace. "What does Bill call you? You missed him at Spring Break."

"Yeah." She knitted her brows. "Why do you ask?"

"So I don't step on his toes, either. You talk often enough; I see the bills."

"He calls me . . . you'd never call me that, anyway." She made a face. "Toots."

"No, you're right; I wouldn't," I grinned.

"Know what?" she sighed, gathering up her work. "I'm done for today. Going swimming."

I opened the envelope from Britain eagerly, even if I expected another rejection, but . . .

> *Brixton Hill, London 2Q81*
> *20ᵗʰ March*
> *My Dear Dr. Durand,*
> *It is with great pleasure that I read of your diary project, both in your query and elsewhere, and I am honored and pleased to say our board has accepted your proposal to publish all eleven days of Capt. Steele's Hill 90 diary in our November 1997 issue of Duckboards if you can get them all to us by the end of this April. We realise the lag time between here and there can be great, and that is the reason for our enclosed postal order that should cover the extra charges for overseas express.*
> *Yours very truly,*
> *Arthur Jones*
> *Acquisitions Editor, Duckboards.*

"SOLD IT!" I shouted to my empty office. I burst out my door, dashed down the hall, seized the first female I found, planted a big kiss on her lips, spun her around, and dashed back to my office.

In a few minutes, my office filled up with people—students, faculty, other staff—all looking at me strangely. The recently smooched, dark young woman pushed her way through the crowd, set her bag on my desk and sternly declared, "now, Doc, I don't get propositioned that often, but I've never been kissed without at least a howdy-do, even on New Year's. I'm Rachel Kemp, twenty-two, fourth year pre-law from Pulaski, Tennessee. I was just smooched by a guy I never met. Just who the *Hell* are *you?*"

I extended my hand. "Rachel, I'm Doctor Curtis Durand, forty-two next week, Professor of History from Cicero, Illinois. I just sold an article to a major WWI magazine."

As far as young women go, Rachel was pretty in a non-model way, but she had a beautiful smile. "Well, congratulations, Curtis. And thanks for the kiss; made my whole day."

Mine, too.

"Shh . . ." Meli held her finger to my lips that morning. "They're waiting outside . . . "

"Waiting for us to be done or to start?" I wondered. Timing precluded full-frontal marital joy, but Meli was accommodating.

"Hard to say," Meli whispered, donning her robe. "It's a school-Tuesday, so Maria's got the boys up."

"How did our children . . .?" I mumbled, pulling my shorts on.

"They know before we *do it*," Meli declared, heading for the door.

"One hopes no details with any accuracy," I said, swinging my feet down.

"Happy birthday, Dad!" read the cardboard banner Jason carried over his head. Other cards and signs followed with Maria and Charlie.

Though birthday tributes for my forty-second natal poured in throughout the day, those in the first hour meant the most.

> This article is based on the diaries of
> Captain Edmund "Ned" Steele, US Army, who
> commanded the American Expeditionary
> Force's 1st Machine Gun Instructor Company
> in WWI. In November 1917, with casualties

at Paashendaele so catastrophic, General
Pershing ordered the 1st to stand a front-
line shift on Hill 90 in the Canadian
sector in Flanders. What should have been
a mere three or four days at the front
turned into eleven . . .

"What d'ya think, Tony?" I asked when he handed me the draft back.

"Amazing," he breathed. "You got all of this out of one diary?"

"Those and his memoirs," Maria smiled. "Took three months to get it all at least partly verified."

"Well, I think you've done it, Curtis," Tony nodded, "with a little help from Maria."

"More than a little," I smiled at her. "She's been most helpful and diligent. The Steele Collection's money is well spent."

"I guess. How's life as a Regent, now?"

"A lot more responsibility for a little more work," I answered, nodding. "Amazing how much *and* how little they get done over the course of a month."

"You dragged Polly onto the Regents, too?"

"We want to change the bylaws so that at least two seats are always filled by faculty."

"Think that'll fly?"

"We'll not only make it fly, Tony, we'll make it sing and dance."

"So, what do we make of this?" I asked the class, putting up an entry from a diary Mickey found in his basement the week before.

> *12th May, Jefferson Barracks, Missou.*
> *Our platoon has more certain knowledge of*
> *our Benoit-Mercier guns than all the others*
> *in the 89th, and the Army has chosen us for*
> *the Machine-Gun Section in the Provisional*
> *Division. We depart for Mexico tomorrow. I*
> *barely have time to write to my family.*
> *Sgt. McTee says I will be an important part of*
> *the section. I believe I will be little more than*

a mechanic.
From this day forward, I shall strive to clean
up my language.

"He's going to Mexico," Sharon said.

"He is. We just got this diary. As far as I know, this is the only enlisted man's diary of the Punitive Expedition to Mexico, even if he'd only make irregular entries afterwards."

15th July, Camp Bliss, Tex.
We drew mules and carts and touring cars for
our machine guns this morning, and will
cross the border and meet the rest of our
section south of Juarez tomorrow. Our
platoon will double the size of the division's
Machine-Gun Section. The [expletive] *dust here*
makes it hard to breathe.

9th August, Mexico.
Our mules are cantankerous creatures; our
horses are not much better, but they are more
particular about feeding than the long ears
that will eat anything. They both suffer from
the heat and a lack of water.
We hear about action with the bandits in our
MG squads, but our HQ Squad doesn't. We
have detached three of the section's six guns
in touring cars so far.

17th September, Between Dublan and Rucio,
Mexico.
I cannot find this God-forsaken place on any
map, but the campesinos call this place
Perrion, which our scouts say means "rock."
They at least provide water for our animals,
though we humans have to filter and boil it
to drink it, it is so foul.
We have been moving every day and have not
set up a tent but one day in five. Every
creature-comfort is in short supply, from soap

The Persistent Past

*to papers. I am tempted to tear out sheets
from this journal to use if it would provide
relief to my behind.*

"Papers?" I asked.

"*Toilet* paper," Larry said.

"They lack even toilet paper?" Beverly wondered.

"Apparently." I answered. "Kinda wonder if they ever solved that problem, because the next time you hear from Ned is this:"

*1ˢᵗ January, 1917, Mexico.
I have neglected my diary for too long, but I
have been busy.
No celebration of any kind for the New Year.
The cold desert is surprising. We have been in
Mexico for nearly three months. I have not
taken a bath of any kind in nearly five weeks
and I* [expletive] *reek. We are all running out of
razor blades and soap. I borrowed a
cutthroat and sliced myself up pretty badly.
We see no bandits, no action, but we hear it
sometimes. One fellow's Kodak has filled up,
but I don't know what he's taking pictures of,
since this is just featureless* [expletive] *desert.*

"A cutthroat . . .?" Elias asked.

"Straight razor," Max answered. "Got the name after the safety razor got popular. Looks like Ned had never used one before."

"The safety razor was patented only in 1905," Brandy nodded. "If he's, what, twenty here? He may not have."

"And not a bath to be had," Beverly said.

The class talked about this entry for some time, I believe, because the changes in sanitation since then were so many and so stark. This kind of privation was unimaginable to those who had never *seen* a new black-and-white TV in a store.

"Then," I said dramatically, "we have . . . this."

*20ᵗʰ January, near the Texas-Mexico border.
Making a machine gun pedestal for the*

supply train's Benet-Mercier from an unrepairable Mallen motor wagon's* rear axle and tie rods was easy if you know what the [expletive] you're doing. I helped Dad clean out that plant after he bought it for his suspension factory. A Capt. Stilwell from the baggage train wanted to see it done, so we did it with Lieut. Able's permission.

Welding two different metals is tricky, but with proper flux and heat, it is not as hard as all that. Met Gen. Pershing while we were making the pedestal. Sgt. McTee knows him well and knew his family before their tragedy. I am glad when officers have a sense of humor, for my jokes can be dry.

An officer with an unpleasant voice, a Lieut. Patton, wanted my view on something military. I gave him my thoughts on the dim future of the horse and the bright one of the machine gun in military operations.

My invention invoked a great deal of curiosity at HQ, but I doubt we will ever see it used since we are ordered out of [expletive] Mexico. Wonder if this receipt would get me more than a cup of coffee somewhere.

I have reduced my profane entries, but not eliminated them. I must strive to do better.

"He was a handy guy," I said lightly, while the class read . . . and read . . . and read.

"He met Pershing in Mexico?" Larry asked. "And Stilwell . . . and Patton?"

"Apparently," I shrugged. "From our research, the timing is right. They were all there, or could have been. Patton's voice has been described as hard to listen to. Stilwell's location during this time is hazy . . . "

"What family tragedy is he talking about?" Bayard asked.

---

* Early term for a truck in the US.

"Pershing's wife and three daughters were killed in a house fire in 1915," I said. "Sergeant McTee might have been Pershing's enlisted aide before that."

"Never heard of a Mallen truck," Kensie said.

"Got this from the Wayne County Historical Society:"

```
From: Sylnettting@usaol.com
Subj: Mallen Auto
Thank you for your query. From our
records, the Mallen Auto firm of Dearborn
existed from 1909 to 1911 and manufactured
only fifteen vehicles before being forced
into receivership. No known examples
exist. The Steele Spring Company used
their building until 1922, when Ford
acquired that firm after the death of the
owner and took over the building.
     Sylvia Netting, Archivist.
```

"One must have made it to Mexico," I declared. "And Ned's father passed by 1922."

"So it appears," Max mused. "Got far enough to be cannibalized for a machine gun pedestal."

"Yep."

"He met Pershing in Mexico . . ." Kensie said.

"He met Patton . . ." Larry said.

"This guy was a Corporal then?" Bayard asked.

"Yep." Silence. "Met Patton and Pershing several times after that, apparently."

"How many?" Larry asked.

"Enough to be promoted to Lieutenant Colonel before he was twenty-two."

"All in these diaries," Beverly sighed. "This is a gold mine."

"And a good part of that gold mine just went by express to England," I declared, shoving the mailing receipt into the overhead. "For publication in November . . ."

VALIDATING THE DIARIES

I asked the class, "So, what do we make of this?" in the next-to-last class of the semester.

16ᵗʰ July, On the road to Reims.
I'm glad our springs are so effective in these touring cars or I'd need [expletive] dentures. We encounter so few Americans up here that we are objects of curiosity. All our trucks and cars—even those hauling the mules—seem so incongruous compared to the long lines of marching Frenchmen with their animal-drawn wagons and hand-drawn carts. The trucks and cars we see headed east are laden with equipment and men.
Then, there's those going the other way; the casualties. So many, so forlorn, so dirty. I can sympathize with them, and especially for those who won't see tomorrow, which is more than a few.
I cannot wait for this madness to be over.
There, I've said it. This [expletive] war is brutal [expletive] madness.

"He's tired of the war," Sharon said. "Tired of the killing, the blood . . . "

"The sight of the wounded," Vihaan answered. "He can't countenance it much longer."

"All true," I said . . . waiting. "What else?"

"Where *is* he here?" Larry asked.

"*Better* question. An eastbound road to Reims wasn't in the American sector in 1918. What else?"

"Most of the French Army is afoot," Bayard observed. "At least there it is."

"Excellent," I said. "And . . .?"

"They aren't used to seeing Americans," Sharon said.

"They weren't used to seeing vehicles hauling animals," Brandy declared. "Not when they're mostly afoot."

"Right," I said. "Now, the first thing you mentioned about this entry was . . . "

"About the end," Sharon said.

"Yep," I agreed. "You saw his profane protests about the conflict *first* because . . . "

"We expected to," Vihaan nodded. "Our social conditioning."

"Decades of peace marches have made us see what we want to see everywhere," I said, "passing over all that other information; important information that only a careful reading would reveal. Now," I sighed, turning the overhead off. "Everyone does it, but we have to resist it. We have to slow down and see the complete source; the details where the Devil hides."

"We cannot research expecting to see anything," Larry said.

"Exactly," I agreed. "Discovery happens when you look everywhere, expecting only what is there, not what we expect to see."

"Like those diaries, Doc?" Vihaan asked. "You didn't expect to see them in that trunk."

"No, I certainly did not," I agreed.

I had several correspondents in Britain by then, but this was a familiar name in Ned's WWI diaries.

> 12ᵗʰ April 97
> Greenock
> My Dear Dr. Durand;
> My name is Archie Talbott, and my father
> knew Capt./Col. Steele during the 1914-18

war. I understand from my granddaughter in America that you have found Capt. Steele's diaries and that you intend to publish them. These would greatly interest my family, as Father's association with Capt. Steele was very important to him, as was the extensive correspondence the two of them carried on after that war.

It is my understanding that Capt. Steele was also in the 1939-45 conflict; I flew Dakotas in the RAF throughout. Capt. Steele was so generous during and after that war, sending our family little parcels of food and cards at Christmas. Father passed in 1965, and I still have Capt. Steele's condolence card. I have many of Capt. Steele's letters to Father in my possession. I also have a memoir Father wrote after the 1939-45 war, when he was an ARP warden in London and Lincoln, detailing his experience in France in 1917-18 where he mentions your Capt. Steele often, and speaks of meeting him in England in 1943. If these would be of any use to you, please let me know. I look forward to hearing from you.

Yours,
Archibald Talbott

So, I asked for copies of his letters and memoir, hoping to fill in more blanks.

"Say, Mickey," I grinned, seeing him as I pawed through the Steele material still in the storeroom. I hesitated to grab too much of it, because he had been a commandant at Camp Penobscot twice, and so technically much of it was owned by either the state or the Army.[*]

"Hey, Doc," he answered, hands in his pockets. "Looking for anything in particular?"

---

[*] That was still being negotiated by the state and the Army, at my instigation.

"Just . . . seeing if he said anything else about . . . France or . . . Germany," I answered distractedly. Ned's diaries expressed reserve in his views about either his enemy or his friends, despite his ability to be very descriptive about battle.

"Well, I can tell ya some things in that regard," he said. "You won't see anything like that in those official papers."

"OK," I said, still distracted. I was trying to just catalog some of the other material; he'd put some Army working notes in diary-like journals I'd grabbed earlier. "Let me finish here and I'll be out."

I found Mickey in the Visitor's Center lobby a few minutes later, polishing the glass on the display case with Angie's apron. "So, what did Ned think of the Germans?" I asked.

He looked amused. "Ya know, I knew him for nearly half a century and I only ever called him 'sir.'"

"How well did you know him?"

"Oh, as well as any employee knows his boss of half a century, I guess."

"He employed you?"

"Kinda, yeah. I worked more *for* him than *with* him. I worked *with* Miss Angie more than *for* her."

"How?"

"The General didn't stand around on ceremony, liked to get stuff done. Not to say he didn't do all the pomp that goes with being an officer; he just didn't pay too much attention to it."

"How did you meet him?"

"His senior enlisted aide hired me after his junior enlisted aide was killed in Luxembourg in December '44." Mickey gazed out the window while he spoke. "The General built a pickup division from scratch in a few days, and commanded it during that Battle of the Bulge. I stayed with him all the way into Germany."

"What did he think of the Germans?"

"I don't know that he thought of Germans as anything other than just people he had to fight when they fought him. Now, the Japs; they were a different story."

"Why?"

He gazed out the window again. "Because he left Miss Angie and his youngest boy in Manila in '41 when General Marshall sent him to Russia."

"What did Marshall send him to Russia for?"

"The way I got it from Miss Angie . . ." He repeated much of the story Carl had told us, then smiled bitterly. "You ain't got that far in his diaries, have ya?"

"No," I answered honestly. "And I don't have his diaries for Korea, either."

"Let me look for them," he sighed. "That memo help at all?"

"It did. What did he make of the French or the British?"

He chuckled lightly. "The Brits he had great respect for; the Canucks, too. He had a lyric for 'em:"

They fight like Hell 'til half-past-three!
But then they stop for a cup 'o tea!
Hinky-dinky parley-vous!

"He and General Brick used to sing that when they got in their cups." He shrugged. "Didn't mean anything by it, I don't think. But the French?" He shook his head. "He used to say that the French couldn't figure out who they were supposed to fight in the second war: themselves or the Brits or the Americans or the Germans, or all of 'em."

"How did you end up here?"

"Well, after I got demobbed in '46, I took a job on a ferry boat between Long Island and Connecticut. It was . . . let's see . . . '49 when I ran into General Brick. We saw each other once in a while after that. Then in '52 he looks me up, says General Steele needed help with his farm up here. Now, I know the General was never gonna ask for help, so I just came up here, see what was what."

"Earlier, you said . . .?"

"Yeah, that was because I wasn't sure of you, sir."

"OK; I'll buy that. So the General took you on?"

"Not . . . exactly. Miss Angie took me in, fed me, and put me up in that little cottage. I'd been about two steps from the gutter for a while, wondering what to do with myself and drinking too much because of it. So the General asked if I knew anything about farming, and I said I was raised *over* a grocery store. 'Close enough' he says, and had me negotiate with the farmers working his land. Then

I was managing his repair business and before I knew it, I was taking care of this place, married and with three kids."

"He had a reputation as a go-getter."

"In the war with Germany, they called him an *operator.* Some called him the best in the business." He shrugged. "Since I only knew one other guy like him."

"Who?"

"Colonel Willis, the supplyman. Could steal your eyeteeth and you'd trade him for spares. I heard tell Colonel Willis was the reason the General was so successful in France in the first war, 'cause he could get anything the General needed. In the second, Hell, wasn't nothing Colonel Willis couldn't find."

So much more to learn . . .

> 21ˢᵗ *July, Villemontoire, France.*
> *Now I know what the effects are of our barrages. This was a standing-to-rolling barrage by two platoons of B Company's guns to keep the Huns from using the road reaching 2ⁿᵈ Division's flanks.*
> *Like Gen. Pershing described, we tore them apart like* [expletive] *tigers in a pit. Two companies of infantry and a 77 battery, all but seven men dead, the aidmen found them hiding under cannons.*
> *The locals have been picking at this area for two days now, getting what they could. The buzzing of flies is dreadful and incredibly loud. We shoo away feasting pigs and dogs, but we cannot chase off the* [expletive] *rats. We saw a forest of ribcages in that* [expletive] *abattoir.*
> *Fire and brimstone and a dreadful scorching wind will be the portion of their cup.*

"God almighty," Vihaan murmured after I turned the overhead on.

"Seven out of how many?" Beverly asked.

"At full strength, it would have been about a thousand, but then, half that. I have a memoir entry that . . . ”

"Still," Brandy declared. "This guy can remember a Psalm?"

"He's been at war for several months by now. This is the first time he's seen the effects of his work on the enemy in the open. It must have been quite the revelation."

"What's the significance of B Company?" Larry asked.

"They're equipped with 8-millimeter Hotchkiss guns, with longer range than the rest of his battalion's .303 Vickers guns."

"Ya don't think of that often," Bayard said. "The pigs, the flies, the rats, the civilians picking through the . . . the . . . ”

"*Slaughter pen* is the term you're looking for," I finished.

"Is there *anyone* . . . downrange?" the loudspeaker asked a third time. The firing range at Camp Penobscot was chilly that Saturday morning; I wore my winter coat, even though it was April. Jenny and Mike got permission for me to watch the annual range practice for their helicopter company's twenty machine guns.

"The range is no longer clear," the loudspeaker loudly announced. The range was much as I expected, but rather than paper targets within walking distance that I was used to,* I saw the rusting hulks of cars, trucks, an armored personnel carrier, and a helicopter hundreds, thousands of yards away.

"Earmuffs and goggles on, Doc," the young Captain next to me five yards behind the line of prone machine gunners said. "You *sure* you want to be here?"

"Yes," I said, nodding while positioning my protections firmly. The Captain had been one of my students.

"Gunners: *commence firing!*" the loudspeaker said . . . and the cacophonous rattling, *roaring* of twenty machine guns started. Even through my earmuffs, the sound *punched* my brain as my sinuses filled with the smell of powder that smarted my eyes, even behind my goggles.

Now, I'd been to a gun range before, and fired a pistol, so that smell wasn't new . . .

---

* My father was in the Cicero Police Department and dragged me and my sisters to the range more than once.

But this was *continuous pistol firing on steroids.*

I looked downrange as targets seemed to disappear in clouds of sparks and dust, the multiple impacts becoming indistinct from each other, merging into a single cloud of destruction.

From somewhere I could not fathom, I heard a dull boom, then another, then another, and another . . .

"One five fives," the Captain shouted over the din. "They're about three miles that way," he pointed to our right. Soon, those targets, torn and battered and rusting, vanished under the artillery shells exploding. I felt those blasts even from thousands of yards.

And I began to understand just a little of what Ned was talking about when he talked about the *bzzz-bzzz-thut-thut-boom-boom-crash-crash* he heard in his dreams, that he lived under, that he was on the receiving end of. He lived through this horror hour after hour, for days at a time.

The firing lasted for perhaps five minutes, but I honestly lost track of time before . . . "*cease fire, cease fire,*" the loudspeaker announced.

Then . . . silence. And I could understand what Ned meant by *blessed silence.* But my ears still rang.

"We do this every year," the Captain announced, taking off his earmuffs, blinking. "Burns up old ammo and gets us our practice."

"The range is clear; clear your weapons," the loudspeaker intoned. Little doors on top of the machine guns flipped open; observers inserted rods in the barrels of each.

"Where'd the cannons come from?" I asked, since I knew nothing of them. After the observers cleared the weapons, the gunners picked up and moved them off the firing line.

"The Guard artillery outfit posted out here," the Captain answered. "They join us every year," he added, taking off his glasses.

"All these guns yours?" I asked casually curious, doing the same.

"For the door gunners," he answered. "Two to a ship and two for ground defense." As the last gunner removed the last machine gun, he declared. "Show's over, Doc. Learn anything?"

"Yeah," I sighed, following him off the firing line, "I learned this is a damned noisy business."

"It is," he agreed, pointing back out at the impact area. "That chopper out there ain't there anymore." It had vanished under the pounding.

Damned destructive, too.

"Mrs. Klein, *thank* you for coming," James said genially. We met on Income Tax Fatality Day* in the Regents Interview Room in the Jenson Executive Building, a room as darkly imposing as the Long Room, but larger.

"Your invitation was well past due, James," Tina said tartly. "I have *plans* for this body." Six of the seven Regents sat on one side of a long table facing Tina, who I thought dressed casually—jeans and a sweater—for the occasion.

"Mrs. Klein," Alan sighed, "we asked you here to answer some questions. I hope you don't mind." I, in my first meeting as a Regent, sat at one end of the table, next to the stenographer.

"What sort of questions, Alan?" Tina asked, arching an eyebrow. "That space next to you, James, will suit me after the reorganization, if that's . . ." My first experience in the Interview Room was with Connie, when the Regents grilled her and I on how *appropriate* it was for a pregnant teenager to be on campus nearly a decade ago.

"It is not, Mrs. Klein," James replied patiently. "You are here to answer questions about a news story in the Port Huron papers." Let's just say Connie proved quite capable of defending herself.

"Port Huron is where?" Tina asked, looking more surprised than questioning. She glared at me with contempt. "And why should I . . .?"

"Michigan," Alan said, "north of Detroit. It's where John Templeton and his parents live."

"And who is this John Templeton?" Tina snarled, clearly annoyed.

"It is clear you know," I said. "John Templeton is your grandson by marriage, Connie's first son."

"Well, I'm not aware I had another grandson, you *poser*, but

---

* 15 April.

to amuse you, let's just get on with . . ." Tina replied, obviously trying to be bored . . . but there was something else behind her eyes.

"An article appeared in the *Port Huron News* on 21 February
of this year, headlined 'Templeton's Adopted Love Child Sought
By Birth Father's Family,'" I said. "It was given to the reporter by
an attorney named Ridge." I stopped. "Sound familiar, Tina?"

"What's *that* got to do with *me,* you *clown?*" She looked at me
as if I were something unpleasant stuck to her shoe . . . but there
was some doubt.

"John Templeton's father is the President of the Port Huron
City Council," Alan said. "This kind of thing can be very damaging
in an election year, not to mention embarrassing to a minor child."

"Which means what, Alan?" Tina sighed, rolling her eyes,
shaking her head. "Impress me with something off the football
field . . . "

"The McCullochs are *screaming* about the breach of their con-
fidentiality in their implicit contract with your daughter-in-law when
they gave up their parental rights," James said. "So are your son and
your daughter-in-law. Now . . . ."

"*Spit it out, James,*" Tina demanded loudly, reaching into her
attaché case. "I have agenda items and I *expect* to . . . "

"The reporter, aware of laws regarding adoption confidential-
ity," I said, "won't shield Ridge after the McCullochs and the Templetons threatened to sue the paper."

"*So what?*" Tina shouted, staring at James, then Alan, then me.
"Stick to your books and papers, you *little* . . . "

"Ridge works for you." I said. "He was questioned by Judge
Walking Elk last week, and he's stated, on pain of disbarment, that
he fed that reporter the story on your instructions."

Tina blinked and calmly stated, "I demand my seat on the Regents. Period. I will litigate until I am seated." She stared at me.
"You, little bookworm, are not entitled to a seat. Only those who
own this mausoleum are *entitled* to seats on . . . "

"That is not stated anywhere in the Bylaws, Mrs. Klein," James
said. "As you well know."

"*Because you removed it,*" Tina shouted. "My attorneys
know . . . "

"Calm down, Tina," Devota Crest Klein emerged silently from the door behind me. "Your lawyers know no such thing."

"*Who invited her?*" Tina asked the air loudly, not looking at her mother. "She's got nothing to do with—"

"She has everything to do with this meeting, and which brings us to why we invited you here, Mrs. Klein," James said at length. "The majority of Corporation stockholders, and that means the Committee of Regents and Mrs. Devota Klein, have found you lack the moral fiber that is required by the Crest community and the accepts your resignation as Chairman of the Crest Corporation."

"*You can't—*" Tina cried. "*I own . . .* "

"Not enough, Christina," Devota said patiently. "Now let's get out of here before I cut your allowance."

No one said anything as they left.

So . . . that was done.

"Hello," I said, answering my den phone the next Sunday. We'd just got back from St. Barbara's ecumenical service.[*]

"Hello," a pleasant voice answered, "Is this Professor Curtis Durand?" Preparations for Sunday dinner were casual; I was hoping for takeout chicken . . .

"Yes," I said, thinking it was a student with some emergency on a Sunday afternoon.[†]

"My name is Barbara Brick Lawson. I got your name from Mickey Parnell . . . "

"Yes," I answered suddenly interested. "Are you any relation to . . .?"

"My grandfather served with General Steele."

"Mike Brick," I repeated dumbly.

"That's him. You've read about him in General Steele's diaries?"

"I have, Miss . . . Lawson, is it?"

"Mrs., Professor," she corrected. "My father was Grampa's second son, born in Manila in 1923. When Grampa passed in 1989,

---

[*] We made it a point to go once or twice a month, making sure that the kids understand there may be power beyond what they could see.

[†] Only my students called me "Professor," and that only at first.

General Steele was an honorary pallbearer, as he was somewhat frail . . . ."

"He had a stroke that year," I added.

"When he heard about Grampa, yes."

"Just out of curiosity," I asked, glancing at the campus map on my wall, "do you know about the Brick Building here on campus?"

"I do," she said. "Grampa was up there to visit General Steele in '64 and looked around the campus. His family wanted to start a law school and name it after my great-grandfather."

"*That's* who it's named after," I said. The Theodore Lawson Brick School of Law at Crest was one of the smallest in the country, but only started in 1990.

"But," she continued, "the Brick family also wanted a lasting monument to its highest-ranking military son some place, so it might as well be there."

"And so . . ." I started.

"So, the family made the donation to finish that building."

"But your grandfather never attended the school?"

"Nope. The only other time Grampa was up there was when the building was dedicated in the spring of '73. I was sixteen, thought the campus was beautiful."

"It's where our Military History Department is now."

She laughed. "Ironic, ain't it? It was an office-something when it was dedicated."

"We call it the Barracks."

She laughed again. "Wild."

"Tell me a little about the Brick family, please."

"Well, the Bricks have lived on Long Island since before the Revolution, made their money first in real estate and hemp, and then in construction and railroads. They were among the original Four Hundred of New York."*

"They're still around?"

"Sure."

"Can I have your contact information?"

---

* The *crème de la crème* of New York society in the late 19th Century.

"Sure. Just . . . the family's attorneys want to contact you regarding what you're writing."

"To censor . . . ?" I started.

"No; to make sure nothing private about the Brick family was revealed. They're very private people."

"In the *Social Register* and they're . . . "

"The Brick family is extensive, Dr. Durand."

"Please call me Curtis."

"Curtis, I'm Barb. But only some members of the Bricks are on that nasty list; I'm not, for instance, and neither are my parents or any of us kids or most of my cousins. Grampa was because he couldn't get off it because of his rank and his medal."

"Medal?"

"Grampa was awarded a Medal of Honor in 1945 for something General Steele said he did in North Africa. He made Major General before he retired. He retired for reasons of health, he said, after General Steele was ejected from Korea."

"You know about that?"

"More than I wanted to. Grampa would rant about it often enough. He hated General MacArthur for just erasing General Steele like that."

We spoke in a similar vein for quite some time. Mike Brick talked about, and wrote about, Ned a lot, it seemed.

The next week, I got a bundle of letter copies from Mike to his wife, Suzanne, and several hundred pages of notes for a memoir.

And I filled in more and more blanks.

7ᵗʰ January, Hotel Deluxe, Paris.
I met my new driver, a Sergeant Hughes. We went out to the battalion, saw everything was in good shape, and came back safe and sound. Hughes drives a Cadillac Touring car as if it were a baby carriage.
Our current headcount is 406 officers and men present and ready for duty, after many came back from the hospital and recovered flu cases. Doc Miller informs me that at least half of the 105 men still in the hospital will

return home and [distorted] *discharged from the Army there.*
Dinner with female companions is a long forgotten treat. Mike seems to be a great deal more energetic than he has been. I have to wonder if that malaise so many flu survivors suffer from is permanent.
There! Not a single profanity!

"What can we glean from this?" I asked.

"This is after the shooting stopped," Beverly said.

"Yes."

"He's cleaned up his act quite a bit," Larry observed.

"The influence of Angie," Brandy said, to general amusement.

"Maybe, but he was aware of his profane habits before. Let's concentrate on the rest."

"His unit's depleted," Bayard said. "He's concerned about his unit strength."

"Why?"

"They aren't sure if they don't have to keep fighting," Larry said. "It was an *armistice*, not a *peace*."

"Right, and . . ."

"There were long-term effects from the flu?" Max asked.

"There were some," I said. "Apparently, *that* influenza could do a lot of damage to the system, even for those who survived it. Encephalitis was pretty common because so many people were infected; still *is* with some flu patients."

"Ya kinda wonder about Hughes, though. Where would he sleep? At the unit or in Paris?" Everyone looked at Larry. "Well?"

"Another good question, but not that . . ."

"Isn't it important? Tells you what kind of guy this Steele was, won't it?"

"I suppose," I nodded. "But for our purposes, let's concentrate on what's here, not what isn't . . . though Larry makes a good point, the careful researcher should follow up on if possible. Now . . . this."

2ʳᵈ January, 1919, Hotel Deluxe, Paris, France.
I started this volume because once again I

tore out too many pages of Volume XIV.
This place is a staircase or two above Le Petite
Rose. My First floor room above the mezzanine
is bright and clean, though a bit worn, as big
as my kitchen back home. My uniforms still
stink of carbolic and phosgene gas, and have
more than a few holes. I brought Rodgers and
ordered Brick to join me. And ~~she~~ Angie—I
can write her name here—is staying here. She
and some of her friends who have been here
the longest got leave.
As a war hero—or so the press back home calls
me—I am a useful ornament to the
politicians and senior officers. I have no
illusions about what my duties will be here:
an overpaid butler to some Washington
functionary or politician.

"What's here?"

"It's six days before that last one you put up," Larry said.

"Yes . . ."

"Explains what happened to Volume XIV," Brandy said.

"He's glad to be alive," Phil said.

"And with Angie," Brenda said.

"What about why he's there?"

"He's with the Versailles conference?" Vihaan guessed.

"Not as a Colonel, he's not," I said. "He believes he's there to escort Versailles politicians."

"Is it why he's there?" Sharon asked.

"I don't think so," I said. "Much of this volume has been destroyed, so we don't know, and the record is silent."

"He couldn't write her name before?" Brenda asked.

"For privacy reasons, in case it fell into someone else's hands. Many diarists did that—do that—I'm told."

"In Victoria's day, a lady's name appeared in the newspapers only three times," Sharon said. "Announcing her birth, her marriage, and her death. I wouldn't expect a gentleman acquaintance's diary would have it at all in 1919. After marriage, perhaps, but . . ."

"Yes, but, they are informally engaged. The Great War changed a great deal. Would they have indulged in premarital sex without the war going on? Corsets disappeared and skirts got shorter. These are Windsor,* not Victorian† or Edwardian‡ times. Ned and Angie didn't get formally introduced as the mores of the time required. Ned and his pals went to a dance in 1917 and met gals without formal introductions. He met several on trains. The war changed a lot out of expedience."

"Vietnam gave us the miniskirt and free love, too," Sharon said. "Without those, the dorms would be dull."

Among other things.

"Huh," Maria said, fanning through the enormous stack of fan-folded print-out from England. "We can find the origins of all our diaries with this."

"Looks like, yeah," I agreed, searching through the stack of photos Mike gave me the same day. Half of the 3.25-by-2.25-inch pictures on the 100-frame roll had been unprintable. Half the rest were mere shadows that Mike's developer printed on contact sheets. But for 24 of them, Mike's guy made not-bad 5 × 6 prints. "Here's Angie and Ned, sweetie."

She looked with a little smile. "Looks like a wedding."

"Yeah. That's General Pershing, and a Colonel who *could* be George Marshall."§

"Who?"

"He'd be very important later. This one's . . . the woman might be Angie's friend Harriet; the man *is* Mike Brick."

"Wedding party picture?" she wondered. "Makes sense; I was in one alone with Mike's best man."

"You barely came up to his shoulder," I sighed.

"Yeah; he's a nice-enough guy who didn't step on my feet when

---

* 1910–Present. Name changed from Saxe-Coburg-Gotha in 1916.
† 1837–1901.
‡ 1901–1910.
§ I only recognized Marshall from another WWI-era photo of him I'd seen just days before.

we were dancing. Who's that?" she asked, looking at another picture.

"I believe the Senator and his wife," I said. "A reasonable surmise, given that these others are wedding shots and they're the oldest civilians."

We shuffled through another half-dozen photos of people posing for the camera, one of a car and driver, another of a sign that read, "Fort Leavenworth, Kansas," before we came to . . . "a baby?" she asked.

"Baby girl," I said.

"How can you tell? She's . . . "

"That bow in her hair; they used to do that when most photos were black and white. This might be Corrine."

"We should send it to her," Maria grinned.

"Or another print from the negative," I said, putting the stack down. As I examined the poorly exposed shadows on the contact sheet, I thought I could see buildings and people, but no identifiable details. In another envelope were the negatives. Then I realized . . . "Verification . . . "

"What?" Maria asked.

"This camera; these undeveloped photos . . . if that *is* Pershing and Marshall, and Ned said they were at their wedding reception with the Senator in his diary . . . that would make many of these images January 29th, 1919."

"Oh!" Maria exclaimed. "The camera is like a *time capsule.*"

"Right," I grinned. "They verify what Ned said in his diaries, because there's *no way anyone* could fake these pictures on these negatives."

"Holy sh . . ." she caught herself. "We just verified everything?"

"Yes, this camera did, sweetie," I sighed.

Those photos, nearly a century old, confirmed a year's work, and all of Ned's diaries.

Sometimes, our work happens like that, and the past is always persistent.

EPILOGUE

T he past is always with us, and as Maria found out, would always affect us, even after all those years. As a history educator, researcher, archivist, husband, father, and grandfather, I've always been aware that the distant past is never really distant, but always quite persistent. My sons learned that with their friends; my daughters with theirs, only with different consequences.

It took time to inventory Mickey's additional material he dug out of his basement and found at the Visitor's Center. The item count soared over 15,000 when we found more boxes in the farmhouse attic.

The Hill 90 article was a big hit, and garnered a great deal of attention to the diaries, and demand for more. Two years later, Crest started a course on America in the Great War; I was the first instructor. During her high school years, Maria published articles about Angie in both world wars.

Steele Farm became a museum for the three-dimensional artifacts for which Crest had been trying to find a venue for years. The Steele Collection bought the Great Ugly Beast for $1,000 and placed it on display in the Steele Farm Museum, next to his WWI secretary. The graveyard stayed where it was.

In less than a decade, Connie's businesses made her one of the wealthiest women in the state. Mike sold his store to go to work for the Crest Corporation, restoring school furniture and woodwork.

Maria and I continued to work on the diaries, and when we found Volume XXXVI, we saw this entry in 1941:

20 October, Subic Bay, PI
Gen. Marshall has ordered me to Russia on a
special mission to find if the Russians will
keep fighting or fall apart, as we expect them
to do. We are sending the trunk with our
personal papers to Sen. Gibson, and I want
Angie and Carl to go with it, but Angie has
duties here and just won't go. Getting hard-
headed Carl to go to the 'States on his own is
just as hard.
All the rumors about Japan are true, and we
will be in this war sooner than later. The
Guard and Reserves have all been called up;
Contraband Clark has built many units with
draftees, and Gen. Marshall is keeping them.
These islands will become battlegrounds, and
the evacuation of civilians won't be possible.
Corky and George are safe stateside, but I
know I have to go to Russia, and I leave with
dread for my family here.

Publishers initially showed interest in the WWII and Korean War diaries (I called that project *Steele's Hammer*) after *The Great War Diaries* came out, but it faded as the war in Iraq dragged on. I got the microform project for Ned's pre-1941 diaries completed before I finally published *Hammer* decades later, including this entry from Volume XLVII:

5 Jan 51, Wonju, Korea.
I didn't expect a brass band at the airport,
and I didn't get one. My French hosts ushered
me to a weapons carrier, and we drove to the
bn. Colder here than Luxembourg in '45, or
maybe I'm just older. My French is a little
rusty and there're no Legionnaires to help
translate, but we got along OK. Food's lousy,
but there's lots of it. We are tied in with a
British bn. on our left on the other side of a
gorge.

Historians often have to get that persistent past out of our heads, to forget all about how we got where we are, because it is often, as Ned's diaries taught us, horrible.

Connie bought a piece of isolated, tree-covered land in the Jenson Mountains with a creek, a fifty-yard beach, and a cabin. By June, we skinny-dip *with* them. Maria brings her friends out there, and the boys bring theirs. Polly, Simon, and their children join us.

But we still go to the Keys at Christmas or Spring Break, or both, when we can.

All those beaches get our heads straight, so we don't have to hear those bullets *buzzing* and *thumping*, see those men dying, if just for a little while, ever living with that persistent past.